The Pain We Allow

S.K. Presley

Contents

For those of us who want a little crazy with our love.

Some unhinged action with our happily ever after perhaps?

This book is for you.

Stay just a smidgen insane so they'll never know what to expect day to day, it keeps things interesting when he's calling you a good girl.

Because, are you really?

I don't think so. At least, not for *this* particular book. So, reader, let's be bad today. Because tomorrow, we can go back to normal like it never happened...

Trigger Warnings

Mental health issues depicting depression, anxiety, suicidal ideation, and PTSD.

BDSM-Sadism/Masochism relationship

Depiction/memory of child drowning, school bombing

Child kidnapping/allusion to child being hurt

Threatening Messages/Letters

Depiction of cancer in a parent, and parent death

Intense descriptive sex scenes to include sex toys

Depiction of murder

Scenes in which MMC purposefully and consensually hurts the MFC to include:

hurting with stapler, choking, spanking, restraining with duct tape, belts, ropes, suspension, whip play, fire play, electrical play, blood play, knife play, degradation, use of thruster machine for pleasure, urine play.

Dear reader, I wanted to pop on here to tell you that though this book is a dark romance, and of course it has a fair amount of smut in it, other topics discussed in this book are serious, emotionally heavy, and I want you to know that at no time are you expected to make yourself push through this book. Please take all the time that you need, remember to be good to yourself, treat that mind well, and as always, take care of your mental health. You're all you've got at the end of the day, so treat yourself with reverence, kindness, love, and respect. Know that I am always rooting for you.

Enjoy this crazy ride,
SKP

Olivia's Note

To You

Birth, trials, sorrow, redemption, and loss.

Life has a way of humbling you. When you think you know what you're doing, a lesson comes to show you that you, in fact, do not.

You don't know anything, least of all yourself.

So, what do you do when you can't trust yourself anymore? When your foundation has been shaken irrevocably and you're left trying to hold together the small pieces and vestiges of your life.

I'll tell you.

You go back to the beginning and allow yourself to be humble,

Broken down,

Allow yourself to be built back up.

Born again.

Strong. Capable. New.

Baptize yourself in the fires of life and you come out of the carnage like a phoenix rising from the ashes.

Brand new.

And when you're reborn, make damn sure that there's no one on earth that you can trust more than you can trust yourself.

Love,

Olivia

ONE
Jar Of Dirt

SITTING AT THE HOSPITAL hours later, both Olivia and Vanessa were passed out against each other in exhaustion. Mary and Beth thoughtfully brought a change of clothes for each of them, and they were currently lying under heated hospital blankets, but the comfort of the heat only went so far.

However, the artificial warmth would never be enough to chase away the chill that had settled so bone deep that the four of them would not be able to welcome the feeling of the sun back into their life after what happened that night.

The sun was gone.

Vanessa had her head in Olivia's lap, and Olivia had her head tilted back and on Colin's shoulder. Colin still stared numbly.

He startled as Jonathan's voice penetrated his musing. He swallowed back bile for the umpteenth time, feeling sick.

"Bro, that wasn't your fault. You had a cover on the pool. It was an accident. I'm contacting the company and suing for negligence first thing tomorrow. I'll handle this for you." Jonathan's warm voice drifted over him, and Colin felt his eyes burning with unshed tears. He looked over at his friend slowly, knowing his face was an impenetrable stricken mask he couldn't crack for the life of him.

Maybe that was the problem. There was no life, as well as no sun.

"Jonathan. If I hadn't been so persistent, if I hadn't pressed so hard...none of this would have happened," he lamented, his voice deepened with grief and terror for Allison.

The doctor suddenly appeared around the corner, wearily. His mouth was pulled tight, his face was pale, and what was left of any vestige of hope snuffed out like a flame that even Olivia's aura couldn't bring back. He groaned, a pained sound, putting his elbows on his knees and his head in his hands, crying proper now.

Jonathan put his hand on the back of his neck, his face just as stricken.

"She's stable," the doctor said wearily, his elderly features standing out in sharp contrast in his face.

Colin's breath hitched in shock as he looked up in disbelief. Jonathan's hand squeezed his neck hard before letting go.

"But we'll need to observe her for a while just to make sure. There's still a chance for dry drowning and other complications," the older man said wearily. Jonathan leaned over and shook the women awake as Colin stood slowly.

"What did you just say, doctor?" Colin asked. His voice sounded hollow to him, feeling the embers of his heart flickering shallowly, not quite wanting to ignite.

"She's stable, son." The doctor now turned to the women, who were both sitting up and blinking the sleep out of their eyes. "We need to keep her for a few days to monitor her brain activity, though. Who's her mother?" he asked, glancing between the two of them, not able to tell with their red hair.

The medical team had informed the doctor that Olivia was the one doing CPR and was in the ambulance. They had to give her a sedative because she wouldn't leave her side for them to work on Allison. She'd been too frantic.

Vanessa said quietly that she was, and the doctor pulled her to the side to speak with her alone.

Olivia looked up slowly in shock, her red hair fell in her face as she slid off her chair to her knees, sobbing. Colin walked over to her and got down on his own knees, pulling her into him, cradling her head to his chest. They were all so exhausted and emotions were running high. He gulped relieved breaths, his frozen heart suddenly beating into overdrive.

"Olivia, I'm so sorry. I'm *so sorry*, baby. Please forgive me," he bit out against her temple, his voice hoarse as he squeezed her hard against him.

Olivia shuddered in his arms; suddenly spent as she took comfort from him.

The doctor and Vanessa walked back over to them. She crouched down and silently put her arms around Olivia and Colin before placing a kiss on Olivia's head.

The doctor, who was still standing next to them, spoke again. "If you hadn't jumped in there and got to her when you did, tonight would have been a different story. I was told that you jumped off a balcony to save her. Those precious seconds meant everything. Good job, you did well." The doctor tilted his head at them in respect, and walked away. His weary countenance betraying just how close they all came to a very different outcome this night.

***

They stayed at the hospital for three days, Colin and Jonathan getting them takeout, as no one wanted hospital food. Allison's room was bursting to the seams with flowers, balloons and stuffed animals. So much so, they started handing them off to other patients on the floor and leaving the flowers in various nursing stations. On the evening of the third day, they discharged Allison and they were able to go home.

Allison proved to be a very resilient child, bouncing back in almost no time. Olivia and Colin temporarily stayed at Vanessa's home with her and Jonathan, who seemed to have moved in with them, abandoning his mansion. Mary stopped by a few times, bringing dinner, and wanting to see Allison for herself as she'd grown very fond of the little girl.

Allison terrorized her mother with temper tantrum requests to see her friends, making everyone's life a living hell being stuck in the house with her so much so that Olivia decided it would be best for them to go back to their home and let her life go back to normal.

They'd come home one weeknight evening the second week of December, as the snow blanketed the property, seeing the house beautifully decorated for Christmas. The sight left her speechless, tears in her eyes. She'd been feeling so down, spending the last couple of weeks trying to repair her relationship with her sister. They'd listened to Jonathan's suggestions to go to therapy, having made an appointment to begin after the holidays.

They tried to bounce back from the fight, all of them feeling guilty in one way or another for the events that led up to Allison's accident.

Olivia often snuck off to the basement, finding a secluded closet where she curled up on the floor and cried a lot. She cried over the guilt from the accident with Allison. She cried because she was unable to share with Colin the true nature of her secrets, and it was eating her up inside. She wanted to trust him, but she was too scared to let him in.

And to top it all off, their sex life was suffering.

If Olivia was truly honest with herself, she missed the all-encompassing sex between her and Colin. While everything else was going back to normal, that still hadn't. And her body craved it, but he wouldn't give it to her. She knew he also felt incredible guilt for Allison's accident.

While they were all holed up at Vanessa's, they all did their best to rally around him, to let him know that no one held any animosity or blamed him, least of all her. She mostly blamed herself.

The day they had an intervention to try to snap him out of his guilt, she got on top of him and made love to him softly, sweetly, trying to show him, in her way, that she cared. He meant something to her. But she couldn't bring herself to say the words.

And what could she say? 'Colin, I love you, I'm a former dominatrix mistress who beat and degraded wealthy men for years to make ends meet. A lot of them are probably your colleagues by the way. Oh, and I'm also a failure who dropped out of school.'

Such a fuck up. How could he, with his status, want something like that? Something so damaged who would give him a bad name? She'd think to herself.

Now they were back home, looking at all the magnificent Christmas trees throughout the house, and Colin's eyes stung seeing her look wide eyed at all of them beautifully decorated, except for one in the lounge by the kitchen. Mary left that one alone for them to decorate together. Looking outside, Olivia silently observed the new wrought iron fence with a padlock that Colin had thoughtfully erected around the pool while they were gone.

It looked stark and depressing next to the white of the snow.

At the sight of the fence, Olivia closed herself in the toilet closet of their bathroom and cried. Realizing that Colin wouldn't bother her when she was in that little room. In there, her tears and emotions were safe to let out. She felt fresh feelings of inadequacy swamp her.

Not a good aunt, couldn't even be a good student, and maybe she wasn't a good girlfriend? Was there anything she could do right? All these thoughts swirled inside her head.

Abandoning the lingering trauma, Colin attempted to lift their spirits by dragging her out of the house and spending a full morning together the next day outside with mugs of hot chocolate, creating snow angels, snowmen, and chasing each other in snowball fights.

Colin tackled her to the ground and kissed her pink lips passion-ately, pressing rather a lot of his body weight into hers and she thought this was it. It was going to end their dry spell. She wanted it rough; she was getting antsy and needy; but still, he denied her what she needed. He then hauled her off to a decorating store, to buy special ornaments for the tree that they spent the night decorating, the movie White Christmas playing in the background while they wrapped presents to put under the tree.

Perfectly and undeniably festive, yet still, she remained incomplete.

Olivia became so frustrated she couldn't even orgasm normally, their sessions pleasing her less and less. And Colin didn't dare com-plain, not wanting to push her. Not after what happened on Thanks-giving. He'd never overplay his hand regarding her and risk anything like that happening ever again.

Christmas morning came, and they celebrated the morning at Vanessa's home with a huge breakfast, fresh squeezed orange juice and so many presents. They were all sitting around the fireplace, a Christmas playlist going as they all exchanged gifts. Colin smirked and scoffed at Jonathan's gift to him; a villa in the south of France. All the housing details were in a festive folder that was wrapped in a green ribbon.

"Who gives a house as a present, bro?" Colin joked, secretly thankful. He couldn't stand buying properties out of the country.

"Uhm, you gifted me my house. Remember?" Vanessa teased.

"Nah, your sister worked that one off already, trust me," he shot back, a wicked grin on his face as he glanced over at Olivia who blushed and looked away with a little eye roll.

Colin was happy to see that the tension between the four of them was completely gone, and terribly happy that he had the foresight to gift Jonathan a brand spanking new blue Ferrari, complete with a big red bow, and a baby seat in the back. The trunk boasted all kinds of baby paraphernalia, and he'd finished the look off with an enormous pink binky hanging from the rearview mirror. He ran for his life when Jonathan saw that. The big guy had a vicious hand for not being in the lifestyle.

One thing they all agreed on, was Allison made out like a bandit. She was completely covered in toys and loving all of them. Now ready to celebrate her sixth birthday in the next couple of months.

Allison's favorite gift was Vanessa and Jonathan telling her that she was going to be a big sister. And Olivia's heart pricked, wondering if it would ever be her turn to have that sort of happiness. Colin was quick to turn her thoughts elsewhere, and she was shocked speechless at her gift of the office building he'd started planning for her. He held back telling her about the meeting with the Architect CEO in a couple days, wanting it to be a surprise.

She looked at him almost like he grew two heads.

"Colin," she smiled hesitantly, "You must have some kind of faith in me, mister," she breathed, passing her hand over the documents to the building almost reverently. As if she was scared to touch it, to want it too much.

Olivia's gift to Colin was a jar of dirt, which made him tackle and tickle her until she almost peed herself. And a framed collage of the two of them filled with three photos of them kissing during Halloween, kissing during Thanksgiving, and kissing in front of their Christmas tree. His eyes pricked as he tried not to cry. She didn't know how much he cherished photographs, and a part of him came so close to sharing a picture of his mother. But he held back, knowing that if he shared anything about his family, then he'd have to tell her about the accident.

And because things were so fragile between them, he didn't want to risk it.

Jonathan gifted Olivia with a beautiful leather-bound, signed, first edition of the Grimm's Complete fairy tale book. Olivia ran to the big man, crying all over him. He chuckled and patted her back affectionately.

Vanessa gifted him with a slapper whip, which he promptly slapped her with. Lightly of course, he didn't want Jonathan to kill him with one of those torture techniques he shared with him that one time. He in turn gave Vanessa a lifetime all you can eat certificate to her favorite Italian eatery. Vanessa gasped, jumping up and down for joy, practically screaming.

Colin shook his head, chuckling at her antics. Food was this woman's love, Lord.

It was a beautiful holiday full of love and joy.

***

Colin was seriously regretting the decision not to tell Olivia about the meeting with the architect when he called her while he was finishing up at the office a few days later. He explained there was a last-minute dinner that he needed her to attend with him. He rifled through the copies of her work that he made, wanting to show the man in person.

Colin had crafted Olivia a short portfolio, complete with the most breath-taking picture of her in the front.

He was taken aback when Olivia told him she was going to take Allison to the theater. She bought her tickets to see a play and wouldn't be able to attend. He froze in his seat, his ankle over his knee as he looked at the framed collage of them on his desk.

"Olivia, I really, *really* need you to come to this meeting. Don't make me beg baby," he said softly, veiling his rising irritation easily, in favor of trying to be sensible. A concept that was coming harder and harder by the day to accomplish. It felt like forever since they played, and he was in serious pain. Denying them what they both needed because after Allison's accident, he didn't want to rock the boat.

She didn't tell him she loved him, didn't even tell him she cared for him and still hid things from him. Not to mention Colin was pretty sure she'd been sneaking off to cry, but he didn't want to press her on the issues after the accident. He wanted *her* to come to *him*, like the day she shared her story about her mother with him. Between those things, and the shit he'd been dealing with already, he didn't want to risk ruining what little foundation he'd come to build with her.

"I'm sorry, but I can't drop this. I *promised* Ally and she's been looking forward to this. *And* I've barely been spending time with her the last couple months," Olivia stated softly.

"What play? Can you get tickets for tomorrow instead?" Colin asked sharply. Holding the phone away for a second and sucking his teeth as he heard her say it was their last night in the theater for the season. His chest burned, and his fingers twitched with the need to snatch her through the phone.

"Olivia," he said roughly, leaning forward in his chair and planting his feet on the floor. His irritation getting the best of him. "I need you there. I don't ask for much," he nudged.

"I know, that's the problem isn't it. You don't fucking ask for anything anymore! Have a nice dinner, I'll be home by ten," and with that, the line went dead. Colin pulled the phone away from his ear and stared at it incredulously, as if he'd dreamt it. His head cocked contemplatively to the side as he leaned back again in his chair. After a bit he got up, jerked the lapels of his suit jacket, grabbed her portfolio, and tapped it once on the desk before walking to the door. He made the decision to attend the dinner and pitch Olivia without her presence, believing her work was good enough. And then he'd go home to prepare for her.

If she wanted it rough, then that's what she'd get.

He got into his personal elevator in his office and headed down to leave for the day, giving himself permission for the first time to let his demons come out to play.

TWO

A Cue To Start The Game

BACK AT THE HOUSE, Colin chilled out for a minute from running his errands after the business dinner with the architect. He sent Beth home with some more food and put on some good tunes to listen to. He had his ventilation system going and was smoking a cigar downstairs in the basement, as he took a second to text Jonathan to make sure Olivia left on time and was on her way before he turned back to his computer screen. Setting himself up at his pool table and leaning over his laptop, he tapped on the keyboard lazily, searching for what he wanted.

Flicking the ash, he glanced up at the multiple monitors he had on the walls in the swimming pool and billiards room.

Colin smiled, momentarily content with some music playing over the system and enjoying a really expensive scotch. So expensive, his dick got hard just from the process of buying it at the store.

He was lingering down in the basement lazily, just spoon feeding the fucking beast inside of him all the filthy things he'd wanted until Olivia came home. His dick jerked in his pants, impatient. Setting his mouth, the features of his face tightened as he made sure his computer synced appropriately to the mounted televisions. Doing a test run, he smiled a filthy smile when he heard the monitors start with the videos he'd selected.

Colin hadn't even changed when he got home, taking multiple trips from his car to the indoor swimming pool, Choosing instead to carry and unload bag after bag of ice into his pool fully dressed in his work suit.

Looking over, he saw the chunks floating, happy to know it was cold just like he wanted it. Then he took his time leisurely cleaning all the pool balls, placing them back into their rack on the pool table and off to the side.

Flickering his eyes to his phone as it lit up with a notification, he saw that she was pulling up the driveway. He pulled up their text thread.

Come straight downstairs. -C

Turning to face the entryway of the basement, he waited patiently, leaning against his pool table in his usual stance with his legs crossed and a cigar lit in his hand. A Gurkah His Magesty's Cigar, at seven hundred and fifty dollars each, his favorite. His eyes narrowed as the door opened and he saw Olivia walk through, her legs looking delectable in some heels that she shouldn't be wearing in this weather.

Olivia froze when she walked through the door and saw Colin.

Her eyes widened, clocking him leaning against the pool table, his suit pants and shoes still on from his fancy dinner. Colin's white button down was opened to his pants, exposing his slabs of hard muscle and big body. The sleeves were rolled up, showing off his muscular forearms and he was puffing on a cigar slowly. His eyes were hard as steel as he watched her.

She let her bag drop to the floor carelessly with a hard thud and turned her head to the side silently as her ears picked up the sultry music.

Colin just stood there, not greeting her. Smoking on his cigar.

Olivia's heart beat painfully in her chest as they stared each other down in the big space of the basement. She swallowed hard as she realized she was going to finally get what she needed. She could tell just by looking at him. He looked different, severe in the set of his body. Her nipples hardened, and she gasped as he lowered his eyes slightly and noticed it himself. Taking an appreciative drink, he suddenly spoke, breaking her of her trance.

"Come here," he said, his eyes never leaving hers. She shivered at his intensity, suddenly feeling very exposed, and very...trapped.

Olivia flinched as she immediately felt her juices saturate her panties. She whimpered as she willed herself to take the steps required to cross the space to get to him. When she was about five feet away, he held up a hand to stop her, taking another deep drag of his cigar, content to stare at her with his searing gaze. Her eyes pricked with tears, her body tightening painfully. She let out a little pained sob in response, starting to tremble.

"Don't you want to know how my night went baby? You're being awfully rude tonight," Colin said, tilting his head at her. His thick forearms rippled as he raised his arm to grasp his cigar, flicking it off to the side where he had an ashtray for it.

He absolutely relished her shocked stare.

"I-I'm sorry. It wasn't my intention to come across rude, Colin," Olivia said, her heart almost choking her words. That magnetic feeling sizzled between them, and the slow flame that was already there burned brighter as he fed the inferno with his casual assessment of her.

"Oh no baby, you're not allowed to use my name. But you know that, right?" he chuckled darkly at her. "You call me Sir, don't you remember?" his voice caressed over her like butter.

"Oh, sir. *I'm so sorry*, sir," she said, sarcasm dripping heavily with her tone. "How was your night, sir?" she said in a little princess voice, causing him to flash her his dangerously dazzling smile. The first real one he'd felt since the accident.

Colin pushed off the pool table and came to her, slightly to her side and stood still next to her, not touching her. She shivered, feeling the danger seep off of him in waves. He stared ahead of him, not even blessing her with his gaze. Taking a deep draw on his cigar, he sighed low in his chest.

"I think it goes without saying that you already know I can more than fuck the sass out of you so.... how's that pussy baby?" he asked, taking another drag of his cigar before turning his face slightly and regarding her closely, his eyes dark, slightly frightening in his intensity.

Olivia inhaled sharply and recoiled slightly at the heat she found in the depths, suddenly overwhelmed. The simple question pierced deep into her brain and her eyes widened.

Colin reached out quickly and easily grasped Olivia by her arm and held her still. His physical warmth sank in, grounding her.

"Answer the question. It's a very simple one. How is it? Is it good?" he asked.

"It h-hurts," she stammered around the lump in her throat. Looking to the side she froze, feeling slightly lightheaded at the ice floating in the pool. He caught the direction of her gaze and turned his eyes to her. Always concerned with her emotions first.

"Is the ice in the pool going to bother you baby?" he asked softly, not wanting to traumatize her. The last time she'd been in a cold pool was during Allison's accident.

Olivia shook her head no slowly. Her eyes narrowed and her lips parted, needing to jump in. To quench this hot feeling that he was making her suffer through.

"What are you going to do to me?" she asked. Her voice quivered, coming out as a whisper. He smiled, almost pityingly. He suddenly moved slowly to face her back, taking his hands and slowly tugging the zipper of her dress down her back, peeling the fabric away from her body.

He ignored her question for a moment.

"Why does your pussy hurt? What have you been doing to it?" Colin said softly from behind her, admiring her flawless skin, the shape of her neck and shoulder, which suddenly shrugged up at his question.

He embarrassed her.

Colin pushed her dress down her beautiful arms, watching as it wisped away from her body.

"It's so hot," Olivia whimpered, feeling like she could fall through the floor. A sob hitched in her throat as he unclasped her bra next. She was so turned on it scared her. She briefly turned her face to try and find him in her peripherals, so he stepped slightly to the side, facing her and giving her the comfort she needed.

"It's cool down here, sweetie," he said softly, tapping her legs to have her step out of her dress. He tossed it and her bra to the side, leaving her in her heels.

Olivia jerked when he suddenly placed his warm big hand against her belly and pressed hard, molding her back to his front. She whimpered at the feel of his big erection against her bottom, and he began to move them in time to the music. Making her gyrate her hips, he stepped them to the beat of the music, the speakers playing a dangerous beat wreaking havoc on her senses.

"Phil Collins In The Air Tonight. *A classic,"* Colin said to her, his lips close to her ears as the man's voice suddenly sang to the opening sound of the snare.

He turned her suddenly, and he pressed close, one arm splayed on her lower back, keeping her flush against his strong hips and thighs. He kept his hand holding his cigar free and would take a drag occasionally, just enjoying slow dancing with her and his cigar. She suddenly flushed, feeling vulnerable. The stark intimacy feeling like he was splitting her open slowly, painfully.

A tear slipped down Olivia's cheek. Her vagina had swelled and tightened painfully, and she was about to scream she needed release so badly.

He ignored her and continued to move them, almost imitating sex with her, him still fully in his clothes. Olivia felt so exposed with no clothes, while he just manipulated her to the music, the lyrics causing damage as he met her gaze while they turned and swayed. He expertly careened them around the basement floor, his body doing incredible things to her imagination.

Colin turned her once more, walking her to the pool table where he held his computer.

"Kick off your heels," he said as he leaned from around her, pressing slightly into her back and using the same hand holding the cigar to wake his screen up and tap some buttons. She lowered herself on her feet, heels off. She jerked and gasped as she heard raunchy moaning, slapping sounds, groaning, the sounds of hard sex coming from the speakers within the large area and she jerked in earnest as it sunk in what was happening.

The man was playing porn.

Oh dear Lord, Olivia thought to herself, feeling like she'd just caught on fire she was so embarrassed.

"Col-" she hissed painfully as he suddenly gripped the hair at her scalp in warning. *"Sir,"* she corrected herself. She squeezed her eyes shut.

Colin manipulated her head with his grasp around her hair, feeling her head turn.

"Open your eyes," he said.

She complied, almost collapsing when she did.

On every flat screen in the general area there was a different porn scene featuring a redhead woman getting railed every which way to Sunday. She cried out, her knees buckling. Feeling her body go up in flames. From embarrassment or desire, she wasn't even sure anymore. It was all blending together in one incomprehensibly rough mind fuck. And he hadn't even touched her yet.

Suddenly she regretted every time she begged, every time she was upset that he took her too gently, every time he ignored her requests.

The man was making sure she was good and thoroughly fucked, from her mind on.

And she wasn't sure how she was going to survive this one.

"I'm going to cool you off baby. Get in the pool," he said in her ear. Knowing her dilemma without her saying it.

He let her go suddenly, letting her find her balance. She walked slowly to the pool, not able to hide from the televisions. Hearing the tap of his shoes on the floor behind her, and the slow drag of something behind them.

She watched as one man had a pretty redhead tied up and was making her orgasm repeatedly. The woman's high screams for mercy not bothering the man in the slightest, she was dripping sweat, mascara running down her face and drool was dripping from her mouth.

Olivia looked away embarrassed as she took the first step into the pool moaning and closing her eyes. Cold, but feeling instant relief from what felt like the fires of Hell licking at her skin.

Colin had grabbed a chair and took it to the side of the pool and sat with his ashtray, balancing it on his knee. Resuming his usual stance of his ankle on his knee, he rested his head on a finger against his temple as his eyes flickered from screen to screen. He'd fired up another cigar and was leisurely dragging on it, sounding like he enjoyed it very much.

Olivia watched him as he leaned his head back and blew impressive smoke rings in the air. She hissed as the water rose to her vagina, cooling her off wonderfully, only leaving an empty sharp ache instead of the unbearable burn.

Olivia plunged into the water, heart swelling as it enveloped her completely. She sunk to the bottom, willing her heartbeat to slow. She glanced up from the bottom of the pool and opened her eyes. Colin was crouched down, taking a picture of her. She floated back up, lungs burning as she broke the surface, flicking her hair back hard and splashing him, giving a little giggle as she got a nice amount of water on him.

Colin just sat there, not flinching, smoothly moving his cigar out the way of the spray. Flicking the tip with that sexy movement of his and letting her have her fun. He grabbed his scotch and offered it to her over the side of the pool.

"Come here, tilt your head back and open your mouth," he said, watching her comply.

Olivia stuck her tongue out slightly as she did, and he hummed deep down in his chest as he smoothly tipped the glass with two fingers holding the ice inside, and poured the liquor straight down her throat. He watched her swallow before allowing her another drink, her pink tongue doing wild things to his imagination.

Suddenly one of the televisions took center stage and she turned in the water, her attention absolutely riveted as it stole her breath.

A woman was tied down, squatting on her knees on a large dildo. Her hips were encased by a leather harness that was hooked tightly to the floor by bolts, and her hands were restrained together by a rope hanging from the ceiling.

A crack rendered the air followed by a groan as some man whipped her back and her buttocks repeatedly. Her juices were copiously running down the dildo and onto the floor and she cried out as she orgasmed, throwing her head back in submission, looking like she was deep in subspace.

Oh fuck, I want that, Olivia thought, her skin heating up again, despite the cold pool water.

Colin tilted his head, watching Olivia's reaction. She was incredibly excited and panting shallowly. Her irises dilated, only leaving a sliver of green.

"Get out," Colin demanded hoarsely, walking to the wall and grabbing several towels he had stocked for the pool. He tossed them carelessly on the pool table and moved his laptop to the side. She walked out of the pool looking like a fucking goddess, her red hair made dark by the water and slicking to her head. He groaned as she walked slowly to him, knowing the effect she had.

Olivia's skin was pulled tight due to the cold, her nipples were rock hard, and her body had a pink flush. He picked her up and placed her onto a towel he laid out on the pool table. Bending down he took her lips hard in a rough mating of mouths. His hands encased the side of her face, warming her up. He groaned as her unique taste invaded him. Pulling away, he turned and snatched up her heels, placing them back on her feet.

She looked at him questioningly.

"It's going to hurt, isn't it?" she whispered. "It's going to be painful," the thought thrilled her, pulsed through her veins, heightening her desire.

His intense gaze bore into her eyes.

"And if pain is what I want to give you, what do you say?" Colin asked, pulling his hand up to grasp her nipple hard, tugging rhythmically. Causing her to make a lovely sound. He waited as awareness slammed into her.

"I'm supposed to say thank you, sir," Olivia swallowed, her body slightly undulating. He helped her onto her back, his big hand warm on the back of her head, lending her comfort. She bent her legs back and tilted her pretty heels in the air. He made her wait as he dragged his laptop back to him and pressed a couple of buttons. Suddenly, all the moaning and porn sounds stopped before an eerily familiar playlist started.

Her brain struggled to make sense of it, the monitors flickered back to life, and the image came into focus right as Colin dipped his head to her pussy and grabbed her whole mound in his teeth, biting her firmly.

Olivia cried out in shock and pleasure, and bucked under him as her brain processed the televisions.

Colin was playing a recorded video of them fucking in the closet that night after the gala. She orgasmed hard as she watched Colin completely take control of her body on the screen. Her helplessly tied to the wall with the belt and him pounding into her. The sound of her screaming his name suddenly entered the room, along with his growls, grunts, and sex groans.

Flesh slapping penetrated her ears and drove deep into her brain, echoing around and driving her crazy.

Olivia drew her knees back further as he'd begun to nibble and work her clit, pressing two fingers into her and twisting, searching. She flinched her hips hard in pleasure. Her gaze torn between watching him work his dark head in between her legs, and him absolutely turning her inside out on the screen. She suddenly gripped his hair and pulled hard, worried she was going to combust.

Colin ate her out for several minutes, his fingers manipulating her G-spot, until she came with an embarrassing groan, knowing she was ruined. He'd fucking ruined her.

He was proving effortlessly that he not only had control of her body, but her mind. And that's what tonight was about.

He got up suddenly, giving her a brief reprieve, his fingers sliding out of her wetly.

"You're perfectly swollen baby," Colin murmured, reaching over and slamming the rest of his drink, not even stopping to swish the expensive liquor around his mouth. He looked down at her contemplating her expression, before leaning over and pulling the ball set over within hands reach. The balls clinked together softly as he moved them.

"Pick one," he said gently, cupping her breast with his warm hand before leaning over and taking her erect nipple in his mouth.

"For what? Sir what are you-" she gasped, arching. He took her hand and placed it on the rack of balls.

"*Pick. One.* And do not make me repeat myself for the rest of the night," he said roughly, a warning in his gaze. He turned his attention to her hand, watching her closely, as if her reaction was important to him. She glanced over, her brow furrowing as she searched through the balls confused.

"What's the matter?" he said, already knowing the answer. He'd leaned forward and was doing distracting things to the inside flesh of her knee.

"Where's the eight ball?" she asked curiously, her hands sweeping over the ball rack once more.

He glanced at her sharply before smiling, making her heart skip a beat. He really was beautiful.

"Oh sweet thing," Colin said, leaning down and taking Olivia's lips in a deep kiss. Raising up to regard her once more. "You must know that when one sinks the eight ball, that means the game is over. *And it'll never be over between us.* I'm working my way in, so it's not available. I'll hand you the eight ball when *I'm ready* for you to sink it," he said confidently; his double entendre not lost on her.

Olivia paused, her heart pounding. Wrapping her hand around the white cue ball she handed it to him, the weight heavy in his hands.

"This is the ball that starts the whole game, and keeps the others in motion," Olivia said, a double entendre of her own.

His neglected erection jerked as desire mixed with sharp satisfaction filled him.

Chuckling darkly, he took it from her. Holding her gaze with his he lowered his hand and held it to her pussy and pressed, making her hiss in surprise.

"Colin!" she moaned wildly, feeling him twist and turn the ball against her private flesh, slickening the resin of the ball and warming it.

He watched her carefully, with a high moan she arched her back and her legs jerked prettily as he pressed it slightly deeper, watching her inflamed tissues part even more for this forbidden act. She squealed and tried to buck her hips as he got it further in.

Feeling her body's resistance, Colin dipped, taking her clit in his mouth and expertly manipulating it, sending her flying into a surprise orgasm on a shocked scream, not letting her up as this time he pressed firmly and with a small audible sucking sound it disappeared into her body. She made a small sound, and he whipped his head up to assess her.

His erection twitched against his pants.

"Jesus, I've never heard you make that sound before. Fucking sexy as hell," he growled in his low voice. He sank two fingers inside of her and pushed the ball deeper.

She lit the area up with her excited screams, mingling with the sounds of him fucking her viciously on the television. Just for good measure, he gave her another orgasm, having to hold her legs back as she slithered across the pool table trying to recoil from the sensation but wanting more. He jerked her back roughly, rising and bending down into her face. She was panting and moaning, sweat beaded on her upper lip and she was trembling. Her fingers clawed into his biceps.

"It's so h-hea-heavy, sir," she panted. Completely shocked at what the delicious pain was doing to her body. A rare warm sensation spread throughout her body, and she marveled in the feeling. The feeling of being free.

Of letting go.

"I'm going to turn that pretty ass red, and if you push the ball out during your punishment, I'm going to stick one in your ass and beat you until I am convinced you learned your lesson. When I ask you to come to dinner for work, you don't tell me no. And if you ever hang up on me again so help me God woman, I will fucking light your ass on fire till there's nothing left to singe," he growled.

She nodded, her eyes wide, the green almost completely gone.

"What?" he said, reaching forward and slapping her breast hard several times in quick succession.

"Yes, sir!" she yelled, moaning as she was assaulted from every angle. His voice, him in her face, them fucking on the tv, the music, the ball, sitting high and heavy inside of her spreading her out so deliciously. She throbbed deep around it, orgasming again at the heavy sensation. She gasped up at him, meeting his stern chocolate stare, feeling safe. Floating on the exquisite feeling.

"If not, I'm sure it'll be crystal clear by tonight," he growled, flipping her over on the table. "Head down, *ass up,*" he ordered.

Olivia hurriedly complied, gritting her teeth as she tightened her muscles painfully, trying to keep it inside of her. She heard his belt buckle before he whipped it out of his belt loops.

"This is going to hurt, and I don't know when I'm stopping, so don't bother to ask," he said, stepping to the side.

Suddenly, she heard a whoosh and felt a sharp stinging pain against her ass. It was decidedly not an easy hit, he meant what he said. She cried out, trying to recoil.

"What the fuck are you supposed to say, when I give you pain?" he growled, his hand snapping forward, the belt hitting her burning flesh.

"Thank you, sir!" Olivia screamed, losing her mind.

She began crying tears of joy, of absolute bone-shattering relief. Looking behind her, she saw he had taken his belt off and had it folded it double, clasping it in his hand.

"See, I think we've forgotten the terms of the agreement and who's in control here. I've been too lax with you. *My fucking bad,*" Colin snarled, gracing her with another stinging slap, making her ass jiggle with the force. She rolled her forehead on the fabric of the pool table and moaned, as she caught sight of her body going limp on the television screen, his beautiful body pistoning strongly, not tiring.

She nodded to herself in agreement, knowing he was right.

Colin went wild.

Yes! he roared in his head, seeing her flesh start to welt slightly, her creamy skin turning bright red. He noticed she pushed back, anticipating every new strike.

More stings as he slapped her over and over, her screams transforming to moans as the punishment did what it should do: service her greater need. He worked her over for long minutes, some hits stinging worse than others, other hits were gentle. Olivia never knew what the next one was going to be. She felt her walls flutter around the ball, and he paused in his slapping of her flesh, rubbing her ass gently, soothing her. She was calm, her mind slipping into a comfortable daze.

The pain felt so soothing that she would swear she was in heaven.

Olivia had no clue how long she floated there like that, her breasts and head pressed into the pool table completely relaxed. The pool ball had served to anchor her with its weight. Abruptly his voice penetrated her subconscious, easing her back up gently. She shuddered as she felt his big hand soothing across her abused flesh oh so gently.

"*Push,* push it out baby. Good girl. That's my baby. I am so fucking proud of you," Colin crooned as he caught the ball in his hand before placing it on a pool towel. He wrapped her up in his strong arms. Shutting off the electronics and carrying her upstairs, letting her come down easily. And when he was ready, he rocked her world in a different way, no less intensely.

***

A couple of hours later they were lying in bed, and Olivia was tossing and turning, not able to settle. Concerned, Colin sat up and reached over to his nightstand. As he flicked the light on he pulled himself up to rest his back against the headboard. He flicked his eyes down her restless form and decided to break his silence.

"Baby, come here," he said softly, watching her push her hair behind her as she turned to regard him sleepily.

"I'm trying to sleep," she said softly, sighing and closing her eyes, stretching out and unable to get comfortable. She groaned.

"Uh huh. You can't rest because there's something going on with you. I've been ignoring it, thinking it's school stuff that you were struggling with, but this is deeper. Come get into my lap please," Colin kept his tone purposefully calm and soothing, not wanting to alarm her.

Olivia sat up with a huff and held the silky green sheets to her breast and rolled to her knees, shuffling to him. Colin tsked and yanked the sheet out of her hand and just shook his head.

"No reason for that," he said softly. He took her arm and pulled her onto him firmly. He took a deep breath and spread one hand on her back and another on the side of her face. His eyes searched hers, trying to see. Trying to understand, to relate to the hurt that was buried inside of her that she was too scared to share.

It wasn't lost on him that the only time she'd safe worded was during an emotional conversation where she felt confronted. He'd have to tread carefully.

"We're about to do the emotional version of page three so there's no safe wording out of this one," he whispered, knowing he was forfeiting a seriously sexy and potentially life changing experience that he only got to indulge in with her permission twice a year per the contractual agreement. His heart tugged but he felt it was worth it, she was worth it, this fucked up shit that was killing her on the inside was worth forfeiting anything and everything physically pleasurable.

Colin's hand tightened on Olivia's face when she recoiled slightly.

"No. We need to talk," Colin took another deep breath. "This is hard for me too. The last time I pressed too hard, Allison got hurt. But I can't continue to ignore that there's something going on with you because I'm scared that something detrimental is going to happen. I'm not going to continue to walk around you, as if I don't know you're hurting. I see it, Olivia," his eyes flickered between hers and he let her see his own hurt.

Olivia's heart thudded painfully in her chest, and tears welled in her eyes. *I can't. I can't…. I can't. Even for you I can't*, she whispered in her head.

Misery pulled her features tight and, as if she was having an out-of-body experience, she heard a strangled sob escape her throat before she slapped a hand over her mouth. As if that could help keep the pain inside.

Colin's hand left her cheek and rubbed her arm. His eyes stayed on hers, widening in concern at the sudden wave of emotions that graced her features. His heart broke. It was bad, whatever it was, was bad. And in that moment, he hated himself for not seeing just how bad it was.

"Baby… *it's me*," his eyes searched hers, desperate for her to see. "I'm safe, I love you. *And I know you know I love you*, and it's ok if you don't love me back," Colin felt his own eyes well up with tears. Olivia began trembling, breathy gasps escaped her fingertips. He gently pulled her hand from her mouth. "But please, just let me love you. I can help you hold this! You're not alone anymore… you can trust me. Olivia, trust me? *Please*. Just trust me baby, why won't you trust me. What have I got to do to earn it?"

Colin's own breath hitched as he fought desperation.

He placed his hand back onto her cheek, his eyes implored as he leaned in slightly. His chest burned as it expanded with a deep breath, and he placed his other hand on the other side of her head, pulling her to him slightly. His thumbs stroked her cheeks, and he leaned forward, pressing his lips against hers softly.

He shuddered, speaking against her mouth harshly. "Is there someone I need to pay off? I will give up everything for you, Olivia. All this shit can go! The money, the house, the bikes, my cars, *everything!* Just fucking tell me and I'll do anything! Just let me in, please. It is killing me to see you like this, mi amor," Colin groaned, feeling a tear slip out of his own eye as she squeezed hers shut and a mournful cry escaped her.

Olivia bowed her head, leaning forward to rest her forehead onto his chest. Curled in on herself, the pain as it left her body was like someone was slowly driving a knife into his heart and twisting it. "You can't fix it Colin! It's already done. Oh my God... *oh God*," she cried out softly, her voice breaking as she sobbed inconsolably.

His arms banded around her hard as she began to rock herself side to side, small wails leaving her as she shuddered against him. He leaned his head back against the headboard and let himself join her in her emotions, feeling tears slick down his own face and wet his beard. He stayed silent, not willing to make this about him.

Even the fact that she was crying like this in front of him was a step in the right direction.

He held her until she exhausted herself half of the night, falling asleep with tears on her face and leaning against him. He tightened his hold around her, refusing to let her go.

Even though she claimed he couldn't fix it, he was determined to fix whatever this was. Colin already knew he was the lock; he was sure of it. He was more sure of Olivia than he was of his next breath, his next heartbeat.

He just needed the key.

***

The next morning, Colin stayed in bed with Olivia, watching her wake out of sleep carefully. She fluttered her eyes open then curled in on herself for a moment, her brain trying to process out of sleep. He ran his hand down her back in great big soothing strokes, letting her take her time.

This beautiful vixen is mine, Colin thought. He was going to call Vanessa and point blank asked her if she cared if he married her. He might have to kidnap Olivia and take her to another country if she didn't agree. He briefly toyed with the idea, but then suddenly Olivia was speaking to him.

"I don't greet you, because you're the one I can't say goodbye to. And you're also the person who, if I say hello, it means you were away for too long," she said softly, shyly glancing up at him before lowering her eyes.

Colin's eyes widened. Trust. She was giving it to him. Maybe he didn't have to kidnap her, he would have to wait and see. With the thought warming his heart, he gave her that rare, dazzling smile, just wanting to enjoy her minor concession, making her squeal as he pulled her to him so she could lay all over him. He rolled her all over the bed laughing with joy, reveling in her trust.

Trust. It filled his chest and overflowed that space inside of his heart that'd ached every day for the last twenty-three years.

Maybe trust was the key?

But it still didn't quite feel like the right key.

THREE
Secret Wedding

NEW YEAR'S EVE WAS upon them, and they'd enjoyed dressing up and going out to a rather lavish party, hiring Jonathan's niece to come and babysit Allison so they could go to Jonathan's friend's mansion. Though lavish, it was a laid-back party, and he'd noticed that Olivia could dance, like really dance.

The owner of the home had observed that she had rhythm and asked her for a simple tango dance, and it broke the whole house into a dance competition which made everyone's night.

Sometime later they were back at Colin's house just relaxing, enjoying each other's company, wanting to count down the New Year together watching, of all things, a boxing match. Jonathan's psychiatrist friend, Alexander, had trained the boxer who was the finalist in the match and they were curious to see if he would win.

They were, for all intents and purposes, relaxing in the lounge with the fireplace going and sipping their drinks when it finally hit him.

Olivia was staring down into Allison's face, as the little girl drifted in and out of sleep with her head in her lap. And Olivia was gently tracing her eyebrows, smiling tenderly at her. He looked over at Vanessa who was curled up on the sofa next to Jonathan and she was pensively staring at Olivia cradling Allison. His breath burned in his lungs as his eyes narrowed.

The key he'd been so adamant at finding suddenly clicked, he wasn't one hundred percent sure, but he'd learned over the years to not ignore his gut instinct.

His chest tightened painfully.

No fucking way.

"Vanessa," Olivia's sister looked over at him in surprise at his sudden recognition. "Will you please take Allison and put her to bed then join us back down here again?" he quipped, taking another deep swallow of his whiskey, having a feeling the night was about to turn nasty. She saw something in his gaze and nodded, carefully maneuvering Allison and walking around the bend and disappearing to where the elevator was.

Colin had already asked Vanessa if she minded if he asked Olivia to marry him, but no one knew when that time was coming. But he did, and everyone in the house could just fuck right on off if they tried to stop him, especially Olivia.

He had the sickening thought he might have to kill Jonathan if the man didn't let him do his thing.

Olivia flashed him a smile before looking over and asking Jonathan about the boxing match that was currently on the flatscreen. Colin took a second to get up and walk to his office, locating the manilla folder out of his safe and bringing it back to the lounge with him quickly, putting it on the side table.

Vanessa had rejoined them and was freshening their drinks and laughing, tucking her hair behind her ear and blushing at something Jonathan said.

But Colin couldn't stop looking at Olivia. Her guard was obviously down, and she was more imbibed than she usually lets herself get. He was grateful that she was finally letting her hair down after the awful events that happened over Thanksgiving, which made it all the harder for what he was about to say.

Taking the remote control and turning the television on mute he'd gotten up and stood in front of Olivia who was currently trading a 'what the fuck' look with Vanessa. Sitting down at the coffee table in front of her, he leaned in and spoke softly.

"When are you going to tell her?" he said, placing his elbows on his knees and clasping his hands together. Olivia's eyebrows furrowed in confusion as she took another sip before laughing softly. Her gaze flickered up and down his body teasingly.

"Tell who?" she giggled, ignorant of what he was talking about. He looked over at Vanessa who suddenly had her stare pinned on the side of his face. Her body tensed up slightly and she'd put down her mocktail drink. The woman was incredibly observant.

"Allison. When are the two of you going to tell her?" Colin replied softly. Olivia gasped, her pink cheeks flushing darker as she quickly glanced at Vanessa before flickering her eyes back to him as they narrowed.

"What are you talking about?" she said rather indignantly, suddenly snatching the blanket a little closer to her chest, tangling her hands in the plush cover.

His eyes probed hers for a second before he got up and retrieved the manilla folder, slapping it down loudly on the coffee table before resuming his seat in front of her. His eyes no longer kind but shrewd. She looked at the envelope, her eyebrows raised slightly before once again sliding her gaze over to her sister and now Jonathan who was currently sitting still as stone, watching Colin carefully.

He ignored them both.

"Look at me. Don't look at them, I'm addressing you," he bit out authoritatively. She gasped, flicking her eyes back to his and stiffening, her head slightly raising in surprise.

"Colin-what are you-" Olivia whispered; her lips parted as her breathing increased.

"I do not tolerate anyone insulting my intelligence. Least of all you. You will answer me, I'm done fucking around," he said softly, not easing the authoritative clip in his voice. A vein suddenly appeared in her forehead as she worked hard to control her facial expression.

A sob suddenly erupted from Vanessa's throat, and he looked over, and noticed her crying quietly. Her gray eyes looking sadly at Olivia, who'd now started shaking her head minutely, pushing herself back into the couch trying to get away from him.

"Ollie maybe we should-," Vanessa started, sounding like she was choking on her tears. Jonathan had placed his hand gently on her shoulder and was giving her small comforting rubs. She took the sleeve of her hoodie and wiped her eyes.

"NO, Nessie!" Olivia suddenly yelled, making Vanessa jump and place her hand on her throat. Her tears fell harder. "We agreed!"

"He deserves to know!" Vanessa said back, louder.

Olivia pushed the blanket off her and tried to get off the couch. Colin snapped, leaning forward and snatching her up by her hair, roughly scooching forward and pushing her back into the cushions. A tense moment passed while she looked at him in horror and Vanessa suddenly cried out.

"What the fuck Colin! What are you doing, let go of her!" Vanessa yelled, struggling to get up but Jonathan easily held her down.

Colin didn't care if they saw, they were going to figure this out.

"Tell her," Colin growled to Olivia who was squirming and crying in his hold. "Tell her I can do whatever the fuck I want to do to you," he said, gazing into her furious green eyes. When it was clear she wasn't going to cooperate, he reached over and calmly opened the folder and handed the agreement to Vanessa, his hand still tight against the back of her head. Vanessa took it tentatively.

Olivia's eyes now changed from furious to frightened and she stilled, pleading now.

"No Colin, what are you doing? Vanessa, don't you dare read that," she whispered, watching Vanessa out of the corner of her eye as she read the first page, ignoring her sister's pleas. Vanessa, no longer trying to get to Colin now, gasped and her eyebrows shot up in the air.

"Oh my God," Vanessa breathed, placing a hand over her mouth.

Colin relaxed his grip, still carefully eyeing Olivia while he waited for Vanessa to get to the good parts. Her jaw dropped and she'd suddenly slapped the paper to her breast, turning quickly to throw a horrid and embarrassed look at Jonathan, who was reading over her shoulder, his own eyebrow raised in surprise. It wasn't every day he shocked the man.

"Olivia, you didn't! No freaking way you signed this," she said simply, eyeing her sister once more before peeling the packet back and flipping the page.

It was Olivia's turn to cry, looking everywhere except them.

Vanessa let out a soft cry of shock as she got lower down the page. Under different circumstances, Colin would have found her reactions amusing. But not today.

"Allah. Friend. Page three? Wooow, interesting imagination," Jonathan suddenly murmured, hitting a certain spot in the paper, putting his hand to the back of his neck and rubbing before reaching over and necking the rest of his whiskey and pouring another bigger drink. He motioned for Vanessa to do the same, clearing his throat and remaining silent.

Colin turned his attention back to Olivia.

"So, I refuse to fuck this one out of you love. We can't get out of this, the agreement is airtight. And I want some answers. I promised to take care of you, and shoulder your burdens, and not just financially. I'm not watching the guilt eat you up anymore. I already know the truth; I just want the why. You deserve peace, let this go. I'm warning you you're going to let this shit go one way or another," Colin said, not having any shame over what was in the contract or having Vanessa or Jonathan to see him talk to Olivia like this.

Olivia's eyes widened slightly, her tears subsiding. He looked over at Vanessa, who had leaned forward suddenly. Her head dropped into her hands as she cried anew, looking so tired. "And you deserve peace too, Nessie," he added, addressing Vanessa now, who looked up and shared a look with him.

"Olivia," she whispered. "It's time. It's really time, sis."

"Can someone fill me in on what the hell you three are talking about?" Jonathan said suddenly, leaning forward as well. Placing his hand on Vanessa's knee in support.

Vanessa looked at Jonathan. "Olivia is Allison's mother, not me," she said softly. She turned her gaze back to Olivia who suddenly began to gasp heaving breaths.

Colin winced as unimaginable pain filled her eyes. Colin leaned forward and placed his hand on her breastbone over her heart. It took her a bit, but she stilled. He swallowed, his heart pounding painfully in his own chest, feeling his own heart break for her.

"I know it's painful, but we're done. We're done ignoring this," Colin said. "Olivia, I love you," he said, letting the pain in his eyes show. She now gasped in surprise, not pain.

Jonathan let out another low "wow," at Colin's fresh admission.

Colin leaned forward and grasped both of her thighs, firmly rubbing all the way up to her hip and back, trying to comfort her through what he knew was an impossible situation she was in.

"She was seventeen," Vanessa said softly. Ignoring Olivia's pained whimper. She'd closed her eyes and leaned her head back, placing her hands on her face. Vanessa slid to her knees on the floor and inched closer, placing her arm around Olivia's hips. Leaning in for a quick hug.

Olivia made a mournful keening sound. Emotions she'd spent years keeping locked away suddenly flooded forward, making their way out.

"I'll help shoulder the burden," Vanessa said softly, "you know that we'll figure this out Ollie...I'll tell him okay, I'll help," she glanced up at Colin as Jonathan slid over into her abandoned seat, getting closer and lending his support.

Vanessa began to speak, and Colin was elated to see that Olivia was finally letting her.

"Olivia was seventeen when she got pregnant as a senior in high school. We'd been living with Grandpa Stephen for four years at that time and I'd just gotten my CNA certificate and married my husband. We'd just bought our house," she started, taking Olivia's hand who was now hiccupping and staring off to the side.

"Then, she was awarded a full ride scholarship to the university through their architectural program. We knew she was talented but damn! And we were so proud because our parent's death hit her the hardest as she was youngest," Vanessa stopped, swallowing past the pain that quickly passed over her face.

"The father of the baby suddenly dropped out of school and disappeared, like literally dropped off the face of the earth. The timing was horrible, we didn't want Olivia to give up her full ride scholarship, so Grandpa and I planned for me to take the baby for just a while until she finished school," Vanessa paused and took a deep breath, tears slipping from her eyes.

"We just wanted to give her a chance, you know?" Vanessa's voice cracked and her breath hitched on a pained sob as she glanced down to the floor sniffling. "We'd already suffered so much. Dead parents, moving in with an elderly man who didn't know how to raise us, then the pregnancy, and then Allison's father disappearing," Vanessa smiled wistfully before continuing.

"It took so much convincing. Olivia didn't want to do it, but the school was across the country and we couldn't uproot ourselves to move. Grandpa wouldn't allow her to give up the scholarship program. So, we went through the courts for me to get temporary guardianship of Allison. My husband Nathan was supportive in the beginning. But then it quickly became clear that Allison had medical problems. He became short-tempered, not wanting to help me with doctor appointments, or with anything at home in any capacity. Soon he just stopped coming home altogether. He moved to a hotel and I was summoned with divorce papers. Then Grandpa's medical diagnosis...and I couldn't keep up by myself here. She had to drop out and she was so close to being done. It was like one fuck up after the other. Neither of us could catch a Goddamn break," Vanessa stopped momentarily to place her hand against her forehead, squeezing her eyes shut at the onslaught of memories.

Colin reached out and placed his hand on her shoulder, giving her a nod and encouraging squeeze.

"Oh Nessie, I'm so sorry. I took so much from you," Olivia said hoarsely, looking at her sister, misery pulling her face tight. Vanessa leaned forward and wiped her tears away.

"I would do it a million times over Olivia, you're my little sis, I love you so much," She said, before sitting back on her heels. "I don't regret anything; I really hope you know that. Like really know it deep down inside."

Olivia sniffled, wiping her sleeve across her eyes.

"Thank you," she said, looking at her sister. "I really needed to hear that," she leaned forward and hugged her, running her fingers down her sister's hair before sitting back again.

Colin watched silently as she turned and drank the rest of her drink. She turned her eyes to Colin once more, taking a deep breath. Then another.

She stared at him forever, her eyes going through a myriad of emotions before speaking.

"I love you too," Olivia admitted hesitantly.

Colin's eyes crinkled as he felt his face break out in a tentative smile. His heart soared.

"I was just so embarrassed and lost. I've been in survival mode for so long I didn't know what to say or do. I just worked. And dealt with the guilt of ruining my sister's life, and not being able to be a mother to a sick child. I had to drop out of school because of Grandpa Stephen's cancer, I had to take care of him because Vanessa had her hands full. And then we had Allison's growing medical bills, and Vanessa almost lost her house. By the time I was able to be present, Allison was already calling her 'mommy' and I knew I'd lost my chance," Olivia closed her eyes on a pained sob.

"I didn't want to confuse her. I'd been working a grueling schedule to help supplement Allison's medical bills. I'd already given my share of Grandpa Stephen's life insurance money I'd inherited to save Vanessa's house, so they'd have a place to live and not on the streets. But the medical bills quickly took over again as the money dwindled," she paused, flicking her gaze slightly between Vanessa and Jonathan.

"I met a friend who introduced me into some...work... and then I took a job at the diner so I could have a proper job and the government wouldn't get suspicious due to what I did as a side hustle. I quickly found I could make a lot of money doing it. But between the diner, the bartending, and the other work I barely had time to eat or sleep much less be a parent. So, I begged Vanessa not to tell her the truth. I refused to let her lose her mommy, the only mommy she knew, because of my mistakes," she said, her voice breaking, her green eyes almost black with pain. "I mean, who wants to hurt a little girl like that? I'd rather cut my own heart out than break hers!"

Olivia closed her eyes, jerking slightly when she felt Colin's lips against hers, softly kissing her. He pulled back.

"You were a victim of some horrible sets of unfortunate circumstances," he said hoarsely, his heart breaking for these two women and the little girl upstairs sleeping peacefully. He looked at her, silently encouraging her to continue.

Olivia's eyes widened as she realized what he wanted. She pressed her lips together, shaking her head slightly.

"Colin I can't, you won't understand," Olivia whispered. She flinched as Jonathan leaned forward and poured a small amount of liquor into her glass. He spoke quietly.

"Olivia, you need to get this off your chest, we can see it's eating you from the inside out. We all care about you and want to see you acknowledge this and start healing. It's the only way to move forward," Jonathan said softly, ever the therapy guru.

Vanessa looked up at Colin's questioning glance.

"I can't help on this one, she never told me. I already told you this multiple times," she said, rubbing her thumb on the back of Olivia's hand.

He leaned forward again, his eyes searching hers, begging her to see that he loved her regardless.

"You won't want me," Olivia whispered, trembling. "Not when you hear. You'll never want to touch me again," she threw the words out vehemently.

"That's not possible," Colin said, seeing nothing but heart break in her eyes.

Her heart was pounding, making her feel dizzy.

Colin sat back, taking his gaze from her eyes. He stood on his feet and grabbed a huge pillow from the couch. He stood and pushed the coffee table back with his foot and dropped it to the ground in front of her. He took a second to release his watch, needing the moment to steel himself for what he was about to do. It dropped to the table with a loud clank.

They all jumped slightly at the sound.

"Kneel," he said, folding his arms and waiting. Her brows furrowed in shock as she stiffened, her eyes slowly turning to Vanessa and Jonathan.

"Eyes on me."

An inaudible gasp escaped her lips as she paused.

"What did I just ask you to do?" Colin said sternly, patiently waiting.

Olivia stared up at him. She leaned over and picked up her drink, they all waited as she finished it quickly, wincing at the burn. Looking like a weight lifted off her shoulders, she slid off the couch onto the dark blue cushion and kneeled before him. He paused a second, letting her adjust before he crouched down and turned her, so she was kneeling with her back to her sister and Jonathan. He stepped next to her and placed his hand on her head, lending her his comfort.

After a tense second, she sobbed, and leaned her head against his thick thigh.

Colin could hear Vanessa's jaw hitting the floor.

He turned his body away from the couple next to him. Stroking her hair slowly, talking to her quietly.

"I've got you, in every circumstance. I won't ever make you do this in front of Allison, or anyone else, but you need our support. They are family, the closest ones to us. I am willing to let them be here to help you through this," Colin said softly, continuously stroking her head as she leaned against him tiredly.

Olivia let the weight go, lowered her eyes to her lap before sighing, mentally steeling herself to utter the next words. "I spent four years b-beating wealthy men for money. Twenty-five hundred dollars an hour, sometimes more, depending," she whispered, so low Jonathan had to lean in closer to hear her.

There was silence before Vanessa spoke first. "What. What do you mean you beat them?" she asked, her voice small.

"I had several clients I would meet throughout the month, sometimes at hotels, sometimes in their homes. They paid me to degrade and beat them. Whips, chains, some liked to be burned until they were physically sick. They liked to be choked, some like to be cut until they bled. I saw a couple of them at the charity gala we went to. Judge Carmichael was a client, among others," Olivia finished quietly.

Biting her lip, she pulled her head away from his thigh and rubbed her hands over her face. Heaving out a big sigh, she moved to stand up, pulling her long skirt out of the way.

"Where do you think you're going?" Colin asked sternly. His hand suddenly tightened on her head, refusing to let her up.

"I'm going to go pack my stuff," she said, simply refusing to meet his eyes. Her heart was splintering into a million pieces, she was so hurt she couldn't even cry anymore.

"The hell you are, Olivia," he said sternly. Raising his eyebrows when she didn't move, just sitting there confused with her hands in her lap. "We still have an agreement. For the next four years in fact," he said, lowering to a squat next to her and getting in her face.

"Do we?" she whispered; a look he didn't recognize shifted across her face.

Hope.

"I'm afraid so Ollie," Vanessa spoke up from her spot on the floor still. The papers were in her hand, and she was flipping through them.

"The way this agreement was written, he made it seem like you had an out, but you don't. You're stuck, beyond the two and a half years plus whatever time you've accumulated according to this. You essentially signed your life away," she said; the papers falling to the floor from her hands before they were snatched up rather roughly by Jonathan, who quickly scanned through papers before chuckling.

"It's not funny but.... motherfucker you really had the audacity, didn't you?" Jonathan said, leaning forward and pulling his phone out of his pocket. "This is the best contract I've ever seen. You took your time with this didn't you?"

"I have all the audacity. I told her that in the very beginning. It took me two solid weeks to write that contract. I have no shame. None. I knew what I wanted," he replied, staring into her eyes.

Olivia blinked silently at him, her eyes swimming in a plethora of emotion.

"So, you better get real comfortable because neither of us are going anywhere," he said, putting a hand against the side of her face. "Do you need me as much as I need you, baby?" he asked softly.

Olivia bit her lip, feeling the onslaught of emotions that were assaulting her. Out of all the confusion, her hesitation about Allison, her fear of not being good enough, her disappointment and heartache, her love for him was the one thing that felt natural. And she gave herself permission to nurture what felt just as painful as it was glorious.

"I do," she spoke softly, putting her own hand against Colin's face, giving him a small smile. He smiled and nodded at her.

"Jonathan, can you call our lawyer and go get the other file on my desk please?" Colin said, his voice rising slightly.

She half listened as Jonathan disappeared into Colin's office as he scrolled through the numbers in his phone before reappearing rather quickly, speaking to someone on the phone.

"Yeah, can you get over here to Mr. McDermont's home? We need that marriage license and your presence, sorry it's such late notice but there's been a slight change of plans. How much? I'll pay for it, let's call it a wedding present," he handed the folder to Colin before sitting down on the chair again, facing Vanessa, who's face now took on a rather alarming expression, shifting from happy to confused, then back again.

Vanessa looked at Colin and mouthed 'tonight?' at him. Colin nodded his head back. She broke out in a goofy smile, the same one that Olivia sported sometimes.

"I'll send it your way shortly, should be deposited into your account by tomorrow. Motherfucker you don't trust me or something? I'm worth five billion dollars... No, to be clear I AM offended, and I just might beat your ass before you make it in the house," Jonathan turned his gaze, eyeing Vanessa. "Ok, Ok. Hey, you got another one of those marriage licenses? Ah...well, I'll try next time. See you in a bit," he hung up the phone, tilting his head curiously at Vanessa.

Vanessa's half choked on her drink.

Olivia's eyes widened as she looked from Jonathan to Colin, her eyes pinging back and forth between the two.

"What's happening? Somebody please tell me what's happening?" Olivia whispered, slowly scooching back up until her hips hit the armchair. She was breathing hard, not able to make sense of anything tonight. She briefly wondered about the state of her mind.

Colin didn't answer her, he was busy flipping through the new document and double checking it.

"Ollie, I think you're getting married," Vanessa said, a stunned expression on her face. She slowly broke out into a smile and a giggle, turning and clicking glasses with Jonathan before leaning back and placing her head on his thigh. He put his hand on her head gently, grinning down at her before leaning in and giving the side of her mouth a soft kiss. Vanessa blushed furiously.

"Colin," Olivia pressed. "Look at me," he moved the document slightly, looking down at her still kneeling on the floor.

"What is it baby?" he said, a slight frown on his face.

"Did you hear what I said?"

"About what?" Colin's frown deepened.

"I beat wealthy men for money. I did sick stuff for work; it was essentially prostitution."

"Yes, I heard you the first time," he said dismissively, looking back down at the document before finding what he wanted, squatting down and handing it to her. "Look here, this is the most important information, I think. The lawyer will go over the rest with you, but I want to make sure you are ok with this before we sign it."

Olivia's jaw dropped. He'd handed her a prenup.

The stipulation he wanted her to look at; 'Olivia Alexandra Cameron will retain all property assets to any business created during the marriage in the case of dissolution of marriage to Colin Ian Mc-

Dermont. In the event of infidelity, all parties shall put the accorded value of the home listed address 7790 Feathers Ln, the home shall be put in a trust for all children of either party to be collected upon the children's twenty fifth birthday. Both parties shall lose rights to the home and all possessions within.' Although dissolution is in place, the contract that was signed September 9th shall remain active and legally binding.

A tear trailed down her cheek.

"That's our home. The one you sold me the blueprint rights to," he said softly, wiping the tear away. "I don't care what you did, if you killed someone I still wouldn't care. I love you. Will you have me?" he asked, going down on one knee and pulling out Allison's ring pop that he stole from her lunch bag. He'd ask for forgiveness later.

They all erupted in shocked laughter at the sight of the blue ring pop that he presented. Olivia took a deep breath and shook her head yes, unable to speak. Standing up he placed it on her finger before leaning in to give her a harsh possessive kiss.

"Thank you for being so brave," Colin whispered against her lips, gently rocking her side to side as he held her against him. "Thank you for being so stubborn and insufferable and giving me a reason to beat your ass. Thank you for being the yin to my yang. Thank you for loving me and giving me a second chance at life. Thank you for being you," he said, pulling back to look into her shining eyes.

Olivia sobbed at his words. They were the most beautiful expressions she'd ever heard.

They got married that night, in a small intimate ceremony in the lounge with Vanessa and Jonathan as witnesses.

Colin promised Olivia that they would have a lavish ceremony and invite all their family at another time. Soon, everyone had signed the necessary documents, and they were back together sitting in the living room. Toasting to each other, slightly in shock. But not unhappy. Jonathan couldn't stop beaming, his bright white teeth soon overtaking his whole face as he was proud of his friend.

As they went to bed that night, he fucked her in ways it really isn't decent to write about.

FOUR

Necessary Evils

A FEW DAYS LATER, after dinner, Colin and Olivia were sitting at the kitchen island cutting vegetables as she attempted to make her first focaccia bread without Mary present. And so far, Colin was pleased to see she was doing a good job. His gold wedding band shined brightly in the light of the kitchen, and he was happy to know that her wedding ring, which he had designed and special ordered, would be here a little after school started. As of right now she'd been wearing a simple band on her finger, at his insistence.

He was quiet, not wanting to break her concentration. Her hair was up in an adorable sloppy ponytail, and she was sticking the tip of her tongue out the side of her mouth, her face almost in the focaccia as she concentrated on making the design perfect. He'd set a moody instrumental playlist over the speakers, and he was reveling in the perfect feeling of just being with her. Her phone rang, making her jump slightly.

He put the knife down and took a sip of his scotch, his eyes roaming over the flour stuck to her messy, scantily clad body, wondering if she'd let him lick it off.

"Hi Aliyah!" Olivia turned the phone and propped it up against a bag of flour facing Colin before coming around with her own drink. He raised his drink in hello before leaning forward to press his lips to her hair. He pulled back as he smiled, amused at the dough stuck in her hair.

"Babe, you are not going to believe this!" Aliyah screeched through the phone, causing Olivia to slightly jump in surprise. Colin moved on his stool, pulling her slightly in between his legs and began to start trying to rub the doughy goo out of her hair.

He wondered briefly if he'd find any of the strands in the baked dough, smiling at his secret thought. His baby was trying so hard to create something in the kitchen and he found it sweet, even if it was costing him a small fortune to get constant take-out and pay Mary extra to make freezer meals and lunches. The woman just couldn't cook to save her life.

"Whhaaaatt, Beau'?" she sang back to Aliyah, now trying to swat him away as he was trying to stick his hand down her pants outside of the camera view. He arched an eyebrow at her as she removed his hand and placed the knife back in it with an admonishing look.

"Our friend Sarah got ahold of me and informed me that Studio Banks has a huge influx of new students signing up for a dance class with you. Girl, EVERYONE saw you on the internet from when you were at that millionaire's party. Can you teach a class this Saturday night?" Aliyah said, her screen going dark as she went into a tunnel.

Olivia gaped at her friend, barely hearing Colin chopping the last of the vegetables. The glass clinked as he finished his drink off. She reached over absent mindedly and poured slightly too much to refill it. He grasped her hand quickly with a slight frown, upturning the bottle and putting it down.

The scotch was not meant to be wasted, but savored.

She leaned into the phone closer. "Aliyah!" she snapped, irritated. Colin's eyes narrowed. "What did you tell her?" she hissed into the phone, her face upset.

As Colin observed the conversation, he too, was becoming upset, as Aliyah seemed to be ruining their good time, and possibly ruining the kinky night he'd had planned for them. He was trying to get it all in before she went back to school, not relishing the thought of her having lingering pain while she was supposed to be focusing on class. He cleared his throat rather abruptly; irritated.

"Uhm I told her yeah, that the GOAT would be in attendance. There's one hundred people signed up for that class because of you what the hell did you think I said?" Aliyah snapped back.

Olivia groaned. "Fine," she said, turning the phone to face her as she resumed the bread design, turning to make sure the oven was turned on first.

Colin snorted. That's an improvement at least, he thought, his eyes turning away from hers as he quickly took another drink.

Olivia didn't see the look on his face as his mind turned to planning their honeymoon. She only had a few free days before school started, so they weren't able to take one. So, he was trying to figure out when their breaks could align so he could plan something amazing, and he'd wanted her all to himself for at least a solid week if not more.

"Can I bring Colin?" she asked, throwing him a look. He raised his eyebrow and shrugged. He didn't care.

"Hell ya, everyone would love him, he's hunky," Aliyah said, the woman being a lesbian just threw that out there as an afterthought.

"Alright, I'll be there. As long as you're there," she said sternly. Her voice making Colin want to choke her to kill that authoritative clip, he didn't like it in their home. His fingers tightened on his glass as he took another sip.

"Be there at six. We can catch up. Love ya," Aliyah said before disconnecting the call.

Half an hour later, Colin had to remind her about the bread, as he was busy experimenting, thrusting a big cucumber in between her legs while she was laid out on the island as they waited for her bread to be done. Thankfully it didn't burn.

They carried her design upstairs so they could eat it while fucking in the bedroom's lounge.

She spent the next few days going to rehearsal, while he was at the office. She'd join him for lunch, sweaty and desperate for a break. She taught the class and then afterwards he drove her home, turned on by the private lap dance she'd treated him to after everyone left the studio.

***

"Colin!" Olivia's cries fell on deaf ears as she screamed through another hard orgasm, she was pushing against him, but he held her tighter, giving her those perfect thrusts that stimulated the sensitive spots in her body and drove her wild.

Colin had driven them home with his hand on her bare pussy, gripping her possessively. He'd instructed her to take her pants and panties off in the car. When they got to the house he parked haphazardly in the front and ripped her out of her seat, shoving her down on his dick in the driver's side.

He made her ride him mercilessly until his truck was rocking with their movements.

Olivia cried out as he stepped out of the truck with her still wrapped around him, twitching in orgasm before he turned and walked them into the house, lowering them and fucking her on the foyer floor with the front door still open, he hadn't even bothered to turn on the lights. Colin flipped her to her knees and was pounding into her so hard she couldn't even think straight.

He placed his hand on her mouth so her screams couldn't carry outside the house.

Caught up in the throes of their passion, and his pleasure heightened by Olivia yelling at him to spank her, Colin took his belt off and whipped her across her ass while he was giving her perfectly measured drives into her beautiful body.

Her heart quickened at his feral smile, and she tried to reach for the leg of the foyer table to steady herself, but he turned and dragged her away, slamming the front door closed. Dragging her by her foot into the elevator, he gave her a bone rattling jerk to pull her the rest of the way in, where he had her straddling his hips again.

She orgasmed so hard she reached out and slapped him in the throes of passion, and in retaliation he'd tied her elbows to her knees and then strapped her ankles down via her head once he got her to the bedroom, the strap tucked under her neck to keep her legs in place.

"Ohhhhh okay, you're fucking hitting me now, huh?" he asked softly. Moving to wedge two pillows under her hips, the position opening her up and spreading her wide for him at the perfect angle.

"I'm sorry sir, I'm just a little overwhelmed, please don't punish me I didn't mean it," Olivia whispered, her whole body trembling in ecstasy at the thought of Colin unleashing himself on her. She got two of her favorite things in one night, dancing and Colin's wild side.

She refused to think about why she was so adamant he hurt her.

Her emotions had been all over the place and she needed a release badly. His words temporarily ripped her mind from her feelings.

"I just know that you can't possibly think that we've even gotten started," he said as he stared into her bewildered face. He'd never tied her up like this before, mindful of her shoulder. But tonight, she'd proven that was a moot point, her shoulder was no longer a problem.

"Colin-" she tried again, her body shiny with sweat, she was struggling through her breaths, he'd already given her several toe-curling orgasms. But he'd already left her and went to their drink cart, mixing them up something. He took his phone and began to scroll through it.

He walked over and sat, letting her drink in peace, tilting the glass to her lips. He put the glass on her nightstand as the music began to play softly through the surround in the room.

He'd put on Lose Control by Teddy Swims. The lyrics raw, rubbing at the synapses in her brain simultaneously weakening and strengthening her at the same time. He leaned down, licking into her mouth deeply, rumbling deep in his throat. He was wrapping his dominance around her like a cloak, pulling it tight against her.

His big hand cupped her pussy and she clenched, feeling that delicious burn she often got down there.

Colin pulled back from her moaning form and his eyes caught her gaze, he raised his hand before roughly slapping it down on her mound and cupping her again, massaging her. She let out a cry at the first pop on her pussy. He slapped her in quick successions, the pops reverberating throughout the room. He cupped his hand around her and squeezed with a soft grunt.

"I want to take your ass," he said, not giving her reprieve from her eyes or his hand. She was wriggling, moaning under his administration. She cried out as his big finger started manipulating her clit in small circles.

"But not tonight. I just want to leave the thought with you," he said, leaning down once more, this time taking her nipple in his mouth in a hot suck. She struggled against the restraints, trying to arch but not able to move anywhere. The music abruptly changed into a softer transition.

Olivia caught her breath, her eyes misting up. He had put on A Gift of a Thistle from Braveheart, the melody tearing through her heart. He climbed back on top of her and thrust into her slowly, his gaze not leaving her eyes the whole time. Groaning contentedly, he thrusted slowly, the deepest he'd ever been inside of her. The music swelled around them as he struggled to contain the emotions he felt for her.

Olivia cried, opening her heart to him. "Let me go," she whispered, needing to touch him.

"Ask me a different way. I don't want you to ever ask me to let you go," he said softly, his brown eyes staring into hers softly as he waited.

"Please undo my legs and arms, sir," Olivia repeated, hissing as he ground against her just a little deeper.

Colin paused, removing her ties and bent down, feeling her fingers sinking into his hair. He resumed taking her mouth in a loving kiss as they rocked intimately to the beat of the music in their own dance, finally having found each other amid all their chaos.

Afterwards, she locked herself into the toilet room in the bathroom, sobbing as she sat curled on the floor, confused by the depth of her feelings. This became a habit, one she became good at hiding from him.

She didn't want him to know that despite their lifestyle, she was still hurting. All the repressed emotions she hadn't wanted to deal with were violently ripped to the surface and she didn't know how to handle them.

***

Colin surprised her by taking her on a five-day honeymoon to Belize and then to Italy. The two destinations wildly different, but each serving a purpose.

They lounged lazily in Belize, the tempo there much slower, allowing them to relax without any pressure. They went snorkeling and he was even able to convince her to go parasailing. Italy saw them going to multiple museums. She refused any attempt to shop, only relenting to get them matching beaded bracelets that only cost twenty-five dollars each at a stand off the street. It was his most cherished possession aside from his wedding band.

She was thankful that she blushed frequently, because it helped hide the tears from her crying in secret.

Olivia didn't know how to explain why her face was always pink. She looked forward to school, knowing that it would help distract her from this sudden bleakness she found that gaped like a black void inside her heart, right where her box of hurts was.

Too soon school started, she began to throw herself wholeheartedly into her studies, subsequently ending their little bubble of relaxation.

Colin felt that nagging feeling come back. They still had a couple of issues that they were both avoiding. They needed to figure out what to do with Allison, and he needed to tell her about the accident. He had a fresh outlook on the fear she felt at revealing how she'd made her extra money, feeling the same fear at telling her about the day that ended in him killing five individuals twenty-three years ago.

Olivia was currently sitting at the kitchen island, books spread out in front of her, and trying to type up something for a class while he was scooping chocolate chip cookie dough onto a baking sheet.

"Are you almost done, love?" he said, throwing her a glance as he placed the cookies in the oven and turned to lean against the counter, a fresh whiskey in his hand. He took off his glasses and placed them on the counter, finding he had to use them slightly more since the constant computer use was causing eye strain.

"Yes, I'm just finishing up a submission for my Architectural, Culture, and Society class," she said, before she finished typing and closing her laptop on a heaving sigh, rolling her head back on her shoulders and moaning. She was having a hard time getting used to the long hours on the computer typing. So, he often sat near her when she had to do these assignments, working quietly on his own computer, catching up on the news or conducting his own business for his company.

She was in a way grateful for the distraction. Due to the complex nature of her studies, she was able to focus on that and not cry so much. Repressing those emotions was the one familiar thing she could latch onto.

Tonight, Colin was baking them cookies to celebrate the end of the week on Friday night. It was a rather brutal one for her with lots of assignments and she'd appreciated his support. Olivia put her elbows onto the island and let her face fall into her hands, just needing a minute. He walked around the island quietly and pulled her to him, resting her head on his chest.

"Colin, do you really think I can do this?" Olivia whispered softly, pulling back and gazing into his eyes, her own filled with tears. "Maybe I bit off more than I could chew?"

"Olivia, you've got this. Academia is just that necessary evil that we all must get through," he smiled kindly at her. "I know it's harder because you were out for a few years and now you're back into it when it's the toughest, but you did yourself a favor starting your studies months early," Colin reached forward to push her hair behind her ear and run his knuckles across her cheeks.

"Come on, stop thinking about it and give yourself a break this weekend. You've been eating, sleeping, and drinking nothing but school for the last three weeks," he leaned down and gave her a chaste kiss, turning to make her favorite drink. He didn't let her drink when she was doing school work and she respected that decision.

A slow smile spread across her face, and he saw her gears switch rapidly.

"Can we talk about wedding planning?" Olivia asked excitedly, turning her wedding ring on her finger, it had arrived a couple of days before school started and it was a stunner. So much so he'd bought her an additional wedding ring for her to wear while she was out at school, as she didn't feel comfortable wearing such a magnificent jewelry piece when she went out by herself.

"Sure," he chuckled, hearing the phone chime softly that his cookies were done.

"Why don't you ever use the timer on the oven?" she abruptly asked, making him stiffen slightly as he opened the oven, waving the surge of heat from his face. He hadn't expected her to ask that question. He gave her the truth.

"I can't handle certain noises like alarms, sirens, emergency lights," he said gruffly, taking a spatula and beginning to lift the cookies off of the sheet and placing them onto a platter.

Olivia scrunched her eyebrows, taking a sip of her drink, her brain quickly contemplating and reviewing the last few months. She hadn't had an alarm set since she'd been with him, not having a need for one. He always rose before her and woke her up if she needed to get up for anything. She'd realized how calming that was, but never thought to ask why.

"So, is that why you were so...out of sorts...the day I got lost? I'd noticed something was off, but I just wasn't sure. I wasn't comfortable asking," her eyes met his briefly. "I guess we were both so out of sorts that night," she trailed off, blushing as she remembered the night he'd taken her for the first time.

"Yes," his eyes hid a small smile as he brushed over her face with an intense look, turning and placing the cookie sheet into the sink. He grabbed them a plate and loaded up on cookies, taking her hand and leading her down to the basement media room.

"So, what's the reason why?" she'd asked, pressing gently.

He'd already disclosed he took anxiety medication and saw a therapist every Monday, but she still didn't know the reason why. Whatever the reasoning was, she knew it ran slightly deeper than the fear she'd harbored over her own secret. The violence of his rare nightmares attested to that. However, she felt a smidgen of resentment that she'd laid all her secrets bare for him to still carry his own.

It didn't seem right or fair to her, but trauma often didn't make sense.

She curled herself up against him on the big sofa, having another moment of feeling small next to him. Sometimes their age gap was glaring, especially on nights like this when she was tired and vulnerable from being mentally pushed all day. In a nightgown that she knew he loved, his demeanor next to her was blaringly male.

He placed his arm around her shoulder, his t-shirt pulling tight across his muscles, he was relaxed in gray sweatpants and bare feet.

Olivia was anxiously biting the skin on her finger. Colin leaned down, placed his own teeth around it, tugged it out of her mouth and kissed her. He reached over to haul her leg over his to settle against his thigh. She slowly caressed his five-o clock shadow and stayed patient as he pulled up her leg the way he wanted it. Her shapely calf looked so little on top of his thighs.

"That's something I think I'd prefer for you to go to my therapist with me to talk about," Colin confessed, handing her a cookie.

"Babe...I don't need to go to a therapist with you for you to tell me what's bothering you," she whispered, not understanding the magnitude of the situation. And Colin told her so, which made her feel irritated and rejected. Trying to pull her leg back, she stiffened as he placed his hand on her knee, curling his fingers around and gripping her tight to keep her from moving. His eyes flashed warningly at her.

"Olivia, I have PTSD around this issue, please just listen to me and don't fight me on this," he said. Her eyes widened slightly, flickering back and forth between his.

She looked away hurt.

"Would you like to talk about Allison?" Colin changed the subject smoothly. "I know yours and Vanessa's therapy appointment is going to start soon. Have you had any thoughts about what you want to do?" he put the plate of cookies aside and leaned into her lightly, placing his elbow on the cushion and leaning his head into his hand. His other hand stroked up and down her calf. He raised his eyebrow at her when she looked at him with an incredulous look.

"Excuse me? You won't share with me but you expect me-"

"Don't do that," he interrupted her sternly, cocking his head at her. His fingers tightened threateningly on her leg. Olivia narrowed her eyes at him, her emotions getting the better of her.

"You're fucking rude," she whispered, meeting his hard gaze with one of her own.

"You're fucking stubborn," he growled back in answer. Leaning in slightly, his rising irritation met her indignant energy and filled up the space between them.

Olivia tried to yank her leg away from him, but his grip was too tight. She hissed at him, pushing against his chest.

"You've got some nerve, demanding me to give you everything and you give me nothing," her head jerked as she tried to recoil away from him. He took his other hand and easily placed it behind her neck to still her, his big hand encompassing it and squeezing slightly.

"I give you everything," Colin whispered harshly. His hard eyes on her wild green ones as his other hand slowly trailed up her thigh to her hip. He squeezed that in his hand too. "You have all of me baby, make no mistake. You have so much of me that you have the power to absolutely destroy me and don't even realize it. And I think it's time for you to give me something in return," he growled, leaning into her face.

Olivia's breath hitched in excitement at his words, she began to struggle anew at the raw primal hunger that was suddenly in his eyes. Before she knew it, his hands were fisted in her underwear as they pressed painfully into her flesh before tearing and falling away. He pushed her back into the sofa, ignoring her small cry as he shoved up her nightgown and off her body.

She startled as she heard the plate of cookies crash against the floor when he suddenly reared over her.

"Colin!" She yelped, as he leaned down to her breasts.

Gasping, she slapped her arms over her chest, looking up at him. She felt oddly too exposed, their harsh breathing the only sound in the room. There was no music to help, the movie hadn't even been turned on yet. It was just them, the muted lights in the room and she felt ripped open for him. That discrepancy between them widened, making her feel somehow smaller and more vulnerable than before.

Colin turned his hard gaze to her, his hands flexing in a warning against her skin.

"Take your arms away," he said sternly, his hands grip suddenly crushing on her hip.

She shook her head at him, biting her lip as he leaned down further, pressing his body weight into her, the width of his hips making her spread her legs wide for him. She started trembling.

"Wife, do as I say," his voice assaulted her senses, making her crazy.

When Olivia didn't comply, he took his hand off her hip and held her wrists together, moving her hands above her head, pressing them into the cushions. His eyes flashed warningly at her before he leaned down. She wailed and jerked as he took a sensitive nipple between his lips and bit down gently, growling as he could smell her sharp arousal flare around them. He moved to her other nipple and gave it the same harsh attention, reveling in her cries.

Ignoring her wiggling, he reached back and lowered his sweatpants below his hips, freeing his erection.

He thrust into her in one smooth motion, circling deeply and agitating her clit. She orgasmed quickly with all the stimulation. He pulled away from her nipple and looked down at her flushed face.

"Look at me baby," he said gently, moving one hand under her lower back and pressing her up to him with each stroke. The wet sounds where they met sounded sharp in his ears, egging him on. "I'm going to give you one more, then I'm going to fuck this sweet ass of yours," he said, holding her stare, noticing her breath hitch in embarrassment.

She turned her face into her arm as he pistoned his hips in and out, giving her perfectly measured thrusts. When she was crazy with need, he let her orgasm and pulled out, feeling her muscles drag against his heavy cock.

"Colin," Olivia begged, her face now looking up at him. She shivered as he began to drag her juices from her opening to the puckered hole in her ass. "Colin, I'm scared."

He leaned down and kissed her, reveling in her plump lips.

"I've got you," Colin said, and suddenly a peace fell over her as she realized he meant it. She hissed and arched as he suddenly pressed, her flesh not wanting to give.

"Let me in," he whispered. "Let me in, Olivia, you're tearing me apart."

Olivia let out a soulful cry as he pressed harder and she opened for him jerking against his hold. He waited, shushing her gently, pressing a tender kiss to her forehead as he inched deeper. She leaned forward suddenly and bit his pec, causing him to groan and press even deeper.

He snarled as her teeth broke the skin through the material of his shirt.

Colin took the pain growling, listening to her squeal as he sank all the way into the hilt and stilled them. They were breathing harshly. He moved, sweeping his hand from her shoulder down her side to her knee and back up, soothing her. He gently moved her head back from her hard bite on his shoulder.

"This is as intimate as we can get," he said, looking at her with pain in his eyes. Her own widened in response to his words. "I'm terrified that when I tell you what happened, you will leave me, Olivia. I need us to discuss this in a controlled environment because I am worried I won't be able to control myself if you try and walk out on me baby. It would kill me. I don't have anything more to offer you to make you stay. You have everything that means anything to me," he leaned his forehead against hers, his own breath catching at his admission. His minty breath fluttered warmly across her face.

She leaned up, taking his mouth in hers deeply, her tongue sweeping, searching for his. She moaned as his dick twitched inside of her.

"Move," Olivia whispered harshly, trying to press her hips up but it was difficult in her awkward position. "Colin, I'm not leaving you. I love you. I love you so much it hurts. If you can accept me and all my faults, don't you have faith in me that I can accept you and yours?" she whispered, pulling at her wrists again.

Colin let her go and her arms came around his neck to press him to her. He began to move slowly, dragging his cock in and out of her on a harsh groan.

"You're so *tight*...feels so fucking right," he said gruffly, groaning as he pushed back in on a low slap of their flesh meeting. He moved his arm, squeezing his hand between them and sunk two thick fingers inside of her vagina as he moved his hips leisurely, placing his lips to the side of her neck as she arched on a low moan. She clenched hard around him, her muscles spasming along his finger and his cock.

His thumb pressed tight circles onto her clitoris, knowing she needed extra stimulation to make this feel good.

Olivia grabbed his free hand, pressing it against her neck. He looked at her for a few heart stopping moments and her hand fell away shyly, thinking that he wouldn't give this to her. Her heart pounded painfully before he'd suddenly tightened his big hand on her neck, watching her eyes flutter closed as she caressed his arms loosely with her hands. After a bit, he eased up and let her suck in air before flexing again.

He felt her body tighten as she silently rode out her orgasm.

He let her throat go, pulling his fingers out of her pussy to lick her juices off before bending down to press his lips once more to hers. They stayed like that until they were both depleted emotionally and physically. He scooped her up and took her upstairs where he stepped them into a bath where they held each other the rest of the evening, only leaving when their skin started to prune.

They stayed in bed most of Saturday, and despite the relaxed day, she felt on edge and had been since they were in the media room. Colin surprised her by making tacos, not commenting on her short replies and lack of talking, thinking that she was just withdrawing after sharing something so intimate. He gave her extra care, cuddling with her in bed, taking a bath with her and settling them in for a movie in bed. They were still trying to feel out each other's intricacies, and he was mindful to pay attention to anything that could be a trigger.

Sunday, they spent the whole day with Vanessa, Jonathan, and Allison, going to see an interactive play.

Colin again noticed how quiet she was, not being her usual animated self with Allison.

Monday came and went, and Olivia threw herself into her schoolwork again. She had such a rigorous afternoon studying that she fell into bed and was asleep before Colin came home from work a little later than usual, having had to move his therapy appointment with Dr. Tyson back due to an extensive work obligation. He confirmed with Mary that Olivia had eaten before going to bed, not wanting to wake her up unnecessarily.

Colin tamped down his feelings of desire, not having had sex with Olivia since Saturday morning and here it was Monday night, and she was already asleep. Tomorrow evening was their first therapy appointment, and they had already gotten the primary paperwork out of the way so they could spend the ninety-minute session talking. He went to his study and spent several hours working, trying to take his mind off his wife in the bed upstairs.

But it was no use because she was always on his mind and in his heart.

FIVE

Scarcity Mindset

TUESDAY MORNING, THEY WOKE up and got ready separately. Olivia's mind was heavy on their session tonight. Having never been to therapy, she was worried that the counselor was not going to understand their dilemma and worst of all judge her for giving up her rights to her child. Especially when she'd technically had an opportunity to get her back, because it wasn't as if Vanessa was keeping her from Allison.

She'd been worried about it all weekend and knew she had been short with Colin. On top of school stress, she was sad that she felt things were changing within the dynamic with her sister and Allison. Though she knew Jonathan was a wonderful man and a much-needed father figure, she felt like she wasn't needed anymore, and she began to start closing her heart off from her daughter even more. It hurt too bad to think about. And she didn't want to discuss it in therapy.

And then there was Colin's secret. She was so antsy she found herself talking back with Colin, and just withdrawing into herself. She hadn't been this irritable since she was killing herself working at the diner.

Colin dropped her off at school and she struggled anew, finding that she'd barely passed an exam for one class, and missed reading an entire chapter for another.

By four in the evening, she'd realized she missed several texts from Colin, having been too immersed in just barely getting by to notice her phone. She walked briskly to where she knew he was parked and gave him a halfhearted smile as he rounded the car quickly to open the door for her. He stopped her with a hand on her shoulder as she attempted to get in the car.

"Hey, slow down," Colin said, grabbing her backpack off her back and putting it into the back seat. She began to try and get into the car again, not meeting his eye. "Olivia, stop. Stop and look at me for a second."

Olivia turned slowly and met his eye, barely holding back her tears. "I don't want to look at you," she whispered.

She kept her eyes on his chest as the tear she'd been holding back all day falling and splashing onto her cheek and she rubbed it away hard, sniffing. Wrapping her arms around her waist, she made herself stay still, waiting for his next move.

Colin walked her until her back was against the open car door and put his forearm on the top of the car and leaned in, affording them a little privacy. Her hackles went up as she realized he wasn't letting her up until he got what he wanted. She glared at his chest before reaching up on her tiptoes to press a chaste kiss to his lips.

His hand grasped her chin and held her still, he tilted her head up until she met his gaze.

The look he gave her was so searingly intimate that her world felt rocked for a split second, and she swayed on her feet. She let out a little whimper and she felt her face flush with emotion. Another tear fell out. Perhaps it was better that she cried before the appointment so she wouldn't embarrass herself in front of the counselor. He leaned down and sealed his lips to hers in a gentle kiss. His tongue sweeping along hers ever so gently.

"I'm taking you to dinner before the appointment," he said softly, he noticed her fingers fisting in her sweater. "It's ok love, do you need to cry before we leave?" he asked suddenly, pressing his lips to the top of her head.

Olivia whined as she broke, all the pent up emotion just leaving her at once at his question. It was like she needed him to give her permission to let it out in front of him. He wrapped his arm around her waist and pulled her into him, and she sank her fingers in his shirt. Crying silently into his sweater. All the while he kept his lips pressed to the crown of her head.

After a few minutes, she pulled back, shivering. They were still outside in the cold, but Colin wasn't complaining, just giving her what she needed. She took a deep breath.

"Thank you," she whispered, feeling him wipe her tears away. He helped her bundle into the car and dropped another kiss on her mouth before closing her door and getting into the other side.

"Colin?" Olivia said softly, as he was putting his phone on the car's docking station. He grunted in acknowledgment, putting the restaurant's address in the GPS.

"Can I pay for our dinner tonight?" she whispered, not looking at him.

He furrowed his brow as he turned to look at her, turning his whole body in the seat to face her. They regarded each other for a second. His stare always seeing too much.

"First, I need you to answer what it's going to matter if you swipe your card, or I swipe mine?" he asked, an eyebrow arching. She furrowed her own back at him.

"What?" she asked, confused.

"Our money is combined, what's mine is yours and all of that. You have access to everything baby, you haven't looked at your account in a while?" Colin asked.

Olivia frowned, digging into her purse and pulling out her debit card. It looked the same. Then took out her phone and logged into her banking app, seeing too many numbers and dollar signs that betrayed that he had in fact merged their finances, without asking her. And she didn't know because she thought she'd been paying for her school lunches and other things with the money he'd given her for the blueprints, not having a need to look at her accounts like she used to.

Olivia felt stripped of her last vestiges of independence. She felt her blood boil as she snapped mentally.

"Olivia-"

"SHUT THE FUCK UUUPPP," she screamed at him so loud she felt like she burst a blood vessel.

She turned her back on him in the seat, facing the window and curling in on herself. Colin wisely kept quiet and took a deep breath, determined to make it through the evening. He knew that a break was coming and had been mentally preparing himself for it. He put the car into drive, and drove off slowly in the direction of the restaurant, attempting to get a handle on what was happening between them.

They sat at a secluded booth at a restaurant he'd chosen, and Colin pissed her off by ordering the most expensive bottle of wine they had on the menu. So, Olivia waited until they drank half of it before she knocked it off the table by 'accident', then promptly helped the waitress clean it up. She settled back in the seat and calmly ate the rest of her soup, feeling minutely better.

He waited until they were in the car before he locked the doors and turned to look at her.

She recoiled at the fury in his eyes.

"You're going to get what you're begging for, but we're going to get through this therapy appointment first. I don't know what the fuck is going on with you right now, but I have been an exceedingly patient man. You need to watch yourself before you bite off more than you can chew, little girl."

Olivia slapped him across the face before she even knew she did it, hearing his groan as his head cracked to the side. He stayed there, his eyes closed and breathing deep. She gasped; eyes wide before she slowly turned to look out the front of the window. She began trembling, her breaths coming out panicked.

"There's no need to shake. I would never retaliate by putting my hands on you back in anger," he said, his tone clipped as he turned back to face the front.

"I'm s-s-sorry, Colin," she whispered, barely able to hear her own voice through the blood rushing in her head.

Colin threw the car into drive and peeled off down the road. The car ride was uncomfortable, he didn't even turn music on to break the tension, not saying a word to her. Soon they were at the therapist's building. It was an indiscreet glass building with no identifiable markings other than a number for the address.

Colin rounded the car and opened her door, she didn't even know if he looked at her as she was studiously not staring at him, too afraid to meet his eyes. He closed the car door with a slam that made her jump and she winced as he placed his hand on her lower back to escort her up the stairs.

Colin had already schooled his face into an impassive yet pleasant expression as he introduced her to Dr. Tyson.

Dr. Tyson was a short, yet intimidating African American male who had the kindest eyes she'd ever seen. She went to sit on the couch next to Colin, carefully perching herself stiffly, taking a peek around the room to relieve herself of the sudden rush of testosterone that took up the space.

Olivia saw a movement out the corner of her eye and saw that Colin had placed his hand palm up on the sofa between them.

She chanced a glance at him and noticed he still wasn't looking at her. She tentatively placed her small hand in his and she felt tears prick the back of her eyes when he closed his hand over hers and squeezed softly, rubbing his thumb along her knuckles. She squeezed his back, leaning more into the seat and crossing her legs.

Dr. Tyson explained that he wanted to keep this session light, just an introduction. He spent time explaining his modality to Olivia, how long he'd been a therapist and wanted to know if she'd ever been to therapy, and what she expected to get out of therapy, individually and as a couple. He also spent some time going over their relationship, so he could get a better feel for their dynamic.

He was not shocked or gave any indication of judgment when Colin explained how they got married, and how quickly they got married... and that they were compatible in that way. The fact he liked to give pain and she liked to receive. The doctor wrote some notes on that, and Colin squeezed her hand again when she was unconsciously trying to lean forward to see his notes.

Olivia relaxed back into the seat. She got really embarrassed when the doctor brought up their age gap, not at the age gap itself but at Colin's obvious pleasure behind it. It was the same pleasure she found that he took in when he spent a lot of money, or really did anything that meant he had power.

But she quickly realized that he didn't abuse that power.

His sadism was only limited to their sexual relationship. Which was apparently very tame at the moment compared to how it could be. When the doctor brought that up, Colin spoke about how he was aware that though they got married very quickly, he wasn't rushing or pushing the dominant submissive lifestyle they were leading; preferring to sit back and observe what Olivia really responded to and what he felt she could tolerate in their early stages of marriage.

He stated that due to her fragile emotions lately he didn't want to inadvertently do something to damage her mental health if she wasn't yet strong enough to tolerate such a dramatic shift in their dynamic.

This information shocked her, at how much he'd been holding back due to her. And she felt comforted and considered.

Olivia appreciated that and expressed so when the doctor asked her.

"Yes," Olivia said, licking her lips and shifting in her seat uncomfortably. "I had only ever been with one person, one time before I met Colin. And I found that I was utilizing other means to satisfy that need inside of me, unconsciously. I worked hard because I needed money, but now looking back, I relished the pain I put my body through. Not knowing what I really needed. I still find myself sometimes, when Colin and I aren't... aren't..." she trailed off. Not knowing exactly how to say it.

She pointedly kept her eyes from straying over to her husband.

"This is a safe space, Olivia," Dr. Tyson said, smiling at her gently. She took a deep breath.

"When we aren't intimate the way I need it...I feel almost like a ticking time bomb when I don't get...my needs taken care of. It makes everything else worse. So much worse," she whispered, knowing her face was bright red. She pulled her hand from Colin's and gripped them together harshly.

"I'm struggling in my studies right now, I'm back in my architectural program and I'm starting back in the hardest classes after having over four years off and I'm struggling," she paused, her eyes briefly flickering up to find the therapists kind ones. "I'm struggling with feeling like a failure. I just found out today I basically failed a test. I feel like I'm disappointing Colin, my sister, and Allison. I've pulled away from her to protect myself," she sniffled and whispered her thanks as Colin handed her a couple of Kleenexes. She wiped her nose and crumpled the tissue in her hand. "And I also feel bad because Colin's opened up a whole world to me and I just want to be worthy of it. So, I can't fail. I never fail! But I just don't know what to do. All I've ever known since I was fourteen years old is to shut off my emotions and work. Succeed at my efforts," she sighed.

"You don't feel worthy?" Dr. Tyson inquired, settling back a little and putting his kind eyes on hers. She shook her head.

"I was killing myself to make fifteen grand a month. For my niece and my sister," she left out that the niece was actually her daughter. "She has a medical condition. But anyways, life has been so hard, and all I knew how to do was work. Then Colin appeared out of nowhere, literally in a storm and wouldn't leave me alone for a month trying to get me on a date. I didn't know he was so well off. With the simple swipe of a card he can buy ANYTHING he wants, things that would take me a lifetime to work for. It just seems so....so...." she paused.

"Go on." Dr. Tyson said, his ballpoint pen poised over his paper.

"Surreal. Like why did I, of all people, hit the lottery like this?" she whispered. "My parents are dead, my d-niece, dropping out of school to take care of my sick grandpa, barely able to make ends meet. Colin didn't know this but... I hadn't eaten in two days when he took me out on our first date. He took me to a restaurant and spent two grand on a meal when all I needed was a three dollar cheeseburger to fill me up," she refused to meet his gaze when Colin turned his attention rather noticeably towards her.

"So, you've been surviving with a scarcity mindset, and the drive of a hustler, and then you up and marry a man- a self-professed sadist at that- within months, who gets off on the power of making money. And having a ton of it at that...and you're surprised why your mind can't settle? Why you're so emotional?" Dr. Tyson said softly, not even scribbling in his notepad. She scrunched her nose.

"Olivia, I love you," Colin said softly. "Even if I was financially broke, I would still love you. My money, yes, is a bonus and I want you to enjoy it. How I built my company is a product of the trauma I have to live with for the rest of my life. I love that someone who actually needs it, who damn sure deserves it, can use it. And won't take advantage of it? You are a blessing to me. You're a gift baby," Colin reached out and grasped her hand once more, giving her a firm squeeze.

She tentatively met his gaze and bit her lip as she tried to decipher the look on his face.

"So, Olivia, you haven't asked Colin to give you what you need, and Colin, you're too afraid to take her there? Why?" the doctor said, shifting in his seat and scribbling on his notepad.

"Tyson, you know me. You know how I am. I'm scared to take her there. I'm scared of running her off. Maybe it's too soon? We're too fragile right now?" Colin whispered, his hand tightening on hers.

"Why do you think I'm going to run away Colin?" she whispered, turning more towards him and searching his eyes. He met her look with a sad one of his own. He took his free hand and racked it through his hair in a small gesture of insecurity that she was not familiar with coming from him.

"Because, when you find out what happened when I was a teenager, and then you find out just how real it can get for us in the bedroom... I'm scared it's going to be too much and you're going to leave me. That's why I had that clause drawn up in our prenup. It really was the only stipulation," he said softly, his hand leaving hers once more and scrubbing down his face.

Her eyes narrowed. "I hit him, shortly before we got here, I lost it and hit him," she said, turning to Dr. Tyson.

"And why did you do that?" Dr. Tyson asked, scribbling now.

"I think it's because.... unconsciously...I want that reaction out of him, I need him to give me what I need. I want him to ground me. I won't leave you Colin. Not because of this," she whispered, opening and desperate for him to see.

Inside her mind, she was holding the lid off her box of hurts and gesturing for him to go inside and explore.

"Colin, she's telling you that she's ready. Do you hear it?" Dr. Tyson said his attention focused now on Colin.

Colin gave them both a short nod.

"Not until I tell her what happened, Doctor," he said, leaning forward and scrubbing his hand once again down his jaw.

Dr. Tyson nodded. "That's fair," he said, closing his notebook. Olivia felt herself deflate slightly, the leather of the couch feeling hot against her body.

"Ok, we're at the end of session, and we can discuss more next time when we can give the topic adequate holding space. For homework I want you each to write down what it is you want the other to know. We will then read it outloud at the beginning of our next session next week," the doctor stood up and shook both of their hands and led them to the elevator.

The drive home was harder than the drive there, if that was even possible. Olivia kept thinking about the slap she had given Colin, knowing that he was going to punish her one way or another.

"Colin..." she said.

"I think therapy is going to be good for us," he said suddenly, taking the turn that led them into their neighborhood.

"Colin-" she tried again, turning in her seat slightly. Her fingers grasped her seatbelt hard, twisting against the restraint, wishing it was another type of restraint.

"No, Olivia. When we get home I want you to take a shower and go to bed. Leave your backpack in the car and leave your phone with me," Colin interrupted, holding his hand out. Olivia placed it into his hand and watched as he pocketed it and hit the button for their gate and drove slowly up the curved driveway.

Olivia let him walk her into the house and then blinked when he continued through and made his way to a door that led to the outside without another word to her. She took the stairs up, hearing the door close behind him. She showered and cried, feeling vulnerable after their first therapy appointment, but not knowing what to do to fix this sudden chasm that opened between them.

Completely mentally exhausted, she fell into bed and crashed. She was so sick of crying.

A couple hours later, Olivia had awoken with a start, and noticed that Colin's side of the bed was empty, the covers not even ruffled, betraying he hadn't come to bed. Rising, she spotted her phone on the nightstand next to her, charging. Colin had come in at some point to check on her. She looked at her phone, seeing it wasn't even midnight yet.

She grabbed her phone and padded downstairs, trying to find him. He wasn't in the house that she could tell.

Taking her phone, she unlocked it and texted him.

Where are you? Did you run away? -O

She was mixing a drink, now wide awake, and a couple minutes passed before she heard her phone ding.

Do you have to be so insulting? I'm in the guesthouse, come here. -C

She went back upstairs and hurriedly threw on a tank top and a pair of sweatpants before grabbing her drink and shoving her feet in a pair of Ugg slippers she usually wore on the grounds around the house. She walked out the backdoor and made her way to the heated path that led to the guest house, seeing the lights on there, with more landscaping lights leading the way.

She was busy bracing herself against the cold air when suddenly music swarmed the space from hidden speakers in the landscaping. The sounds of a deep bass and a skilled guitar riff filled her ears. She had a prickle of awareness as she walked, sipping her drink to help calm her nerves.

Sliding the door open, Olivia took a second to let her eyes adjust to the dimmed lighting of the small house. Turning, she saw Colin standing in the middle of the room and shredding a guitar against the sounds of the music track. He was in a deep gray T-shirt and loose dark jeans. His muscled arms worked the guitar vigorously, the veins in his forearm standing out in sharp relief.

Olivia's eyebrows raised as she looked around in shock.

He was in the big space that would normally be used as the entertainment center, and he'd seemingly converted it into a small studio. The space was dark, intimate, and a slightly dangerous feeling settled over her as the space seemed to pulse with Colin's aura. The notes he was playing were a skilled piece, and Olivia found herself raising an eyebrow at him when he caught her eye, extremely impressed.

His fingers worked the strings in a complicated rhythm, and Olivia felt herself getting wet just watching him.

Her breathing became ragged at the unparalleled sexiness of him wielding the guitar and the strength in his body being aimed at the instrument, knowing that he unleashed that same power on her. She kicked off her shoes and walked over to the plush sofa. He caught her eye as she folded her legs under herself, and he transitioned his song into a track she recognized from a famous movie. Surprising her even further, he leaned into the microphone stand and began to belt out the lyrics, his rich voice growling into the mic.

Olivia's jaw dropped in shock as she watched this man lose himself singing to the music.

Looking around, she really took stock of her space once more, seeing what looked to be thousands of dollars of professional equipment lining the walls around them. Colin had never once alluded to her that music was a hobby or passion of his, however looking back, she realized it made sense. Music was always around them; he asked her to make personal playlists for him, he'd had an expensive sound system all throughout the house ready to go at the touch of a finger.

He even fucked her to musical playlists he'd carefully curated.

Thinking of fucking, Olivia felt her body get hot, her heartbeat pounding against her chest. She took a healthy drink of her liquor and winced feeling her body overheating. The sounds of the bass and guitar were pounding into her body. She put her drink down, maintaining eye contact with Colin as she shimmied out of her shirt and sweatpants. He held her eye contact the entire time, his eyes smoldering into that hot intense look that intimidated her, tortured her, and that she loved so much.

He didn't miss a beat as she leaned against the plush pillows and arranged her hair around herself, feeling it flow down her arms and breasts, tickling her waist. She looked over him hotly, pulling her legs up and smoothing one hand to cup her breast, and pulling her other hand down to smooth over her mound.

Watching him work his guitar, she licked her lips and began to play with herself like he played with his guitar. She could not believe how turned on she was and looking down saw her pink nipples poking out through her hair. She twisted one and gasped sharply, tensing as her fingers also grasped her sensitive clit. She felt the wetness on her fingers and moved up her hand to lick it off seductively, slightly embarrassed but knowing he liked that.

She heard the minute mistake in his playing as she did and knew that she was affecting him.

Olivia closed her eyes, moaning as she sunk a finger inside of herself, pumping hard. Imagining it was his cock, his fingers, or his tongue inside of her instead. Her mind filled with dirty images of them together, and the sound of his voice filled her ears as she arched off the couch with a cry. The fierceness of the orgasm took her by surprise. Her skin felt like razor blades were being pulled across the delicate flesh she was so sensitive.

She'd briefly doubted her sanity at doing this so blatantly in front of him, especially when he hadn't gotten his after her bratty behavior during the day. Her thoughts took a left turn, remembering them doing anal at the beginning of the weekend and realizing that's why she'd been on edge. She'd been left reeling, feeling incredibly vulnerable after their moment on the couch in the media room.

Dazed, she blinked slowly and began to close her legs, feeling more exposed than she was comfortable with.

"Keep them open mama," she heard Colin growl through the mic.

He turned and clicked a button on his laptop, putting his guitar down on a stand, the instrumental music resumed as normal through the speakers. He grabbed the mic and lowered it, picking it up and placing it next to her head on the side of the couch. She looked at him in alarm.

"Colin, what are you doing? I'm not singing!" Olivia looked at him in alarm. Her voice echoed around the room through the mic. She might be talented at dancing, but she could not sing to save her life.

"Incorrect, you're about to sing me a special song," Colin grated out in his rough voice, and Olivia noticed his face was pulled tight. He ripped off his shirt and she realized he was barely restraining himself. His movements betrayed the barely suppressed violence of his actions.

"No, I can't!" Olivia gasped, suddenly trying to get up. She looked at him with wide eyes as he shot out a hand and pushed her back down with a big hand on her chest.

"Open your legs and bend your knees back. You've been too mouthy with me, and I don't appreciate it. You've forgotten your place, huh?" he asked, cocking his head at her. That invisible string between them tightened, strengthening just a bit more.

She whimpered as she complied. His voice taunting her, echoing around her in the small space, pulling against her and hardening against her defenses.

"Bend your knees back further. Further. Arch your back harder. Don't fucking test me, Olivia," he growled down at her.

Olivia whimpered, hearing that through the mic as well as she quickly jerked her knees back, holding them tight with her hands. Her body quickened again at his veiled threat, her heart pounding hard. She reddened in embarrassment and started shaking her head, tears filling her eyes at the magnitude of the moment. Having kicked his pants off he laid his body on top of hers, placing a hand on the side of her head to still her movements.

She bit her lip as she smelled her arousal, she was dripping.

"If you even think that because we're married that it voided our original agreement, you are sadly mistaken Olivia," he said down to her, his authority scratched at the already overstretched and sensitive nerve endings of her mind and body. "You will do as you're told."

He moved, notching the thick crown into her slit.

"I'm going to bruise this pretty cunt," Colin said, his dark eyes flashing at her. "This is going to hurt. And if you don't give me what I want and try to close off those sexy screams of yours, I'm going to make it hurt worse."

Olivia arched hard, pressing her chest into his as she clenched suddenly. His words too much, tipping her off into an orgasm that reached into the deepest recesses of her mind. And instinctively she knew that the next orgasm was going to blow her to so many pieces she wouldn't be able to put herself back together again without any help.

Fuck.

Colin waited patiently until she lowered back down to the couch. He looked deep into her eyes before his abs tightened and he slammed himself home in one solid thrust so hard he'd shoved her up the couch on a growl. Her wild screams pierced the room, echoing through the help of the microphone stationed by her head as he proceeded to fuck her harder than he'd ever fucked her yet.

He was pissed and unleashing his frustration onto her willing helpless body.

The sharp slaps of their bodies meeting, mixed with her screams, broken moans, and cries filled the room. He growled, the sound echoing loudly around them. He persisted, not letting up on the pace, and his lungs burned for air as he tugged her hips off the edge of the couch and really put his back into it, shoving all of his body weight into her. Fresh cries pierced the air at this new angle.

The couch slammed hard against the wall, and he briefly thought about Jonathan and the check he had to write to cover the expense of the damage he and Vanessa did to his guest room that required him to contract work out to fix the drywall. He pounded into Olivia harder at the thought and silently reveled in her sharp scream.

Colin looked down into her shocked face, his brow furrowed and his face was tight with tension. He grunted, thrusting hard in between each sentence, their flesh colliding sharply. Olivia's heart beat wildly at the sound of his voice, harsh and gruff as he spoke down into her face.

"You've been back talking me."

Slap. Slap. Slap.

"Being fucking moody."

Slap. Slap. Slap.

"Picking fights with me."

Slap. Slap. Slap.

"Then had the nerve to hit me? It's like you're fucking itching for it. Keeping this greedy cunt satisfied is like having a full-time job. You better be glad I like work, baby," Colin snarled on a vicious downstroke that had her arching her body off the couch. He pushed her down hard, stunning her.

"Colin." Olivia shrieked; her cries falling on deaf ears. He blatantly ignored her. Her safe word was on the tip of her tongue.

"I don't even care that you're going to be sore, imagining the look on your face when you lower yourself into the seats at school because you're going to be too tender to sit down right is what's going to get me through the rest of the week. Yeaaah," he groaned, the low sexually charged sound rumbling through his chest, the primal sound awakening something even more wild inside of her that she couldn't explain.

Her safe word dissipated, and she snatched her one opportunity to get what she truly craved from him.

"You're not fucking me hard enough," she snarled up at him, her eyes flashing defiantly at him. Her fingers clawed into his back.

Colin narrowed his eyes and reached forward and slapped her cheek, not a true slap but a stinging one. She gasped and narrowed her own eyes back at him. He slapped her again, his eyes wild on hers.

He wanted a reaction, so she unclasped her hands and tore at his hair, pulling hard and screamed again, this time in shock and fright as they fell to the floor with a crash. They tore at each other like animals, and suddenly Colin lowered and bit into the juncture of her shoulder and neck with his teeth, breaking the delicate skin of her neck.

She screamed, bucking under him, trying to tear him off her or pull him in closer, she wasn't sure. "Slap me Goddamnit it!" she screeched, clawing at him again.

She rejoiced when she felt the hot stinging pain burst across her face and she arched violently, screaming so loud she lost her voice.

The mic stand fell to the floor with their actions, and she raked her nails down his back hard, overcome with lust. He roared with pain, reaching for her arms and slamming her hands into the floor above her. He lowered his head and took a straining nipple into his mouth in a harsh bite, tugging and pulling.

She felt the room spin as her orgasm hit her so hard that she screamed in a panic as her vision wavered, feeling her body completely blow apart, arching and bucking wildly underneath him.

Heaving screams left her body, tortured sounds that she'd never heard herself make before. Her orgasm felt like it broke her in half, and the only thing grounding her was Colin's teeth on her nipple and his hard dick nailing her to the floor, holding her together, tethered to him.

It lasted forever, and he just waited patiently as he rubbed out her pleasure, making it last even longer.

She lay there underneath him, shivering, feeling like her body was caught on fire. He looked down at her, his own chest heaving as he paused in his brutal thrusts. He reached for her face suddenly and roughly scrubbed his palm across her jaw and mouth, wiping the spit from her chin. Her eyes closed, and she tried to turn her face, shame suddenly filling her.

"Don't you dare look away from me," he growled, forcing her face to him once again. "I fucking love making you lose control. We have nothing to be embarrassed about, do you understand me?"

Olivia gave him a nod, and blinked the sudden rush of tears away. She gave a pained whimper when he ground himself into her hard. His hand flexed hard on her wrists as he began to thrust again.

"I'm not done," Colin said, leaning down to take her mouth, this time swallowing her cries. She moaned as he began to twine the extension cord from the mic around her neck, holding her in place for his brutal pounding.

He loved to punish her this way, and loved that she loved it as much as he did.

SIX

Difficult Conversations

THE NEXT DAY, COLIN dropped her off on campus as she couldn't drive comfortably, telling her he would meet her at the campus dining hall for lunch. He made sure she was ok before he drove off. In her first class, she lowered herself into her seat gingerly, hating she was a couple minutes late due to the need to walk slower than usual.

A classmate named Stella threw her a questioning glance and wiggled her phone at her, wanting her to check her phone. She really liked Stella, and she was fast becoming more than a study buddy.

Girl are you ok, why're you walking like that? What happened? -Stella

Olivia bit her lip at the message, her face turning pink. She couldn't tell her the truth.

My husband took me ice skating, =). -Olivia

Aw that's sweet, my husband takes me to do fun stuff like that too. We should do a double date! -Stella

Olivia smiled, thinking she would like that. So far, they'd only hung out with Vanessa, Jonathan, and the occasional rich friend's party over the holiday. She was dying to do something normal, something that didn't require two-hundred-dollar bottles of wine and a rich friend's mansion.

Okay, let me talk to Colin, and I'll get back with you on planning something. He's meeting me here for lunch, so I'll talk about it with him then. -Olivia.

Both women put their phones away and paid attention to the instructor. Olivia turned on her recording cassette she used to review lessons to help her with her work. She had a natural talent for architecture but was finding herself caught up on the unnecessary academia.

She popped an extra strength pain pill and saw her phone light up with a text from Colin stating that he was waiting at a table by the window in the dining hall. Smiling, she gathered her belongings and walked to the dining hall with Stella, gossiping about a show before entering the enormous room.

She spotted Colin quickly, who was busy shooting off a text on his phone, sitting in front of the food he'd already thoughtfully ordered for her. Her grin spread at how delicious he looked in his suit, with his ankle propped on his knee as he typed away at his phone. He looked completely out of place however, and it wasn't lost on her that most of the college students were unabashedly staring at him when they'd walked past.

"Hi there," Olivia said softly as she approached him, bending down to give him a swift kiss on his lips before sitting. She squealed softly as he reached forward quickly and snatched her back down and took her mouth once more, too thoroughly for campus.

"Oh my God, baby! Are there pigs flying? I actually got a hello out of you?" he teased, leaning back and placing his phone on the table. His eyes flickered over her form intimately, throwing her off balance.

She blushed hard as she attempted to sit again, biting her lip and groaning as she lowered to a certain point and then suddenly plopped down, her legs giving out. She looked up at his low chuckle, seeing him staring at her with barely contained mirth.

"Stop laughing at me!" she whispered, tearing open a dressing packet and ignoring the curious looks at other campus students staring at them as they walked past, knowing their age gap was glaringly obvious here, especially as Colin stood out so handsomely in his expensive dark gray suit. She looked at her salad in appreciation; he'd made it exactly how she liked. Extra cranberries and strawberries on the side.

Her hackles went up as a woman in a nearby table was blatantly staring inappropriately at Colin. Olivia threw the woman a filthy look as she stabbed her salad. She looked over at Colin who was tucking into a burger. He looked sexually virile even doing something as mundane as eating.

"Thanks for meeting me here, babe. But you didn't have to," she said, reaching forward to touch his hand lightly before picking up the water bottle he gave her. He gave her a look while he chewed, his throat working around it on a swallow.

"Of course, I had to," he said lightly. "Yesterday was a lot for both of us, and I'm not even just talking about the sex, our therapy appointment was pretty intense. And I wanted to make sure you're ok. I'll be having lunch with you every Wednesday after our appointment. It'll be part of our aftercare," he took a healthy drink of his own water, before swapping it out for coffee.

"But yes, I know I took you too hard last night. Too hard and too long for a school night. I fucked you for hours, and then you had to get up at seven. I'm sorry," he cleared his throat. Not used to apologizing for his behavior. "I truly wanted to connect in person to make sure you were ok," his eyes slowly turned to the female who was still watching him, and Olivia watched quietly as he cocked his head at her and threw her an unusual back off look. Making the woman turn away quickly.

"Are your studies getting any easier for you?" he asked, biting into his burger again, eyes on her, softer now.

Olivia bit the side of her cheek and shook her head, her cheeks pinkening again this time in embarrassment instead of desire.

"It's just the academia part...the endless reading and making sense of the words. I have to work extra hard to get through this class," she mumbled, putting her fork down in irritation. She leaned back in her seat and crossed her legs, looking out the window momentarily.

"It's just that in this field of work I will be communicating with everyone involved in a project. From the various engineers, the clients, the contractors, the foremen, the local government, the landscape architect, the interior designer...and so forth. It's a lot, and very hard to get back into after being gone for so long. I swear I picked the hardest career to get into," she said, pushing her plate away.

Colin nodded thoughtfully, pushing her plate back towards her.

"You are talented, and you are more than capable. I will sit with you every night until you get through this. And if you need guidance, I will find it for you. No giving up, ok?" he reached over to cover her hand with his, squeezing reassuringly.

Olivia smiled at him thankfully. She picked up her fork once more, stabbing and swallowing a bit of her salad, suddenly noticing that Stella was walking towards them with purpose. She smiled brighter at the sight of her friend, who threw down her bag rather roughly and huffed before sitting in the chair across from them.

"Do you two mind? I won't be long," Stella said as she took a bite out of her apple and left it in her mouth as she hurriedly got out her phone and opened it.

She took the apple out of her mouth and took Colin's outstretched hand and accompanying "Colin", shaking it before giving him a rather hard once over, even tilting her head to see his shoes. Colin raised his eyebrow in amusement as she went back to her phone, searching for something.

What the hell? He thought, tilting his head to look at his own shoes briefly.

"I'm Stella, nice to meet you, Colin," Stella said, her eyes trained on her phone. *"Aha!"* she suddenly said, turning the right way in her seat, facing them both now, her long braids swinging as she moved. She handed her phone to Olivia who took it with interest.

Colin had finished his burger and was sitting back watching Stella in amusement. Relaxed after his meal, he slid an arm across the back of Olivia's chair. His fingertips stroked her shoulder lazily as he listened to the woman.

"We're trying to plan a double date, so you don't kill her ice skating," Stella murmured, now getting what she considered to be her first good look at him. Her eyes raked over him thoroughly from head to toe once more. Colin furrowed his brow before smiling at her, raising his eyebrow.

Stella did a slow smile and threw Olivia a 'holy shit you did good' look.

"Ice skating?" Colin said with interest, looking over at Olivia who was looking at Stella's phone and picking at her salad. *"Eat,"* he ordered quietly, squeezing her shoulder lightly and watching her place a strawberry in her mouth.

"Yes, Stella asked why I was walking like this, and I told her about our ice-skating date last night," she said smoothly, smiling prettily and handing Stella her phone back.

"Ahhh. Yeah, Olivia couldn't quite get her bearings. Rather unfortunate since we're going to have ice skating lessons multiple times a week," he looked over at Stella again and flashed her a dazzling smile, momentarily stunning her but she recovered quickly.

"Well, I would like to invite you two mini golfing with me and my husband this weekend. It'll be fun, we can go at night, get a little tipsy off cheap beer! It'll be so much fun!" Stella smiled excitedly and Colin found himself instantly liking the cheerful woman. He hoped Olivia could become close to her, and that she wouldn't be so withdrawn sometimes.

"Only if I can provide our ride. We will pick you up and drop you off, since you were so kind to extend an invite," Colin interjected smoothly. Olivia smiled to herself as she finished her salad dutifully.

"Sure, if you insist, that would be nice. We could actually enjoy having a drink together for once instead of one of us having to be the designated driver. But we get to pay your way in since you're providing the ride," she said coyly, finishing her apple and wrapping it up in a napkin.

"We'd appreciate that so much, thank you. What does your husband do for work?" Colin asked again, taking another healthy drink of his coffee.

Olivia witnessed how he good naturedly humored her friend and noticed that generally he was a people person, never treating anyone different due to his status. He placed her hand on his thigh, rubbing and pressing firmly.

"He owns a security company; he contracts out bodyguards for the rich folks around here, and elsewhere too," she answered, having not been filled in by Olivia about her husband's status. Or her new status, thanks to him.

Colin smiled. Olivia paled.

"Yeah, those damn rich people can be something else huh? Real snobby," he ribbed back, clearly having fun with her friend. Olivia relaxed slightly.

Slightly.

They shared a laugh, before Stella got up quickly to leave them alone, texting Olivia their address and confirming a reservation time for Friday night.

She looked at Colin, who was still sipping slowly on his coffee.

"You do realize that YOU are 'the rich people'. Right?" she said with a soft laugh as she finished her own water. He reached a hand over and she caught the hint when he turned her secondary wedding ring on her finger.

"No baby, WE are 'the rich people'," he smiled warmly at her. "And the first thing you have to do as a rich person is make sure people don't extort you for money. We're going to have fun on Friday, I'm looking forward to it," he said, getting up and collecting their trash while she grabbed her bag. "And by the way, tonight we'll switch out your ice skates for roller blades instead," he chuckled as he pulled her close, pressing his lips to her hair and dropping her off in the hallway. "I'll be here at four to pick you up, baby."

Colin watched her get into an elevator before he sauntered off and headed back to his office to finish out his day. Sitting at his computer in his office, the thought about her last violent orgasm last night made him wonder if they were ready to take it to the next step. He'd contemplated taking that next step this weekend, after they went mini golfing with her friend and her husband.

Feelings of doubt crept into his subconscious.

At the end of the day, he closed down his office, thinking about how he wiped the spit off her face last night, and how good it felt to even be the reason to put it there to begin with.

He thought about the look on her face when he'd slapped her face lightly, realizing she was telling the truth to their therapist. She did like it rough, she liked it messy, and she loved him dominating her.

A few hours later he picked her up from school and realized her demeanor was a lot softer than it had been over the last few days, and figured he'd pencil in more sheet clawing grinding sex into their schedule. She leaned into him and didn't protest when he took her mouth in a seriously indecent kiss in her school parking lot. He let her go with a groan, adjusting his erection in the seat.

He moved his hand to her pussy and squeezed possessively, through her pants, loving her hitched breath.

She had taken out one of her architect books and was furiously scribbling in it. He realized she was doing that because she didn't plan on trying to resell the book, and wondered if she was taking a tentative step in the right direction regarding money.

"How was work sweetie?" she said, scribbling so hard it sounded like she was trying to tear the paper up.

He threw her an amused glance, cupping her slightly harder.

"I had a rare, rough day today," he said, turning into their neighborhood. She threw him a look, pausing in her scribbling.

"And you came to have lunch with me?" she asked incredulously, her green eyes comically wide. She paused, holding her book aloft, still staring at him from across the seat.

"Yes, you are obviously more important," he mused, smiling as they rounded the gate and drove up the driveway, heading to the back of the house. He noted that Mary was gone for the day.

"I mean, work is work though. I don't want you to be bothered with me when you have real stuff going on Colin!" she admonished gently, putting her book back in her bag.

He parked efficiently, easing in next to her Porsche. He turned to her, resting his hand on her headrest.

"Olivia, you are not a bother, and you are not a burden. You are my greatest asset. Haven't you figured that out by now?" he said, staring into her eyes. "And you're real, you're my wife," he growled, leaning across the seat and forcing her chair into a reclining position. He started dragging off her leggings and underwear.

"Bend your knees back. Now!" Colin bit out as her pink pussy came into view. She obeyed and squealed as he maneuvered her further down the seat.

He leaned over and roughly pulled the neckline of her shirt down and bared a round breast. Mindful of her soreness, he thrust two fingers into her slowly at the same time he lowered his head and took her nipple into his teeth, rolling it and nibbling. He groaned at the first spurt of her pussy on his hand, loving the warm wet feel.

He tugged her nipple sharply with his teeth and then bit harder, feeling her clench down on him. He gentled his hold on her breast as he spread his fingers inside her mercilessly.

"Colin. *Uhnnn,*" she moaned, arching and gasping at the feeling of him stretching out the sensitive flesh between her legs.

He picked his head up to look at her, thoroughly enjoying hearing the wet sounds of his fingers thrusting into her pussy.

"We're going inside to eat dinner, then we're going to take a short nap before you do your homework. I know you're tired from last night. I just wanted to give you an orgasm to relax you," he said gruffly, his thumb agitating her clit in circles.

He leaned down to kiss her knee before nudging her leg out of the way and sucking her nipple into his mouth again. After a few hard pulls, she climaxed on a low moan, her body sagging into the seat.

"Thank you, baby," she said, breathing hard, lowering her legs. He helped her sit up gently and grabbed her clothes.

"You're more than welcome," he replied, a small smile on his face.

Colin went around to her side of the car and pulled her out, scooping her up and taking her into the house. He settled her on her feet before patting her ass on the way to the office with her school bag.

"Go put on a robe and meet me back down here for dinner," he instructed, throwing her a sexy grin as he rounded the hallway to his office, disappearing inside.

She took the elevator upstairs and walked into their bedroom before veering left into the closet. She undressed and took a second to brush her hair out. Sighing at the admission that she was not just tired, but exhausted. Yawning, she put on a silk robe that left most of her cleavage bare and tied the sash just under. The robe made her look very womanly and sexy. She heard her phone ding.

Hey Red, this is G, I hope you don't mind but I'd saved your personal cell from when you called me one time from it. I wanted to let you know that Judge Carmichael has been causing trouble asking about you. It's pretty serious and we had to drop him as a client. I just wanted to give you a head up just in case. Hope you are doing well, I'd love to hear from you and know you're doing ok. Love, G.

Olivia's eyebrows raised in surprise at hearing from her powerful former boss. Her heart began to pound, knowing she was going to have to inform Colin and was worried at what his reaction would be. She frowned at the contents and responded back.

Hey G, thank you for the heads up, I am doing ok for now. I hope you are well. -O

Leaving her phone in the bedroom, she made her way downstairs and heard Colin in the formal dining room. Veering off again, she walked through, seeing the lights dimmed and candles lit on the table reflecting off the huge picture window. He had jazz playing in the background, a bottle of wine chilling in a bucket of ice on the table, and two plates of small racks of lamb with a rosemary and wine reduction sauce, baby mashed potatoes, and asparagus, courtesy of Mary.

Tonight, she found herself truly grateful that they had help, she didn't think she'd be able to manage dinner on top of everything else going on.

She gave her thanks and sat at a chair that he had pulled out for her, suppressing another yawn. She smiled at Colin who'd put his glasses on, finding he often liked to wear them in the evening and the habit betrayed that he'd spent too many hours on the computer that day. She thought they made him look very distinguished and sexy, and if she had more energy she'd crawl under the table and suck him off.

But she needed to talk to him about the text she'd just gotten.

She leaned forward and grabbed the wine and poured his glass first, a healthy amount. She spoke as she started pouring herself another smaller amount.

"Colin," Olivia paused, the glass hadn't made it to her lips before she finished. "Gypsy texted me on my personal phone. Said something about Judge Carmichael causing trouble asking about me, and they had to drop him as a client. I just thought you should know…" she trailed off, putting her glass down untouched and picking up her utensils.

Olivia cut a small piece of lamb and put it in her mouth, chewing slowly as her eyes drooped slightly, suddenly wishing that she might have told him another time.

She looked up to see him staring at her.

"When was this?" he said, sipping his own wine and leaving his food untouched. Again, she was struck by how competent he looked, how much older and masculine he was.

"Just before I came down, she texted my personal cell," Olivia whispered, closing her eyes against the burning gritty feel. She put down her silverware and rubbed her eyes, blinking against the sting there. He'd screwed her till almost four o'clock in the morning, then she had to get up at seven for school and she was running on fumes.

Colin grunted and began to eat.

"I'll handle it. Thank you for telling me," he said, his hand coming out to grab hers reassuringly, and she believed him. She knew he wouldn't hesitate to use what influence was at his disposal to ruin the judge.

"I just...I don't want to be an embarrassment to you," she said softly, putting another forkful of asparagus in her mouth. She winced as he threw his utensils down rather harshly. She watched as he placed his elbows on the table and tented his hands together, in a rare moment of introspection, he sat there silently thinking.

"Colin?" she said, arching an eyebrow at him, not used to seeing him so lost in thought. He turned his eyes to hers.

"Olivia, I love you. I don't know how else to say it. You are not an embarrassment to me, your past is not an embarrassment to me. Do you think I would have brought you into my home, into my life, into this agreement and married you if I thought you were an embarrassment? I don't ever want to hear those words come out of your mouth, I'll punish you the next time I hear you say anything like that. I'm only not doing that now because you look like you're going to fall over from exhaustion," he said softly, his eyes tight on hers.

She nodded once, spearing another bite of her food and chewing it slowly.

"About Allison," she whispered, changing the subject, the tired feeling overcoming her and making her want to talk about issues that she'd not wanted to before. He leaned back in his chair, snagging his wine glass and giving her his full attention.

"Would you think any less of me, if I said I didn't want to regain custody of her?" she whispered, her eyes watering as she stared rather unseeingly at her plate.

Fucking God why can't I stop crying? It's every day, she lamented to herself, bowing her head as she wiped a lone tear away.

There was a tense moment as he took a slow sip of his wine and placed his hand on her chair, scooching her to him easily. He placed his palm against the side of her face and turned her head to him.

"Is it because of me? Because you're worried about how I would treat her? If I would accept her? Because you don't have to worry about that," he said, his voice taking on a hard edge.

She peeked up at him with a slightly shocked look on her face and slowly shook her head no. They stared at each other hard and Olivia tightened her lips, seeing a myriad of thoughts cross his expression before he decided to reply to her.

"I wouldn't," he said gently. "But I would like to hear your reasoning when you are ready. Because this is a loss. And I think this needs to be discussed in length with Vanessa and Jonathan. I know that they said they would continue to raise her, but maybe we can discuss something along the lines of contributing to her care; and if you would ever like to tell her in the future, what that would look like," he said, giving her a sad smile. "But no. I don't think any less of you. This is a hard, multifaceted situation, no matter how you slice it. And I'm truly sorry that I couldn't have found you sooner to help amend this before it got to be too much," he stroked her cheek before continuing.

"But I would like to discuss the possibility of having more children with you. When you are ready of course," he said, both of their meals were effectively forgotten.

Olivia stared at him with her green eyes, welling up with tears again. She nodded once, looked away and reached for her wine glass, cradling it against her breasts and looking rather pale and shocked. Colin cleared his throat.

He stood up and held out his hand, leading her upstairs where he pulled down the black out curtains in the room and made them take a nap for a couple hours, both needing rest.

SEVEN

BJs and New Friends

THE REST OF THE week flew by, and Colin called the architectural firm to see if Olivia could do a tour and speak with a couple interns and full-fledged architects who worked there, thinking that maybe it would help her get over this bout of difficulty at her school.

Soon it was Friday, and Olivia solidified plans with Stella before they left campus. She'd had to drive to school that day, as Colin had a business lunch and a full day of work.

She called him before she took off.

"Hey love, I'm headed to run an errand, and then home. When are you getting to the house and what time do you think we'll be heading out?" she asked, making the merge to get on the highway.

"Olivia," Colin rasped in his husky voice. She could hear him settling down further in his chair and the muted sound of what she knew was his glasses hitting the desk. "Are you looking forward to seeing me baby? You hardly ever call, you mostly text me."

She gave him a little giggle.

"I am looking forward to having some fun tonight, yes." she admitted. His buttery voice doing dangerous things to her imagination. "It's much needed, this week has been especially difficult, you know. Thank you for taking such good care of me."

"It's my pleasure," Colin waited a beat before he asked the question; Olivia knew he would catch it. "So where are you going, you said you had an errand to run?"

"Ohhhh, can we just keep this one thing secret? I'm picking up a gift for you," Olivia said gently.

"Hmmm...you know I don't like secrets, but I will relent if you text me the moment you get there, and the minute you leave to head home. I won't pry and look at your location, you may turn it off if you'd like just for this," his dominating presence radiated out through the phone, causing her to blush. She made a small sound in her throat as she turned into the parking lot of the jewelry store.

"No need for that, Colin. I'm already here. I'll text you when I'm headed home."

They hung up and she walked through the store to get the embellished tie clip that she special ordered just for him. It was an engraved, simple silver piece that said 'OM' on the front, and on the back had an engraving. To my very own Clark Kent. With love, Olivia. While she was there, she browsed around their men's ring department and found a piece that screamed Colin. But it was very expensive, hosting a series of black diamonds.

She stood there for a moment, and Dr. Tyson's voice appeared in her head. His scarcity mindset comment had been bugging her since the appointment.

Colin's voice now entered the picture, speaking about how much of a turn-on it was for him to have money and the power associated with it hit her hard. Gritting her teeth, she asked the man to check the size on the ring; it was Colin's of course. Feeling her heart pound, she purchased both the ring and the tie clip and fought back a wave of nausea at the price, so she added insurance just in case.

Carefully stowing the bag into her purse, she made her way to her car and texted Colin she was on her way home.

Walking into the house she greeted Beth and Mary who were currently packing up to leave for the day and gave them both a kiss on the cheek on the way to their bedroom. She went to the bathroom and stowed the boxes on the vanity before changing her mind and taking it into their walk-in closet and pressing the button that released his watch, cuff link, and ring drawer. She took the gifts out of the boxes and then stowed them side by side, closing the drawer back.

She picked out her outfit, a cream cashmere sweater with a matching skirt and red fuck me jimmy choo heels, laying the items on the bed. She jumped into the shower quickly, doing her business so she could focus on her hair, blowing it out into big shiny waves that tumbled down her back.

Olivia heard the moment Colin got home because music played through the speaker, an easy relaxing tempo. She hoped that had meant he'd had a good day, she was looking forward to having some much-needed time with him tonight on a fun outing.

She was putting the last of her makeup on, standing in an expensive hunter green lingerie set when Colin appeared in the doorway. He stopped and leaned against it, moving his eyes down her form and making an appreciative noise in his throat. It was so blatantly sexual of a sound, she stopped applying mascara for a second to stare at him, doing her own once over. He'd removed his tie and jacket, unbuttoned the top two buttons revealing his chest hair and the top of his tattoos, and rolled up the sleeves of his crisp white button up shirt.

"God you're so sexy," he said, rubbing his jaw and staring at the front of her reflection in the mirror. She smiled and attached a ruby red stud earring to her ear.

"You're sexier," she said, licking her lips as she attached the other earring and turned smoothly to face him, closing the distance between them and smoothing her hands down his chest.

"It's a pity the driver's going to be here soon, we could have had a quickie," she whispered. He graced her with a slow dangerous smile.

"You're not topping from the bottom pet, not tonight. I'll decide if we have a quickie or not," he whispered, leaning down to take her mouth in a rough kiss. Olivia was glad she didn't put lipstick on. She'd noticed earlier on that lipstick would be a rarity, as Colin almost always had his mouth on her.

"Where's my gift?" he said as he pulled back, giving her that intense stare that was also mixed with something new, a fresh excitement that made him look slightly younger. She melted a little at the sight and felt so silly that it took her so long to do something nice for him. She penciled in wanting to give him a gift at least weekly, something that would make his week a little brighter.

Olivia flashed him a wide smile and lightly pushed him through the door. Pulling him into their closet, she studied him, chewing her lip and nervously wringing her fingers.

"You don't have to like it," she blurted out. "I literally got it on a whim and-"

"Olivia," Colin interrupted, but she kept speaking as if she couldn't hear him.

"We can take it back, it's not too late. I have insurance on it, and I can sell it or something," she finished breathlessly. She grabbed onto his forearm anxiously. Her cheeks were pink.

"Give. Me. My. Gift. Now," he growled, folding his arms and widening his stance. He gave her a filthy 'don't fuck with me' look that had her scrambling to open the drawer. She winced as the drawer flew out then caught, before slowly sliding back in. She moaned, tilting her head, wanting the floor to open up and swallow her whole.

"It's there," she whispered, trembling. She was way more nervous than the time she'd gifted him with the tie and beard set at the beginning of their relationship.

He looked at her and gave her a crooked smile as he pulled the drawer open wider. She could tell the minute he saw them, nestled amongst his other belongings. His breath hitched and stopped as he reached in slowly to take out the clip and ring. He saw her initials before turning it and reading the inscription on the back. His nostrils flared and his eyes flashed as he suddenly whipped his head to her.

He seared her to the bone with that look. "Get the fuck on your knees," Colin snapped, placing the items back and closing the drawer.

"Colin-" she gasped, confused. She licked her lips, her weight shifting to one foot as he suddenly unbuckled his belt.

"Get on your knees before I push you down there myself," he bit out. Olivia's eyes widened in excitement at the vision of him pulling out his beautiful cock.

Olivia whimpered as she felt her panties flood with moisture, her mouth suddenly filled with saliva and she hit her knees hard, attacking him. Mouthing the tip, she licked along the seam and then took him deep. She squealed as he suddenly grabbed her head and pushed hard, fucking her mouth so relentlessly that she fell back on her ass with the sudden onslaught and scooched back as he pistoned his dick in and out of her mouth.

Looking up wildly at him she moaned as she felt the back of her head hit the island in the closet, she was trapped between the cabinet and his body. He fucked harder, pressing deep until he reached the ring of her throat.

Olivia cried out around his thickness, fighting her gag reflex. She was acutely aware that her mascara was running, spit dripping off her chin. He suddenly reached down to grab her jaw and he angled her head higher before his thighs suddenly flexed and he pushed a couple inches past the ring in her throat, making her scream wildly.

She dug her nails into his thighs as her desperate moans and whimpers mingled with his harsh sex sounds. She heard the back of her head repeatedly knocking against the cabinet, and the pressure built in her groin at how viciously he was taking her. Just like how he wanted. Her body ached and screamed for him to fuck her like that.

"You're going to swallow every drop," he ordered. She felt him swell and pull back several inches until he was on her tongue. His face tightened briefly as if he was in pain, a low groan rumbling in his chest. She felt Colin's dick twitch before spurting on her tongue and she moaned as she swallowed, licked, and sucked down his uniquely male essence.

She continued to lap at him gently as he spread his hands on the island above her and his chest was heaving, trying to regain control of himself. After a couple delicious minutes, he straightened himself and leaned back, putting his dick away silently and buckling his belt.

Olivia stayed on the floor, slightly in shock at what just happened. Her body thrummed happily but her mind was reeling. She started slightly when he'd suddenly bent down and grabbed her under her arms to haul her up off the floor. He perched her on the island top then stepped forward and buried his face in between her breasts, banding his arms across her back. Olivia blinked in surprise, her own hands coming up to sink into his hair.

"Uhm C-Colin..." she said hoarsely, wincing at the ache in her throat. "Does that mean you like it?"

She gave a tentative smile as he chuckled darkly in between her breasts, pulling back to look at her. She gasped, his eyes were shiny, the crinkles around his eyes betraying his emotion.

"I know how hard that must have been for you, to pick something so expensive. I love you baby," he said, his own voice betraying his own emotion. Her eyes widened as she barely got to see him vulnerable. It seems like he was giving her a gift of her own. He turned to grab the ring, sliding it on his right ring finger, then turned back around to face her.

"Can I help you, make yourself back to being presentable?" he offered hesitantly, his hand reaching out to smooth down the back of her hair.

She shook her head no slowly. "I got it. Will you go downstairs and make us a quick drink while I finish? I won't be long."

He nodded and leaned forward, kissing her softly, his big hand palming the side of her head. She leaned into his touch reverently. He pulled away and walked out of the closet leaving her alone.

After a minute she felt a goofy smile break out on her face. That was the feeling she couldn't figure out. Pure feminine triumph. Her heart soared at being able to see how she could make a powerful man like him lose control. She jumped off the island and did a little happy dance. She hurriedly freshened up, brushing her teeth and throwing clothes and heels on before heading downstairs.

Colin was dressed slightly more casually than his suit, but still ever the killer in a fresh pair of slacks, black button down shirt, and a pair of Graysons. He was leaning against the sink, sipping from a glass of whiskey. Her heels clicked loudly as she rounded the corner and headed straight to her drink. She necked it down and licked her lips, heading to the fridge and pulling out a few grapes and a piece of cheese.

Fully aware that she was blushing and unable to meet his eye after what just happened in the closet.

"Do you want some?" she asked quietly.

"No, I want to talk to you about something. I'd like to play next weekend. We're going to talk about stuff at our therapy appointment and I'd like for us to be more vulnerable with each other," Colin said. She turned back, looking at him over her shoulder.

"What?" she said, meeting his gaze and shivering.

"I want to play how I want. Are you ready?" Colin asked, not requiring her permission but wanting it.

He smiled slowly at her blush. She nibbled on the piece of cheese before taking another swallow of her drink. Just then the phone beeped.

"Driver is here," he stated, pressing another button to open the gates for him.

He put their glasses in the sink and grabbed his keys, escorting her to the front and chuckling at her exclamation.

"You got us a limo to go mini golfing!?" she'd admonished excitedly.

She reached up and smacked an excited kiss on his mouth before trying to run down the stairs in her heels. Terrified for her safety, he hauled her up short by her arm with a firm grip, making her go slow so she wouldn't break her ankle. She was practically bouncing in excitement.

The driver pulled away when Colin gave him the address to where they were going. He'd looked at the neighborhood ahead of time through Google maps and deducted that Olivia's friend and her husband did well for themselves.

Not that he was judging.

Twenty minutes later they'd pulled up into a gated community, one that was smaller and not as rich as theirs but still leagues out of what Olivia could have imagined just half a year ago. She bounced excitedly in the chair next to him, and he felt his heart swell as he looked at the ring she'd gifted him on his finger. She was too much.

They pulled in front of a very nice house that looked similar to the one off of Home Alone, but more modern and with very pretty landscaping.

She rolled the window down to stick her head out the door and Colin was gifted a very pleasing view of her backside as she began to wave vigorously. Stella, who'd just appeared out of the house, was waving back excitedly with a big smile on her face. Colin looked past Olivia to see that Stella was doing an excited little bounce of her own, her husband appearing out of the door next to her. He turned to lock up the house before she took his hand and tried to bulldoze her way to the limo. Olivia opened the door and unfolded herself from the limo, running to her friend and snatching her up in an excited hug.

Colin chuckled as the tall African American man bent down to give Olivia a half hug. Stella's husband's face broke out into a wider smile at Olivia's excitement, keeping his hand firmly around his wife. They entered the limo and settled in their seats. Colin reached forward and gave Stella's husband a firm handshake.

"Colin. Nice to meet you," he said pleasantly, feeling in a very good mood due to Olivia.

"I'm Vincent. 'Sup man?" Vincent looked at Colin and gave a respectful nod towards Olivia. "And you're the friend I've heard so much about," he flashed her a smile, his teeth gleaming white in the muted light of the car.

Olivia smiled back, liking the man's energy, seemingly a lot like Jonathan's.

"Better be ALL good things!" she said teasingly, sipping on her drink she heard Colin tell the couple to drink whatever. There was a shuffling as Vincent moved quickly to make Stella a drink, and then held it to her lips. She leaned forward and sucked at the straw, moaning slightly as he tilted the glass away and put it back in the holder.

Colin met the man's eye who gave him a discrete nod at his look, seeing him put his arm around Stella and holding her close.

Colin peeked at Olivia who was blinking rather confusedly, a small smile on her face as she looked between the couple. She hooked one of her legs around Colin's, a thrill going through her as he placed his hand on top, curling his fingers around and digging in slightly.

The men started to talk about Vincent's security company and Olivia leaned forward slightly to speak to Stella.

"Hey, did Dr. Ferguson give you a bad grade on that test we got at the beginning of the week?" she said quietly, the girls had been comparing teachers and grades, both seemingly struggling in the same area.

"Yes, I got a D, can you believe it? It's so foul," Stella lamented back, reaching forward to grab her drink and pursing her lips as Vincent quickly took it and held it to her lips.

Colins ears pricked as he heard a small clicking noise.

Stella leaned in again. "Are you still spending hours a night trying to get through the text?" she whispered, pushing back her heavy braids that had fallen between them.

Olivia leaned further forward and nodded, "Yes. Colin has sat with me damn near every night while I try to figure out the texts. I didn't struggle this much when I was in the program a few years ago. It's really disheartening. Freaking embarrassing," she said, a sad look passing her face.

Colin suddenly pulled her back and turned her face to his. He stared at her for a moment before he leaned down and licked into her mouth lewdly, tightening his grip on her when she tried to pull away embarrassed. He waited her out until she softened in submission and relaxed in his hold. He pulled back to feather a thumb across her cheek and searing her once more with his gaze.

"I would appreciate it if you didn't talk about school tonight. I don't want any sad looks on your face for the rest of the weekend," he ordered.

"Yes sir," she breathed, not even realizing she said it. She was so overcome by the intensity of his eyes.

Stella interjected softly.

"Something tells me ice skating isn't exactly what I think it means?" she asked questioningly, leaning forward once again to sip from the glass Vincent held out. Stella reached forward suddenly and stilled his hand as he attempted to take it away too soon.

Colin's ears pricked again as he heard another two clicks. His eyes widened in recognition, meeting Vincent's and gave him a knowing smile.

"My man," Colin said with a thoughtful grin on his face. "You're in the lifestyle too?" he questioned, smiling even brighter when Vincent replied they were.

Olivia looked between the two men again, hearing their exchange that quickly quieted as the limo slowed, approaching the adults only mini golfing arena.

The women got out and practically dragged the men to the front where Stella pulled out a card and got them all tickets.

"There are two levels, a MASSIVE food court, an arcade, music and dancing! This place is like Disneyland for adults!" Stella shot back to the men excitedly. Colin leaned towards Vincent.

"Is she always this excitable?" he asked, flashing him a good natured smile as they followed the women into the big building, taking a second to crane their heads up and look around the massive space.

Vincent looked at him with a weary look. "Yes, she takes quite a firm hand to manage. What about yours?" he asked Colin.

"Same, we've only been married about four weeks, so I'm trying to not be so hard on her. She's new to the lifestyle, I'm trying to figure out how hard to push her."

He looked at Vincent who was already pulling out his phone.

"Send me your NDA, and I'll send mine. We'll sign them real quick through DocuSign." Vincent said first, already reading Colin's mind.

Colin grinned, making up his mind about this man; he had a good feeling about him. They exchanged information quickly and sent the necessary signatures. With a nod, they rejoined their women who were busy trying to figure out where to go first.

They went to the area to grab their clubs and Olivia practiced swinging. Colin had to jump out of the way at her violent upswing. His chest was tight as he sidled up behind her. For not the first time, he thought about the fact that this woman spent years beating wealthy men, the exact thing he so badly wanted to do, yet prevented himself from doing to her.

His erection strained against his pants.

"Slow down, I know you must have a vicious swing, but you need to take it easy," he whispered in her ear. He got behind her and wrapped his hands around hers, gently pulling her arms back and hitting the practice ball. It rolled into the hole. He tightened further at her smile; she really had a delightful smile.

He groaned quietly, pushing her hair back behind her ear and leaning forward to place a kiss on her forehead.

"Let's play for real," he said in his smooth voice, jerking his head and leading his way to the first hole.

An hour and a half later they were in a vicious competition. Colin and Vincent were neck and neck, not even willing to concede and let the girls fake win. They were apparently not those types of men. Colin looked back, Olivia and Stella were tipsy, giggling and laughing at something on Stella's phone, unconcerned.

Vincent sauntered over and placed his hand on top of the screen and Colin observed his actions curiously.

"Are you ogling at other men, boo?" Vincent teased, leaning forward to take Stella's mouth in a hard kiss. "Can you pause for a second to watch your husband kick this guy's ass? I'd appreciate it," he said softly, leaning down to muzzle her ear.

Olivia looked away and smirked, catching Colin's eye. He was leaning against a sturdy wooden fence that was the theme of this hole, waiting. She drank the rest of her drink heartily, and cheered good naturedly as Vincent won the game by a hair's breadth.

She skipped over to Colin and threw her arms around his neck.

"I'm just being a good sport," she said against his mouth, kissing him and licking her tongue along his lips. She pulled away to give Vincent a high five before linking arms with Stella.

"Food court," Stella yelled over her shoulder, and they took off in a hurry, leaving the men to catch up.

"Yours a brat?" Vincent said suddenly, catching Colin's eye as they walked.

He shook his head no, with a wry smile.

"No, she's a masochist. But Stella being a brat, that explains the clicker," Colin answered, turning the ring on his finger.

"Ohhh...you're a sadist, huh? Well, I guess that makes sense considering she's a redhead. They got some sort of interesting reaction with pain," Vincent said suddenly, turning teasing eyes onto Colin's and bumping shoulders with him in a brotherly way. "Us doms have to stick together. You let me know if Stella is rubbing off on her. I'll correct her."

Colin threw him an appreciative glance.

They caught up with the women at the food court, snagging a circular private booth. The women went to two different lines and came back with a crazy amount of food and plates for sharing. They helped the women unload everything then go back for drinks before settling back and started to divvy out the food.

Colin wrinkled his nose at Olivia, who was mixing some cuisines that probably shouldn't be.

Stella and Vincent were also looking over in shock, trying unsuccessfully to hide it. He threw them a slight apologetic glance, placing his hand on Olivia's back and rubbing slightly.

"Alright now," Stella said with an amused smile on her face as Olivia took her first bite and moaned. They all laughed lightly at her.

Colin once again slightly rolled his eyes, wondering if she would ever not eat in her weird way. He placed his hand on her thigh and curled his fingers in hard, relishing her gasp. He dug in a little harder, hearing her soft moan, looking over and seeing her face flush.

"Are you ok love?" he said innocently, putting a bite of chicken in his mouth and grinning. She nodded, putting another bite of food in her mouth.

"You can't eat or drink too much, I have plans for us later," he whispered against her ear, kissing the shell and biting her lobe. She squeaked and dropped her fork, snatching her napkin and placing it higher in her lap.

"Colin, I'm in a cream outfit! You're going to make me drop food on myself," she hissed back, taking another big swallow of her drink and protesting when Colin took it out of her hand and smoothly threw it in a trashcan nearby.

"I said no," he said, not even trying to hide their dynamic. She pouted prettily as she continued to eat. Only her flushed cheeks betrayed her excitement and anger. She flickered her eyes nervously to the couple seated across from them.

"Well," she said haughtily, turning to pierce him with her green eyes. "It better be fucking worth it then."

Stella whistled across the table. Colin briefly heard Vincent admonish Stella before he turned to pierce Olivia with a look of his own.

Colin's jaw clenched as he bent into her face. "It's going to be worth every welt, scream, and tear I get the pleasure of wringing out of this pretty body tonight, best believe it," he whispered, hearing her sharp inhale. Leaning in, he inhaled slowly.

"I smell you, did you just come?" he growled quietly in her ear. He briefly felt her slight shake of her head. "Are you ok? I know how wet you get," Colin ignored the way she hunched her shoulders up in mortification and leaned in rather indecently, pushing her slightly forward with his movements.

"Colin, no... I'm ok," Olivia whispered. She turned bright red, her voice coming out whiny as he suddenly wedged his hand under her bottom to feel if her skirt was wet. He didn't want anyone seeing any evidence of her desire. He grunted happily.

"Good girl, not so messy this time, huh?" he said softly, for her ears only.

Olivia peeked through her hair and saw Vincent and Stella momentarily submersed in their own world, not paying them any attention. Stella was giggling as she was holding a bite of food to her husband's lips to eat, and laughing harder when he would bypass the fork and take a bite out of her neck with a growl.

Olivia smiled, not feeling so put into the spotlight. It suddenly clicked.

"Colin," she whispered. "Are they like us?" She turned to him with a questioning look.

"They are in a dominant and submissive relationship, yes. But he is not a sadist, and she is not a masochist like you. However, she is a brat, and if you'll pay attention, she pushes him to get a reaction. Look at them, don't they look happy?" he interjected, running his hand down her arm and pressing her to him.

Olivia nodded, a weird peace settling over her. She didn't feel so alone after seeing another dynamic in person. She looked at him again.

"I want it. I can handle you, Colin," she whispered, lured in by his magnetizing gaze. "I want the pain that I believe only you can give me."

He nodded, taking her hand and kissing her knuckles.

"Then let's go," he said, signaling Vincent. They stood up and cleared the table, taking the women's hands and walking them out of the building to the limo waiting for them outside.

He was relieved to see the trust between them being nurtured. It gave him hope for the next week ahead, when he would tell her about his past, and the accident that changed his life.

***

They had a fun time driving Stella and Vincent back home, blaring nineties hip hop and rap music and trying to outdo each other lyrically. Colin won this round, with Vincent coming in a close second. As they pulled up to their house, he shared a friendly hand clasp and back pat with Vincent, who promised to contact Colin about hiring security in wake of what Gypsy relayed to Olivia regarding Judge Carmichael.

"I don't want security following me! I'm going to look like the biggest freak at university!" Olivia lamented as the couple left, and it was just the two of them. Colin shrugged out of his blazer, spreading it on the floor in front of him and relaxed back into the seat. He cocked his head in that dangerous way of his, his arms rippled with his tattoos standing out in sharp relief.

His brown eyes pierced hers. "Come here, Olivia," he said, tension thickening the air and stealing her breath away. She glanced down at the blazer before looking back at him.

"In the limo?" she whispered. Swallowing hard as he gave her a sexy grin. He reached over and grabbed her arm, pulling her not so gently to her knees on the blazer in front of him.

"You ready for a workout, baby?" he murmured softly, leaning forward and placing his hands on either side of her hair and taking her mouth in a raw kiss that left her flooded. He sucked at her lips for long seconds, groaning into her mouth, letting her know how good she tasted.

"A workout?" she teased, "Are you taking me to the gym?"

"No baby, I'm about to take you to church, because we're going to need to repent for our sins tonight. We may need to invest in some holy water to cleanse you of the filthy things I'm going to do to you," Colin whispered, opening the door and ushering her out and into the night air of their property.

Olivia walked beside him, his words repeating a thrilling echo around her brain. Knowing she would follow him straight into hell if he asked her to.

EIGHT

Broken Hearts = Shattered Trust

SATURDAY MORNING CAME AND Jonathan called Colin with an emergency business trip to Russia. He kissed Olivia and told her he would be back Tuesday night or Wednesday morning at the latest and to spend some quality time with Vanessa and Allison.

Olivia saw him off, waving at him from the front before heading upstairs to pack herself a bag. She pulled out her phone to text Vanessa.

Hey sis, impromptu girl's weekend! I'm packing my bag now. Do you need me to stop on my way in and pick up anything? -Ollie

She took out a duffel bag and began to stuff items into it. Seeing her school backpack, she tried to dismiss it from her mind. Colin had asked her to take a break during the weekends for now because school was consuming her and so much studying could be counterproductive. She looked at her phone as it pinged twice.

I love you, please have fun this weekend. I'll be checking up regularly so keep your phone close baby. -C

Yes, can you stop and get some vodka? I know it's your favorite, but we ran out, and if you could get me something for this mocktail recipe that would be fire. See you in a bit, we need an all nighter! Should I ask Jonathan's niece to join us so we can have adult fun after hours? I know I can't drink but we can go dancing!!! -Nessie

Olivia bit off a giggle as she responded with a bunch of demon head emojis.

Hell yes sis! Going to stash my bookbag in the guest house and I'll be headed your way in a bit.-Ollie

Olivia finished packing her bag and grabbed up her backpack, determined to make time to carve out space just for her schooling. Colin was right, she didn't have much of a school and personal life balance and so she decided to take a page out of his book and designate a space just for her studies and architectural work.

Olivia looked out the window seeing the guest house was glowing, giving her an idea. She'd utilize one of the rooms there, so she could have a clear delineation of space. The only time she'd work on studies was in a work room.

Feeling like a huge weight had been lifted off her shoulders, she picked up her backpack and headed downstairs.

Letting herself into the guest house, she glanced around seeing all of Colin's music equipment put away neatly, and the couch put back into place. There was a very nice bar and kitchen that led to a hallway. Heading down that way, she passed a bathroom and two bedrooms facing each other at the end of the hallway. Poking her head into one, she saw a very lush bedroom and smiled appreciatively, never having taken the time to explore the whole house.

She turned to the other bedroom door and tried to turn the knob; it was locked. She looked down and saw a touch pad for a code. Frowning, she glanced around at the other doors, not seeing any keypad to their entry.

The hairs on the back of her neck stood up as she put her bag down and whipped out her phone. Colin had previously given her every code to the house in an encrypted file that she kept on her just in case she needed to get in somewhere and couldn't get in touch with him.

Olivia scrolled through the codes; front door, codes for every car, codes to the cellar in the basement, code to get into the master closet, code for the various safes in the home, etc. No guest bedroom code was present. She huffed, her curiosity peaked. She put her phone away and leaned down to try the code to get into their closet. Access denied.

Code for the safe. Access denied.

Code for the cellar. Access denied.

Code for the front gate. Access denied.

Irritated, she stood back and tapped a finger to her lips.

She tried his birthday. Access denied.

Olivia tried the code to his computer. Access denied. Then a warning sign. She'd almost utilized up the number allowed before the door locked for twenty-four hours. About to give up and shrugging her shoulders, she decided one last code couldn't hurt, then she'd leave to go to her sisters.

She typed in her birthday off a guess.

Access granted.

Smiling in excitement as the lock disengaged, she swung the door open, suddenly surrounded by darkness in a windowless room. She felt around blindly for a light switch before finding it, her brow furrowed as the room suddenly illuminated in harsh LED lights. Her eyebrows raised and her lips parted on a harsh inhale.

Oh. My. God. What the entire fuck? Olivia's brain struggled to process it all.

She took a hesitant step into the room before turning her head back to look down the hallway again, suddenly feeling frightened. She leapt forward and grabbed the lone wooden chair tucked under a desk that hosted a monitor and jammed it against the door, paranoid that it would close and she would be locked in.

Her eyes swept the expanse of the room, not knowing what to settle on first. There were a ton of newspaper clippings and articles on the wall behind the monitor, and on the opposite wall were huge canvas pictures of what Olivia could only guess was Colin's family...though she thought he didn't have one.

There was a much younger Colin standing with a man and a woman, the resemblance to his Latina mother striking, however he had his father's bone structure. A picture of Colin as a child in a superman cape with his arm thrown around a dalmatian, laughing as the dog licked his cheek. A portrait of Colin's parents posed together in a beach picture; Colin next to them as a toddler playing with a ball in the sand.

Then, in the very center of all the photographs, was Colin in a candid portrait of what looked to be him standing alone in front of a beautiful cherry wood casket in a massive church, standing close to a picture of his mother. It was his mother's funeral. Olivia felt tears prick her eyes at his loss. He never spoke of his parents or his family to her. The look on his face was tortured. He was so young.

Barely an adult, if he even was one.

She pulled out her phone and typed a quick 'I love you' text to Colin before turning to the other wall, preparing to leave because she felt like she was snooping on something extremely private. But an article on the wall caught her eye.

It was a clipping that hosted a red headed family.

A mom, father, a teenage daughter, an adolescent boy and a baby girl. They were scrunched together in the photo smiling brightly in matching white tops and dark blue jeans. The adolescent boy and teenage girl had green eyes like hers.

She stepped closer. Her phone suddenly rang, but she was too enamored by the text on the newspaper clipping to answer it.

'**Local teen Colin McDermont (16) responsible for the death of a Connecticut family of five. McDermont will stand trial, but it is yet unknown if he will be tried as an adult. Details are unclear but McDermont hit the family going well above the legal speed limit and the car fell off into an embankment, killing the family instantly.' Details as to whether the teen was drunk driving, or distracted driving is yet to be released.'**

Olivia felt her body heat up and her flesh broke out in goosebumps. She put her hand to her mouth, swallowing bile.

He didn't. No fucking way he didn't, and then married me, knowing how I feel about my parents, she whimpered as she looked around the wall, seeing more clippings of the family, funeral details, and more articles about the wreck.

It was never made clear what happened. Tears welled into her eyes, momentarily blinding her. Seeing the computer, she figured that it would host the answers, since it was locked in the room with the rest of the information.

Olivia swallowed her nerves, stepped forward, and wiggled the monitor awake. She bent slightly, pulling the keyboard up from the rolling shelf that was under the top of the desk. She paused briefly, seeing another password prompt. She put her birthdate as the password in again and breathed a sigh of relief as it let her in the first attempt.

Her relief was extremely short lived.

She saw multiple electronic folders and clicked on the one named Olivia. The date was late August, around the time of the storm when they'd first met. She clicked on the folder to open it, seeing image after image of herself. Sitting in her car at the diner, sitting in her car at her apartment's parking lot, looking up to the heavens at the food bank she went to for assistance. Images of her at the bar. There were videos of her leaving her clients' houses, and a video from the night of the gala where he had recorded the interaction with the judge.

More pictures of her from their time together, all taken while she was unaware.

Pictures of her and Allison, her and Vanessa, studying on the floor in his office, staring out the window of his building, her sleeping in bed, her in the kitchen making bread with Mary. Olivia started shaking, turning and running to the bathroom; she barely made it before she vomited, staying hunched over for long minutes until there was nothing left, and the dry heaving was over.

Moaning in distress and pushing herself off the floor, she heard her phone pinging repeatedly. Her mind burned with lightning hot betrayal. She felt used, taken for a fool.

He picked me because he thought I would somehow fix him killing that family. He didn't want me! I wasn't worthy, after all! I was just the vehicle for him to use to absolve himself of his sick fucking life, she screamed in her head.

Olivia's heart broke as she realized it was all a lie from the very beginning. She tore off her wedding ring and threw it on the computer back in the room and turned, leaving her book bag by the door. She looked at her phone. Thirteen missed calls from Colin and several texts. She blocked him without looking at them.

Racing to the main house, she ran back upstairs and yanked down another duffle bag, packing it as quickly as she could. She turned and got into the safe under the island in the closet and pulled out her passport and some spare cash. It wasn't much but it was something.

She pulled out her phone with shaking hands again, running to the bed and ripping her charger from its port in the nightstand. She scrolled through her phone until she found the name she wanted.

Gypsy, I need your help. It's an emergency. -Olivia

She grabbed her purse and raced downstairs to the garage, throwing herself into her car and trying to click the lock for the garage doors to open. They wouldn't open. She threw the car into reverse and didn't blink as she smashed his favorite bike into smithereens, taking out several other bikes in the process. Sirens filled the garage as the bikes' alarms started going off.

"Fuuuck!" she screamed. Her car beeped, notifying her of an incoming call from Jonathan. She answered, uncaring of the sirens blaring in the background.

"Jonathan, you tell him to fucking open these doors right now! He can't lock me in!" she yelled into the phone, opening her car to walk to the garage doors to see if there was a way to get it open manually. She couldn't see any.

"Olivia, please slow down and let him explain," Jonathan clipped through the phone, sounding like he was running. She could hear his muffled "I got her," to whom she assumed was Colin.

Olivia hung up quickly and blocked Jonathan, then in turn blocking Vanessa. Then blocked Aliyah too, just in case. She went through her phone and blocked everyone: Mary, Beth, Sara, Stella, and even Vincent.

Her heart was racing, and all she could feel was her heart breaking, and the burning sting of betrayal tearing her life apart right before her eyes. She hadn't felt this kind of pain since she realized she'd lost Allison and when her parents died.

She grabbed her bags from the car, leaving the keys in the ignition and the doors opened and went back through the house and out the front door. Taking out her phone, she called Gypsy who'd answered rather quickly.

"Gypsy, it's me. I need a huge favor. Can you pick me up? I'll text you the address and explain on the way. I need a ride to the airport. Thank you."

She hauled ass down the long driveway, pulling up an uber app on her phone. Breathing a sigh of relief that the gate code still worked, she hurriedly paid online for a cab service to get her immediately and took her to the address she'd given Gypsy.

Thanking God that her debit card still worked.

***

Six hours later Olivia was sitting in an airport terminal.

She'd withdrawn a bunch of cash and moved her two hundred and fifty thousand dollars from one bank to another that was completely in her name, fully knowing that the transfer might not go through until next week. Hence her need for cash. She'd gotten a burner phone at the airport, tossing her cell in the trash after programming necessary numbers. Looking over her documents, she'd glanced again at the fake ID, passport, social and travel documents that Gypsy was able to give her on the fly, due to her lawyer connection.

The process took a little longer than Olivia expected, she'd wanted to be in the sky and well on her way out of the states by now. While she was in Gypsy's lavish apartment waiting for the lawyer to process her documents, she took advantage of the extra time and dyed her hair a deep mahogany brown.

She fought like hell to keep the tears at bay, calling on years of practice oppressing her emotions to assist her in not breaking down in public.

Gypsy hugged her goodbye at the security checkpoint and promised to send a slew of clients her way once she knew she'd landed safely. She would also send her the address to the small bungalow that she'd found for her, in Macau, China. A hot spot for their touristy clients.

Olivia looked over her itinerary. She'd have to fly to Los Angeles, then to Hong Kong, before hopping on another connecting flight to Macau. Gypsy let her know that she'd paid to have a taxi pick her up at the airport and take her straight to the bungalow.

She felt completely disconnected from her body as she checked her bags in and took her carry on to the plane, barely making it on time. She refused to think about Colin and what he was assuming right now, placing him into that box of hurt that she'd ignored for weeks now, nailing it shut. She sat in the window and listened to the air hostess go through all the security measures before they took off.

Olivia felt her heart break for the final time as she let go of Allison, Vanessa, and Colin.

NINE

Colin

Denial...

No

***

Nothingness...

God, please help me.

***

Grief...

Sobs.

***

Faithlessness...

"I don't want to do this anymore..."
"You have to, Colin. You have to hold on for her."

***

Anger...

In their closet, Colin leaned over his phone, watching the video of them kissing in front of their Christmas decorations. He'd tortured himself watching the onslaught of videos they'd taken together and his hand shook with anger. With narrowed eyes, he threw his phone across the room with a shout.

"You fucking bitch!" he yelled.

Sinking to the floor, Colin angrily kicked over Olivia's basket of used laundry that he'd ordered Beth not to touch. Crying big heaving breaths, he slowly gathered all of her clothes off the floor and into his arms, dumped them on their bed, crawled in between the sheets, wrapped himself around her clothes, and pressed his face into her pillow. He let himself cry for long minutes until he heard the master bedroom door open.

"Mijo?" He stilled, hearing Mary's voice. "Mijo, it's Mary."

He tensed and fisted his hands around the fabric he was gripping, hearing Mary come into the dark room. She'd moved into the guest bedroom down the hall temporarily, as no one had trusted him enough to be left alone after Olivia left.

Colin stayed silent, clenching his fingers harder around her clothes as he felt Mary's presence getting closer and closer, approaching his back. He winced as she clicked the bedside lamp on and leaned over him, putting her hand on his hair as she stroked it lightly. Groaning past the deep throbbing cavern that used to house his heart, he attempted to speak past the pain. *"Madre..."* He squeezed his eyes shut as he clutched her clothes impossibly closer.

"It's ok, mijo, I've got you." Mary crawled into bed next to him and propped herself up on the headboard and pulled his head into her lap, clothes and all. "El dolor no dura siempre, mi amor."

Pain does not always last, my love.

"Mary, was I such a bad husband? Why did she leave me? *Am I really that easy to abandon?*"

"No Mijo...she was hurt, baby. You both were. She'll be back."

"I don't think so, Mary...you have no idea how hard it was to earn her trust. I knew better. *I fucking knew better,* but I was going to tell her. I was going to tell her everything. Our therapy appointment was only a few days away. Less than a week. I was going to tell her everything."

I was going to tell her everything.

***

Terror...

Colin's eyes went wide, seeing the body laid out in the hospital room. They were about to pull the plug on the redhead but were trying to exhaust all familial opportunities. He was their last call.

Jonathan looked over at him.

"Brother, we're going to find her. We need you to stay strong."

Beep....beep.....beep....

Colin's chest caved in. He couldn't breathe. He turned on his heel and walked out of the room, out of the hospital and into the night.

"Leave me the fuck alone. *Get away from me!*"

He turned and swung at Jonathan, who had run and caught up to him down the parking lot where he was headed for the highway.

"I'm not fucking letting you do this to yourself, you dumbass!" Jonathan roared, ducking another punch and hurling himself into Colin's torso, knocking them both over onto the concrete. Jonathan straddled Colin and gave him three almost bone shattering punches to the face.

***

Hopelessness...

Colin bowed his head, sobbing. Vanessa sank down to her knees on the floor of the living room with him as she her arms around him. She looked over his shoulder, catching Jonathan's eyes, tears in her own.

"Vanessa, the body they found... it wasn't her...she's still alive," Jonathan said gently, lowering to his knees in front of his friend.

His broken friend.

Colin clutched Vanessa tighter, groaning.

"It's going to be okay. We're all going to be okay," Vanessa whispered, trying her best to soothe him. "We're family and we're going to make it through this."

Her own voice broke, unsure of her words. Hoping it was true.

***

Emptiness...

"We're done wallowing. Come with me. If you don't, I'm calling emergency services and having you committed tonight. I mean it this time."

Colin turned his head from his spot on the floor in his windowless room, his eyes haunted as they met Jonathan's.

"I'm just going to let him beat the shit out of me, get it over with," he said quietly, his voice hollow.

"Then let's go. Alex is waiting." Jonathan's voice was hard as he stood there above Colin. His arms were crossed and his brow remained furrowed, letting his friend know he meant business.

Jonathan waited until Colin pushed himself off the floor before exiting the room.

***

Numbness...

Colin made his way into the luxury boxing gym behind Jonathan, veering into the locker room to stash his things while Jonathan greeted the tall, well-built psychiatrist. Alone momentarily with his thoughts, he wrapped his hands quickly before pulling on his boxing gloves, trying to think of something, anything other than his missing wife.

His runaway wife.

The wife that ran out on him because he *betrayed* her. Colin's eyes stung with unshed tears.

He'd stopped crying almost a week ago, and shortly after, Jonathan became scared.

Colin blinked, feeling hollow. However, he was definitely not scared.

He turned to make his way to the boxing ring.

***

Pain...

Colin watched as Alexander faced him head on, assessing him carefully before speaking. In a rare move, Colin scrunched his nose in displeasure at how violating his eyes were.

"Now, I'm going to let you decide how far this goes tonight. All I'm going to promise you is that I'm not going to hold back. It's your face, your body. Jonathan paid me well to provide this service and I'm nothing if not thorough. If you get beat into the ground tonight, then that's on you. Not me."

Colin stood in the middle of the ring, leaning against the ropes. Numb, he eyed the tall, brown-haired athletic psychiatrist with the wicked jawline and strong disposition.

He felt no fear.

Pushing off the ropes, Colin threw Jonathan a rather nasty look as anger suddenly sparked within him, wanting to beat his ass instead for making him do this.

Alexander strode up to him swiftly, getting into his face. Colin met the man's abnormally striking blue eyes boldly. Any other person would find him intimidating, but not Colin.

The only eyes who had ever intimidated him were his wife's.

Colin's lips tightened as his nostrils flared, his blood pressure rising just thinking about her. He blinked, feeling a tugging at his hands as Alexander pulled his gloves off roughly.

"If you're going to die, die like a man. And fight me like a man. Make her proud as you go, coward," he said to him deathly quietly, his eerily cold blue eyes flashing.

Colin's eyes snapped to Alexander's as his fist flew up, hitting air as Alexander ducked easily out of the way.

"That's what I'm talking about. *Let's go*," Alexander swung forward fast and Colin felt his head crack to the side. Grabbing his cheek hard on a shocked grunt, he turned his head slowly to look at the cold ass psychiatrist.

He felt secure in the pain Alexander provided.

He felt solace in something his wife loved. For once, he embraced the pain tightly, letting it keep him alive instead of destroying him.

Letting it nurture him.

TEN

Thirteen Weeks Later

COLIN STARED RED EYED at the big manila envelope that Mary placed on his desk in the study, seeing his name and address, but no return address. He was trying to get his heart to calm down, but he'd just left the gym after an almost three-hour brutal workout.

He took a deep swig of his whiskey and ignored his phone pinging, knowing it was Jonathan texting him again. He took a pair of scissors and cut through the bubble wrap layer inside of the envelope, his gut churning as he saw hundreds of hundred-dollar bills spill out, with a piece of paper. There was no name inside the contents, but he knew it was from Olivia.

> **OWED**: $2,232,000.00
>
> 5/11/2024 Deposit $50,000.00
>
> Total owed: $2,182,000.00
>
> Next Deposit date 5/31/2024
>
> $2,000,000.00 Vanessa
>
> $112,000 Student loan payment
>
> $90,000 School Tuition
>
> $30,000 miscellaneous
>
> I will be keeping the petty cash from the safe as you tore up my $15k the day you brought me to your house. I know I owe you, but you owe me too.

Colin counted fifty thousand dollars in all cash. He picked up his tumbler and threw it against the wall, hearing glass crunch everywhere. He picked up his phone and called his PI.

"Howards she made contact," he said, picking up one of the hundred-dollar bills. Already plotting his revenge.

"Tell me what you know," Howards replied.

Colin smiled, his first in months since the day she'd left him thirteen weeks ago. Sitting back down in his chair, he jiggled his computer mouse, prompting the screensaver to appear. His eyes landed on his green-eyed wife pictured on the screen. Instead of softening, they hardened. Colin gave himself permission to let his demons out full force when he got her back. Nice Colin was gone.

I AM getting you back. I'm coming for you, baby. Just wait. You're going to get what you're owed alright. We both are.

ELEVEN
Mistakes

Six Weeks Ago. Seven weeks after leaving Colin

OLIVIA WALKED UP TO the little ramen shop and pushed her way in, hearing the tinkle of the bell on top of the door. She paused and took in the smell of broth, spices, and the sounds of the people seated around little tables eating hot bowls of ramen. Most were Asian locals, however there were a couple tourists who'd recently found the spot and loved it. It was almost closing time as she walked into the little ramen shop that was only a fifteen-minute walk from her bungalow, ready to learn how to make a ramen dish from the little lady named Ying who ran the place.

The older woman took a liking to her as Olivia started coming in every night for a hot bowl of soup. Shortly, the two of them started talking, and Olivia mustered up the courage to ask for her to teach her to make the dish for herself. Eventually they struck up a friendship and she rather enjoyed the woman imparting her wisdom to her. She'd been there almost every night, learning to cook from Ying.

She gave the man at the front register a wave before making her way to the back kitchens where Ying was currently placing ingredients on the long table next to a steaming hot pot of soup. Olivia had been there the night before, putting in the various cuts of meat and aromatics for the broth to simmer overnight. She was back tonight to finish it up.

"Here, let me," Ying motioned with her heavy-set arms for Olivia to turn around and bend down.

Ying took her hair and twisted it up into a high bun before shoving a chopstick into it, holding the heavy mass there. Olivia fought back familiar tears of sadness as the woman manipulated her hair. However, thanks to Colin, she didn't have a knee jerk reaction like she used to at someone doing her hair.

Thinking of Colin, a tear fell out and her breath hitched on a sob. She pressed her hands into her thighs over the purple pleated skirt she was wearing and stood up as Ying tossed an apron over her head and tied it at her back before giving her a heavy pat on her shoulder.

Olivia turned and began adding ingredients to the flour.

"What is it, beauty?" Ying asked, ever observant. She was sitting back in a small chair at the table and watching Olivia manipulate the flour. She'd gotten good at making dough over the last couple weeks and Olivia attributed it to Mary's teaching her how to make focaccia bread. At the thought of the older Spanish lady, Olivia cried anew, leaning back so as to not get tears in the dough.

"We can talk while we make the bao, beauty. What are you running from?" Ying asked softly.

Olivia sniffed. "Who said I was running?"

The elderly lady tsked.

"Cooking has a way of bringing emotion to the surface. You come in here every night and cry. Also, I can tell you don't cook, so maybe you couldn't have known that. You can't come back here and not be emotional, beauty. The food won't turn out right. It's done, now we can roll out the dough and add the ingredients," the woman's kind voice caressed her and made her feel safe. The smell of the broth reminded her of her mother.

Olivia and Ying took time to pinch off small pieces of dough before taking a thin wooden roller and rolling the dough out into small circles. She added a small scoop of pork filling before pinching the dough closed.

"No, like this. See?" Ying said, taking her own dumpling and showing her how to twist and pinch the dough correctly.

Olivia nodded and opened her dumpling back up, mirroring the woman's movements. She had about four dumplings set aside before she began to speak.

"Ying, you're right. I am running," Olivia said softly, glancing at the kind woman's round face. She barely had any wrinkles. Ying's kind brown eyes settled on hers softly and Olivia was again grateful to find there was no judgment there. However, the woman quickly let her know in these last few weeks that she was not above doling out gentle chastisement..

"Are you going to stop any time soon?" she asked as she rolled another piece of dough out.

"I don't know," Olivia whispered, her head tilting to the side as she contemplated her question. "I don't know if I can,"

"You know what happens when you don't stop running?" Ying asked, gesturing for Olivia to start putting the dumplings in a small pot of broth. Olivia dropped them in carefully, seeing the dark broth swallow the dumplings, the little tip of the dough sticking out of the surface before being swallowed, taken under.

Olivia turned back to Ying, her eyebrow arched. Ying leaned forward.

"You die, from exhaustion. Stop running. Whatever you did, it can be undone. So stop being scared. The fear is ALL over you, and it makes you a target!" Ying said rather loudly, pointing a weathered crooked finger at Olivia's chest. "Learn to face your fears head on, only then you will have peace."

Olivia's eyes smarted.

I did the wrong thing. I shouldn't have left him like that, she thought to herself. Feeling her cheeks burn.

They sat there in comfortable silence and ate. After a short while, Ying spoke to her about her younger adventures and how her children were doing, who were consequently in America.

An hour later, they were sharing a cup of tea when a man's voice interrupted them.

"Hey Ying, how are you Auntie? Olivia, sorry I'm a couple minutes late. You ready to go? Did you save me a couple?" her bodyguard Erick came into the space with them and bent down, snagging a dumpling and biting into it.

"Hmmm," he said appreciatively. "Olivia, did you make these? They're getting so much better!"

Olivia smiled, glancing up at the man's chocolate eyes briefly before looking away, wishing those chocolate eyes were someone else's. Her heart swelled painfully.

"Yes, Ying is a wonderful teacher," Olivia replied, leaning forward in her wooden chair to give the older lady a hug. "I'll see you tomorrow, Ying. Ramen this time?" she smiled, giving her a little kiss on her cheek.

"Yes, I'll be here," Ying said softly, walking them to the door and seeing them out.

Olivia and Erick walked back to her bungalow, talking about their day and sharing their adventures. Gypsy had graciously paid for Erick to look after Olivia while she was there and could get back on her feet.

They reached her bungalow and Olivia paused before opening the door, feeling herself sway into this tall man who reminded her of Colin. Except he wasn't. Her eyes watered.

"Thanks," she bit out tightly, giving him a small smile as she went into her home and closed the door behind her, locking it.

She slid down the door, wrapping her arms around her knees and let the tears fall where she sobbed for two hours straight before wearily crawling in the bed. She had to prepare for another day of vetting potential adoptees of children that she'd saved from being stolen, killed, or sold off by Asian black-market dealers. She was paid quite a pretty penny for snubbing the black market. No one messed with her here, her reputation somehow preceded her, thanks to her client's whispers. Folks knew about the hard-hearted dominatrix who beat and did sick things to men... all the way in China.

Olivia couldn't bring herself to submit to providing beatings any longer. Colin said she was done with that.

So, she would be.

***

Olivia twitched in her sleep, restless, dreaming about her husband.

"I love you, Amor," Colin said as he stroked his knuckles down her cheek softly.

They were in bed, and he was lying on top of her in between her spread legs. Every now and then he would give her a deep slow thrust, but then he'd just stay there, looking deep into her eyes.

"I love you too Colin..." Olivia whispered.

"You couldn't have...why did you leave me like this?" Colin said, reaching a hand up to place it over her chest. "Our glow is gone, baby. I can't feel it anymore. Can you?"

Olivia woke with a gasp, sweating, holding her hand to her racing heart. She pushed her hair out of her face and looked at the bedside clock.

8:00 AM.

She fell back to the bed and shuddered before letting out a body wracking sob that carried out of her bedroom. For a long time she cried, eventually hauling herself into her shower where she continued to cry. She placed both of her hands over her chest, trying to feel that glow.

He was right; it was gone.

She let out a pained whimper as she got out of the shower and slammed her brush into her head with every pass through her hair. Tying her hair into a shrewd bun at the back of her head, she roughly pulled her clothes on and made her way to the front of the house where she grabbed her purse and her phone and headed out the front door to the black unmarked car waiting for her.

***

Olivia walked into the small dilapidated house off a dank alleyway and looked behind her, making sure her bodyguard Erick and their driver were still behind her. Hauling her tote higher on her arm, she resisted the urge to press her nail deep into the spot where she used to be injured. She took a deep breath, keeping her expression somber, yet open. She winced as a worn out looking middle-aged woman opened the door cautiously.

"Who are you?" The lady asked in Cantonese. Olivia tilted her head as Erick translated for her.

"My name is Olivia, and I got a tip that your little girl was about to be sold on the black market. We would like to purchase her at a premium price and take her to a reputable organization to be put up for adoption." Olivia waited as Erick translated for her, and she saw the woman's eyes widen before nodding hard at the two of them, opening the door and gesturing them in.

Twenty minutes later, Olivia walked out of the house with a basket. She put it into the trunk and climbed into the unmarked vehicle and she waited until they were on the main road before opening the middle seat and reaching into the trunk, pulling the basket through and opening the top.

She stroked the baby's black hair tenderly, feeling a tug in her heart. Missing Allison.

'Don't worry, precious, we're going to make sure you go to a beautiful home where you can have your own fairytale."

Olivia pulled the sleeping baby out of the basket and cradled her tightly to her chest, giving her love and letting her feel her heartbeat for comfort. Though at this point, she was unsure if her heart was even working properly. Its glow was gone; extinguished, overshadowed by pain and hurt.

Somehow, she was able to finish the drive without crying, having depleted her tears earlier in the day.

TWELVE

Coming To Collect

Present Time. 13 weeks after leaving Colin

"HOWARDS, SHE MADE CONTACT. It's just an envelope with no return address, filled with money. Fifty thousand dollars," Colin said shortly into the phone to his private investigator.

Standing up from his office chair in his study, he felt his chest tighten with a burning pain spreading uncomfortably throughout his body. She was alive. Colin closed his eyes and let himself feel relief.

"Currency?" Howards asked, his tone just as clipped.

"American. What can we do?" Colin gritted, placing a hand on the back of his neck, squeezing hard.

"We might be able to run the serial numbers on the cash to see what country the money was last run through. Send me pictures of some of the bills real quick. Let me call my government connect and I will be in touch when I hear something."

"Howards, make it quick please," Colin stated before hanging up. He hurriedly did as Howards asked, then immediately dialed another number.

"Hello?" Jonathan's deep voice sounded relieved as he answered.

"Jonathan, it's Colin—" he started, immediately being interrupted.

"*No shit,* motherfucker. I certainly didn't think you were Donald Duck! *Any update?*" Jonathan asked quickly, dismissing any niceties.

Colin had been on a rampage for three weeks straight and Jonathan thought he might have to fight the man himself.

"Yes, I'm on my way. I'm waiting to hear back from my PI. I'm putting the plane on standby; will you be able to fly out with me?" he said, seeing a text from his PI come in. He read it as Jonathan replied, seeing that Howard's government connection was currently running pictures of the bills as they spoke.

"Of course. Where to?" His best friend replied.

"We're still trying to figure that out. I'm on my way to your house." Colin ended the call and grabbed the envelope, stashing everything back in before taking off toward his garage. For the first time, he felt a little life enter him along with bone searing relief.

You're alive, and I'm coming to collect you, baby. Best believe.

***

Colin walked into Jonathan and Vanessa's new home fifteen minutes later, rounding the foyer, seeing Vanessa walking straight to him. The tall, curvy redhead threw herself into his arms, crying.

"Oh my God, *Colin!*" She sobbed, her tears wetting his jacket. Her fingers clutched at him desperately and he hugged her back as hard as he dared without squishing her swollen stomach, mindful of the baby she was carrying.

"I know," Colin said hoarsely. "I need Jonathan. Where is he?" He pulled away from Vanessa gently, turning towards his study.

"He's upstairs, putting Ally to bed." She sniffed, wiping her eyes and glancing at the staircase.

Colin took the stairs two at a time, banking a left and heading towards Allison's room, knowing exactly where it is. He paused, hearing Jonathan's deep voice filter through the crack of the door. He knew Jonathan was in there, reading her a bedtime story. His phone beeped just as he was getting ready to walk into the room and he paused, pulling his phone out.

The currency places her in Macau, China. We're still trying to figure out how and where. Her name does not show up in any database for any plane, no bank statements showing cash used, no cell phone, nothing. We originally ran both her maiden and married names with no luck. She's likely under a false identity. We have to dig some more. -H.

Eyebrows furrowed, he read the email again. *China?* Colin thought. His lip curled.

The bitch.

His hand tightened on his phone and he grimaced on a rough inhale as that word came back. He'd called her so many names the first few weeks after she left, silently and to himself, of course. But then the first local redheaded woman showed up dead and he firmly stowed away any bad thoughts he had about her. He refused to taint her memory like that, worried the next red headed woman would be her, though it wasn't. Then the next lady showed up dead and he started truly panicking. After the fourth local redhead showed up, Jonathan threatened to put him in a seventy-two-hour psychiatric hold if he couldn't get control of himself.

He'd ID'd every one of them. Each trip to the morgue killed a piece of his soul until he felt he'd never be the same again. Consequently, Colin began to torture himself in the gym to keep the anxiety that was his ever-present companion at bay. Then he moved on to broadening his sleeve tattoo, the hum of the needle and the pain overtaking his mind, canceling out his thoughts just enough to be bearable. Between the bodily torture, boxing with Alexander, renovating a small room off their closet, and the endless hours of work, he'd managed to make it through these fourteen weeks by the skin of his teeth.

How could she do this to me? Colin thought for the twelve thousandth time. With shaky hands, he knocked and pushed himself into Allison's princess themed room. He gave her a little smile, seeing she was tucked in for bed and Jonathan was sitting next to her in a recliner with his legs propped up, reading her a bedtime story in the glow of her pink princess lamp.

"Uncle Collie!" Allison smiled brightly, looking happy and content, tucked securely under the covers with her stuffed animals. Her normally gray cheeks glowed pink like her room. Finally, she was looking healthy. He bent and gave her a hug and a kiss on the top of her head, ruffling her strawberry blonde curls gently. However, Colin's smile wavered when he heard 'Uncle' and those familiar feelings of insecurity came back hard.

"Hey, lil' bit," Colin said in greeting. He sat in a nearby chair and typed out instructions on his phone for the flight crew to have the plane ready to be boarded as soon as possible, and then messaged his personal assistant to get the hell up and pack, as she was coming too. He listened while Jonathan finished Allison's bedtime story and closed the book, leaning down to kiss her forehead.

"Goodnight, daddy," Allison said, yawning, curling into her pink bunny. "Goodnight, Uncle Colin,"

"Night princess." Colin winced against the endearment as he made his way out of Allison's room, hearing Jonathan shut the door behind them as they entered the hallway.

"Update?" Jonathan said shortly, his eyes flickering over Colin's form tightly.

"She's in Macau, China!" He hissed, throwing him a filthy look and pacing down the hallway with quick steps.

"Wow, she *ran* ran, huh?" Jonathan said, his steps quickly overtaking Colin's as he hurried his way into the expansive primary bedroom, entering his and Vanessa's closet and pulling down a suitcase that he began throwing clothes into.

"Seems so," Colin said. His eyes stayed tight on Jonathan's marble top island as he contemplated, for the billionth time, what she was doing with herself if she wasn't dead. *How'd she get fifty grand so soon?*

The same question he'd asked her for months before having to drag it out of her.

"Hey," Jonathan said, pausing briefly in his packing. "She's alive. That's the most important thing right now. Now let's go get the girl back so she can stay that way."

Colin nodded and waited as Jonathan finished up before they bid Vanessa goodbye and took off into the night towards the airport where their private plane was waiting.

***

EIGHT DAYS LATER. Macau, China. 10pm.

Olivia followed her friend and bodyguard, Erick, to the front of her bungalow. It was late, and he was once again walking her home from the local ramen restaurant.

She took out her keys and went to unlock the door, pausing for a second to glance up at the man, whose brown eyes were so similar to Colin's. Feeling that familiar, haunting ache in her chest, she spoke quickly before she lost her nerve. "Hey, want to come in for a small nightcap before you go? I have popcorn, and I could use a friend right now," she asked with a touch of sadness in her voice.

She wasn't lying, her nights were becoming increasingly worse, and she knew if she didn't have a night soon where she didn't cry herself to sleep, then she was going to have to get on depression meds, and she didn't want to do that. Her eyes burned with unshed tears.

Erick was nice, but he was no substitute for Colin, and Olivia knew she was just using his looks to appease herself. She missed her husband and her family and for the millionth time she wondered if she hadn't misjudged the situation, only reacting out of hurt and extreme heartbreak. But the writing had been quite literally on the wall. How could she have misinterpreted it?

"Sure, but I gotta get back to my house soon," Erick said, putting his hand at the back of his neck and squeezing. He briefly thought to himself that he couldn't let himself go all the way with her as this woman was clearly damaged. He wondered about her. He didn't have the whole story, but just the look in her eyes and the stance of her body made him wary. She'd been through something painful and he wasn't sure he wanted to get near her with a ten-foot pole.

No, he'd accept his generous checks from Gypsy and go about his business as usual.

Olivia nodded with a small smile that never reached her eyes and opened the door, seeing her lamp glowing on a side table next to her kitchen. She threw her keys and her phone on the side table, placing her purse on the countertop and grabbing a bottle of water from the fridge, tossing it to him playfully.

God, anything to get my spirits up, she thought, feeling the familiar pang of grief glowing in her heart and making her chest tight. She was hopeful some company would help.

"Hey, find something on the television. I'll be right back. I need to get out of my heels," she said, padding her way into the space to the hallway. Sniffing, she scrunched her brows, noticing her place smelled different, slightly too familiar.

What is that? she thought, feeling that glowing, gaping feeling in her chest burn hotter.

Making her way through the dark and into her bedroom, her skin prickled as she went deeper into the room, gasping as her heel caught on something. Stumbling briefly, she was distracted from the niggling feeling as she bent down to extract herself.

What's this duffel bag doing here? She thought to herself, holding up the strap and seeing it attached to a big black bag that was packed.

Her eyes narrowed, and she startled in fear as she saw movement across the room by her bed. Suddenly her bedside lamp clicked on. Terrified, she let out a blood curdling scream before the light fully illuminated the space. Falling into the dresser behind her, she gasped as her heart crawled into her throat and the figure came into focus. Her eyes widened in recognition.

Him.

Looking murderous in a plain white T-shirt, his tattoos dangerously standing out against his arms. Her eyes roamed, seeing Colin had broadened his sleeve on his right arm in her absence. Her heart pounded and she went slightly lightheaded at the look in his chocolate colored eyes.

Her eyes flickered, finding another figure. "J-Jonathan?" she sputtered, just as her sister's fiancé came into view.

"I see you still can't say hello to me, wife." Colin growled with a thunderous look on his face.

Jonathan had a slight smirk on his face that quickly disappeared when Erick came crashing through the doorway with the bat she had stashed close to her room. Seeing the three of them, he went for Jonathan first as he was closer, swinging wildly. Colin kept his eyes on Olivia's, and she couldn't take her eyes away from him, even though they were both painfully aware that Jonathan was currently being attacked. There were a couple of grunts and a sharp blow, and Erick fell to the ground gasping in pain as Jonathan sank his fist so hard into his stomach he gagged, almost throwing up on her carpet.

She snapped out of her spell, turning her eyes to her friend and Jonathan.

"Jonathan, *stop!*" Olivia yelled, her heart racing for her friend.

Jonathan had wrestled the bat away easily, using some complicated kung fu moves, and snatched the man back up to his feet before letting him go. Erick stumbled a few feet before making his way over to Olivia. Her eyes flew to Colin's once more and widened as she felt her heart fully stop. She gasped in fear and toppled back a few steps, placing a hand on her racing heart, seeing he'd pulled out a deadly looking gun and was currently training it on Erick with a look she'd never seen in his eyes. White hot, furious rage. Her loving husband was gone, replaced with someone she didn't recognize. Someone who had a coldness and darkness about him.

Ruthless.

"You fuck my wife?" Colin asked simply. There was no stress in his tone revealing his anger or displeasure, it was as if he could have been asking Erick to hand him a piece of paper. The calm of his tone terrified Olivia. Colin had obviously had weeks to come to terms and deal with her absence.

Her eyes flickered greedily, seeing how his white t-shirt stretched across his chest with his movements, his tattoos looking dangerous as he welded the gun rather expertly. But his eyes.... she couldn't meet them, and he wasn't yet trying to meet hers either.

Olivia noticed he put on several more pounds of muscle in her absence, no doubt working his body to the bone to deal with her leaving him. Olivia couldn't help it, she bit her lip as she felt her panties flood with desire as his possessive claim sunk into her brain. She was sick, just as sick as him. Had to be. She shivered violently, feeling like she was in a fever dream.

Her breath hitched, feeling that spark suddenly ignite inside the cavern of her chest, bringing her back to life. Just then, his eyes slid to hers for a heartbeat length of time before he looked away dismissively once more.

Oh God baby please don't kill him! Her teeth chattered.

Erick held his hands up and inched away from Olivia carefully.

"Nooo," Erick said slowly, his eyes sliding slowly to Olivia, who was currently shaking so hard that the dresser was barely holding her up. She could mentally hear him yelling at her to say something, to explain this situation that looked so bad was completely innocent.

"C-Colin, this is Erick. He's been w-watching out for me since I've been here," she whispered, feeling like she was talking through a frog in her throat. She let out little panting gasps, feeling the edges of her vision start to go hazy as it hit her she was about to cause a man's murder. A man who'd done nothing but help her since she got to Macau.

"Oliv-," Erick started to speak, but was quickly interrupted.

"You say her fucking name again and I'll blow your brains out all over this room. Motherfucker *I dare you*," Colin said, his voice calm, resigned.

He stepped forward to them and cocked the gun against Erick's head. That simple movement spiked the tension in the small space and Olivia whined as she finally collapsed, overcome. She gasped in shock as Colin shot out his free hand and wrapped it around her throat, preventing her from hitting the floor. He hauled her up and against his rock-hard form. Olivia's eyes stared wildly into his as he finally turned his chocolate eyes onto hers. She pulled in a panicked breath at the absolute misery and depravity she found within the depths of his gaze.

He smirked coldly at her, tightening his hold slightly. Jonathan moved into her eyesight, making her eyes flicker to him.

"Ollie, Allison had her liver transplant. We made it through," Jonathan said kindly. Somehow knowing what to say to soothe and ground her. His eyes bored into hers for a second before he turned to Erick, who was still standing there with his hands up.

"Go on, I'll see you out," Jonathan said softly to Erick, waiting for the man to turn and head to the door before walking two feet to them. He turned slightly to put a heavy hand on Colin's shoulder, efficiently grabbing the gun from him and leaning forward to place his lips on Olivia's temple.

"Welcome back, Ukhat," Jonathan whispered to her, stepping away and turning to walk to the door.

Sister.

"Don't be too long because we've got a plane to catch. And don't hurt her either. I'll fuck you up." He threw over his shoulder as he closed the bedroom door with a click.

There were a tense few moments as they regarded each other, greedily drinking in the others' appearance. Olivia trembled, feeling her body flush hot with fear and desire as he regarded her silently. Her eyes widened at the pain expressed within his and her lips quivered, feeling his fingers tighten slightly around her throat in warning.

Olivia made a small sound, slapping her hands onto his shirt and gripping hard as they both moved at once, lunging and clutching at each other as their mouths met roughly. Olivia squealed as he picked her up and slammed her roughly down onto the dresser, shoving up her skirt and ripping her panties off, grunting as one edge of the elastic caught in between the heel of her right foot and her shoe.

"Who is Erick to you? Your pimp... drug dealer? Connect?" he bit out, his voice laced with jealousy and bitterness. Her blood sang as he opened his belt buckle and took his phone out of his pocket before shoving his pants down just enough to free his erection. She whimpered as he suddenly jerked her hips to the very edge of the dresser, causing her to have to lean back and support herself on her elbows.

"How did you find me?" She gasped, her blood rushed through her veins at the feel of his fingers crushing into the flesh of her thighs.

Colin ignored her. "Has he ever fucked you? Has he had his cock inside this sweet body? *MY body?*" He snarled, as he spread her legs roughly, looking between them. His fingers bruised the inside of her thigh in a crushing grip. "You had better goddamn answer me when I ask you a question! *I ASKED YOU IF YOU FUCKED HIM!*" His eyes snapped to hers and she balked at the anger she found there.

"No! No Colin, he's my bodyguard," Olivia whispered, flinching as he suddenly lowered his head and spit between her legs, making her face flame with embarrassment at the unexpected action, the feeling flooding her from her head to her toes leaving her slightly breathless. He cut his eyes to her as he took his cock out. The sight of it cooled her off a little as it was so angry looking and swollen with need. A thread of precum hung from the tip and he notched it into her opening before looking up at her, hearing her groan at the hot feel of him against her.

"C-Colin-"

"Pathetic," Colin interrupted, the one word her undoing as he suddenly thrust hard.

Her scream echoed around the room as he mercilessly bottomed out inside of her. The dresser banged loudly against the wall with the force of his thrust. He pulled back and slammed back in roughly, drawing another wail from her, and a harsh bang from the dresser. It burned. She hadn't had anything or anyone inside of her since she left him. She wasn't able to go there, still feeling too raw.

She winced as he reached forward, grasped her hair, and pulled her face up to him. His eyes roamed her brown hair, displeasure was present on his face, plain as day, and she pursed her lips at the sight, feeling shame mix with her arousal.

"Shut your *bitch mouth*. I don't want to hear it," he said, his words ringing harshly throughout the small space.

Olivia's eyes widened in surprise at his harshness before narrowing in anger, and she reached forward and pushed at his chest hard. "You fucking asshole!" she yelled at him, growling low in her own throat as he let go of her hair and snatched her wrists up, grasping them in one hand. His other hand went back to her throat, wrapping around and squeezing the sides, cutting off her air supply.

Colin's eyes flashed as he bared his teeth at her. "I have coddled you, I have bent over backwards for you. And you fucking left me, even after assuring me you wouldn't while we were at the therapist. I trusted you and gave you everything that I had, all that I was, even *changed* myself for you. No fucking more," he whispered harshly, slamming into her on another painful thrust, making her cry out.

Olivia tilted her head down as she felt a series of hot shivers race up her spine and her eyes fill with tears at the truth of his words. He verbalized what she'd been thinking. Though she was hurt, her trust betrayed, she'd reacted like a child, causing everyone around her undue pain. She sucked in a breath when he loosened his grip enough and felt tears spill onto her cheeks.

"*I know*, I know, I'm so s-sorry baby I was wrong!" Olivia cried out, trying to jerk her head away, but his hold on her throat was too tight.

"I didn't mean to hur-" she tensed up as he suddenly reached forward and slapped her across the face, the movement making her clench hard around him in excitement. He roughly yanked her head back to look at him, and she narrowed her eyes at him, panting.

"Goddamn you for making me like this...for making me love you," she hissed at him.

"You have no fucking *choice*, amor," Colin replied in a rough tone that made her heart race with excitement. "You're going to like it *whether you fucking want to or not.* You're going to fucking love me because you have torn my heart out and stomped all over it and left me fucking bleeding. And by the way, *I don't fucking like your hair.* That was a bitch move," he growled into her face, still thrusting. "And if you don't want to come back as what we agreed to in our contract, then you are damn sure going to come back as what we agreed to in our marital vows as *my wife.* I'm not letting you out of it that easily." He suddenly reached for his phone, unlocked it, and placed it on her chest.

Olivia gaped up at him in embarrassment as he never slowed, the little slaps of their bodies meeting clear as day in the room.

"Mr. McDermont," a woman answered the phone.

Olivia's eyes widened as she hurriedly placed her hand over her mouth to stem her moaning. Her core tightened viciously; she was about to orgasm. She cursed in her head as she became wetter, the slapping sounds echoing louder as she coated his erection with her essence. Her heart leapt in her throat as Colin suddenly reached forward and pulled her hand away, slapping her lightly on her face once again. She turned furious eyes to him as she gritted her teeth as she orgasmed, locking the muscles of her throat down, trying to be silent. Her nails clawed into the dresser as she tried to recoil away, and he yanked her back, grinding heavily into her pussy.

A tear escaped her eye at the pain of it.

"Sylvia, I need you to go to the drugstore and buy some hair dye stripper and have it on the plane for me. And I need at least ten days worth of plan B pills, and five pregnancy tests. And some duct tape. *Now!*" Colin said, not even trying to hide the hard sex sounds that were in the background. The woman was quiet for a second as the slapping sounds ensued. Olivia threw her head back, gasping as she felt her body break out in sweat, overstimulated and not ready to have another orgasm. Colin slowed his movements, thrusting harder, causing her to moan as he pressed deep into her.

"Hmmmm fuck me," she whispered as low as she dared, feeling her toes curl in her shoes.

The woman on the phone stuttered for a second, obviously hearing them.

"Y-ye-yes sir. How many boxes do you need?" Sylvia said, sounding like she was moving very fast.

"Four, five. I don't give a fuck as long as it works, just figure it out! That's what I pay you for," he said sharply, hanging up on the woman. He clicked a few more buttons and Katy Perry started singing about Riding Harleys in Hawaii. The song he'd played when he met her at the diner. She gasped in recognition and licked her lips as he leaned down to her face.

"Fourteen mother fucking weeks," he said, slapping his hand across her face again, making her gasp.

"I hate you. So much, Colin!" she threw the words at him mercilessly, whimpering as she felt a seriously painful orgasm looming.

"That makes the two of us. How fucking dare you leave me? *How could you, Olivia?"* he looked at her, his eyes cold. She narrowed hers at him, staying silent.

"I missed you though," Colin suddenly said, yanking her top down and exposing both of her breasts. His eyes trained on her bouncing globes and erect nipples for several minutes as he beat his flesh into hers. The beat of the song provided the perfect tempo for them. She flinched, finding their situation incredibly sexy.

"Now, are you going to cum for me, huh? Be my little cum slut? That's all you fuckin deserve right now." He yanked her head back to stare at him as he lowered his face to hers. "You sure don't deserve me as I was." With a groan that he quickly cut off, he silently orgasmed at the first hard clasp of her vagina, his fingers digging deep into the flesh of her thighs. She shuddered, resting her head against the dresser mirror and taking a minute to breathe deeply. His flesh slipped from hers too soon, still hard, and he stepped away from her, his chest heaving slightly.

Colin regarded her coldly as he took a second to pull himself back together. "You're packed up already. We're going home. Pull yourself together and meet me in the front," he said, leaving no room for argument.

"You can't fucking order me around-"

Colin moved fast and Olivia gasped and recoiled back away from him, pressing her back into the mirror and turning her head as he'd suddenly crowded into her space. Colin's scent permeated her senses as he pressed his chest against hers. They were silent for such an uncomfortable amount of time that Olivia's heart began to race, not knowing what was happening. Confused and slightly scared, she made a small sound as he tilted his head. Placing his lips to her ear, he spoke softly in a low tone.

"If you don't get your fucking ass off this dresser and do as I say, then neither one of us is going to be the same after tonight. I promise to God, Olivia, you do not want me to go there. *Get. The. Fuck. Up.* I won't tell you a third time," he breathed into her ear, deadly serious. He pressed his lips to her neck right over her pounding pulse and despite the rough hate sex they'd just had, Olivia was ashamed to admit she could go again. "Tell me right now, and I want the truth. *Did you fuck that man?*"

There was a tense few seconds where they just breathed into each other's space and Olivia's heart pounded uncomfortably hard in her chest, making her pant, desperate whines escaping her throat. *This is him. This is sadistic Colin*, she thought with a hot thrill racing through her body at seeing her husband as he truly was for perhaps the first time.

"No," she answered quietly, knowing her eyes were pained as they flickered away from his intense gaze.

He nodded once, not saying another word.

Olivia glanced around nervously, seeing that all her personal stuff was gone. She hopped off the dresser and inhaled sharply as semen and her essence visibly slicked down her legs. Her eyes flew away from him embarrassed, as she turned and went into the bathroom, limping. She unhooked her panties from her shoe and blushed, thinking her husband literally just fucked her like a whore, her underwear hanging from her shoe, all while he made a phone call at that!

Taking a few minutes to wash up, Olivia ventured from the bathroom a little later to see Colin gone and the bags removed out of the room. She walked through the hallway and into the living area seeing there were several men in the room with them, including Jonathan. He threw her a quick assessing look, averting his gaze quickly at what he saw, making her run her hand down her hair self-consciously; blushing.

Did all these men hear what just happened? She thought to herself, tugging her rather short skirt down.

The men headed out of the house and Colin clocked her gaze and jerked his head to the front door, signaling her to silently follow them. Olivia cast another quick look around before walking to the little table and grabbing her purse. After a quick search, she noticed her keys were gone. With a fission of trepidation mixed with hope blooming in her chest, she followed the security detail out of the home and into the waiting vehicle outside.

She was thankful that Colin allowed her to stop at the ramen shop to say goodbye to Ying, who announced she was happy to see her stop running and promised to make her stay in touch. The simple concession touched her, and made her hopeful that however they moved forward, it would be at the very least amicable.

***

Jonathan settled himself in the barrel seat of their private plane, wincing as he heard a crash come from their back bedroom where Colin and Olivia were. He glanced in apology at the airplane stewardess as her eyebrows rose, handing him his whiskey. He pulled out his phone, connecting it to WiFi and dialing Vanessa. Putting it on speakerphone, he placed it on the table as he opened his laptop.

"Hello?" Vanessa's soft voice filtered through his consciousness, making him settle for the first time in a week.

"We've got her, baby," he said, taking a sip of his drink and shaking his head slightly as he heard a soft cry followed by a series of slaps and Colin's deep rough voice sounding sharp, muffled by the bedroom door. He turned the volume on his phone up and stuck ear pods in his ears.

"Oh my God, Jonathan," Vanessa suddenly cried, her voice hitching. *"Is she okay?"*

"I think so, not sure how much of her is going to be left by the time we get home though," he said wryly, hearing a sudden silence come from the bedroom. After a few seconds, he heard Colin's muffled voice speaking again with Olivia's voice clearly yelling back at him. Vanessa paused.

"Well, tell him to leave something for me to attack. That's not fair. Fucking bitch just up and left for *months!* We thought she was dead," she whispered rather harshly through the phone.

"Baby, I'm going to tell you the same thing I told Colin. No one can blame her for reacting the way she did. What she found in that room...I can only imagine what it must have looked like to her. Now they're both going to have to figure out a way to put the pieces back together, if they can," Jonathan said quietly as he typed on his laptop, going over work for his business.

The week in China had cost him several million dollars, and he winced as he realized again that Colin also took a major financial hit for the last fourteen weeks he'd been going crazy trying to find Olivia. Jonathan had to step in and help run his business. He sighed tiredly, typing out an email to Dr. Tyson on Colin's behalf, reinstating their therapy appointments for the both of them. Colin hadn't been going since Olivia left. Too much longer and Jonathan thought he'd have to place Colin in a psychiatric hold.

"Yeah but...he wasn't drunk Jon. Why didn't he just tell her?" she whispered; he could feel her heart breaking for Colin.

"No...it's complicated but she didn't stick around long enough for an explanation. And he wasn't exactly forthcoming with the information. How's my girl?" he changed the subject.

"Ally's doing good," Vanessa said.

"My boy?" he said, now referring to their baby still in her stomach at seven months.

"He's kicking me to death. He's going to be strong, just like his daddy," she whispered reverently.

"And you? I can't wait to see you, love," he whispered back. Wishing he could feel her soft skin against his.

"Just missing you. Trying to settle into this big mansion you dragged us into," she giggled through the phone.

"Well, enjoy it because when I get home, we have a lot of making up to do," he said with a small smile, bidding her farewell and ending the phone call. He took a sip of his drink, turning back to his work and trying to ignore his absolute maniac of a best friend and his wife.

***

Slap, slap.

Olivia roughly shrieked into the duct tape that was wrapped tight around her mouth as she sagged into the chair she was strapped to. Her body quickly tightened again as she saw Colin stop and shake his arm slightly before he paused to take a deep drink of his scotch. She let out a series of sobs, her breaths coming out hot through her nostrils as he made her wait for the next blow. His arm snapped and the mean flogger landed.

Right on her clit this time.

Throwing her head back, her eyes rolled into the back of her head as she silently suffered through the worst orgasm of her life. Her body twitched hard in the restraint; her mind still not believing he'd restrained her like this.

Colin duct taped her around the chair in the bedroom of the plane, several loops around her torso, looping around the back of her chair, then around her thighs, holding her up and splayed open for him, her feet hanging on either side of the arm rests. She tilted her head back, her hands clenched, shaking.

Her pussy was pink and swollen from the flogger's constant manipulations.

He teased her with fluttering slaps mixed with hard flicks. Olivia moaned as she felt herself dripping onto the seat beneath her. He'd yet to touch her, aside from the flogger. She wanted his mouth more than anything in the world, but she couldn't say it. She could only wait for the pain right now. She thought about giving him the hand signal to get him to stop, only so he could unbind her and she could tell him to put his mouth on her.

However, she instinctively knew if she safe-worded to get him to do something else, then she would be in more trouble than she was in now.

Colin sat on the bed in front of her, regarding her trembling, helpless form. With every strike, he felt more and more of his control coming back. He breathed deeply, inhaling her unique scent.

"You look so beautiful, mama," he rasped, his Latin flair coming out thicker than normal, betraying his desire for her. He leaned forward to cup her swollen, stinging flesh in his big hand, and she whimpered as he ground the heel of his palm into her clit. She was red; he'd been spanking her pussy for a while, alternating the blows from the top of her mound to her clit, and sometimes to her breasts, her thighs, her feet, and her arms. Not giving her a clue as to where it was going to land next.

Suddenly the bedroom door flew open, and Colin cranked his head to the side, narrowing his eyes. Jonathan appeared with his hand clamped over his eyes.

"Yo, what the fuck," Colin hissed, tilting his head back and regarding his friend.

"Ukhat, are you ok?" Jonathan gritted, not addressing Colin, but Olivia.

Olivia squealed into the tape around her mouth, her eyes flashing at Colin, who was turning a nasty shade of red himself. He'd suddenly turned his head and looked at her, a disbelieving expression on his face. He leaned forward and slowly peeled the tape off her mouth.

She almost choked, taking a ragged breath. "I'm. Fine. Jonathan," Olivia gasped, feeling like she could faint with embarrassment.

"You hear that Dr. Fucking Phil? She's *FINE!*" Colin suddenly bellowed at Jonathan, making her flinch. This was the second time in one night she'd truly heard him lose his temper and his tone was scary.

"Olivia, do you have a safe word?" Jonathan pressed, refusing to leave.

"Yes!" *Oh my God, get out.*

"Then why aren't you using it?" Jonathan almost growled, still angled away from them.

Olivia glanced at Colin again from her helpless position. *Because I need this. Because I'm sick in the head, maybe? Because this man takes me to hell and back and I skip happily right along with him, my little demon husband. Fucking liar.*

She couldn't say any of that, so she said. "Because I don't need to, Jonathan," she said softly, her green eyes staring into Colin's. She wondered if she imagined his eyes softening as he treated her to what she figured was a truly evil smile in return.

"You heard the lady. Now, if you don't get the fuck out of this room Jonathan, I will kick you through one of these exit doors and watch your happy little inquisitive, nosy ass fly away!" Colin growled at his oldest friend.

Olivia heard the door click shut as Jonathan left them alone.

"Now," Colin leaned forward, licking his lips and replacing the tape over her mouth.

"Wait!" she gasped, but he'd already firmly put the tape back in place and was currently sinking to his knees in front of her.

"No," he dipped his head and swallowed her clit without warning.

THIRTEEN
Mile High Talks

OLIVIA'S ENTIRE BODY SHOOK uncontrollably as she swiveled her hips on top of him. She'd been riding him endlessly, secretly eating up the feel of his crushing grip on her hips as she screwed their flesh together. She threw her head back and gasped, feeling a hot bead of sweat roll down her spine and she clawed her nails into his chest as she locked her muscles against her impending orgasm.

"No!" she gasped as he reared forward and latched hard onto her straining nipple. She let out a little shriek, feeling herself gush wetly on him. Her hearing faded slightly, replaced by a ringing sound. *"No Colin, no!"* She tried to jerk away and then pushed at him, failing to loosen his latch on her breast. She shuddered as her sex tightened up, spasming on his thick length. Colin groaned, the sound vibrating through her nipple down to her clit. "Oh God I'm going to pass out!" she whimpered, beginning to push in earnest against him now.

The ringing in her head became louder and she felt her world tilt on its axis as he grabbed her arms hard and rolled them fast so she was underneath him, her legs spread wide as he bounced off her pussy unrelentingly. The bed was squeaking in protest and the sheets had long since half torn off the bed in their passion for one another. Their joining was messy, and she wouldn't have it any other way.

"The hell you are," Colin growled, shoving back through her sensitive tissues, making her keen and cry out for mercy. He settled himself on top of her and licked up her cheek before grasping her head and holding her still. "Now I know you're young and we have sixteen years between us, and though it turns me on so fucking much that I'm older than you, I still have so much to teach you," he punctuated his statement with a deep grinding thrust that had her eyes rolling into the back of her head. "What I'm not going to tolerate is temper tantrums, much less one that lasts thirteen fucking weeks. So, until I am fucking satisfied you've learned your lesson, you better be letting me know you are paying attention, baby. And God help your ass if you don't stay present. So if you pass out, I'm just going to wait until you come to and then fuck you a different way, until my ego is appeased. You feel me?"

Olivia gritted her teeth and groaned through this orgasm, feeling it work its way torturously from the inside out. She barely had the energy to flinch as he tilted his head down and latched onto her neck, biting her hard and sucking the vulnerable flesh into his mouth.

"You and your fucking ego can go straight to hell," she bit out, knowing she was goading him.

He let go of her neck and she screamed as he yanked her leg up and delivered ten harsh slaps to her ass, making her clench around him harder.

"If I'm going to hell, then you best believe I'm dragging you with me."

***

A few hours later, Colin disengaged from a barely conscious Olivia and yanked his clothes back on. He went into the little bathroom off the bedroom and washed his face and hands, not wanting to smell too much like sex when he went out front. He went back into the bedroom and pulled the covers higher over her now sleeping form, and pushed her now red hair away from her face. Earlier, he'd thrown her into the little shower and followed her in with the hair dye strip boxes, ignoring her protests for privacy. He'd be damned if she was going to miss any spots.

He just wanted the brown shit gone.

He'd also made her pee on all the pregnancy tests, his harsh look daring her to defy him as he held out a test one by one, crowding her in the bathroom to make sure she peed on all of them, not giving her any privacy. She saw some of the coldness leave his eyes as they all showed up negative. Not much, but some.

Colin closed the bedroom door and walked to the front where the seating area was, ignoring Jonathan who was on his laptop with his ear pods in. He went to the drinks cabinet and poured himself a healthy scotch. Turning and taking a seat perpendicular from Jonathan who'd taken out his ear pods and was giving him a rather assessing look.

"What?" Colin snapped. His eyes flashed as he returned the look, tilting his head back and ignoring the burn as the alcohol went down. He rubbed his aching chest.

Shit, he thought. He hurt everywhere, and his dick was still hard. Not to mention he was still incredibly pissed about Jonathan's interruption earlier. He knew that he was responsible for that, having almost leapt off the deep end several times in the last few weeks but the man really couldn't think he'd hurt Olivia. Not really. The woman held his soul in the palm of her hand.

"Vanessa said to leave something of Olivia for her to rip apart when we get home bro. Can you lay off for a little bit?" Jonathan said, his eyes turning back to his computer when Colin threw him a wry look.

"Fuck that. Vanessa can have what I *let her have,*" Colin said, flinching as he took a rather big gulp of the scotch. "How much longer until we land? I'm losing track of time,"

"Nineteen more hours. We've been in the sky for five," Jonathan replied, his eyes boring into Colin's. "You're not even ashamed, are you?" he said, taking a drink of his own whiskey and leaned back in his seat, getting comfortable.

Colin's lip curled. "Why should I be? She's my wife," he snarled across the seat at him.

"She's not your *property.*" Jonathan raised an eyebrow.

Colin stiffened. They differed in opinions, and in Colin's viewpoint, he damn near owned her, and she owned him. Jonathan knew that.

"All I'm saying is, you might want to actually talk to her about the reason why she left before you screw the poor girl to death." Jonathan nudged. "Bro, we still have to get home and stop by my house. Vanessa wants to see her, and Allison needs to see her." He held up a hand, halting Colin's reply.

"No, I don't want to hear it. I just spent a fucking week in China with you looking for her. I've lost millions and you have lost hundreds of millions in the last fourteen weeks. We're stopping by my place first. Get your shit together and let's get back on track!" Jonathan's voice came out hard.

Colin narrowed his eyes at Jonathan. "We'll go to your house, *only* because of Ally," he bit back in a reply as he signaled for the stewardess. "Can I have something to eat please?" He requested of her rather rudely, suddenly starving. He'd barely eaten since they'd got to China. He had been so adamant to find Olivia.

"Yes, sir. I'll have it to you shortly," the brunette said, her eyes flickering down his form greedily, lingering on his tattoos before she turned to head to the front of the plane where the small kitchenette was.

Jonathan watched her walk away. "Whew, that woman wants you," he teased, trying to lighten the mood. "She wanted to put you on a plate for herself. If only she was aware of your particular brand of kinky." He chuckled, ignoring Colin's filthy stare aimed his way, unimpressed. He poured himself some more to drink. "You ok bro?" Jonathan asked, closing his laptop and placing it to the side, giving Colin his undivided attention.

"No," Colin snarled back. "I'm going to fucking tell her after she wakes up. Get it over with. Will you stay please?" he said, not wanting to show weakness but really seeing no other alternative. He didn't want to risk her running again. And what was she going to do? Parachute off the plane? He knew she was talented, but he doubted she could pull that stunt off.

His chest ached and he felt like he'd aged ten years in just the three months she'd been gone.

"Of course, man. Whatever you need. Probably best to get it out the way because I can't say what's going to happen to Olivia when Vanessa gets her hands on her," Jonathan said, his eyes softening towards him. The stewardess put a plate of roast beef carrots and potatoes in front of both Colin and Jonathan and disappeared. Colin ate and sat back, staring contemplatively out the window.

At some point he and Jonathan both fell asleep.

***

A couple hours later, Olivia woke up and moaned, just lying there, feeling like she'd been hit by a truck. She had no clue how long Colin had been fucking her, but it exceeded any other time they'd done it before. She shivered as she sat up, wincing at the pang in her vagina. The man was a machine and was single mindedly focused with all his fury on her, intent on nailing her to the plane.

She brushed her red hair out of her face, rather relieved to see her color was back to normal, she'd hated being brunette.

Getting up, Olivia disappeared back into the bathroom, seeing a towel and a linen dress laid out on the small table. She hissed as she got back into the shower, wincing as the water felt like needles against her sensitive skin. She worked diligently to wash the smell of hard sex, sweat, and Colin off her body before rinsing thoroughly.

Then she washed a second time just to make sure. She was embarrassed that her husband just railed her like a whore for the security officers, his personal assistant, and Jonathan to hear; she didn't want them smelling her as well.

Olivia brushed her hair and left it wet, pulling on her bra, not finding any underwear.

Well then, she thought, her eyebrows raising. Her stomach growled and she bit her lip, eyeing the door that led to the rest of the plane. She frowned, not knowing what she was facing when she went out there.

She got out the phone Colin provided her and scrolled through it before remembering that she was on a plane and couldn't use it. Wobbling over to the door, she cracked it, seeing the small hallway and another powder bathroom. She tiptoed barefoot to the end and spotted Jonathan reading a book, facing her, and Colin was in a chair across from him with his back to her, asleep.

Olivia waved, getting Jonathan's attention. Walking further in, she sat at a little table nearby and waited for him to join her.

"Hey," she said softly, tucking her hair behind her ear and giving him a small, shy smile as he settled into the seat next across from her.

"Hey," Jonathan said, his dark eyes assessing her. He wisely didn't say anything about her appearance or said anything about him interrupting her and Colin earlier.

"Is there any food on this plane," Olivia whispered, "I'm starving."

Jonathan nodded and smiled as he signaled for the stewardess. "Yeah, what do you want? We have roast beef or chicken and rice?"

"Chicken and rice please," she mumbled, wanting something not so heavy on her stomach. *The only way to solidify my place as the most fucked up wife ever hall of fame is to throw up while Colin is fucking me. No thank you.* She poured herself a cup of sprite and sipped it, trying to calm her nerves. Her eyes slid to Colin who was still sleeping peacefully.

"That's the most peaceful I've seen him since you've left," Jonathan said quietly, seeing her gaze on Colin. "I'm sorry I walked in on you two like that...I just wanted to make sure you were ok," he admitted, stunning her.

She winced. "Did he tell you what I found? Why I left?" she said, needing him to understand she wouldn't just abandon her family without good reason.

"I know what you found. I know the whole story, Ukhat. I was there through it all from the beginning."

Olivia glanced down at the table, taking a deep breath and trying to steel her resolves. "Jonathan...can I trust this man? He had so many pictures, almost like he was stalking me from the beginning. And then the newspaper clippings of that family? He knew how my mom and dad died. I feel so *fucking foolish,*" she paused for a second and then took a gasping breath. "He made me love him and then broke my heart. I felt so blindsided," she whispered as a hot tear slid down her cheek.

"Olivia, I'm sorry you had to find out the way you did. I can only imagine how awful you must have felt. How betrayed. And I know we all have to handle things in our own way. I don't judge you for leaving, I hope you realize that," he ran a hand through his thick black hair and took a deep breath before continuing.

"Yes, we were all incredibly upset, and there was a lot of damage control that needed doing, especially with Allison. But trauma doesn't make sense. We know this. Everything's happened so fast for us all I think, that we're trying to find our own way to navigate life. It's hard and won't always be perfect," he gave the stewardess a smile as she set the food down in front of Olivia. She said thank you and tucked in, eating heartily.

"Marriage isn't perfect, but you do owe it to him to let him explain himself. Everything isn't always what you think. He wasn't stalking you. In the beginning, I think he was trying to feel you out because you wouldn't give him the time of day for anything, and he's not used to not getting his way. He followed you to try and figure out if you were in a relationship or gay and whether or not he had a chance," Jonathan chuckled at Olivia's cough.

"But then he quickly saw that something was wrong, and wanted to help but didn't know how to approach you without being so direct. You know Colin, he just barrels through with solutions," he smiled at her kindly.

Olivia nodded and they continued to talk quietly about Allison and her liver transplant and how she was doing until Colin suddenly stirred. He always rose before her; she never got to see him when he arose for the day. She saw the change happen gradually. He sat up and stretched his arms, the muscles even thicker than before, giving them a little shake. His face which was relaxed in slumber, hardened and chiseled itself into the man that she knew. He took a second to check his watch before standing and turning, seeing her and Jonathan at a table behind him.

His eyes hardened as they landed on hers and she glanced at the tabletop shyly, feeling ashamed of herself. She'd put everyone through so much. She felt her cheeks pinken as he came around to sit in the chair next to her. He leaned back, crossing his ankle over his knee and extended his arm to slide behind her back in the barrel seat she was in.

"Five more hours until touch down. I hope we all got enough sleep. We still have Vanessa to deal with and I don't know about you two but I'm going to need several drinks to handle that," Jonathan quipped, getting up to refresh his drink and make them their own. He came back cradling three glasses in his big hands before setting them on the table.

"Did you eat?" Colin said softly to Olivia, sliding her drink towards her cautiously, almost as if he was worried she would throw it on him. Her green eyes flickered to him, almost dark with the plethora of emotions that were on her face.

"Yes," she whispered, blinking back tears. *How can I love this man?* "Did you?" she asked back softly, seeing Colin nod his head yes in response. Grabbing her drink, Olivia tossed a healthy amount back and winced as she sucked on the lemon that was on the side of her glass, grimacing as she felt the burn spread.

"We need to talk," Colin said, his own face reflecting his worry and emotion.

Olivia jerked in her seat facing him. Licking her lips, she took a quick breath before she began to speak, her words coming out more rapidly than she cared for them to. "Colin, I don't hate you. I know that I was upset but I didn't mean it when I said it," she said softly, wanting to lean into him but not ready to give him that yet. "I just felt so *betrayed*," Olivia's face broke as she looked away, hiding herself from him on a pained whimper.

She cried harder as his hand settled on the back of her neck. Jonathan pushed a tissue into her hand and she whispered thank you. Pressing the napkin to her eyes, she wiped her nose feeling like a wreck, physically now and not just mentally. She sagged in relief as Colin turned his eyes onto her, softer now.

"I didn't mean it either, Olivia. I was just so mad. We thought you were dead, baby. Until the money started coming. Then the fury came right along with it. I'm sorry that you felt like you had to run instead of coming to me. I wanted to try and tell you so many times, I just didn't know how to without losing you. But then I lost you anyways, except I couldn't even give you my side of the story. I know what you found looked really bad. But I have that stuff as a reminder of my pain, and what I work so hard for," Colin said, his voice coming out rough and hollow.

"Is it because I'm a redhead? You thought by picking me and pulling me into this fairytale life that you would be absolved? I mean, what exactly was it?" she whispered, unable to meet his eyes, not wanting him to see into her soul when he broke her heart further.

Apparently there was still enough soul left there to shatter.

"No baby, I think it was just a lucky coincidence. Fate. I really was out there about to end it all when I saw you. It was almost like the heavens decided that it was time for me to move on, and they made my ultimate blessing look like the source of my torment. Because that was a sign. And I needed something obvious because nothing was helping," Colin replied. Olivia was aware of his eyes on her profile, but she wasn't quite ready to face him.

"True, I've almost had this man committed more times than I care to talk about. He was doing okay for a while but began to spiral with the guilt that was eating at him," Jonathan chimed in, clearing his throat, and sitting back further in his seat.

"What happened, Colin? I need to know," she said, finally turning her eyes onto his. She slightly recoiled at what she found there.

"Will you leave me again? If I tell you?" he said hoarsely, his hands fisted hard, turning his knuckles white. She leaned forward and placed her hand onto his thigh.

"No," Olivia said honestly. She loved him, even though what he was about to tell her was probably going to destroy her mentally. "I think we're stuck with each other. You just drug me back from one of the most obscure places on earth," she gave him a small smile, feeling his thigh tense.

Her smile faltered as he turned in his seat to regard her with eyes that looked tortured, bleak, desperate, and absolved. She gulped a desperate breath of her own, feeling her lips quiver as she waited for his next words.

"Baby if you don't want me anymore after I tell you this, you can go. You don't even have to pay me the money back," he said, his voice coming out hollow. She briefly wondered if he really even meant it.

Ouch, Olivia thought, feeling her heart crack further. She didn't want him to say that; she never wanted him to give her an inkling that he'd ever let her go.

Olivia took a deep breath. "Colin, were you drunk when you hit them?" she asked, letting the words linger in the air around them. Jonathan took a deep drink of his whiskey and leaned forward, gazing at the two of them intently.

Colin stared at her for a second. Because how could he tell her this without talking about his mother. The one person he'd never wanted to talk about again. His face tightened.

"No. No, I wasn't," he said, his voice coming out gruffer than he intended. He glanced over at Jonathan, who nodded his head encouragingly at him. Colin turned his eyes to the table in front of him, momentarily steeling himself to set his secret loose. His hand shook as if the physical action would be enough to keep the mental grip on his internal torment. He turned his eyes back to Olivia's, finding a small measure of comfort that she was still staring at him in the face.

"It was late, and storming. I was driving home from a friend's house. I had just delivered his money from selling his supply of coke, and had gotten my cut," his eyes were tight on hers. She stared back, not even wanting to blink, surprised that he used to be a dealer.

"My mother had been in treatment for health problems, and I was selling drugs to help my father pay for her hospital bills. Sounds rather familiar, doesn't it?" he said quietly. She nodded her head, her eyes widening.

"It was around the time that modern cell phones were just coming out, and they were still the little Nokia phones, with the keypads that you had to press multiple times to get one letter out. Well, my father had texted me to let me know that my mom had suffered a heart attack and was being rushed to the hospital. I was reading the text message and began driving too fast to rush to be by her side when I hit the car with the family inside. I didn't see the stop sign through the rain in my haste and t-boned them going ninety miles an hour. The mom and dad, teenage daughter, child, and baby all died on sight. I don't know how I made it," Colin whispered, blinking back his own tears, breathing hard. Not wanting to relive that moment.

Oh My God, Olivia thought, her eyes holding his in disbelief as something flowed between the two of them and her head bowed under its force.

Olivia's heart finished shattering. Feeling it painfully splintering to pieces, she scooched closer, placing her lips on his forearm. She looked startled as a tear splashed on his arm; she was crying.

"I killed five family members that night and wound up in a room at the same hospital that my mom died at just hours later. I couldn't even say goodbye because I was strapped to so many machines to monitor my brain activity. I was so close, but couldn't even say goodbye. I lost my father shortly after too. His whole life ended up turned upside down by grief, and he moved to another state," he paused and scrubbed a hand down his face.

Colin took a deep breath before continuing.

"I had to move in with Jonathan. I haven't seen my dad since before my mother's funeral. I know you saw the picture of me next to her casket. I had to arrange it myself with Jonathan and his family's help. My father abandoned me before the funeral and didn't even say goodbye. He made sure to call me a killer before he left. Apparently, mom was doing ok after her heart attack, but when the nurses told her that her son got into an accident, killing an entire family and I was laid up in a nearby room, she'd had another fatal one. It was my fault." Colin's body tensed and he looked away from both Olivia and Jonathan, unable to face either one of them as he struggled to get a handle on his emotions.

Olivia felt her jaw drop as her stomach flipped. Her hand went to cover her mouth and she let out a shaky exhale. Her grief turned into rage and she bared her teeth as she felt herself turn red. She started trembling, her blood pressure shooting through the roof.

"No!" she gritted out so violently both men slightly jumped. "I refuse to let you believe that. That's a sick man who would turn his back on his son like that! To pick up the pieces by yourself? To call you a killer when it wasn't even your fault! Heart attacks happen. Cancer happens. Fucking liver disease happens!" she almost screamed this last part, and Jonathan and Colin both reached for her at the same time, slightly alarmed by her outburst.

'No! Let go of me. Tell me tell me you don't think you killed your mom. Tell me!" Olivia implored, reaching forward and grasping both of his arms in her hands, clutching hard. He turned red eyes to her, his pain plain as day on his face. "Baby please..." she whispered now, digging her nails into his skin.

God I've been so blind. How did I not see this pain? she thought sadly.

"It doesn't *matter*, I killed that family, and my mother died shortly after she found out. Facts are facts Olivia," he said harshly. His eyes were back to being hard, and he was closing himself off once again.

Olivia shook her head, feeling like she was underwater. She was back in that pool, feeling like it was her drowning instead of Allison. She gasped and sat back in her seat, her eyes widening. "Wait...your dad abandoned you. Do you feel like..." she turned eyes full of heartbreak onto him. She felt nauseated, truly scared she was going to be sick. She blinked, feeling a lone tear slide down her face.

"Allison. Do you think *I* abandoned *her? Have I been fucking triggering you this whole time with my situation?*" she half whispered, her eyes bouncing back and forth between Colin and Jonathan.

"Wow...this has taken quite a turn," Jonathan said ruefully, sitting back in his seat and folding his arms tightly.

Colin remained quiet, unsure of what to say. He hadn't expected the conversation to go this way. He kept his eyes on the table in front of him, unwilling to meet her eyes.

Olivia leaned back and took a deep breath, thrusting a hand through her hair. "Oh my God we're so fucked up. This is so fucked up. You can't even answer my question," Olivia whispered, her eyes staring unseeingly at his chest. She began to cry silently. "What do we do?" she asked. Her green eyes imploring, looking over to Jonathan who looked just as stricken. Her friend who usually had all the answers was suddenly mute.

"I can't say that's made me exactly comfortable, that my best friend is raising Allison," Colin offered as politely as he could, carefully meeting her gaze. Her mouth tightened.

Colin felt his hands shake as his blood pressure spiked. Tightening his fists, he desperately tried to ward off the looming panic attack, thinking this was too much to pick through in one conversation.

"You know why," she suddenly hissed, slapping a fist into her palm sharply. "Do you think this is easy for me?" she said louder, her eyes flashing as she leaned forward in her chair.

Colin suddenly moved, his fist thumping into his chest hard. "It's not just *YOU* anymore! Allison should have been OURS," Colin suddenly yelled, his eyes snapping on hers and narrowing. "And yet I have to listen while she calls *him* daddy!" his eyes flashed angrily at her as he pointed a finger at Jonathan, who was now sitting back and pouring more whiskey into his tumbler, still remaining quiet because what could anyone say to that?

Olivia let out a little sound and placed her hands over her mouth, curling her knees up to her chest in the seat. Her eyes went wide.

Colin was so angry, a vein was beating in his neck. He leaned forward even closer.

"What exactly is it that you want me to say to you, huh? How the fuck is it supposed to make me feel?" he gritted bitterly, getting in her face. "I have been going there every week keeping up your Sunday visits and making excuses, torturing myself staring into her green eyes that are just like yours, telling her excuse after excuse about where her Aunt Ollie is while she calls me Uncle," he leaned back in his chair slightly, trying to control his temper. "It is one thing, to have a child who is five years old, who barely carries memories from that time in their life, and compare them to a teenaged boy almost in their adulthood. I have to remember every fucking thing. I don't have the luxury of forgetting a single thing. I had a mother who loved me, who died. And a father who is alive and wants nothing to do with me. There's no fixing that, the damage is done, we can't compare these two scenarios at all. But we can fix this, and you won't even entertain the idea," Colin breathed deeply, leaning forward once more, further into her space. "So you're motherfucking right I can't answer your question. This conversation is over," he said as he pushed up from the chair and left to go into the back room, slamming the door.

Olivia sat back in the chair, stunned. Jonathan said nothing, sitting there looking just as tortured. She broke, her face crumbling as she drew her knees tighter, wrapping her arms around her legs and sobbing. Jonathan got up and sat next to her in the empty seat, pulling her into his chest as she cried.

"Ollie, it's going to be okay. We'll get through this Uhkat."

Olivia shook her head. "I don't know Jonathan. I know I was hurt but I acted like a child. I don't even know why he'll want me after this. I don't even know why he still wants me."

"Olivia, *Colin loves you*. He meant every vow he spoke with you the day you two got married. You will get through this but you'll have to acknowledge that it'll take time to build back trust together," Jonathan said softly, reaching forward to squeeze her hand. He let her cry on him for as long as she needed until she wore herself out.

They spent the next four hours in silence, not speaking to each other.

***

The three of them were still silent after Colin's raw outburst as the hired driver took them to Jonathan and Vanessa's new home straight from the tarmac. They'd bought a huge mansion about ten minutes away from them.

Olivia was tense, not even able to take in the beautiful property as the car slowed to a stop. She took a second to wipe her tears, her heart beating wildly at the thought of reuniting with Allison and her sister.

She hesitantly followed Colin out of his side, stepping onto the intricately laid drive with ivy growing between the slats. She startled as she heard a loud slam and a *"Where is she?"*

Vanessa.

Olivia's eyes widened as her sister rounded the corner of the drive and half flew down the pathway underneath archways of white climbing roses, her bulging tummy leading the way. Vanessa was crying and visibly shaken, her bare feet padded loudly on the stone as she came closer. Olivia stood stunned, wringing her hands in fear as she came up to her.

She cried out as her head snapped sharply to the side before her sister yanked her to her harshly, maneuvering around her big belly. Vanessa was sobbing.

"You're such a fucking *asshole* Ollie! We thought you were dead you bitch," she bit out. Olivia winced, her cheek stung, and Vanessa had her hands in her hair and was pulling her to her by the strands that she swore Colin had ripped out when he was stripping her hair of its dye.

"I'm sorry Nessie," she half whined, her whole body now smarting from all the abuse over the last twenty-four hours. "I was just hurt big sis," she said, relaxing into her arms. Suddenly, she felt a kick on her stomach and she pulled back gasping.

"Nessie," she whispered, placing her hands tenderly on her sister's bump. She squealed with excitement as she felt the kick again.

"I know, he's very active!" Vanessa said, her spark back in her eyes.

"A boy?" Olivia said, a dreamy expression on her face. "I'm going to be an aunt," she whispered, crouching down to put her face into Vanessa's belly.

"I'm going to spoil you *rotten*, you little thing. Just you wait!" she said, wrapping both of her arms around Vanessa's tummy and squeezing tightly.

"I'm going to get Allison," Colin said, his face tight as he walked away toward the side entrance that led to the couple's mudroom and kitchen.

Jonathan came up next to them and put his arms on both of their shoulders and pulled them in for a hug. The big guy was such a softy.

Too bad Colin isn't, she thought.

Just then, he came out with Allison in one arm. Olivia's heart tugged as Allison screamed so loud and pushed against Colin when she finally saw her, that Colin had to dip quickly to settle her on the ground before he stood up again, his brown eyes flashing slightly as they met hers in a silent recognition of his words to her from earlier.

He meant what he said on the plane.

Allison crashed into Olivia so hard, screaming with excitement and clawing at her, that they both fell back to the pavement. Olivia had to make sure she kept her legs pressed together to not betray her lack of underwear, feeling her dress slip up her legs. She pulled the little girl to her as she felt more tears fall down her face.

"Tee Tee! Tee Tee! You won! You're back!" Allison pulled back slightly, straddling Olivia's hips and placing her hands on either side of her cheek. "Tell me all about the monster! Was he scary?" she said seriously, her brows furrowed, and a serious look graced her face. Olivia gaped at her and glanced over at Colin, Vanessa, and Jonathan who were all standing next to them, looking slightly amused.

"The monster?" she asked with raised eyebrows, trying to dig for a clue.

Colin squatted down next to them, placing his hand on Olivia's back. His upset at her on the plane dissipated as he concentrated on the little girl in front of them. "Aunt Ollie defeated the monster! Your daddy and I were able to go get her, as she was then set free," he said rather seriously, his hand coming out to ruffle her red hair.

"Uncle Colin told me all about the monster and how you had to leave to keep us all safe! And every Sunday he would come and tell me stories about your conquests!" Allison said breathlessly, her excitement was evident.

"And I knew you were getting closer to beating the monster, because daddy said we were able to move into this house because you were getting closer to defeating it and being able to come home!" Olivia turned sharp eyes to Jonathan before looking back at Allison.

She was unsure of what her face looked like.

"And then you sent a bunch of money and now we have three horses outside that I can't wait to show you! And then I got a liver so I knew it was going to be any day that you came back! And now you're here! You're back. I love you, Ollie. You did so good! But can you not go away anymore, I missed you so much, I cried a lot," Allison pressed her lips against Olivia's and then snuggled up under her chin. "You're so wonderful, first you save me from the water, and now the monster. You're so brave, Tee Tee. Don't leave me anymore,"

And that was it.

Olivia broke down crying so hard that Jonathan had to take Allison into the house and distract her while Vanessa and Colin tried to get her off the drive. But she was having a breakdown and didn't want them to touch her, their soothing touches somehow making it worse.

"I can't be a mommy, I can't!" Olivia pleaded to Vanessa, gripping her arms hard enough to leave bruises. "I can't, I can't!" And that's all she remembered before blacking out. The stress of the last twenty-four hours blanking her mind, leading her into the safety of nothingness.

FOURTEEN
Focus On Us

OLIVIA MOANED AS SHE stirred on the couch, she'd been dreaming about one of the nights her mom had stayed up late to brush her hair.

"Mom. I keep making the wrong decisions. I keep hurting everyone. I don't want to let anyone close," she said, her eyes meeting her mother's green ones in the mirror.

Her mother smiled at her softly before bending down to give her a soft kiss on her cheek. She met her eyes in the mirror. "You know what to do my sweet girl, just look deep inside," her mom whispered, placing her hand over Olivia's heart. "I love you Ollie, and never forget I am so proud of you."

Olivia awakened with a gasp.

Her chest was heaving as she struggled out of sleep. She looked around, seeing she was in a beautiful living room, and smelling her mom's chicken noodle soup. She got up, clutching the blanket around herself and turned in a circle, taking in the beautiful dark tones of the wood and moody paint of the living room she was in. The fireplace glowed with fake candles as it was the middle of summer, not appropriate for a fire.

Picking up on more details, she noticed the television was off, helping to blanket the room in silence, and as she turned, she saw a great big shaggy golden retriever lounging close to where she was laying. Her jaw dropped and the dogs' ears perked up as it saw she had her attention. Leaning forward, she looked at the collar, seeing the dog's name engraved as Shadow.

Go figure, Olivia thought wryly, thinking about how Vanessa's favorite childhood movie was Homeward Bound.

She looked around for any more animals and saw a gray cat staring back at her from its perch on a library shelf. Giving the friendly dog a little pat, she'd turned and followed her nose to the massive kitchen. Colin, Jonathan and Allison were crowded around the center marble island and tearing apart biscuits from a massive pile of dough. Instrumental music was playing on the surround sound and Vanessa was stirring a big pot of soup at a huge gas stove.

Clasping her hands together nervously, Olivia hesitated before walking into the kitchen, staying safely in the shadows of the little hallway she was in. She was embarrassed that she broke down so badly in the driveway and wasn't sure if she wanted to join them.

Jonathan spotted her first, as Colin was helping Allison tear her ball of dough in half to make it more manageable.

"Come on Ukhat, join us," he said, taking a drink of his whiskey and turning to grab a wine glass from an overhead cabinet, pouring her some from the half-drunk bottle of wine next to them. Colin turned from Allison and gave her a rather interesting onceover before his eyes landed on hers. He stepped off his stool and sauntered towards her lazily, his pants gripping his hips, and she swallowed down the rush of desire at the sight of his dick print through the material of the sweats.

Colin came up to her and pressed her deeper into the hallway, hiding them from the others in the kitchen. He wrapped his arms around her and pressed himself close. He smelled of soap like he'd had a shower and his hair was slightly damp as she sank her fingers in to feel. He leaned his head down and pressed his lips softly against hers.

Their tongues danced and tangled for a while before he pulled back, his warm eyes searching hers.

"Are you ok baby?" he breathed, his eyes flickering between hers, showing nothing but concern. Olivia swallowed, seeing the mean sadistic Colin seemed to be firmly stowed away for the moment.

"Yes," Olivia whispered. "I'm embarrassed you all had to see me like that. I'm so sorry Colin," she said again, closing her eyes and resting her forehead on his chest.

"Baby it's okay. Let's enjoy your sister's chicken and dumplings." Colin's hand came up to stroke her cheek. "I have missed you like crazy. I hope you got enough rest because you aren't sleeping tonight. And no, before you even fix that smart ass mouth to say anything, fucking you in your bungalow and on the plane wasn't enough," he said, his hands trailing down her body to cup her ass and pull her up to him.

Olivia made a small sound as her pussy heated. "Colin! I don't have any panties on!" she gasped, not wanting to make a mess on her legs.

"I know," he growled as he bent down and nuzzled into her neck, sucking and pulling at the skin, making her squeal slightly and try to recoil, giggling.

"There," he said, pulling away, his own eyes sparkling. "That's what I want to hear right now anyway. Later might be another story," he warned as he turned and patted her ass to walk into the kitchen.

Allison was sitting in Jonathan's lap and trying to convince him why they needed an extra huge biscuit. Hence, why she kept tearing off too much.

"But daddy, Shadow needs a biscuit!" she said, whipping her head around to look at him.

"Peanut, Shadow is a dog and shouldn't have flour. How about we make him a special treat since you love him so much?" Jonathan said, standing up with Allison in his arms. They walked over to the fridge, coming back with a piece of meat wrapped in white butcher paper.

Olivia clocked the price, seeing it was a forty-dollar lamb chop. Her mouth fell open. "Jonathan! You're not?" she said, a hilarious giggle erupting from her as the man began to unwrap the paper before reaching above them and grabbing a skillet hanging from a rack. He took it to one of the many burners and turned one on, setting the skillet on the fire.

"I definitely am," Jonathan replied confidently with a shit-eating grin on his face.

"Bro, I hope to be as rich as you one day," Colin teased, as Jonathan instructed Allison to pour a dollop of oil in the skillet.

"What? The girl wants Shadow to eat good, so eat good Shadow shall," Jonathan said happily, grinning down into the little girls' eyes and bopping her gently on the nose. Vanessa looked at them together and smiled, dropping the biscuits into the soup.

They watched in comfortable silence as Jonathan put the chop in the skillet and cooked it to rare, before setting it on a butcher block to rest. Colin and Jonathan discussed work a bit, as they were behind on some things. Olivia took the time to observe Allison. She looked healthy. Her cheeks were glowing, and her body was filling out like a five-year-old little girl's should. She watched as she clambered onto a stool with her trusty pink bunny in her arm. Observing that its ears had been sewed back on, the black thread peeking out against the pink felt of the bunny's fabric. She blinked back tears; it was only fourteen weeks that she was gone but it might as well have been a lifetime.

"Now," Colin said, reaching for a knife and sliding the chop closer to him. He began slicing the steak in even cuts, the knife going through the meat easily. "What do we say?" he said in a practiced tone as he picked up a piece of steak and handed it to Allison. She scrunched her nose up at the rare meat.

"Never feed a dog anything that you wouldn't eat yourself," she parroted back. It seemed to be a thing between the two of them. Which would explain why she was trying to make the dog the world's biggest biscuit. Allison bravely took the steak from him and put it into her mouth, her bright green eyes lighting up at the flavor. Olivia watched as he snagged a rare piece for himself, popping it into his mouth and smiling at Allison.

"Yum!" Allison said, smacking her lips and hopping off the stool. She disappeared for a minute and came back with a silver dog bowl. Putting the bowl on the counter gently, she proceeded to dump all the meat into it and then went to the refrigerator.

Olivia watched quietly as she yanked a shelf open harshly, pulling out some pre-cut sweet potato and dumping it in there with the steak before disappearing again and yelling for Shadow. "Holy shit," Olivia breathed.

Vanessa smiled at her, putting a bowl of steaming hot chicken and dumplings in front of her. "She's quite the capable little girl," Vanessa quipped, sharing a brief look with Colin before sliding him his bowl. Jonathan reached over Vanessa with a bowl, placing it in front of her at the island with a spoon before placing his hands on her belly and rubbing, placing his lips to her neck.

"So," Olivia broke the silence. "There's no kibble and bits in the house, huh?" she smiled as everyone broke out into laughter.

"Nope," Jonathan chuckled, turning to grab his own bowl.

"Jesus Nessie, this is delicious," Colin remarked, licking his spoon.

"Thanks," Vanessa said before piercing Olivia with a look. "So, why Macau, *China?*" she inquired, staring her down with her cat-like eyes.

Everyone went quiet, Colin and Jonathan both pausing in eating to look at her.

Olivia swallowed hard, her eyes dropping down to her bowl in shame. "Do we have to talk about this right now, Nessie?"

"Uhm yeahhh," Vanessa scoffed as her eyes met Colin's for a second. "I think we do. You *at least* owe us that," Vanessa said calmly, keeping her eyes trained on Olivia. "You have no clue what the hell we dealt with these weeks you've been gone so, I think you can at least give us the courtesy of answering a simple question."

Olivia took a deep breath before looking up, pointedly ignoring Colin's stare. She knew the conversation that was going to be had with him once they were alone was going to be a much different one.

"Because that was Gypsy's contingent plan for all the girls in the underground ring, if anything were to go wrong. Everything was already set in place," she said simply, her eyes falling back to her bowl. Ignoring their silence, she ate the last bite and then picked the bowl up and brought it to the sink, washing it quietly. She missed the look the three of them gave each other. However, she noted their continued silence from behind her and couldn't blame them for their reaction.

She turned. "I don't want to be the only one getting ripped into. I may have reacted badly, and I am so sorry for how this made you all feel, but I was lied to about something I consider being incredibly serious. While you all are over there being *perfect and judging me for it.*"

Jonathan spoke up. "No one is blaming you for feeling the way you feel Ollie. But next time, come to *us*. Don't just take off. You have a family that loves you, you don't have to do it by yourself anymore. We would have been more than happy to bring you into our home if needed. Don't ever think you don't have a place here."

Olivia met Jonathan's stare silently before nodding, wrapping her arms around herself. She flicked her eyes to Colin, who was watching her with an unreadable expression, and his demeanor was way calmer than she expected. It hit her then that he wasn't worried about her leaving. He wouldn't be letting her.

"Are y'all up for a movie after dinner?" Vanessa said, breaking the quiet as she spooned a rather alarming amount of food into her mouth, making her cheeks puff out. Jonathan chuckled at the sight.

"What movie do you have in mind?" Colin asked, slightly more animated than he had been. Olivia smiled shyly, happy to be around her family for the first time in weeks.

"Get Him to The Greek!" Vanessa said through a mouthful of biscuits.

The night went on and they put Allison to bed before joining them in the lounge and watching the movie. The couples relaxed against each other. Olivia and Colin were snuggled under a blanket, her ear was pressed against his chest, and she sighed contently for the first time in weeks as she found herself listening to the soothing sound of his heartbeat more than the movie.

"Hey you two, I'm going to get her to bed. She's passed out," Jonathan said quietly, referring to Vanessa who was snoring softly in his arms. "Colin, you know where your guys' room is. I'll leave you to it. Goodnight." Colin nodded and took the remote from him before he got up with Vanessa in his arms and carried her away.

Olivia placed her head back on his chest and snuggled deeper, sighing.

She tensed as Colin suddenly turned the movie off and put on a sensual playlist. He ran his hands up her body, dragging her dress up and caressing her bare ass under the blanket.

"We're sleeping here," he said, his voice coming out hoarse. "We'll go home tomorrow. I just thought you'd like to be close to them tonight."

Olivia's head tilted up to find his eyes. She gasped as he suddenly turned her to lay flush against him. She was hyper aware of his erection pressing against her stomach.

"We're ok, love. We're going to be ok. I'm sorry about my outburst on the plane," Colin said, his chocolate eyes searching hers for under-standing.

She looked away and licked her lips before responding.

"Colin, I'm sorry. I've not consulted you on how you've truly felt in this scenario. I'm sorry for judging you, baby. I caused a lot of hurt by responding to something without all the full facts. I turned everyone's lives upside down, and you did such an amazing job doing damage control while I'm sure you were worried sick about me." She paused as her voice caught in her throat and she lowered her forehead against his chest. She let out a small, pained noise, feeling her body temperature rise with embarrassment and sadness. "I'm so, so sorry. I was so stupid. You treated me so well... and I couldn't even give you the courtesy of explaining yourself b-be-because," Olivia choked on a sob, unable to finish her sentence as she shuddered hard, her body racked with tears. "I don't think I deserve it, but can you forgive me?" she asked, her eyes welling up with tears that overflowed easily onto his chest. "I don't deserve you," she cried out again, her voice catching on another sob.

Her fingers clutched desperately against his ribcage and she dug her nails in deep, trying to sink into him.

"I'm such a fuck up, Colin. I don't even know why you want me still," she whispered, echoing her thoughts that she'd shared with Jonathan on the plane.

She heard his chest rumble before his hands banded around her arms and hauled her up his body.

"I don't want to ever hear you say that again," he said, his eyes flashing dangerously as his fingers searched along the bottom curve of her right butt cheek. She cried out as he pinched the flesh there harshly. "What do you say?" he growled, pinching harder.

Olivia gasped and squirmed, feeling tears of desire flood her eyes. Her nipples hardened, and she became even more slick in between her thighs.

"Yes sir," Olivia moaned as he took his other hand and fisted it into her hair, lowering her head to his. She moaned as his lips pressed into hers, parting them as his tongue swept in reverently. Almost worshipfully. He pulled away reluctantly, placing a hand on the back of her head. He took a second to look into her eyes and spoke.

"I am not too prideful to admit when I am in the wrong as well. Yes, some might argue that you had a gross overreaction when you left the way you did but, I know how hard I worked to earn your trust," he paused, sadness and regret filled his eyes. "And I should have told you sooner. Much sooner than I did. I was worried too, because deep down inside I knew you were going to react the way you did." He swooped his thumb over her bottom lip that she'd pulled in between her teeth. "I waited too late, because I was scared. I should have told you about my past *before* we married. And for that I am sorry, I will never lie to you like that again, amor. That is a promise."

Olivia sniffled, wiping her tears away, giving him a tentative smile.

"And, in the thread of honesty, part of the reason I am so hurt and couldn't address this the way I should have is because my father is still alive out there somewhere. And that bothers me a lot more than it should...because despite how badly he hurt me, I miss him so much. I think about him all the time," Colin admitted on a deep breath, dropping his head back against the sofa as he closed his eyes against the pain of the admission.

Olivia's eyes widened, and she tilted her head forward, kissing him under his chin. "I think everything's going to be okay, baby, I'll support you in whatever you want to do. If you want to find him…if you just want to leave him be…whatever it is you want, I'll be right by your side. No more running, ever. No matter how hard it gets. We'll just have to incinerate each other and complain about it later," she said as Colin tilted his head back down on a laugh, catching her lips with a harsh kiss.

"What would make you feel better, baby?" he asked quietly, pulling back and assessing her facial features. Olivia remained quiet, however, trepidation filled her eyes. He licked his lips and pressed. "Would you feel better if I punished you?" his heart skipped a beat at the heat that entered her eyes, chasing away the trepidation. He winced as the razor-sharp edge of desire shot its way through his body and he burned from the top of his head to his feet at just how visible the shift within her was.

Tilting his head forward on a groan, Colin swallowed her shocked gasp at his question, and he'd moved his hand to between her legs and grasped her clit.

"Fucking God. You're swollen, amor," he growled into her mouth as he flicked her clit steadily, not giving her a reprieve. She moaned into his mouth as he worked her flesh steadily, flinching as he applied more pressure instead of easing up.

"Colin, I need you! I missed you so much… you talking to me, loving me, touching me. It was so hard to be without you. I cried every night," she whimpered against his lips, feeling his hand move from her nape to yank her dress over her head, exposing her bra. He undid the clasp one handed and freed her from its confines, enjoying the sensation of her breasts settling heavily against his chest, their weight welcome.

"Oh, don't worry, I'm taking my time with you tonight. I've already ordered Jonathan and Vanessa a new mattress. We owe them one for the damage they did to our bedroom when they first stayed over. It's our turn now. You're not sleeping tonight," he said hotly, his eyes boring into hers as he reached lower and speared her with two fingers. Her moan intensified as he pressed all the way in to his knuckle and then pressed even harder, giving her hard thrusts that sounded wet between them. He was content to look into her eyes as she struggled to not freefall into the abyss so quickly.

"I'm just going to warn you, I'm not going to go easy on you when we're home alone. Just so you aren't thinking my leashed temper is something permanent. I don't want you to delude yourself," he said harshly.

Olivia gasped as he hauled her up his body, and caught her gaze just as he took her erect nipple into his mouth. She yelped as she suddenly squirted on his fingers and her mouth opened in embarrassment.

"Oh god, I'm so sorry," she whispered, feeling her face flame as he pulled back from her breasts.

"Did you not hear anything I just said? You're getting ready to flood their mattress, baby. I'm going to be wringing you out all night," she squealed in shock as he suddenly picked her up in his arms. She wrapped her legs around him as he carried her down a hallway in the opposite direction from the main bedrooms. He walked through the door, turning the lock and pressing her roughly against it.

"You remember the first time I gave you an orgasm?" he asked, his eyes on hers hotly. Blushing, she nodded, remembering very clearly.

"Yes. I tried to orgasm so many times after that, that I broke my vibrator. I couldn't orgasm, you had me so fucked up in the head even then that I couldn't get off without you," she whispered, sinking her fingers into his hair and gasping as he suddenly yanked his sweats down and she felt the broad head of his big penis notching itself into her opening.

"I remember your pretty green dress. When you lowered your sleeves and exposed the tops of your breasts, I almost came right then and there," he said, bending forward and grazing his tongue from her collar bone to her other nipple. He paused. "And when your nipple broke free from your bra, I knew I couldn't fuck you even if you invited me in because I knew I was going to *absolutely break* this sweet cunt. It was just too good, beautiful," he whispered, listening to her excited cry as he bit into her nipple at the same time he thrust her down onto him. She sucked in a breath and orgasmed in shock around his thick length.

"Colin!" she screamed wildly, clutching at him. "It's so big! It's too b-big!" she yelped brokenly. She sucked air through her teeth at the feel of his hands tightening on her hips, making her body bob up and down harshly with his movements.

Her hips beat against the door as he sucked her nipple and thrust into her harshly, ignoring her sharp cries.

"It doesn't matter," he growled as he beat against her steadily. "No one can hear you scream on this side of the house, and we've got all night beautiful."

Olivia's eyes widened as she saw his tattooed arms flexing heavily as he yanked and pushed her on and off him. She hooked her heels behind him and sank her fingers into his hair as she felt sweat break out over her body. She threw her head back and cried out again as he pulled her down tight against him and ground incredibly deep, circling his hips lewdly.

"Unhook your legs," he said darkly, tilting his head to stare into her eyes as his hips began circling deep again. "*Unhook your legs* and hold them wide open for me, Olivia. *I* control this, *not you.*"

She swallowed hard, unhooking her heels like he instructed and immediately feeling too exposed as she spread her legs wide for him, bending her knees up and out like he liked.

"*Yessss,*" he growled deep in his chest, and she bit her lip at the first wet slap of them joining together, betraying she was extremely swollen and wet. "You hear that?" he said as he thrust again, listening to her whimper in her throat.

"Colin, it hurrrts," she said, gasping as he circled his hips again before bending his knees slightly and lowering her further down the door. The pleasure was sharp, cutting through her like a knife and leaving her flayed open for him.

Colin's heart skipped a beat at her admission. "*Good,*" he quipped as he pulled back all the way out and then slammed back in on a snarl. She squealed, trying to recoil as he set a steady slow tempo for long, almost unbearable minutes. He stopped, hearing a muted splash between them.

She'd just squirted on the floor.

"Hard and slow. You remember what you told me?" Colin asked, as he pulled his back and repeated the harsh movement, drawing a groan from her. Her fingers clawed as she pushed against him with her forearms, completely overwhelmed. "That's a new sound. It's beautiful. Just like you, my pretty girl," Colin groaned as he spent long minutes thrusting into her body.

Only when she was shaking and dripping down to the floor between their legs did Colin move suddenly, taking them to the ensuite bathroom and grabbing a couple towels. He threw one over his shoulder before walking with her still wrapped around him and him deeply embedded in her. He tossed the other towel on the floor to clean up the mess that dripped onto the floor. Shy, she buried her head into his neck while he pulled the bedsheets back and leaned over, placing her onto the bed and the towel he'd spread out. He pulled her face from his neck.

"All night Olivia. I'm wearing this pussy out. And when your pussy's done, I'll take your mouth, then your ass," he said darkly, as he crawled down her body and settled between her legs, ignoring her sharp cry as he suddenly jammed three fingers into her pussy, twisting and pressing hard as he settled his teeth onto her clit.

"*Nooo!* Colin it's been weeks. I can't," she cried as she climaxed yet again, grinding her teeth together against the bone-shattering pleasure he was giving her.

"No isn't a word in our vocabulary tonight. I'm going to show you just how much I missed you. Get comfortable baby," Colin murmured. He ignored her fresh screams, feeling her body seize up. Relaxing into the mattress, he got good and comfortable, just like he advised her to do.

God she tastes amazing.

***

Olivia moaned as she woke up the next day, looking at the clock and seeing it was almost noon. She placed a hand over her eyes and rubbed, slightly disoriented. The memories of the night came back in a flood. She immediately blushed, hoping Colin wasn't there to see her in the light of day after all that transpired between them last night. She peeked through her fingers at her side of the bed and bit her lip. No such luck.

Colin was sitting up in bed next to her, holding a cup of coffee and watching her wake up. A rather peaceful yet amused look on his face. She closed her fingers, cutting herself off from him.

"Oh my God, please don't look at me," she whispered, as the sensations started settling in. She moaned again, feeling completely worn out.

"Would you like a bath, amor?" Colin spoke in a sex roughened voice. The sound gave her a sick pleasure because she didn't want to be the only one who looked like they'd been absolutely ran through last night.

"Yes please," she said softly, her hand falling from her face as she felt her body elongate into a satisfying stretch. She collapsed back into the bed with a huff and got a good look at her surroundings for the first time. Unlike the rest of the house she'd seen so far with its wooden features, and moody painting and murals, this room was decorated in light creams and blues. It was beautiful and lush without being too princess looking.

He leaned forward and kissed her softly on the forehead before rolling out of bed naked and disappearing into an adjoining room. She heard a bath start and took the time to try and sit up, wincing against the lightheaded feeling. She shot an arm out, blindly grabbing for her phone until she found it.

'Can you die by being fucked to death?' Olivia put into the search engine of her cell phone, starting to worry because it didn't look like Colin was going to let up. She scrolled through all the ER horror stories, and some funny ones, seeing that there really was nothing wrong as long as she got her rest and got sustenance. Which Colin made sure she got.

She pulled up her texts.

How much sex do y'all have? Sorry to ask but I'm trying to see something. -O

A lot. Soooo... you're about to do the walk of shame in a bit I'm sensing? -Nessie

Not sure I can walk yet. I think we ruined your mattress, I'm sorry. Colin said he'd already ordered another one though. -O

Olivia sent her a blushing emoji face.

Right on cue, Colin appeared through the doorway, still naked as he walked up to her.

Olivia's eyes widened and she recoiled, trying to roll away from him. "No leave me alone you *fiend!*" she gasped, clawing at the sheets as he grabbed her foot and dragged her easily across the bed towards him. Her face flushed as he leaned down and wrapped his arms around her chuckling, picking her up and walking with her to the bathroom and lowering her in the tub. She groaned with pleasure, sinking deeper and sighing. Colin got in behind her and hauled her up into him, settling her comfortably against his chest.

He pulled her hair to the side and kissed her neck, inhaling and sighing on a groan. "You smell like rough sex," he whispered into her ear, licking the shell. "How do you feel?"

She hummed in her throat, grateful he couldn't see her face.

"Turned slightly inside out," she said. She ran her hands down his thighs, feeling the crisp hair and hard muscles underneath. She relaxed as he took a huge natural sponge and began to wring water all over her shoulders, one hand rubbing circles onto her belly.

Like music to my ears, he thought as a sharp flash of pleasure raced through his body at her words.

"You're probably going to feel like that for a few weeks," Colin said unapologetically, his hand moving up to grasp her breasts. "I have a plan B pill for you, and then we need to get you back on the pill. We don't want any accidents that will prevent me from ravaging this body the way I need to for at least the next year and a half."

Olivia moaned as he took a sensitive nipple between his forefinger and thumb and rolled. She took pleasure in the fact that he wanted her body to himself for a while. She'd felt unsettled since their conversation months ago at the dinner table regarding children and realized that maybe part of that was the catalyst to her fear; she had so many unknowns with this man. She tilted her head harder against shoulder, realizing that yes, underneath his hard demeanor and his harsh ways with her, he'd taken to Allison very well and he was protective, kind, and gentle with her.

"You're going to have my babies, Olivia," he rasped in her ear. His other hand tilted her head to the side so he could meet her eyes. She whimpered as he tightened his fingers on her harder. Removing his fingers from her jaw, he lowered his mouth to hers at the same time he lowered his hand and cupped her pussy possessively. He swallowed her moans as he licked, sucked, and molded his mouth to hers.

Olivia burned. He wasn't doing anything but tweaking her nipple and cupping her pussy while he kissed her, but she felt laid bare. As if he'd still had her duct taped and spread eagled for him on the plane. He kissed her for a long while, and while he was busy reinforcing their intimacy with one another, she also felt as if he'd crawled into her heart. Her chest felt raw, like he'd opened her up personally and slid his way in.

Her ribs ached; her breastbone throbbed.

Shit, is this love? She thought. Her hand came up to settle across her heart and a whimper escaped her as a tear fell out of her eye. With effort, she pulled away to look at him.

"You came for me," she whispered, her eyes searching his. "Even though I left in such a horrible way. I fucked your bikes up. I messed my car up. And disappeared for over three months," Colin's eyes stared back, no less intense in the light of the day in the bathroom they were in.

"I told you once before; I will always find you, Olivia," Colin rasped again. His eyes hardened suddenly, the skin tightening around them and crinkling in that way she loved. "But the bikes," he sucked his teeth. "Oh, you are paaayyyyyiiinnng *dearly* for that when we get home, missy. You took out six bikes, and my favorite one at that."

"Well," Olivia swallowed, a small smile on her face. "I would do my worst if I were you. I totally did that on purpose. I may have to take out more bikes if you don't pay me back well enough," she said her tone and face turned serious.

"Careful, sweetie," he said with a warning tone, his voice just above a whisper. He tilted his head further to regard her with his own serious look, arching one dark eyebrow. "You don't get to top from the bottom in this relationship. You know how I feel about the tone you take with me."

Olivia gasped as with a quick twist of his wrist he'd suddenly inserted two thick fingers high and hard into her. She heard water splash on the floor as she arched hard, sucking her teeth in pained pleasure before she relaxed on a low, long moan.

"*Jesus*, I had to work to get them in baby. You're so fucking tight and swollen. Tonight's not going to go well for you, huh?" he retreated and thrust back in gently. Not a complete monster, it was reigned in for now.

"Colin," his name came off her throat, sounding strangled.

"What. Is. My. Name?" he whispered in her ear, his voice clipped.

"Sir," she moaned, her pussy clasping weakly.

"That's right. Sir first, Colin second." He thrust into her for long minutes, grinning wickedly against her mouth as she grimaced and circled her hips in the tub. Her orgasm evaded her, but he stayed with her, nipping at her lips and his growl rumbling deep in his throat. But yet it continued to be a slow build. She whimpered and furrowed her brow in frustration, her mouth tightening. Her nails bit into Colin's forearm.

"Oh baby, this is good. I love you making me work for it," he growled, spreading his fingers slightly and swallowing her squeak. His thumb circled her sensitive clit tightly, ignoring her small wiggles to try and get away.

Feeling sweat drip down her temple, Olivia gasped, feeling like she was on fire. She was surprised the tub wasn't boiling. "Sirrrr...," she moaned, tilting her head back further. Suddenly worried that he'd let her slip into the water and drown on her orgasm, he might be that sadistic. Her thoughts took another turn, and she was suddenly happy he wasn't like the main characters in her spicy books she reads who said "come" and then all of a sudden the woman came.

"Stay with me, Olivia. Whatever thoughts you're having, dismiss them and focus on us," he said, sensing she was withdrawing in frustration. He bent forward and clamped his teeth on her neck, agitating and pulling her flesh. That did it. Her lungs seized up on a painful gasp and she jerked her hips as she felt her orgasm suddenly attack her from behind, picking her up harshly and tossing her off the cliff.

She heard an embarrassing moan echoing around the bathroom. Her blood rushed in her ears and she relaxed after a tense minute. Her hips lowered back to the tub, nestling against him once more. In her desperation she'd hooked a leg over the side of the tub and arched her lower body out of the water, Colin's arm banded hard around her chest to keep her anchored to him. With a hitched breath, she realized fingers were still seated firmly inside her. She made a low pained sound as he removed them slowly and with effort, panting.

"Now that," he said in his hoarse voice, "was the most beautiful fucking thing I've ever had the pleasure of seeing in my life. Jesus, you're going to kill me."

Colin made them linger in the tub for a while longer, until he was sure she was physically recovered before he activated the drain and lifted her out. He sat her on the vanity and blow dried her hair, giving her small kisses, lingering looks, and soft touches on the marks he'd left on her body.

Olivia felt shattered, and though she missed Allison and her family dearly, she was ready to go home. She just felt too vulnerable and needed some alone time to process what Colin told her on the plane. Colin agreed, and he worked fast, stripping the bed quickly and disappearing down the hallway, leaving her to get dressed. They walked to the front of the house, hand in hand, and Olivia was grateful that Vanessa and Jonathan treated them with much more grace than her and Colin did when they were caught in a similar position when they'd first spent the night months ago at their house.

"I love you, sissy," Vanessa whispered in her ear after a long hug. They'd spent time saying goodbye to the three of them before climbing in the car and pulling off. Colin placed his hand on her knee in his familiar way, and she covered his hand with hers, breathing deeply and listening as she called in a dinner order from Louis' Lunch. She stayed in the car, not fully trusting her legs, as he went in to grab their food. She took a second to appreciate his sexy walk as he disappeared into the restaurant and pulled out her phone, quickly finding Aliyah's number and beat out a quick text, feeling her heart beat painfully as shame filled her once again.

Beau, it's Olivia. I am so incredibly sorry at how I left and not contacting you. I couldn't risk being found. I'm back home, just wanted to let you know. I love you and hope to talk to you soon. -Olivia

Olivia then sent out almost the same text to Stella, noticing that Colin had put all her contacts into the new phone, minus Gypsy. Feeling a similar pang, she realized she must have left everyone confused and reeling and wondered if she'd get her friendships back. Staring at her phone, she waited several minutes, disappointed when neither of the women replied. She blinked back tears, acknowledging she'd fucked up, plain and simple.

Colin reappeared with two humongous bags of food and slid easily into the driver's seat, buckling his belt. He turned briefly, seeing the change in her, and his eyes scanned her face in concern.

"What happened?" he said tightly, pausing in his movements, not putting the car into reverse yet.

"Nothing," she whispered as she kept her eyes averted from his, not wanting to bother him especially so soon after returning home. It was her mess, and he couldn't fix everything. There were some things she'd have to do damage control on herself.

"I don't believe you, but I'm going to let it go for now," Colin reassured her, aware that she was emotionally exposed, still trying to process their interaction on the plane. Their style of sex was raw, ripping them open and leaving them bleeding. He knew to only push so much.

He'd just got her back and wasn't willing to rock the boat quite yet.

Pulling off onto the road, he turned on a relatively light playlist before placing his hand on her knee, and by the time they pulled up to the house they were laughing and singing along to the songs. Content to just be silly together for a minute after the seriousness of the last couple days.

Pulling the SUV by the fountain, he parked, tossing her the keys to open the door while he grabbed the bags.

"Why didn't you pull into the garage?" Olivia asked, wincing as she realized it was probably still a mess from her destroying around half a million dollars worth of bikes and the back of her Porsche. Seeing his face she continued, "Never mind," she said quickly, walking carefully up the stairs and ignoring her shaking legs.

He tossed her a wry glance as he headed through the door ahead of her, juggling the bags.

"Why so much food? There's no way we can eat that much! Unless you plan on feeding me a burger in between sex-capades. What did you get?" she teased, closing the door behind her and pausing as she realized how much she missed this home. She threw him a goofy smile as she heard some playful fun music filter through the surround system.

Olivia hugged herself. *He came for me. Viciously, with some punishments, and my legs feel like jello. But he came, and told me the truth.*

Walking deeper into the house she rounded the kitchen, hearing more music blast through the open sliding doors that led to the terrace outside. Colin jerked his head that way.

"Look outside," he said, starting to unpack the food and place it into the kitchen warming drawer. She tentatively walked out onto the terrace and her mouth opened in shock as she heard a huge splash.

Aliyah, Sara Banks from the studio, Vanessa, Allison, Jonathan, Stella, and Vincent were all in the pool, splashing each other. Vanessa and Stella were floating on some ridiculous unicorn and flamingo floatation device. There were little balloons everywhere and pitchers of premade drinks and a little ice cream vendor that had a three-tiered cake on ice in a frosted covering which Mary was in front of, accepting a chocolate ice cream cone from the vendor.

Olivia looked at Colin in confusion, too stunned to process what was going on.

"HAPPY BIRTHDAY!" they suddenly screamed from below, cheering and waving at the couple as they saw them on the balcony above. Olivia's jaw dropped and she looked over at Colin with her brows furrowed before slapping her forehead.

"OH my *God*," she whispered. "It's your birthday!?" she hissed, blushing. "I didn't get you anything!" she said, horrified. So much had happened in the last couple of days that she'd forgotten what the date was.

Of course I didn't, dummy. I wasn't supposed to be here. If he hadn't come for me I'd still be in China, she thought to herself.

Colin arched a brow as a grin graced his face. He pulled her closer with a hand on her waist and leaned into her, his lips brushing her jaw.

"Yes, you did. I got my present the day before yesterday, on the plane, and multiple times at Jonathan and Vanessa's. And I'm looking forward to tonight's presents too," he said darkly, pulling her flush against him and nipping at her earlobe. He pulled back and patted her on the ass.

"Let's go get changed and join them. I've been waiting a very long time to show you the grotto. And I desperately want to see your ass in that purple bikini Vanessa brought you," he growled, taking her hand and yanking her back into the house.

They changed quickly. Olivia had to smack his hands away several times, not even sure that she could endure another orgasm like the one she'd had earlier so soon. Her body was hungry for his still, and her nipples were sticking lewdly through the bikini top much to her horror and much to Colin's amusement. She'd put on a sheer coverup and wrapped it around herself to try and help before they padded downstairs making their way to the pool. She'd put on a pair of sunglasses and Colin pulled her to a stop at a lounge before grabbing a bottle of sunblock.

"We're not burning this beautiful skin," he said, taking the time to slather her liberally before tossing her into the pool.

Colin spent time walking around and opening multiple umbrellas around the pool with Jonathan's help, providing shade in various places around the perimeter of the water. His heart swelled in his chest when Stella and Aliyah pulled Olivia to them at the same time for a hug that left them all choking and sputtering as they were a flurry of girl limbs, red hair and braids. Mary leaned down to give her a motherly kiss on the cheek, which Olivia had to pull herself out of the pool for, her hair long enough to cover half of her ass, dark and heavy with the pool water.

The men got out of the pool and joined him at the little outdoor kitchen area to let the girls talk and catch up. Jonathan's niece was currently playing with Allison in the deep end. Vanessa and Jonathan splurged on her having the best swim lessons shortly after her liver transplant and she was a natural. They all cracked open a beer and sat on the couches, relaxing.

"My man! Happy birthday dude. Your birthday present is with Stella somewhere, sorry I don't do great with these things. I usually let her take care of that stuff," Vincent said in his deep voice, leaning forward and clasping Colin's hand hard.

He'd been a huge help with his security contacts, giving him the team that followed them to China for a week and found her bungalow. Colin appreciated the man. He and his wife held no ill will towards Olivia, only worrying and wanting to help find her too.

"Nah brother, you didn't have to get me anything," Colin admonished, leaning back and taking a deep drink of his beer. He was seriously relaxed for the first time in months, his gaze slid from Vincent's to Olivia in the pool who was currently leaning against the little bar where several pitchers of mixed drinks were, pouring herself a healthy amount, and some for Aaliyah, Stella, Sara, and Vanessa who had their own pitchers of mocktails.

Man they are about to get trashed, Colin thought as he rubbed the back of his neck, feeling content.

"I'm surprised that you even allowed anyone here considering.... well, I would have thought you would have wanted to have some alone time with Olivia without a bunch of prying eyes," Vincent said, sitting back and stretching his legs out. His dark skin glowed in the light of the sun. Jonathan chuckled.

"Oh, he's managed to work it in. Trust me, I got to hear a lot of it," Jonathan joked, sipping on his beer slowly. Vincent flashed him another white toothed smile that took up much of his face.

"My man," he said, tipping his beer to him.

"That's why we're really here V, he needs a break before his dick falls off," Jonathan laughed roaringly, jerking out of the way of Colin's playful punch.

"That'll never happen," Colin said vehemently. The more he fucked her, the more he wanted her. He wanted to crawl into her skin until there was nothing left but himself there and he truly didn't care who knew it.

"So, you punish her for fucking up your bikes yet? Your expensive luxury bikes man. I was sick for you when you told me that. I got a spare clicker in my car if you need it," Vincent said, a small smile on his face. His inner dominant secretly eating up the drama with the reward of punishing a submissive. It made his blood hot. Made him want to snag Stella out of the pool for a trip to the guest house.

Colin's eyes slid back to Olivia who was currently disappearing into the grotto with the women.

"Oh V," he tsked, "She did that shit on purpose, so her punishment is going to be well thought out and purposeful. Mama's got it coming, don't you worry your pretty little dominant heart," he said, using his term of endearment that normally only came out when he was extremely turned on. Vincent grunted in brotherly acknowledgment; satisfied.

Truth was, if he hadn't had been so worried about her safety, coming home to see his bikes wrecked like that and the back of her car torn up would have sent him off the deep end.

Jonathan just shook his head, a slightly annoyed expression on his face. He made it no secret that he didn't understand their lifestyle.

"Now, let's crash their little party because I told her that I wanted to show her the grotto and she just can't listen," Colin said, standing up and heading into the pool with his beer. The men followed and joined the women in the space, the lights were on and glowing a purple pink.

FIFTEEN
Vulnerable Admissions

A FEW HOURS LATER, after they'd swam enough, eaten all the burgers, fries, milkshakes and birthday cake, they'd all finally left, giving them privacy. The sun was down and fireflies were out in the yard, casting a romantic vibe across the property. Colin looked down at her as she was waving to Mary, who followed the rest of them out to her car. She sighed, feeling content, happy that the day hadn't been ruined for him. He took her hand and instead of taking her back into the house, he pulled her the rest of the way down the stairs and around the house to the path that led to the guest house.

"Colin," she said, her brows pulled together. "What are we doing?" she asked, a little anxious.

He stayed silent and opened the door and led her in, pulling her through the house and down the hallway to the door that housed his secrets. He paused, turning his face to her.

"I want to show you this myself, not because you stumbled across it," Colin said, hesitantly. His eyes searched hers.

Olivia bit her bottom lip and tucked a lock of hair behind her ear.

"Well...more like broke in. Wouldn't you say?" she whispered, a small sad smile. She'd felt bad and probably would for a bit.

"Semantics," Colin replied, a little half grin on his own face. He turned back to the door, typing in the code and opened the door. He flicked on the light before ushering her in, closing the door behind them. She did a slow circle, seeing a hole in the drywall that wasn't there before. She flickered nervous eyes to him, knowing he put that there with his fist. She wasn't sure which wall to turn to first, the wall with his family, or the wall with the family he killed.

She turned to his family.

He assessed her for a quick second as she stared at the photo of his mother. She was a beautiful, dark Latina woman. With dark hair, Colin shared a lot of her exotic features, however his build was strong, like his dad. His mom was petite and curvy. She had long flowing black hair, and her smile was so youthful and vibrant. Her heart broke.

"You look like her," she whispered, half turning to Colin and wrapping her cover up tighter around herself.

"Yo soy lo único que vive de ella," he said softly, his hands reaching out to touch her face in the picture reverently.

I am the only thing that lives on of her.

"Her name is Elena," he whispered. Not was, is.

Olivia's eyes widened, but she remained quiet for several seconds. "That's a very beautiful name." She reached out and grasped his hand in her small one, bringing his knuckles to her mouth to kiss. She stepped closer to him and leaned her head on his shoulder. Her gaze moved to the picture of him next to his mother's casket. He looked so alone up there by himself.

"You're the bravest person I think I know, Colin," Olivia spoke again, a hint of awe in her voice. She meant it. She didn't know how she would have gotten through her parents' funeral without Vanessa and her grandpa. She couldn't imagine having to do it alone, having to deal with the finances and all the other logistics it took to figure that out.

Her gaze snuck up to him, finding him watching her intensely as she stared at his family pictures.

She smiled slowly. "Can we put one of us up here?" she asked.

Colin smiled in return.

"Here, in the main house, everywhere. You're going everywhere baby," he said, leaning down to kiss her lips sweetly. Pulling back, he turned her to the other wall, his expression serious, before turning pained. The man really was traumatized, and she could see it clear as day when he looked at the family of five, staring back at them from their article on the wall.

She shivered as she stared at the adolescent boy, who had red hair and green eyes just like hers. She peeked up at him, frowning at the look on his face. *It wasn't right.*

"Colin," she said softly, reaching out to turn him to her. She pressed closer, wrapping her arms loosely around his waist, feeling the slabs of hard muscle under her fingers. She craned her neck to look up at him, her eyes flickering back and forth between his chocolate ones.

"They would be so happy, that their lives were the example that has surely helped millions of people all around the world live safer lives. Who knows how many you've saved with your software? You have reinvented what it means for safe driving. Kind of like how Prince Harry is reinventing how social media is regulated. I wish that this was more well known years ago; maybe my parents would still be here. But guess what, if they were still here, then Vanessa and I probably wouldn't have you and Jonathan. Allison might not have been able to get the care that she needed. Life is a domino effect and we really have no say in why things happen. But we can control how we pick up the pieces and move on. My love, you've done such a good job at picking up the pieces of your life. Look what you've done with your trauma. Look at what you've turned their deaths into. It wasn't meaningless. You honor them every day."

Colin's breath hitched, and he turned his eyes once more to the family before nodding once and pulling her the rest of the way to him. There in the windowless room he let go, holding on to the love of his life. Finally forgiving himself.

They were walking back to the house before he spoke again. "We need to talk about Judge Carmichael," he said suddenly, really hating to bring him up, but he needed to inform Olivia of how serious the situation was.

She glanced sharply at him. "What about him?" she asked hesitantly, really detesting the man at this point.

"Gypsy has been in touch with me. He's unhinged, Olivia. I'm going to have to give you a security detail." He held up his hand when she rounded on him with a shocked look on her face. "No. Listen to me," he said sternly, hardening his gaze and crossing his arms. She softened.

"The man is unhinged," he repeated. "Sources, or rather *spies*, have reported erratic behavior. I planned on leaking that video of him assaulting you that night at the gala but he seems to be doing a good job at ruining his career himself. I wanted to wait until I had more ammo to put with the video to really solidify the deal, but he's been careful to make sure nothing gets back to his name. He's got other folks doing his dirty work."

"Okay, but what's this got to do with me? No one's come after me and I've been gone for fourteen weeks," she said, pissed. She didn't want to have a security detail tailing her.

"Baby, three redheaded women around your age have gone missing since you've been gone. That's another reason we thought something happened to you. I was about to go to the man's house and kill him in cold blood. It was only when your money came that I realized you were alive," he said, his voice coming out harsh. Olivia shivered.

"Okay but...the redhead thing could just be a...a..." she trailed off as her excuses sounded lame. Even to herself. Three redhead women going missing in the area was a huge red flag even she couldn't ignore. She looked at him helplessly.

"But Colin, I don't *want* security!" she whined, almost stomping her foot. Her eyes widened as he stepped towards her with a harsh look on his face. Her temper tantrum tested him and she knew that. She stepped back cautiously.

"Well thank God I don't care to talk about what you want right now. But what I would like to talk about, are my *bikes*," Colin growled, never ending his predatory steps against her. His face tightened in a slightly harsh expression as her eyes widened even further.

She shook her head slightly and her steps became more hurried.

"Your bikes?" she said nervously, licking her lips and sideswiping a table with an umbrella.

Biting her bottom lip as her calves hit a lounge, she fell back rather gracelessly before scrambling to the other side. He faked to her right, and she dove to her left, still walking backwards. She screeched when she took another step feeling the concrete suddenly drop off. Her stomach dropped when Colin reached out a hand and grasped her by the middle string of her bikini top. He let her hang there, arched over the edge of the pool backwards, her arms flailing.

"Yes, my bikes that you so thoroughly fucked up. All six of the ten in the garage, including your Porsche. It looks like you took great pleasure in annihilating them," he hissed, getting in her face, his knuckles pressing in the space between her breasts. Olivia's eyes flashed.

"You'll just fucking have to get over it then, won't you sir?" she hissed back.

They stared off at each other in a clashing of wills before he suddenly unclenched his fist and dropped her into the deep end. She screamed before landing with a splash, coming up sputtering. Colin stepped in after her, barely making a sound as he sliced through the water, coming up silently behind her. She was still trying to rub water out of her eyes.

He banded an arm across her torso and dragged her underneath the waterfall of the grotto and into the expansive space inside.

When they got inside, he crowded her against the wall and voice activated 'Olivia's nasty playlist' which had her arching her eyebrow. He placed his hands on the lip of the wall on either side of her and pressed close, his mouth skimming her jaw as a seriously indecent song came over the speakers. She turned her face slightly away from him, her breath hitching as Colin rubbed his large, masculine body on hers. Whimpering, she slapped her arms across her chest as he suddenly untied her bikini top, peeling it from her body slowly.

Colin lowered his eyes to hers. "Lower your arms, Olivia," he said in his deep voice.

He waited patiently as she caught her breath, her arms falling away from her breasts slowly. The rumble in his chest deepened the more flesh she exposed to his gaze. She shivered at the look in his eyes as he stared at her erect nipples, he raised a hand slowly over her ribcage until he cupped a breast in his big hand. His arms looked thicker than she'd remembered, betraying hours spent in the gym these last few weeks. Her face flushed deeper and her sex slickened, thinking of his big hard body being unleashed on hers yet again. He caught her eye again, a slight smirk on his face as he suddenly moved and grasped her nipple harshly between his fingers.

Olivia cried out as he manipulated the nub between his fingers.

"Now," Colin said sharply, his teeth flashed with a dangerously feral smile as he crowded her space. "Let's have a very important conversation. We need to come to an understanding, and quickly."

Olivia trembled as he pressed his hips deep into hers, grinding and pressing her unforgivingly against the stone wall behind her. Her hands came up to lightly rest on his biceps.

"You ever, under *any* circumstances, fuck up my bikes again, you will regret it whole heartedly. I will punish you and won't even say a word. Not a warning. You won't even know it's coming. And there won't be any pleasure involved in it for you. Just straight up pain. Understand?" he growled in his deep voice.

Olivia swallowed thickly, her eyelashes fluttering as she looked up at him.

"Yes," she whispered, slipping her bottom lip between her teeth. She sucked in a sharp breath as his fingers suddenly pinched her nipple harder. His eyes hardened further; he was not playing with her.

"Yes what, mama?" he rasped, his accent thick.

"Yes sir," Olivia panted as he brought his other arm up behind her, sweeping up her back to cup her nape. Colin's hand tightened threateningly. She keened softly in her throat. He pressed even closer, getting good and even with her face.

"And if you *ever* leave me the way you left me again, you will be begging for mercy when I find you. I will relish tormenting you. I wouldn't even let you know you were found at first, I'd play with you the way a cat plays with a mouse when it's caught. I will break every bone beneath my teeth as you lay limp in my mouth. Even God himself wouldn't dare interfere. And then I'll put you back together just to delight in breaking you down again. Over and over," he whispered, his lips skimming her jaw as his mouth moved to her ear.

"Take off your bottoms, Olivia," he said, giving her ear lobe a little nip.

Olivia whimpered, the cool water around them feeling like it should be boiling, the heat and tension was so thick between them.

"Colin," she whimpered, gasping as his hand flew up and popped her in the mouth. Not hard enough to be a slap, but hard enough to warn. Her heart banged excitedly, and she briefly toyed with the idea of asking him to do it again, except this time harder.

"I didn't tell you to speak, and that's not my name right now. It's *Sir*. Nod your head yes if you understand, woman," he said, pulling back and giving her the coldest once over she'd ever felt from him.

It dawned on her then, that this was the first time they'd been truly alone since he'd found her at her bungalow, on the other side of the world.

Olivia paled, her fright warring with her extreme desire and making her feel lightheaded. She tried to scooch to the side, squealing as he roughly yanked her back, fisting his hand in her hair and pulling her head back until the muscles and tendons twinged in her neck. She cried out in pleasured pain.

"I said nod your head if you understand," Colin repeated, baring his teeth slightly. She then realized his control was extremely close to shattering, she couldn't nod with him holding her like this.

She used all her strength and jerked hard against his hand, eyes watering as her hair pulled tight. He took the hand that was on her nipple and moved it to her side, where her ribs were.

"Spread your legs and bend your knees up," Colin instructed, his chocolate eyes still boring deep into hers. "When I'm sinking into you, keep those green eyes on mine. Do not close them. I know you're nice and swollen from the last two days of fucking, and I want to see the look in your eyes when you realize how hard this is about to be. For both of us," he hissed, leaning down and pressing his lips against hers. He sucked her bottom lip into his mouth and bit down harshly.

He busied nibbling at her for a bit, while she did as he ordered and got herself into place for him.

Olivia panted as Colin pulled away from her mouth, placed a hand on the edge of the wall by her shoulder and lowered slightly, making room for the length of his dick. His eyes stared intensely into hers as he notched the broad head of his erection into her opening. Olivia started shaking, she could feel her swollen muscles protesting. His face tightened as he worked the first few inches in before stopping.

"What's your safe word?" Colin suddenly asked, his brows drawn. His hips remained unmoving. and he grimaced as he felt her clench around the tip of his cock.

Olivia paled before flushing again.

Oh no. She whispered in her head, the blood began roaring in her ears. "Bunny," she whispered, her eyes filled up with tears of equal parts trepidation and excitement at knowing how relentless he was about to be.

He grunted as he nodded, pressing his hips into hers harder, her flesh protesting.

"Jesus, you're making me work for it again, huh?" he suddenly bit out, his eyes flashing.

Olivia let out a series of strangled moans as he sawed himself in and out of her against that secret spot inside of her. Her mouth fell open as she suddenly felt her bladder feel like it was going to explode before a hot wave of pleasure suddenly slid through her body, so intense that it stole her breath. Her skin pebbled with goosebumps and she felt the soles of her feet burn.

Olivia's eyes widened at Colin's wicked, knowing grin. He knew what he was doing to her. Letting out a surprised shriek, she had no warning before he fisted his hand in the skin of her ribs hard, and suddenly thrust sharp and firmly, seating himself all the way inside of her to the hilt. She threw her head back in a silent scream as the pain of his action mixed with her severe arousal and she orgasmed, her body twitching. She clawed at him unseeingly, feeling her nails rake down his shoulders, chest, biceps as she lost control of herself.

He suddenly lashed forward, his hand leaving her ribs to wrap around her throat, squeezing, pulling her face back down to his. He squeezed until her shuddering stopped and all that was left was ragged moans leaving her pink lips.

"Are you quite done? We have a lot more of that to get through," Colin gritted, loosening up his grip and listening to her as she inhaled rather harshly.

"Yes," Olivia gasped, her eyes struggling to stay on his as she panted. *"Sir,"* Another gasp of air before he tightened his fingers again, this time on the sides of her neck, cutting off her circulation but letting her breathe. He leaned down to her face as he pulled all the way to the tip and thrust back in with a sharp snap of his hips, and Olivia rejoiced at the feel of her buttocks beating against the side of the pool.

"Now, I'll make love to you later. But right now, I'm itching for a good old fashioned *raw, hard, fuck* with my wife, you irritating bitch," he growled, the water splashing around them as he made good on his promise.

"Call me a bitch again," she gasped, biting her lip hard as a tiny thrill shivered down her spine.

Colin leaned forward placing his mouth to her ear. "You're *my bitch*, understand?" He treated her to a harder than normal thrust as they both fed into their desires of leaning more into the degradation clause of their contract they hadn't utilized much. He missed a beat in his rhythm at how hard she tightened around his cock at his words.

He punished her for throwing him off by hooking her leg over one of his arms. Yanking her wider, he treated her to several hard grinding shoves of his hips into hers, making her cry out.

All Olivia could do was dig her nails in and hang on as he beat his flesh into hers, listening to his growls and sex groans as he unleashed himself. A tear splashed out on her cheek with the intensity of the moment and he chuckled darkly, leaning forward to lap it up before placing his lips to her ear again.

"What's the matter, love? Don't want to be fucked by the big bad wolf anymore?" he taunted, before lowering further and latching onto her neck at her jugular with an animalistic growl, biting down hard. Olivia jerked in shock, pushing against him with her hands as she orgasmed, a high-pitched wail resounding around the grotto as he thrust harder.

"Scream all you want to baby, no one can hear, and no one is here to save you from me. I love the way you cry for me, I swear it makes me stronger," Colin said, never ending his harsh thrusts into her body. He gave her two more mind blowing orgasms, ignoring her fists beating into him before he disengaged with effort and carried her sobbing from the pool.

"Beautiful," he said as he walked them at an unhurried pace to the house.

"You're fucking evil," she whimpered, her head lolled against his shoulder as he carried her into the house. He stopped by the refrigerator and grabbed two bottles of water before turning towards the elevator. She stayed limp in his arms, already resigning herself to a night that seemed like it was going to be even more raw and intense than their night at the gala.

Colin turned her head and caught her eye.

"I'm going to let you in on a little secret baby girl. *I never claimed to be good*," he whispered down at her, a grin tipping the corner of his mouth. She shivered as he opened the elevator door, shooting them up to the top floor. He banked a right, walking them into their bedroom.

Olivia kept her face buried in his neck, still feeling too shy. Too raw. But of course, Colin wasn't having that. He sat down their water and pulled her head away from his neck easily.

"I want you to sit on my face for a while," Colin said darkly, turning them towards the bed and ripping down the covers. Olivia flushed as his words registered.

"What do you m—" she started.

"Exactly what I said," Colin interrupted.

He tossed her onto the bed and then crawled in after her, reclining to his back and snatching her wrist when she tried to retreat. The music continued on into the bedroom, the filthy playlist lyrics making her blush even harder. His demand made her feel even more shy.

"But...but I get really wet, Colin," she said, stuttering around her words and pulling against him futilely. "Wait!" she cried out as he suddenly yanked her on top of him and maneuvered his big shoulders between her legs, hooking her calves and heels under his arms. His hands wrapped threateningly around her hips and tightened. Olivia awkwardly kept herself raised over him, averting her eyes as her face reddened even more. She cried out in surprise as he slapped her ass cheek several times in succession, the stinging and burning feeling spread throughout her thigh and back.

"What the fuck is my name?" he barked, his eyes glittering up at her.

"Sirrr," Olivia moaned, wriggling on top of him. "Oh, *God,*"

"He can't save you, Olivia. Now *Sit. Down!*" Colin snarled, feeling his control snap. He snatched her hips and yanked her down to him, sucking her clit into his warm, wet mouth before he tightened his teeth on her and drawed it out slowly, biting at her and giving her another burning sensation for her to suffer through.

Olivia screamed, the pleasure of the pain shocking her further, feeling herself squirt on his face and his neck.

She jerked above him as he attacked her pussy with gusto. His loud groans and sex sounds mixed with the sounds of him smacking against her like she was the greatest snack he'd ever found. He pulled back and licked her gently through her orgasm before settling his lips around her again in a tight suction. She felt herself bobbing, her thighs clenching and unclenching as he helped her on and off his mouth lewdly. His slight beard scraped against her inner thighs, his breaths puffing over her mound and her lower stomach, making her clench, wanting something inside of her. Her skin misted with sweat and her toes curled, waiting.

The wet, smacking sounds amplified. He gave her abused flesh a little nibble with his lips and she broke again, trying to flinch away from him and the indescribable pleasure he was giving her. His fingers tightened further as his elbows drew her legs in securely against his torso. He suddenly sank all of his fingernails into her ass and gripped her harshly. Olivia moaned and flinched at the pain, knowing she was going to be bruised tomorrow.

He pulled away suddenly, glaring up at her.

"How does it feel, princess, to know you can't get away?" he said again, taunting her.

His mouth went back to her swollen clit as he twisted his head slightly and did something with his lips and teeth that made her eyes cross and her whole body tighten up. Her fingers clenched tightly as a sheen of sweat misted on her skin. He kept with the movement, not letting up. Her pelvis twitched as all the nerves in her body suddenly felt like they congregated to that one spot between her legs, and he was taking a whip and striking all of them at the same time. Her breath froze in her lungs as she jerked on top of him silently, unable to draw a breath.

The tight feeling in her legs relented, and she inhaled on a ragged gasp of air, once, twice before arching her back as her muscles froze again. Without warning her, he locked his teeth on her clit hard.

"Oh my fucking *God!* Sir! *Nooo!*" Olivia screamed, her shouts echoing throughout the room and yet he still persisted.

She threw her head back and let out a series of broken moans, unable to speak, jerking and flinching anew in his grip, not caring about the clutching force of him holding her to his face like this.

Her breasts swelled to the point of pain, her nipples almost numb. Overwhelmed and desperate for relief of any kind, she brought up her hands and clawed at her breasts, squeezing tight to relieve the pressure. She felt tears splash to her chest as she gripped both her nipples in her fingers and rolled. Her vision went hazy as she heard a grumble deep down in his chest.

He was watching her desperately play with herself.

Olivia sounded like a damn animal thrashing above him. She was grinding on him, trying to get him to cease that evil latch he'd had on her clit, but in response he tightened his fingers even further into her flesh, keeping her poised exactly where he wanted her.

"Fucccck," Olivia cried, feeling herself squirt again, more than she'd ever had before.

Her inner thighs and her knees were wet, and she sagged as she realized she'd damn near flooded the bed beneath them. He unlocked his jaw and with a gentle suckle, he let go and pushed her down to a dry area. She was so weak she couldn't move, helpless to fight against him. He efficiently positioned her on her back, with her head hanging off the bed and made her face the floor-length mirror. Olivia keened as she got her first look at his hard body poised over hers in the reflection.

She was nothing more than prey for him.

Her legs were splayed wide, and her knees were hiked high as he towered over her. Her nipples, neglected, were pulled tight and pointing to the ceiling. They were both breathing hard when they met each other's eyes in the mirror. He gave her another wicked grin, chuckling at her distress before leaning down to take her right nipple in a harsh nibble. Her sex clenched painfully. And right then and there, she vowed to never leave this man.

The making up was too raw.

Colin grunted as he thrust inside her clasping pussy with effort. "Let me in," he demanded, meeting her eyes in the mirror once more. Fisting the sheets in his hands, his eyes narrowed threateningly at her.

Olivia's mouth dropped open as she saw her juices gleaming on his chin, his jaw, his neck, and his chest.

"I'm *trying*," Olivia whimpered, her voice coming out in a whine.

She knew she was swollen, she felt split apart and he wasn't even halfway inside of her. She cried out as he fitted his arms into her knees, rolling her back further and wrapped his hands around the tops of her arms, holding her immobile. He looked down at her sternly and her heart fluttered at his reprimanding look. She licked her lips with nervous excitement.

"I'm going to break this pussy and there's not a fucking thing you can do to stop me, is there?" he said, his deep voice penetrating her brain and making her throb hard around him. "Did you think I was just going to take it easy on you when we got back, *hmm? Answer me.*"

Olivia shook her head. "No sir," she whispered.

"If you did, you know me way better than that at this point. I am not taking it easy on you, I don't care if it's been fourteen weeks since you've last had my cock in you, you should have thought about that before you ran." Colin leaned down closer, scraping his beard against her jaw, making her whimper. "But thank you for tightening it up for me in my absence. Your cunt feels amazing."

Olivia's jaw dropped in shock at his words before her face pinched and she inhaled on a ragged gasp.

He tightened his abs and mercilessly jammed the rest of his heavy thick length inside of her. She let out a strangled, desperate scream that she quickly cut off. She tasted copper, having bitten her lip with the effort to not scream. He lowered his head once more and took a tight nipple into his mouth, sucking hard, licking, biting. Every nip sent a zing of fire to her pussy. She was so sensitive and wound so tight it felt like if he bit hard enough, she'd break in half.

Nibbling at her in earnest, he'd begun those delicious drives, bouncing off her pussy. It was so sexual, so untamed, that she orgasmed just off the sight of his hips beating off hers. She purred, her teeth baring, flinching as he moved his mouth to the other nipple and bit down. A hot flash of unbearable teeth grinding arousal suddenly hit her and her mouth dropped open as she swung her head up, tears falling from her eyes.

She stared wildly into his chocolate eyes as her body bobbed violently up and down with the force of him taking her.

Her heart raced in panic.

"Nooooo, sir please, *please!* I'll be a good girl. *I promise! I'll be a good girl for you!* I'll be a good girl, I'll be a good girl!" Olivia's whispered words crescendoed into a scream as she lost her mind, her nails dug sharply into him, feeling manic. Suddenly scared that he was going to kill her like this. That one of the orgasms he was going to give her was going to make her heart fail.

Her nails clawed into the mattress and she felt one tear as he suddenly leaned forward into her face, growling.

"Oh *now* the bitch can be a good girl, huh? You haven't been acting like a good girl, so I'm going to treat you like what you are. You're my fucking *whore ass wife*. So shut the fuck up, and *open up,*" he said roughly, moving one of his arms higher, hitching her leg up further and snatching her head back by her hair. This movement widened her hips even more and he somehow ground a little deeper, drawing a hard flinch and hiss from her. She moaned, her sex spasming.

She loved when he talked dirty to her.

"You want me to go easy on you, after what you did to me?" he snarled at her, slinging his hips against hers repeatedly.

"Yeeesss," she cried. He leaned into her face once again, staring into her green eyes.

"Well guess what mama? I. Don't. Give. A. Fuck," Colin whispered, his own eyes wild as he serviced her body with his.

Olivia could feel that every retreat of his cock took effort as her pussy was clamped so tight around him that it was making little sucking noises with the movement. He lowered to her breasts once more.

"Jesus fucking Christ your body's amazing," Colin said sharply, his sweat drops hitting her body and mixing with hers.

She stopped breathing as she suffered through another orgasm, this one way different than the others. Her toes curled and her body bowed under his, the hot feeling saturated her from her head to her toes. Her eyes rolled into the back of her head, short gasping sounds leaving her mouth. He looked up and slapped her across the face rather harshly, bringing her back.

"No fucking passing out for you, amor. Don't give up on me yet, we're not done," he drawled, sounding like the devil himself.

"Sir," she whispered weakly, her hands feeling for his thighs blindly.

"I'm right here Olivia, and I'm never letting go. By the time tonight's through you're going to understand that. Or your body will, whether your mind wants to or not," he whispered darkly, leaning forward and licking into her mouth. His drives slowed, becoming more sensual and less crazed as he circled, twisted, and screwed his hips into hers, finally making love to her like he promised. He just had to get that raw hard fuck out of the way first.

Now they had all night.

***

Hours later, Colin reclined against the pillows and the headboard with one arm propped under his head and his other arm cradling Olivia against his chest. She was currently nestled in between his legs, her soft body lying on top of his. He could feel her belly expanding against his inner thigh and she rested her head on his stomach. He smiled as he felt a droplet of drool hit his skin.

He'd put her to sleep alright.

Colin reached orgasm twice before finally letting her go, reluctantly. Her body was spent, and though he knew he was depraved, he wasn't evil like she claimed he was earlier. So, taking mercy on her in his own time, he'd laid with her afterwards, kissing her, and rubbing her hair. Giving her care until he was sure she was lucid enough to carry into the shower. He'd sat her on the little bench in the shower and soaped her from head to toe before washing himself, feeling sad to take her scent off him.

Colin's cock twitched when he remembered how he'd roughly slammed her reluctant body onto his face, and the feel of her juices gushed out on him. He'd missed her so much he wanted to drown himself in her. He refrained from telling her that though, seeing as she was still shy with him, despite their very raw style of lovemaking. His hand came up from rubbing her back to caress her hair in long strokes, feeling her snuggle even deeper into him.

Colin smiled as he replayed her crying out repeatedly how she would be a good girl for him if he'd just stop, knowing that the pleasure was making her delirious. He fucking loved that, ate it up. He wanted to fuck her right now to see if he could get her to beg him like that again.

It was so sweet, warming his sadistic little heart. He dropped a kiss to her forehead, seeing her cheek smashed against his pec, her breathing coming out steadily through her plump lips. Her eyes moved behind her lids in a dream. She was in REM sleep, looking peaceful and content. She smiled suddenly with a small giggle, before her face relaxed again. He wondered what she was dreaming about.

He'd put on fifteen pounds of muscle since she'd disappeared, needing something to occupy his mind; to take his thoughts away from the what ifs. So he tortured his body for hours more in the gym than he was used to. He frowned as he realized his sweet girl wasn't used to his stamina, having barely been used to it before she'd ran. Curious, he tugged the sheet lower, seeing a bruise form on her ribs where he fisted her skin in his hand as he slammed her down on him in the pool. Tugging the sheet more, he revealed more bruising all over her hips in the shape of his handprints. His dick immediately became hard again.

She stirred slightly before resettling.

Colin scooted down further in the bed and closed his eyes, careful not to wake her up. Ignoring his hardening erection, he breathed deeply, inhaling her scent. He'd missed her so much he didn't want to let go of her, even to sleep. It took some time, but he fell into slumber with her still cradled against him, having the most peaceful sleep he'd had in almost four months.

SIXTEEN
Say My Name

OLIVIA WOKE UP AND couldn't move, couldn't even stretch. She just laid there, blinking slowly up at the ceiling. She startled as she felt a warm hand land on her head, stroking slowly. Colin.

She turned her head and found his eyes. He was sitting up in bed, in just a pair of loose shorts and nothing else, drinking a cup of coffee. She turned red; he looked so delicious with his tattoos and muscular body. His brown hair was rumpled in a sexy style, and he just looked so masculine.

"Hey baby," he said, taking another sip of his coffee. "You're alive," he smiled, his eyes crinkling at the edges.

"Barely," she whispered, flushing as the memories from last night came flooding back.

Oh God I begged, I really begged. And the sounds I was making! Olivia thought, moaning miserably as she tugged the sheet over her head. She gasped as Colin ripped the sheet back down and hauled her up onto his lap, naked. He groaned as her warmth sunk through his shorts. Shuffling, he pushed them down freeing his dick, lifting her then lowering her onto him, feeling she was still slick from last night.

He hissed as her tightness strangled him. Olivia cried out, pressing her hard nipples into his chest as she went limp against him.

"Better?" he chuckled into her ear as he began moving her hips, grinding her body against him, ignoring her soft sobs.

"You're going to fuck me to death," she whined against his neck, her warm breath washing over him.

"Maybe. I just missed you, and I've got a lot of energy to expend. And who better to expend it on than my beautiful wife's helpless body. Giving her orgasm after orgasm and making her take all my cum?" he grinned wickedly as he felt her stiffen.

He made her roll her hips, her clit pressing sharp against his pubic bone. He groaned as she bit down hard onto his shoulder as she came gently, with a soft soughing sigh, as if she was too weak from the night before to give much else. Holding her buttocks, he lifted her several inches and dropped her, her wetness making the glide smooth. He knew she had to be sore, and the knowledge that he was making it worse, chafing already abused tissues fed the sadistic beast inside of him.

"God, knowing this is uncomfortable for you is really fucking doing it for me," Colin said harshly, nudging her back so he could lean forward to suck a nipple into his mouth, lifting her up several inches and slamming her back down, pressing up and grinding deeply against the back of her sex. He reveled in hearing her sharp yelp. He groaned deep in his chest as he lifted her up and down onto his cock for long minutes, the wet slap of their bodies meeting and her nipple between his teeth his undoing. He came hard, flooding into her. He buried his face into her breasts as he rocked into her, his arms banding around her waist, feeling the little ripples of her vagina as she succumbed to another smaller orgasm.

They stayed locked together that way for a while, him seated deep inside of her. He pulled back to reach for his coffee once more. Taking a deep gulp, he offered his cup to her, surprised when she took it. He normally drank it black. She sipped quietly, still feeling him deep inside of her.

Would he want to carry me around the house like this while he did his everyday routine? Maybe. Maybe he should just staple me to his body and ensure I can't go anywhere. She giggled, her face scrunching as the coffee hit her taste buds.

"Yuck." She complained, giving him back his cup.

"What's so funny?" he mused, taking another deep sip and sitting back quietly, sinking a hand into her hair, content just being with her. She moved to raise herself off of him and he tightened his hand on her hip with a warning sound. She lowered back down.

"I was just thinking how you'd be perfectly content to walk around all day with me wrapped around you. You'd have to strap me to your body," she said softly, running her hands over his hard chest and abs, getting her first real feel of him since they'd been together. His muscles bunched beneath her hands.

Colin made a deep sound in his throat.

"Not a bad idea actually, I've thought about it several times," he said. His eyes glittered at hers from over his coffee cup, making her blush harder as he took another drink. She watched his throat work around it as he cocked his head at hers, his half hard erection twitching inside her as she so blatantly assessed him.

"You can't go again," she whispered, arching one eyebrow.

"Can't I?" he whispered back, placing his coffee cup on his night-stand. He placed both hands on her thighs and rubbed, giving her a dangerous smile.

"Nooo," Olivia complained, feeling him become increasingly hard inside of her. She squealed as he suddenly flipped her onto her back and rolled with her, encasing her wrists with his big hands, holding her arms down to the mattress.

"You know what I think?" His voice deepened slightly as he pressed his body down into hers. Olivia panted for air.

"I think those last two orgasms you had weren't good enough, and you owe me. So I'm not stopping until you come so hard I want to feel you bend my dick with how hard you tighten around me," he punctuated the sentence with a hard thrust, stealing her air and making her arch her back, gritting her teeth.

"Sir?" she bit out.

"*Yes,* Olivia?"

"I'm not screaming for you this morning. It's too early for all of that." She taunted, wrapping her legs around his waist and tightening her knees against him.

"Well, baby," Colin said, placing his hand on the side of her head, his thumb fluttering over her mouth. "I guess it's a good thing I didn't say you had to scream. I said you had to tighten to the point you bend my dick. And you've seen how big my dick is, right?" He circled his hips deep, smiling as he drew a strangled cry out of her throat. He slipped his thumb in her mouth, pressing against her tongue. "You think that's going to be easy? We're going to be up here all day beautiful. I sincerely hope you appreciated the sleep I let you get."

Colin's hand moved lower to wrap around her throat, and he tightened hard, cutting off her air supply as he began to rock them.

It took most of the day, and in the end Colin ended up almost breaking the damn thing off himself, unable to get enough of Olivia's skin, her smell, and her taste. He carried her downstairs for a late lunch, as she couldn't walk from the marathon of sex he'd subjected them to for the last twenty-four hours. He let her nap again for around an hour before he woke her up rather violently, thrusting into her from behind and snatching her head back by her hair. Pissed all over again that she'd ran away, wondering how long it would take for him to get over it.

He fucked her sometimes to keep from crying, or to keep the anxiety at bay. He would never tell her just how off the deep end he went when he'd come home to her gone, his garage in disarray, the guest house room open, and her car with the keys still inside. So many sirens had been blaring that day that he had the worst panic attack of his life. Jonathan had to take him to the hospital.

He had never felt pain like that before, even when he lost his mother. This was different. This woman didn't know she had the power to break him. And he supposed it went the other way too. That was why she left in the first place. He'd broken her heart, and he'd be damned if he let it stay cracked open.

So until they could begin counseling again, sexual healing was on the menu. Copious amounts of it.

Downstairs in his study, Colin groaned deep in his chest as he dripped with sweat. He sniffed and leaned harder into Olivia, who was currently sobbing almost uncontrollably before letting out an ear-shattering scream that shocked him. She was wrapped tight around him while he banged her hips roughly against a wall that held pictures of him and several celebrities and friends.

Through the pain in his back and the blood rushing in his ears, he heard a picture fall and break with their movements.

His heart thudded uncontrollably, and Colin wondered briefly if he needed to worry about that. Mentally reminding himself to schedule a doctor's appointment, he pulled back and gave her several more hard strikes, wincing as his own orgasm took him by surprise.

Weak. Colin chastised himself. He pounded a fist into the wall next to her shoulder as he stiffened and forced himself to suffer through it silently, his face tight and his lip curled.

He loosened his hold on her thigh from where he had her leg draped over his arm.

"Colin, I can't!" She cried weakly, holding him to her with her arms and legs. "*Oh God p-please,*" he smiled to himself as it came out "puh-lease," she was adorable. "Bunny, bunny, bunny."

She safe worded.

"I know baby," he reassured, trying to tamp down the gasps that were escaping from his own mouth. "We're done. For now," Colin bit out, his voice sounding hoarse as he tried to fight through the fire in his lungs, wondering if maybe he overdid it this time.

Looking down between them, he pulled out from her body and checked them both for blood just in case. Nothing. He felt relieved. His dick was finally soft enough for him to not feel like he had a steel iron shoved in his pants. He looked back at her, still struggling for air and took in her red stained cheeks, with big fat tear streaks running down them. She was trembling.

"Let's get cleaned up," he said, pulling her to him, thankful once more that he'd spent hours at the gym and his body was in its best shape.

Colin carried Olivia up to the bathroom, and they showered with her sitting down on the bench again. He knelt down before her and wrapped his arms around her waist, soothing her, stroking her hair, kissing her stomach. He praised her for how well she'd taken everything, for how wonderful she was, let her know that he loved her, and most of all, thanked her for seeing him and accepting him when he wasn't sure at times that he could even accept himself.

They shared a sweet, loving kiss. Her hands wrapped around the nape of his neck as the water worked to soothe their aching muscles and sensitive skin.

Olivia and Colin washed up before napping a couple of hours. Waking up, Olivia put on a black silk robe and him a pair of matching silk pants. They went downstairs and to the kitchen, pawing through the refrigerator and cabinets, ravenous for food this time, instead of each other.

***

"Oh my God," Colin mumbled around a bite of noodles. Turning incredulous eyes on to Olivia, who was sitting there, sipping red wine and sitting back in her chair looking very satisfied with herself. They were in the dining room with two lit candles, and a big bowl of Asian noodles with a reduced savory sauce, chicken and vegetables.

He'd set the table while she cooked, nervous the whole time for obvious reasons. He glanced at his plate again, twirling his fork around more noodles, chicken, mini corn, watercress and snap peas before sluicing the whole thing in the sauce on his plate and putting it into his mouth. He groaned.

Jesus that's good. Colin thought to himself.

"You fucking learned how to coo-" he coughed, pressing a fist to his mouth, forgetting himself. "You learned how to make this in China while you were gone?" he said incredulously, mentally kicking himself for almost revealing the most hilarious family secret they all kept.

His wife just wasn't cut out for the kitchen.

Olivia smiled prettily at him, and his heart almost stopped at the sight. She was just too beautiful. He reached over to push her hair behind her ear as she poured a little more wine into her glass before giving him some as well.

Fuck I missed her so much. Colin winced, the squeeze in his heart becoming deeper.

"Yes, Erick connected me to a small hole in the wall cook there and she taught me how to make bao, and this dish here," she said, rolling her lips as she saw him narrow his eyes.

Shit shit shit! Olivia thought, she was in for another retribution fuck. Or would it be a revenge fuck? She was starting to lose track as they'd been screwing each other to death for an entire day. She put another small bite of noodles in her mouth, chewing slowly, knowing it was coming.

"I swear to God, I think I would have killed him if you had been taking him back to your bedroom, Olivia," Colin whispered, leaning back and snagging his wine glass. He closed his eyes momentarily as he attempted to get the thought of the two of them out of his head. She told him that she hadn't slept with anyone while she was gone and though he believed her, he just couldn't help imagining it.

She twisted her lips in amusement. "You have no faith in me?" she teased, sipping more wine herself. "I don't believe that you would kill someone in front of me like that, Colin." She tsked, setting down her glass.

"Have you seen yourself? Like really seen yourself, baby? You're a goddess. Men would do anything to get in between your thighs. You're like a fucking siren. I was so lucky the day you agreed to go out with me. I was getting desperate. I'm not used to being told no," Colin said, taking another bite. He groaned in appreciation. He knew Mary would be happy to have a break cooking, because he wanted Olivia to make this dish at least once a week.

"So," she said, speaking around a bite of food before swallowing. "I didn't know you could wield a gun like that. Like you had *practice,*" she asked curiously, changing the subject with her eyebrow raised. Her fingers twirled nonchalantly in her hair.

He stared at her for a second, biting his bottom lip as he tried not to break out into a smile.

"I used to be a sniper for the marines. From oh seven, to two thousand and thirteen," he said simply, raising his wineglass and sipping with a rather proud look on his face.

"I'm sorry what?" she asked, both eyebrows raised. "You were *what* for the marines?" she gave him a goofy smile before giggling at him. "Come on Colin, that one really takes the cake! Be real please."

"You don't believe me?" Colin scoffed. Finished with his food, he sat back and placed an ankle over his knee, twirling his wineglass in his fingers. He watched her dark red eyebrows raise incredulously.

"Well...I just thought...you and Jonathan did the software car taking-over-the-world thing this entire time I guess?" she mused, grabbing herself a little more food. He smiled at her appreciatively, she'd gained a little weight while she was gone, and he was happy to see it, loving her curves in his hands. He felt his cock stir and he mentally tamped it down. They had to be able to get through a dinner without fucking. He ate another bite, sitting back and watching her chew her food. His dick hardened further. He cleared his throat.

"Well, we had a life before that love. Joining the marines was the best thing I could have ever done for myself, at the time. Jonathan and I actually joined together; he was in the torture division. Super top-secret confidential stuff. I just got out later than him. I enjoyed it too much to want to quit. Jonathan was busy building a car brand and wanted to take me along for the ride. No pun intended." He gave her a cheeky grin. "I must say, I'm glad I listened. I owe a lot to him," he said, sipping deeply. "Now, put some more on my plate, wife! You've really worked up my appetite," he said, his eyes becoming hooded with renewed desire as he leaned back deeper in his chair, eyeing her appreciatively.

Olivia smiled mischievously as she stood up and leaned over to twirl some more pasta on the serving spoon and put it on his plate. She picked more chicken, veggies, and sauce to top it and replaced the cutlery. Turning to sit back in her seat, she let out a surprised gasp when he grabbed her by her waist and jerked her back to him roughly.

"What's so funny?" he asked, staring up at her dangerously. His hand gripped her buttock tightly.

"Nothing, I just find that I love serving you, Colin," she whispered down at him as he nuzzled her robe apart at her breasts. She inhaled in pleasure as he found her nipple with his hot tongue and sucked it into his mouth. He spent a minute nipping her with his teeth and sucking softly before pulling back. Her robe had gaped open, one round breast bared with a dark pink nipple wet from his lips, teasing him, driving him crazy. He plumped her breast with his hand.

"Say it again, except this time with the name I prefer," Colin whispered up at her as his tongue lashed out at her nipple before his teeth grabbed it and tugged.

"I love serving you, sir," Olivia said shakily, his teeth rolling her nipple and making her juices slick down her thigh.

Oh God, why do I like this so much? She lamented. Letting go of her with an audible pop, Colin's nostrils flared as his eyes flashed, his expression looking almost angry. Her face paled.

"Down!" he snarled, pushing her roughly to her knees.

Olivia's mind raced nervously.

Colin tore open the ties to his silk bottoms and yanked his dick out. Her mouth instantly flooded with moisture. He was hard again. How he maintained this level of stamina she'd never know. She whimpered at the sight of his thick flesh in his hand, the veins in his hand and arms protruding deliciously underneath his black tattoos that encased almost the entirety of his arm. He pumped his fist roughly, a drop of precum settling on the tip.

"This is your fault," he said, leaning forward and grasping her jaw, prying it open with a finger, then hooking his thumb around her bottom teeth before pulling her to him. "Now, I don't want to take your pussy again because I know you're tender, but you will open your mouth and do as I say. Suck it. All the way Olivia. Don't fuck with me," he hissed, his control clearly gone for not the first time today.

She whimpered, desire deep down in her belly making her hot, she tore at her robe, baring herself from the waist up as she dropped her mouth over him, tasting his clean musk that was uniquely him. His scent and taste made her damn near feral.

Olivia moaned as she rose off him and leaned forward, her tongue lashing along his fingers, licking up his knuckles. She found a vein and licked it all the way up his arm, across his shoulder, and up his neck before ending with a little nibble on his earlobe.

"You taste like my dirtiest fucking wet dream come true. You want to come in my wet, hot, mouth baby? I think you deserve it from beating my cunt up so well over the last couple days. You want to come down my throat like a good boy?" Olivia whispered with a little giggle before sealing the words inside his ear with a little kiss.

She squealed as he snatched her by her hair and slammed her mouth down on his cock with a growl that echoed throughout the dining room. He scooted the chair back with his harsh movement, the sound of the chair scraping against the floor loud in her ears, her eyes watering as he shoved her down on several inches of his cock.

"Oh God," she mumbled around his thickness, earning herself several more inches of cock into her mouth as he pressed hard against the ring of her throat. She gagged and he let up, cupping the back of her head tightly. Breathing deeply, she pulled back before flicking the tip of his erection several times and then lowering. She repeated this process before she relaxed her gag reflex and took him past the ring in her throat. She froze in shock before screaming around him. He'd thickened even further. She wiggled on top of him, struggling to control it.

"Stop and breathe, my love. Concentrate," he gritted above her, his scent sharpened in her nose as he broke out in a sweat.

She paused, her breath coming out hot and fast through her nose. Her eyes were wet, and she realized how messy she was being. She was startled as he suddenly pressed a napkin to her nose, collecting her tears and snot.

"I know you don't like that, so now you can stop worrying about it and take me the rest of the way inside so I can fuck your mouth the way I need to," he said in his deep voice. He hissed, throwing his head back as she suddenly lowered more, pressing her nose into the crisp hairs of his pelvic. After a few seconds, she began to bob, making greedy sounds. She hummed deep in her throat and felt his thighs tighten in response.

"You're such a good little slut. My baby," he said hoarsely above her, his hands went to hers and gripped, showing her that he was right there with her. Affected by his words, she sucked hard on an upswing, and he made a deep growling sound before thickening even further in her mouth.

That sound was her undoing. Olivia pulled all the way off of him and ignored the exclamation of surprise and his order to get back on her knees. She threw herself at him, tackling him so hard that the chair tipped over and dumped them both on the floor. Turning fast, she righted herself and pulled herself up by the table.

"*Olivia, get back here!*" he snarled as he pushed to his feet himself, like a predator. She sidestepped quickly, hurriedly putting him where she was with her back to the gleaming cherry wood table. They assessed each other greedily. Olivia moved first, throwing her body through the air making him stumble back into the table. She crawled up his body and slapped him sharply across the face, stunning him momentarily before she reached over and took her empty wine glass and broke it, taking the sharp stem and suddenly placing it against his neck.

They stared at each other wildly. He let out a dark chuckle, completely unconcerned with her actions and placed his hands behind his head, relaxing as if he didn't have a sharp wine stem at his jugular.

"Tell me, baby, what's wrong?" he goaded, rolling his hips tightly into hers. She straddled his lap, her robe had gotten in between them so they weren't touching skin to skin.

"I don't want you to come in my mouth, I want you to... to.." she couldn't say it. Her eyes narrowed at him as she struggled mentally. She pressed the stem harder into his neck but still he didn't react.

He tilted his head as all the air seemed to leave the room, leaving her panting.

"All you have to do is say my name. You know this, Olivia," he whispered. "So ask me nicely, with my name attached to the request, and tell me what you really want. And I will deliver. Oh and this had better be good for you to lose your fucking mind the way you just did, you've got a piece of glass in my neck. So if it's not good, you better fake it till you make it baby," his words came out stern, he bared his teeth at her in a feral smile. Ready to pounce, but holding himself back, needing her to tell him what she wanted, needing her to trust him again.

"I want you to fuck me like a whore."

"Noted."

"And I want you to...to..." she whispered, words failing her.

"Tell me Olivia," he rasped, feeling the fires of hell beginning to lick at him at her sudden mortified expression that crossed her face. He let himself have a moment of secret pleasure. Though degradation was in their contract, he hadn't utilized it much until he found her in China, and he'd gleamed just how much it turned her on to be forced to be embarrassed and vulnerable with him.

"I want you to whip me like that red headed woman that was in that porn video you showed me."

"Where?" Colin growled.

"On my back."

"My way?" he licked his lips.

"Yes."

"It's going to be filthy. I might scare you. It's going to be much worse than that video," a little grin graced his mouth.

"I'm terrified," Olivia said sarcastically. His eyes flashing was her only warning before his hand shot out and grabbed her throat cutting off her air supply. Her nails dug into his chest as she squirmed on top of him, gasping.

"I'm going to let the disrespect slide. Now, I want you to put it all together in a lovely little sentence, with my name at the end. And your wish shall be my command, little girl," he said, his fingers loosening enough to let some air in. She wheezed for breath, suddenly uncertain.

"I want you to whip my back, and then fuck me mercilessly like I'm a dirty whore, the way you like it. And no safe word. I want you to take me exactly how you want, Sir," her eyes rounded as he suddenly tightened his fingers once more.

"No safe word huh?" he said quietly, his eyes boring into hers tightly. Olivia shook her head no. "Gahdamn," he whispered, a truly evil grin graced his face. "It feels like Christmas," his fingers loosened then fell away. "Get the wine glass out of my neck," his eyes flashed dangerously. With a gasp, she unclenched her hand and the stem fell to the table, shattering in half. There were a tense few heartbeats of time before he spoke again.

"Now while I love that you begged me so sweetly, I cannot make good on your request tonight," he held up his hand at her indignant gasp. "No. You are much too tender; I've been fucking you almost nonstop for twenty-four hours. I'm not risking damaging you, it would be incredibly irresponsible and I don't think you'd forgive me," he said, easily righting himself and sitting up on the table.

She sputtered angrily on top of his lap, before hopping off and storming out of the dining room.

"Fuck you, Colin! Fucking jerk," she said, flipping him off over her shoulder. He chuckled darkly at her as she rounded the corner. He fisted his hand in his dick and pumped it a few more times before spilling his seed on his hand. He walked to the powder room and washed it off. Smiling as he went back to the table, righting his chair and then quickly finishing his food.

Upstairs, Olivia was seething. *Jesus, didn't he know how hard that was for me to say?* she thought.

Huffing, she stomped to their bedroom before opening and slamming the door shut and then going into the bathroom and slamming that door too. Starting the shower, she went to the sink and put her hair in a clip and began the process of brushing her teeth. Irritated that she was scrubbing her mouth of his scent to be spiteful, she untied her robe and kicked it to the side uncharacteristically of her, hoping if he came after her that he'd slip and fall.

She rinsed her mouth out and hobbled her way to the shower, moaning lightly as she settled on the bench that seemed like it'd been her home for at least five showers since she'd been back. She didn't have the strength to stand up long enough to let the water work its magic so she stretched out on the bench, laying flat on her belly on the white ceramic tile, her arm drifting down to the floor. Closing her eyes, she breathed the steam in deeply as the water pounded down on her back and her hair as she relaxed into almost a trance-like state. Her hair growing heavy, its weight made more noticeable from soaking up the water hitting her.

With an irritated eye roll, she silently conceded that Colin was right. Taking stock of her body now in its relaxed, heavy state she realized that her body had taken a beating. They just couldn't keep their hands off each other. And if he'd done what she'd asked right away, it might have tipped them both over the edge. She pursed her lips in irritation that he hadn't come after her right away, and realized that their physical need for each other was borderline psychotic.

She wondered if this hot and heavy phase they were experiencing would fade soon. They'd need it to if they were ever to have a hope of being functional.

Olivia sat up and began to wash herself, paying careful attention to be gentle on any sore spots, which was basically her entire body. Finishing up and stepping out of the shower, she dried herself off before making her way to the guest bedroom, wearily crawling in between the sheets and sighing as her head hit the pillow. Mentally shrugging off the fresh wave of guilt for leaving the dining room a mess, she promised herself she would just take a quick nap before getting up to go down and clean.

***

Colin walked into their bedroom quietly, not seeing Olivia. He back-tracked and went down the hallway, seeing the guest bedroom door closed. He cracked it open, walking in and seeing her knocked out on the bed.

He tsked and went to her, pulled the blankets off carefully and picked her up. Carrying her to their bedroom, he put her on his side of the bed before pulling the sheets back up and pressing her lips to her forehead. Turning, he went into the bathroom and started the shower, still seeing a lingering humidity from her shower earlier. He had come up, wanting to talk with her but he saw how peacefully she was laying there on the bench and decided to leave her be while he cleaned up downstairs. He thought about her requests, and how sexy those words sounded falling from her lips.

He started formulating a plan to give her what they both desired. But he needed her one hundred percent with him mentally and phys-ically, not worn out from an entire day's worth of hard sex.

When he was fucking her downstairs in the study against the wall, she'd screamed so high that he thought he'd broken something inside of her. Colin winced, knowing he overdid it, hating himself for want-ing to wake her up and take her again. He glanced down at his cock as he fisted it in his hand and hissed, seriously overstimulated. He didn't think that either one of them could handle another session right now. Drying off, he walked naked back into the bedroom and laid down on the couch, not wanting to be next to her, smelling her, touching her. They needed a full night of sleep to recover, at the very least.

Groaning slightly, he pulled the blanket over himself and closed his eyes.

SEVENTEEN
Carmichael Confrontations

"Damn girl, you look like you feel like *dog shit. What the hell?*" Vanessa said as she walked in with Jonathan, putting a big folder on the island. Her swollen belly looked like it was ready to pop any minute, and embarrassingly enough, Vanessa's waddle resembled the one she was currently sporting.

Olivia winced, placing a hand on her back and arching, trying to rid herself of the deep ache in her muscles.

Jonathan waved a hello before she pointed him to Colin's study, where he was sitting, going over some paperwork for his company. He'd been walking and looking fresh as a daisy all morning. Olivia, however, was not. She looked thoroughly ran through. By one man, who ironically didn't.

"Yeah well, disappear for four months and see how you can walk again once Jonathan gets ahold of you," she mumbled in reply. She limped over to the folder, ignoring her sister's amused giggles at her walking issue.

"That's YOUR fault, babe." Vanessa giggled, settling herself onto a stool and bending her head over the open folder and showing Olivia the first page.

"So you're having a home birth, after all?" Olivia said surprised. She knew her sister had been contemplating this decision for months. "I am so not getting in the tub with you to help you push," she said, almost mentally gagging at the image.

"*Bitch.* But yes, we're going to have a doula, and we want everyone there. Allison, and *you* obviously. And that includes Colin. How do you think he'd feel about that?" Vanessa asked Olivia softly. Vanessa knew from her conversations with Jonathan how Colin felt about them raising Allison. She didn't want to rub salt into a wound she couldn't see.

"Well, I think he might say yes," Olivia said slowly. "Let's ask him?"

They both shuffled to the office door, shooting an embarrassed glance at each other before breaking out into laughter. Because how truly embarrassing. Olivia knocked on the office door, waiting for permission to be let in, having no clue what he and Jonathan were getting up to in there and wanting to save herself from any more embarrassment.

"You don't have to knock Olivia, you can come in," she heard Colin call to her as she opened and she and Vanessa walked through the door into the study together.

"Hey guys, sorry to interrupt but, *uhm*, we have a quick question for you Col-*babe*," she corrected quickly at his stern stare. At her self correction his face softened immediately.

Jonathan was sitting in one of the seats across from where Colin sat at his desk, his eyes flickering over Olivia in amusement before landing on Vanessa. Jonathan patted his leg, and Vanessa walked over, settling down on his lap with her arm around his shoulders. They shared an affectionate look.

Olivia smiled, walking over and sitting in the chair next to them. Ignoring Colin's knowing look at the reason why she didn't come over to him. They'd barely touched today in an unspoken agreement, knowing that the couple was coming over to discuss birth plans. They could surely go half a day without having sex.

Couldn't they? Olivia, lost in her thoughts, startled when Colin cleared his throat, breaking her from her daydreaming.

"You had a question for me, amor?" he said, his eyes crinkling as he tried to keep from grinning. He was relaxed back in his seat, leaning slightly to the side with his elbow propped up on the armrest, his fingers rubbing his lips as he waited, his head tilted.

Olivia felt her vagina clench. He was just too sexy.

She licked her lips. "Vanessa would like to know, if you would want to be present while the baby's being born."

Colin's brows furrowed. "What?" he said, confused. His eyes landed on Vanessa. "Are you two serious?"

"Yes," Vanessa smiled. "You're family, bro," she whispered, leaning her head on Jonathan.

"Without you, none of us would have found each other. You're special, Mr. Matchmaker," Jonathan ribbed, rubbing Vanessa's belly. The baby started kicking and Olivia leaned over to feel as well, smiling at the thumps. She leaned forward to press her lips against Vanessa's stomach.

"Stop that peanut, stop kicking your momma!" she teased, murmuring into Vanessa's stomach for a bit. Vanessa's belly suddenly moved from one side to the other as the baby readjusted.

Colin frowned, his eyes widening.

My God, he thought, a new appreciation for mothers overcame him and his eyes slid to Olivia once more as he suddenly imagined her pregnant. A little grin broke out on his face and he started wondering if she'd forgive him if he started stealing her birth control pills. He'd have to talk to his therapist about those thoughts, they were mighty intrusive.

"Another thing, we decided on a name for the baby," Jonathan spoke up, sharing another smile with Vanessa before turning his eyes onto Colin, who was now gracious enough to gift him his full attention.

"Oh really? I thought you'd never land on one. Olivia and I were resigned to calling the baby peanut," he joked, crossing his feet on the corner of his desk in an uncharacteristically relaxed move. He smiled at Olivia again, who giggled because it was true. They were actually going to call the baby peanut anyway, but the couple didn't need to know that.

"*Ian.* We're going to name the baby Ian. After your middle name, Colin," Vanessa said, tears coming to her eyes. She didn't let them fall though.

Olivia gasped, putting her hand to her mouth.

"We wanted to get your permission first though, just in case you two decided to have kids of your own. We didn't want to take away your chances of using the name for your own kid..." Jonathan trailed off softly, trying not to make things uncomfortable.

Olivia stayed quiet in the chair. Her eyes finally landed on Colin's who suddenly seemed incapable of speech or movement. He sat in the chair still as stone, just staring at the three of them. She decided to speak up.

"I think Ian is a beautiful name. When we have our own kid, maybe we can name him Sinclair after you Jonathan, unless Colin wants a junior as a boy's name? If we have a girl, then I'd like to name her after Colin's mom, Elena," she said softly, her eyes welling up with tears as they stayed on his. Jonathan smiled a big toothy grin as he gave Colin a discreet wink before leaning down to kiss Vanessa's belly.

"Vanessa, I would love to be there for Ian's birth. Thank you for offering, let us know what we can do to help during. And of course you know that we'll help with Allison. Now, can you two give me and Olivia a minute alone? We won't be long, I promise," Colin said, his deep voice sounding tight.

Jonathan helped Vanessa up before they exited the room, the door clicking shut softly.

"Come here," he said softly, his chest expanding tightly as he regarded her slight form, sitting curled up on the chair on the other side of his desk. She got up with effort, a wince passing her face before she schooled her features quickly into a calm expression. He could tell by her breasts that her breathing was slightly erratic. She was just as nervous as him.

He held his arms open and waited until she settled into him before he tilted her head back on his shoulder, looking down at her.

"I love you," he breathed, his lips coming down to press against her nose, skimming down to her lips. He kissed her gently, his hand moving to her hip and squeezing lightly. He pulled his hand around to her top and slipped under, pressing against her belly.

"It doesn't have to be now. We can wait a while, until you finish school. We can take time to enjoy each other. There are trips I'd love to take you on. So many things we can do before really settling down," he said, staring into her beautiful green eyes.

"I know. I love you too. I just wanted you to know that I'm open to having kids with you Colin. I want your babies," Olivia's eyes flickered back and forth between his, her hand coming up to caress his face, her fingernails scraping through his slight beard at his jawline. Her face was serious, her brows scrunched.

"But not too many babies, ok?" she corrected, feeling his chest shake with barely contained laughter.

"Ok sweetheart," he chuckled, leaning down to kiss her once more before he helped her off of him and they walked out of the office. He grinned as they made their way back to the kitchen where Jonathan and Vanessa were reading over a set of papers next to an open folder, proud that they didn't wind up screwing each other on the desk. They could talk about the future and be vulnerable without being inside of one another. That had to be a good step in the right direction.

They spent time going over the birthing plan, deciding that they would move in temporarily a couple days before the expected birth of Ian, wanting to be close in case they needed support. Olivia would be there to help keep Vanessa company, and Colin of course would be there to help any way he could. He just knew he wasn't letting Olivia out of his sight for a while.

Colin's phone pinged. Vincent.

He opened the email on his phone.

My man,

I got the security detail you requested for Olivia ready, two men who are trained in torture techniques, sniper skills, and kidnapping. They are all specialized fighters who have been in private security for over 20 years each.

Names are Byson and Zero.

Per order, they will rotate shifts, and on the days that she leaves for campus or an outing, there will always be someone tailing her. When school starts back up and they're on campus, they will be in plain clothes. I've also got one guy for you personally, as well. There will be two men who flank your property at all times. I have a set of six men to rotate these shifts. One set in the morning, one set in the evening, and one set during the night. I sent the invoice over for you to review and their specs are attached to this email for your approval. I also spoke with your P.I, Mr. Howard. Nice man.

Information was not nice though; another red head went missing. A woman in her early thirties. This one had green eyes this time. And her toddler was found dumped about a quarter of a mile away.

She was found decapitated, naked in a woodsy area about half an hour from your place. The man is definitely sending a warning. A huge one. Jonathan's team is ready as well for Vanessa.

Contact me if you have any questions. I'd like to schedule a time for us all to meet so we can have you and Olivia formally meet the team.

Vincent

P.S-Stella is bugging me to death about going out to karaoke since apparently you can sing. She wants to do a duet. Have Olivia contact her with some dates you two are available. No negotiations-this is not a request. Peace.

Colin's eyes hardened as he glanced up sharply, catching Jonathan's eye. The women were currently on Vanessa's small laptop, looking at baby furniture.

"Have you checked your email?" he gritted, his eyes flashing. A muscle was ticking in his jaw.

Jonathan shook his head no and pulled out his phone. His eyes scanned the email fast, pausing when he got to the place about the child. Jonathan froze, he looked at Colin and jerked his head to the terrace. They quietly stepped out together before Jonathan leaned against the railing and pulled up his email app.

"Son of a bitch," he bit out, angry. Jonathan hardly ever got angry. He dialed a number, keeping the phone on speaker.

"Hello, Ewing Academy, Jasmine speaking," a woman's soft, cheery voice came through.

"Hi Jasmine, this is Jonathan Sinclair, Allison Reed's father, how're you doing?"

"Well, thanks, what can I help you with?" The woman sounded like she was typing in the background.

"You can start by connecting me to the principal's office."

"O-Oh...well I think he's in a meeting-"

"Okay, so tell him there's been an urgent matter and I need him to end the meeting to pick up the phone," he growled.

Colin frowned. He hadn't heard him sound like this since their marine days.

"Uhm...I don't think I can-"

"If you value your job, you will."

Colin whistled.

"I'll see what I can do, sir. Please hold." The line went to some cheery music for a couple minutes before an older man came on the line.

"Mr. Sinclair, Principal Felkins speaking. Is everything okay? I hear there's something urgent that you need to speak to us about?" The older man sounded calm. Probably used to dealing with rich assholes.

"Absolutely, I need to know who is on Allison's emergency pick up list and I also need the school's rule on visitors who come in and out of the facility. Are there security measures in place for extenuating circumstances? Are there metal detectors and so forth?"

"Well....let me look at her chart real quick. While I'm doing that, I'll have you know we are a peaceful school, and obviously promote no violence, though we do have two fully armed security officers at the school. We do not have metal detectors, but we do have a state-of-the-art security system on the outside of the buildings that includes the grounds of the buildings and there are cameras in every hallway and in the office. The only places that do not have them are the bathrooms, the teacher break rooms, and the classrooms. In order for a visitor to enter the building, they have to be buzzed in by a staff member, and sign in. They also need to be an approved visitor on an attending child's chart. May I ask what prompted the question, sir?" Principal Felkins' voice sounded confident and sure over the phone.

"Yes, there have been multiple deaths of redheaded women over the last four months around our area, we have reason to believe that my sister-in-law is a target, and these deaths are related to her. Allison is her niece, and we cannot rule out she is a target as well. Last night, there was a redheaded toddler killed with her mother about thirty minutes away from my sister in law's property, and about ten minutes from the school. I would like to have my own security officer accompany Allison to class every day. I need him added to the list. Can I come in tomorrow to give you the information and get this handled please?"

Colin smiled. No ifs ands or butts about it. Jonathan was a bull-dozer.

"Sir-we cannot have an officer who is not through our security company-" Principal Felkins stuttered, sounding slightly offended.

"I need you to really think about your next words, Felkins. Because if anything happens to my daughter while on your property and you've refused my request, I will dismantle your institution with you in it. You feel me?" Jonathan growled down the phone with his deep voice, his face flushing darker as he seethed.

"Sir, there's no need- "

"Oh, there's *every* need. I'll be by tomorrow with the head of the security agency, we will get the school board all the needed information. You will make this happen. Be at your office by tomorrow by 7 a.m. sharp, we'll be waiting,"

And with that, he hung up. Not even waiting for Allison's emergency list.

"You're such a good father," Colin said, no malice in his tone. His anger at their situation had dissipated at some point. He reached his hand out to clasp Jonathan's, feeling his strength. He'd been by his side through everything since he was sixteen years old, and if they had to find themselves in this situation, he couldn't think of anyone who would have his back more.

"Thanks man," Jonathan said, his eyes sorrowful. "Bro... I never told you this but... Ezra was pregnant when she died of her heart attack," his voice came out strained. "Three months."

Colin's eyes widened in shock. The news hit him hard, knowing that Jonathan had been grieving an extra life, unbeknownst to him.

"Jonathan....brother I am so sorry. No, I didn't know," Colin stepped forward and clasped his hand on the back of his neck, squeezing. He was strung tight, and Colin realized he had deep seated fear too, he just handled it better. Probably because he'd already suffered a major loss.

"Man, I want to hunt Carmichael down and fuck him up so bad. He's hunting our girls," Colin breathed, his fist clenching as that ever present cloud of anxiety loomed closer. "I want to kill him, Jonathan. For even have the nerve to touch her, to look at her. To want her when she's not his. Now all these women are dying and...*a child?* What the fuck man?"

"We have to be still and let Howards and Vincent do their thing," Jonathan clipped, looking over at him. "Don't be going off and doing anything reckless Colin."

"Jonathan, come on man. You know I won't."

Jonathan was silent for a heartbeat. Colin bristled, already antici-pating his smart-ass reply.

"Yea...but I also know you want to. And we all know how you are when you don't get what you want," Jonathan mused, looking over the expansive property.

"And can you blame me?" Colin growled. "We finally find a taste of happiness, and look. Just LOOK!" he barked, his eyes flashing.

Jonathan turned to face him head on. "You call me...when you get that urge. You don't need to be alone," Jonathan gritted, face tight.

"Fine. I'll skin that punta *alive,* Jonathan. I'm not going to take many more dead redheads with no results. No justice. The man sits on the fucking bench of the highest order for Christ's sake," Colin gritted, folding his arms and turning away from him slightly. His heart pounded. The thought of the judge hurting Olivia, Allison, Vanes-sa...he just wouldn't tolerate it.

"Not for long. That's why he's becoming reckless. Think about how desperate he must be to kill a child. And besides, you know I'll help you. It'll be like the good old days, yeah?" Jonathan turned an amused smile at his friend.

Colin grunted.

"Bro, I hate to be inappropriate, but what the fuck did she do to the man? He was a client for four years, right? Jesus, well, she drove him legit crazy. He's turned serial killer obsessed and killing children and she didn't even fuck him? Is she a witch or something? Could you imagine holding the amount of power he has and lose your fucking mind like that over a woman you haven't even stuck your cock in? It's kinda eerie," Jonathan half laughed, his cheek twitching from trying to hold off a smile. The situation really wasn't funny, but he had a dark sense of humor.

Colin turned an arched eyebrow at him. Thinking about his and Olivia's sex life. He got a very sickening trickle of fear that he would kill over her. And not just the judge either. He opted not to answer. Jonathan already thought he was losing his mind half the time anyway.

He cocked his head, contemplating ordering her to give him one of the sessions she gave the client. He wasn't into being beaten, but when she put the broken wine glass stem to his neck he definitely got a taste of her wild side and liked it. And when she spoke in his ear after sucking his cock, he realized her tongue was possibly just as bad as her bite. He just hadn't ever given her the chance to show him. He hardened his jaw, feeling it ache.

"Let's get back to the women. Think we need to discuss this shit with them before we upend all of our lives," he said, turning his back on his oldest friend and making his way to the door.

The women were finishing up going over everything they had added to the cart. Vanessa opted not to have a baby registry or formal baby shower. She wanted to have a vacation weekend with Olivia, Aaliyah, Stella, Sara and her former work friend named Elizabeth. She'd asked Jonathan to let all his business associates and friends know that if they wanted to send gifts, the greatest gift they could give is a donation to their local hospital that conducts liver research. Vanessa asked for charity donations instead.

Colin gave the biggest donation, of course.

Jonathan and Colin both fretted over the women going on a trip with all the issues that were going on with the murdered redhead women, and with Vanessa being two months out from her delivery date. However, now with them hiring a security detail and several other women going, they decided they felt slightly better about that decision.

"Excuse me ladies," Colin rumbled in his deep voice, sneaking a glance at the computer and seeing the price tag. His chest visibly swelled at the dollar amount and he smiled. There was no rationale for him to feel the way he felt about spending money.

Both Olivia and Vanessa looked up at the men as they rounded the island to face them.

"Where'd y'all wander off to?" Olivia said, her eyes flicking briefly back to the screen. That's how she'd been coping, not looking at him. If she didn't look at him, she couldn't succumb to his stare. And if she didn't succumb, then she shouldn't be spreading her legs.

Right?

"We both received an email from Vincent," Jonathan said matter of factly across the island. He turned to open up the refrigerator and saw some deli meat and cheese roll ups stacked in a nice little bundle. Courtesy of Mary. "Is this-"

"Yes," Olivia harshly cut him off, with an extremely annoyed look on her face. She swore one of these days she was going to buy a pork hot dog and shove it down his throat.

She grinned, the thought immediately making her feel better.

"Anyways," Colin said, throwing Olivia an amused glance, his eyes raking over her form. She was wearing a burnt orange strapless dress, her gold necklace that said Ally, and simple diamond stud earrings in her ears next to a pair of pearl earrings that she'd never gotten a chance to wear.

Colin remembered the day he took her to get the diamonds. He wanted something much more expensive, but she saw these and fell in love with them. So, not being able to deny her anything, he bought them even though they were one tenth the price of the ones he'd preferred. Then she shocked him by driving them to a tattoo shop where she'd gotten a second piercing in her ears, before she let him take them back to the jewelry department and he'd bought her an expensive pair of real tear drop pearl earrings.

She'd left before her ears were healed up enough to switch out of the starter studs and into other earrings, and he was pleased to see that the pearls were dangling rather nicely next to the small diamonds in her ears. His heart swelled with pride.

Colin watched her tuck the heavy lock of hair that had fallen over her brow and dangled down, curling against the island marble top. She'd had her hair in a deep side part, sort of making herself look like Ariel off the Little Mermaid that Ally loved. That paired with the pearl earrings made him want to buy her a ridiculous mermaid tail. One of those expensive realistic looking ones and then make her do a photo shoot on top of the grotto outside. He grinned, mentally playing the image in his head. He may even play the soundtrack to the movie over the speakers while she poses.

He wondered if he could get a lobster floatation device for the pool.

"Dude what the fuck are you thinking about right now? Jesus," Vanessa said, her eyebrow raised as she frowned at him over the computer.

Colin shook his head of the thoughts as Jonathan munched on the deli rolls and offered him one. He refused.

"I told y'all he's crazy," Jonathan murmured, ignoring the filthy look that Colin threw him as he crossed his arms and looked back at the women across the expansive island.

"Anyways, Vincent just emailed us both. The two of your security details are ready. We'll be going tomorrow after Jonathan and Vincent go to Allison's school to meet the team. Starting tomorrow evening, we'll all have security and Allison will have personal security at school. You'll each get two personal guards. Allison will have one. Both our households have a rotation of two security guards at the house in morning, evening, and night shifts,"

Vanessa looked at Jonathan.

"Jonathan, isn't this a little nuts? That means we'll have three security officers tailing us personally, and six people on the property every day? Can we even have our own security officer at Allison's school? I mean, is that even necessary? It seems like the two of you might be overreacting a little bit," Vanessa said, a frown gracing her face as she sat back to take a sip of water.

"Well," Jonathan said, clearing his throat around a bite of food. We'll actually have seven. Colin and I both have security as well," he said, narrowing his eyes at Vanessa, who'd suddenly hit the keyboard harder than normal, paying for the items in her cart.

"I want to know what you two aren't saying," Vanessa said, closing her laptop and folding her hands on the island. Her curly hair showed beautifully in the light of the kitchen, pregnancy made her absolutely glow. "Because this is fucking ridiculous, to be honest."

Colin clenched his jaw and rolled his lips in between his teeth. He leaned his hips against the counter behind him and crossed his legs. His eyes flickered over to Olivia, who had placed her elbows on the island and threaded her fingers together, leaning her chin on them and regarding him silently.

Jonathan shifted uncomfortably before shooting Colin a quick glance. Both men were trying to wait each other out.

"I know one of you had better answer the fucking question. We're *waiting*," Olivia whispered, her voice tight. Colin's eyes snapped back at her and narrowed.

Not in their home she wouldn't be using that tone of voice. A muscle ticked in his jaw and his fingers twitched. She saw the action and raised her chin at him in a dare.

There was a tense second while they had a rather uncomfortable battle of wills.

"Don't fuck with me Colin," she breathed, her facial expression hardened. She looked wild.

"A green-eyed redhead in her early thirties was found murdered, naked, and decapitated about thirty minutes from here, and ten minutes from Allison's school. The woman's toddler was also found killed, dumped a short ways away in the woods," Colin said, his cold stare hard on hers.

He expected her to pale, but what he didn't expect was the absolutely feral look that came over her face. Her lips pulled back and her teeth bared. She let out a ragged exhale.

"Baby-" Colin said, almost stunned with her transformation.

She turned without a word and disappeared before he heard her slam the door that held her purse. She went back into the kitchen without a word and passed all of them, heading to the mudroom that led to the garage. Vanessa exchanged a panicked look with Jonathan before scrambling off the seat.

"We need to follow her. Let's go," she hissed, snatching her own purse and heading to the front where her and Jonathan's car was situated.

Colin grabbed his own keys racing to the garage as he heard her car door slam and the engine start. Audibly cursing, he flung himself out of the way as she backed up violently, crashing into his bikes again, only taking out three this time. He threw himself into his car and backed out just as the garage doors opened. She revved her engine hard, the tires squealing as she almost clipped the top of her car on the garage doors.

He called her phone over the car. She ignored him. Cursing, he took his phone out of the docking station so the cops wouldn't be alerted to reckless driving.

He peeled out after her, seeing Jonathan's Land Rover pull in easily behind them. The gates opened and she clipped her passenger window. It hit the side of the car hard before flapping in the wind.

Jonathan called him over the speaker. Colin answered.

"Bro, what the fuck is going on? Do we need to call the police?" Jonathan said angrily over the speaker.

"My gut is telling me no. Do you have a gun on you? Mine isn't in this car," he cursed, promising himself to go ahead and order guns for all the vehicles so he didn't have to worry about this again.

"Of course, I stay strapped. Any idea where we're headed? She isn't answering the phone for Vanessa."

"I'm going to take a wild guess and say we're about to see Carmichael," he said, knowing deep in his gut he was right.

"Fucking God, this woman!" Jonathan bellowed.

"I tried to tell you guys she was crazy too!" Vanessa hollered in the background.

"I'M HAVING YOU BOTH FUCKING COMMITED-" Jonathan yelled down the phone. Colin quickly ended the call, revving the engine to keep up with her mangled Porsche. He hated to admit that the big guy was probably justified this time.

He sent Jonathan his location just in case they got separated, but looking into his rearview mirror, he realized that wasn't going to be a problem. If he tapped his breaks too hard, Jonathan would easily rear end him.

Baby what are you thinking? he snarled to himself, his own car almost touching hers as she swerved into the oncoming traffic to pass a slow car, he stayed with her, not even wincing at how close the three of them came to hitting a car head on. He prayed silently that there wouldn't be any cops, trying to figure out a story to tell them as to why they suddenly found themselves in a car chase with the police.

Because he knew she wouldn't stop, and if she wouldn't stop, then he'd be damned if he'd stop either. Vanessa being pregnant was their only out and he would use it unashamedly.

Fifteen minutes later, they rounded into a seriously nice residential neighborhood and he paled as she reached over and typed in a code. The gates opened and she backed up almost slamming into the front of him and she revved her engine so hard he was scared she would blow up her engine. Her car shot forward and she rounded the bend before turning again, and a vast mansion behind a wooden gate loomed in the distance. She revved her engine impossibly harder, and he sent a hail mary up, pressing his fingers into the beads of his mother's rosemary he'd been carrying around with him these last several weeks while he was trying to keep his sanity intact.

"NO!" he yelled out at no one in particular, knowing that she couldn't hear him.

Her car shot forward and he saw her hair slip out the open window of her car as she raced for the gate and crashed into it. She bounced off, denting it hard on its hinges, and she backed up. Colin could hear the car complain as she ripped through the gears, flinging herself forward and barreling completely through the gates in an almighty crash. He followed, watching carefully as she flew into the main yard of the house, ruining every bush flower and shrub as she parked on the walkway. He parked close, leaving his car open in order to get the hell out of there with no problem later. Jonathan pulled in on a squeal behind them, slammed his car door and then they both roared out for Olivia at the same time.

Olivia continued to ignore them. Feeling like she was about to drop dead of a stroke or a heart attack. Her blood was rushing so fast through her body that she felt like any more pressure and she'd implode. Trying the front door and seeing it was locked, she bent down and grabbed a rather large rock with both hands, feeling her right arm strain as she swung it back and crashed it through the window.

"Olivia! You fucking stupid girl," Vanessa screamed, running towards them.

Colin got to her the second she clambered through the window, hearing the alarm system go off. He cursed under his breath, grabbing the sill and climbing in after her, taking a few seconds to take in his surroundings. Olivia was screaming for Carmichael as she walked to the front door, unlocking and opening it. Apparently, she was a tiny bit calmer than he gave her credit for.

It fucking infuriated him. He tamped down those emotions, planning to take it out on her later.

Jonathan barreled in just as soon as Carmichael appeared at the top of the staircase.

Carmichael's older face looked shocked before settling into a sick expression of pleasure and delight at Olivia at the bottom of his stairs. A maid came running from the back of the house, with a dishrag in her hands and a startled look on her face.

Carmichael glanced at her.

"We're fine. I've been expecting them," he said to her. "You can continue cleaning Charlotte," he said, his eyes never leaving Olivia, who was currently breathing so hard she sounded like she could hyperventilate any minute. Carmichael began to walk down the stairs, and Colin reached forward to snatch her to him, backing her up a few steps as the older man approached.

Carmichael didn't look the least bit scared of the four of them in his house. He pulled out a phone and tapped a button, the alarm system stopping. Colin's chest relaxed a tiny amount, and he pulled Olivia back further. His eyes narrowed as she yanked out of his arms and marched up to the man, her head cranked back and she narrowed her own eyes at him.

"Guest house. Now," she snarled up at him, turned on her heels and walked out the door, not waiting for anyone.

Colin gave Carmichael a filthy look as Colin swept his hand out, gesturing for the older man to go ahead of him. He wasn't putting his back to him.

Jonathan gave him a "what the fuck" look as they all filed out of the house, following Olivia to his guest house at the back of the property. She let herself in, stepping through and turning on a light.

Soon, they were all standing in the lush foyer. Colin's eyebrow raised rather judgmentally as he spotted a huge oil painting of the man in his robes, his eyes looking sternly down at them all. Everyone was silent except for Olivia, who continued to pant, fueled with anger and adrenaline.

He tightened his lips, suddenly scared he might beat her to death when they got home because this was beyond a temper tantrum. But then he thought back to the information he'd shared with her and his lips tightened.

Can't blame her, he thought. He stayed on high alert, trusting that Jonathan would know when to use his gun if he needed to.

"You wanted my attention? Well, you've got my *full attention*. START TALKING," Olivia yelled, making Vanessa jump.

Carmichael smiled at her. And Colin's eyes widened at the expression in his face. *Holy fuck, he's crazy.* Colin thought to himself, sharing a look with Jonathan. Of course he's crazy, he's killing people to get to my wife.

"I just want you back, Kat," Carmichael said softly to Olivia, his eyes softened, his demeanor softened, even his crossed arms relaxed.

Colin looked down further before his body tightened in anger. Not everything on him was soft, apparently. He rolled his eyes, he would let Olivia see what he had to say, then get their security team in place and let the man think that they were backing down after this little fiasco. Then he'd pay the man his own visit. He wanted Olivia to get hers first. Because he instinctively knew if he didn't, then their home life was about to suffer in a major way.

She walked a couple steps towards him. "You will never have me," she hissed at him. They stared at each other.

"Kat-"

"You leave my fucking family alone. Do you hear me? You see that woman right there?" she pointed behind her back to Vanessa, who was currently half hiding behind Jonathan, rubbing her belly. Carmichael's eyes shifted to Vanessa and Jonathan stepped the rest of the way in front of her, shielding her from his gaze.

"You get a good motherfucking look at her. I know you think what we had was love, and if you ever thought your love for me was real, then you will leave that woman right there alone. Kill *every* fucking redhead on the planet if you want to. But if you touch her, I'll pay you another visit and this time I'll eat your fucking flesh RAW motherfucker, *WHILE* you're still alive. And you want to know the first cut I'd make?" she whispered, sounding deranged.

"Ew," Vanessa whispered, scrunching her nose.

Carmichael shook his head, something flashing in his eyes.

"Your *tongue*. I'll rip it out of your fucking mouth and eat it happily while you watch," she said softly.

Colin winced, believing her. The weird shit and the weird way she ate convinced him she would actually do it. He frowned again.

Carmichael raised a haughty eyebrow at her, a slight grin on his face.

"I will become your worst nightmare. I wasn't Gypsy's head bitch because I was weak, Carmichael. I was the top dog in a ring of thousands of women. You're stupid, trifling, disgusting, low down, tore back country bumpkin wanna be having ass doesn't scare me," Olivia said with pure disgust, like she just swallowed shit.

"If that's the case," Carmichael said, his eyes narrowing at her. "Then why did you struggle so badly?" he cocked his head at her.

"If I didn't have responsibilities beyond my control, I'd be *ruling* that fucking ring right now. Don't mistake Carmichael. We all have a weakness. I'm apparently yours. Don't fuck with mine. It won't be pretty. I promise you. Colin can't save you from me, the law can't save you from me, no one will be able to save you from me if you don't stop. You should be truly careful which buttons you push. Because if you push the right one Carmichael, I will burn this whole world to the ground," she whispered, staring him down with an expression he couldn't place before turning and walking to the door. She stopped, giving his imposing oil painting a little stare as she hesitated in the doorway.

"Oh, I'll have a tow truck come by momentarily to get my car. If you go to the police about ANY of what's transpired today, I will leak the video of you assaulting me at the gala, and all the times I've recorded our sessions where I've made you tell me about trails that you've falsified and the illegal shit you've been doing in our government."

Colin furrowed his brow deeper, he didn't even think to ask her if she had any dirt on the man they could use.

Carmichael took a step forward, his hands splayed in a gesture of submission.

"Kat-I love you. Why would you do this to me? We're supposed to be together, and yet you're fucking *HIM* when I've been begging you for four years to be with me," he half yelled.

Vanessa gagged.

"There's a very thin line between love and hate, Carmichael. You've overplayed your hand way too soon, in my opinion. Gotta be better than that," and with that she walked out without another word for any of them.

"You're just mad right now!" Carmichael yelled out after her. She flipped him the bird and kept moving. Jonathan confidently sidled through the doorway with Vanessa first and Colin paused before turning back to the old man.

"I only let her do this because she needed it and would be hell on wheels if she didn't get what she wanted. I'd think very carefully about what she's said if I were you. I'll be seeing you around, Carmichael," Colin said, raising his eyebrow against the hate in the man's face.

He walked himself to his car, seeing Olivia already in the passenger seat of his SUV and calling a tow truck. The Porsche was beyond ruined. His phone pinged with a text from Jonathan.

Ya'll deserve each other, that was admirable. Let's meet for lunch, follow me. Vanessa's hungry. -J-Dawg

Fine. -C

***

Thirty minutes later they were sitting at a booth, eating their food at a Mexican restaurant.

Jonathan was looking rather green at Olivia taking a bite out of her order. Braised spicy pig tongue tacos. Colin bit the inside of his cheek to keep from smiling.

"I'm just practicing," she said, before taking another bite and closing her eyes, savoring it.

Colin took a bite of his ranchero steak, watching Vanessa who was attacking her nachos with gusto.

"Sis, watching you smash through that gate was epic, like watching something straight out of a movie. But when you crawled through that window, I about had a heart attack. I did get a little of a lady boner, though. Sorry, you're crazy, but I think you're also my hero," Vanessa said, shoving an impossibly large mouthful in her mouth and moaning. She sat back and rubbed her belly.

"I guess we don't need to lecture you about how dangerous that could have been?" Jonathan said across the table, wincing as Olivia bit through a piece of gristle, her teeth grinding. She swallowed.

I don't give a fuck if you lecture me or not. The point stands, Jonathan. He fucks with what's mine, then he'll get what's coming to him. You guys don't understand what I'm talking about. But I guarantee you that he does. He can decide whether or not he wants to take that risk," Olivia chirped back, seriously looking like she didn't just have a manic episode, burst through some gates, trashed her car, and broke into a man's house. Just thirty minutes ago.

She looked like she was glowing. She'd been in her element.

"The point was, for him to stay away from the three-*four* of you guys," she stared rather blatantly at Jonathan.

"Allison," Jonathan breathed.

She nodded her head.

"If anything, I've bought us some time to get the team going, to iron out any kinks, and to get a new schedule in place if we need to," she whispered. Throwing down her last taco, not wanting it as she was full.

"So would you-would you really do what you said back there?" Jonathan said, conversationally, as if they weren't talking about cannibalism to a woman who was just eating pig tongue.

She smiled, folding her arms under her breasts.

"I'm surprised Jonathan, you of all people should know that when a person gets pushed beyond their limits then they'll do crazy stuff to survive. Right?" she asked, tilting her head and regarding him tightly. He'd shared a few stories with her about his past as a torture specialist.

They all finished their food before walking outside to the parking lot.

"Vincent and I are meeting at Allison's school tomorrow at seven in the morning to get the security shit figured out, then we'll all meet up at Vincent's office to meet with the teams and go over protocol, correct?" Jonathan said, wanting confirmation. He placed his arm around Vanessa and held her close.

Colin nodded, taking Olivia's waist and pulling her close as well. The woman was magnetic. He agreed with Vanessa that what she did today was straight out of a movie, and he didn't think he'd be erasing that particular scene from his head anytime soon.

However, she was still going to be punished for doing it. And he began to formulate a plan.

EIGHTEEN
3, 2, 1, Zero

"OHHHH SIR," OLIVIA WHIMPERED as Colin thrust nice and slow into her.

It was early the next morning, still dark outside, and he had her on her knees in the shower and had been fucking her for well over an hour this way. He did not care about how wet she was as the water was pounding down on them, washing it all away anyways. She was shaking, the hard thrusts he was treating her to jiggled her ass and her breasts, her hair hanging wet and wild down her face.

She'd lost count of how many orgasms she'd had. Her chest hurt, tightening painfully in preparation for another one. She let out a ragged whimper, feeling herself clamp down impossibly tight around him.

"Stop shutting me off Olivia, open up and take it beautiful. Your creamy pussy takes such a good beating, doesn't she?" Colin growled.

Imagining her teeth bared yesterday as she threatened the judge, he thrust harder. He yanked her butt cheeks apart, spreading her mercilessly. He'd never tolerate her looking at him like that. The thought made him absolutely feral.

"Oh *God*!" Olivia complained, arching her back and lowering the rest of the way to the floor, the side of her face and her breasts pressed into the tile as he circled his hips on a deep grind, giving her several hard thrusts slightly to the right, brushing her cervix making her scream.

A thrill raced through him at the sound and he repeated the movement, observing the muscles on her back stand out in sharp relief as she tightened up. He grabbed her hair and snatched her up, arching her neck back.

The water splashed erotically around him as he pressed hard down on her hips, splaying her against the shower, grinding her pussy into the tile. He threw all of his body weight into her, bouncing off her pussy with every hard stroke. He let go of her hair and grabbed her breast with one hand, and her throat with the other. He pulled out and pressed into her anus.

"Colin!" she screeched wildly, trying to buck against him, forcing him to lock himself around her harder.

"Hmmm?" he growled into her ear as he pressed hard, feeling her flesh give. She suddenly stilled, her eyes wild.

Oh my God, why's he fucking me like this? she thought. She shuddered, feeling her heart race as she attempted to calm herself down.

"What's the matter baby?" he whispered into her ear. "Did you have something you wanted to say to me?" Colin bit out, licking into her ear. He gave her nipple a roll and sharp tug as he pulled out and pressed forward, slapping into her.

"I'll fucking kill him, Olivia. Before I ever let him get his hands on you. I'll kill us all before he ever gets to taste this body. You know that don't you?" he said, letting his evil side come out to play.

Colin let go of her throat and pushed her hair out of the way before resting his hand heavily on her back. He gave her steady pressure, digging his palm into her flesh. He suddenly raised his hand and slapped it down hard onto the upper left side of her back, causing her to jerk and scream in surprise. She turned to look at him with wide, shocked eyes.

"Turn your head back *around*," Colin gritted through his teeth. She obediently turned and placed the side of her face back on the tile. He rested his hand there on her back again, before repeating the stinging motion.

Olivia shrieked again at the burning pain of his hand, meeting her flesh repeatedly. He did this for long minutes listening for her safe word if she so needed to use it, his palm hitting every inch of her back until her cries turned into moans.

"This body's fucking mine. Not his, *it's not even yours*. It's *mine*," Colin said with an eerie growl that reverberated throughout the shower. "That's everyone's fucking mistake right now. You all think this body is yours to do with as you please. It's not! And one day soon, I'm going to show you just how serious I am," he snarled, his palm hitting her flesh, rubbing then repeating the motion.

"Colin!" she screamed, tears escaping her eyes.

He continued with the hard thrusts and the hard slaps on her back, not even reprimanding her for using his name.

"Shut up!" he shouted. "What's even worse is that I can fucking relate to the sick son of a bitch. If you went away and were with another man, I'd probably be doing the same thing he's doing. Killing everybody, losing my fucking sanity, knowing another man was sinking his cock into you. What the fuck are you doing to us?! Fucking bitch driving us crazy!" he half shouted, delivering another sharp blow to her back as he thrust impossibly deep, drawing a high scream out of her. He fucked her for several long minutes, his blows on her back becoming less and less frequent as she slipped into subspace.

A series of broken moans sounded from her as Olivia shivered, his words, and his manipulation of her nipple throwing her off the cliff as she orgasmed with a weak moan. Her body sagged weakly, but still he thrust, trying to find his. Refusing to not be satisfied.

He pulled up her hips suddenly and yanked her back on him, she screamed anew and clamped down on him so hard his eyes rolled, and he grit his own teeth, snarling as he thickened and combusted inside of her.

He laid himself on top of her, breathing hard as they both splayed on the shower floor, feeling the water getting colder as they struggled to regain their senses. With a groan he got up, slapping his hand against the control panel and turning off the spray. He bent down and picked her weak form off the tile, carrying her back to bed.

"In a little bit when you're settled, I'm going to brush your hair, Okay?" he said as he sat on the bed next to her, his thumb caressing her cheek intimately. Listening to her low whimpers. He might have said too much in the shower, but he meant every word, even though they came out sounding half crazed with jealousy, possessiveness, and lust. It was truly motivated by fear.

He crawled in next to her and curled himself around her trembling form.

It was a rare day that he had them do anal, he was a very big man, and it wore her out sometimes beyond reason. So, he chose carefully what days to do this on. Today was just one of those days. Her freak out yesterday bothered him more than he cared to admit, and he woke up early with a full on panic attack. He'd had a dream that Carmichael kidnapped her and was raping her in front of him as he lay there dying. And that was his last sight on earth, his wife being violated while he lay dying, unable to save her. And he'd be damned if that ever happened.

He inched closer, pressing his lips against the hair at her ear, nudging it away until he found the bare skin of her neck.

"Such a good girl, mamacita," he murmured to her in her deep voice, calming her, giving her kisses. He rubbed his hands down her arms, her stomach, her hips, cradling her until the trembling stopped. Colin looked down at her. "I'm going to go get the brush, it's going to be an emotional day and I think we both need this baby. Can I? Will you let me?" he said to her again in his deep voice, leaning down to press his lips against hers firmly.

"Yes," Olivia said softly, looking up at him through shiny green eyes observing another tear slip out. She was emotional, as she always was after he'd had her the way he did in the shower. Her breaths rose and fell with small whimpers, and she moaned when he dipped down and sucked her nipple into his mouth with a desperate groan. Not able to get enough. It was never enough. Would never be enough.

Colin turned, placing himself between her legs and lowering his weight into her.

"Maybe just one more, to settle you first," he said, taking her lips in a wet smacking kiss before lowering his head to her nipple once more, thrusting up and into her gently. Hearing her cries as he circled his hips.

"We're not getting up until I know you're okay," Colin said, raising his head and looking deep into her eyes. Feeling his heart tug for his wife, this beautiful woman.

Whoever said gingers had no souls were lying. They had their own and were adept at stealing everyone else's apparently. Lord knows Olivia had a firm hold on his. Moving firmly inside of her, their green silk sheets falling and rising with his hips, he maintained his gaze with hers as he thought about this woman's spirit and her bravery yesterday.

He moved up that visit he planned on paying to Carmichael.

***

Colin was downstairs in the kitchen, making scrambled eggs for egg sandwiches, waiting for Olivia to come down. She was taking her time this morning getting ready. He thought about what he said to her in the shower, hoping he didn't scare her. He put the top on the pan of eggs to keep them hot as he snatched up his phone, leaning his hips against the counter. It was almost seven forty-five and he'd been waiting for Jonathan to text him about his meeting with Allison's principal.

What's going on brother? -C. Kent

And a message to Vincent, who was with Jonathan.

Hey Vincent, Are we're still on to meet in an hour?-Colin

He put his phone down and looked out the window above the sink. The sky was not looking like it was going to turn that beautiful blue it normally does, however, there was supposed to be a bad storm later on in the morning. He then took a second to call Mary, asking her to please make sure that the lanterns and lighters were all out in one spot in the lounge so they could get to them easily if they needed to and then told her to go home early.

Colin had a generator but you just never know, could never be too careful. He took out four slices of bread and began to butter two pieces, and put mayonnaise on the two along with a slice of tomato. The butter was for him, mayonnaise was for Olivia. A lot of the time, he still thought the way she ate was revolting, but he'd come to love her for it. He knew she was going to not be happy with so many carbs early in the morning, but she'd get over it.

We're finishing up at the school. They let us bring in our own security officers. You good?- J. Dawg

Yes, it's just been a long morning already. Olivia's nervous. The thought of having a security detail is fucking with her head. -C. Kent

Vanessa is thankfully not taking it too hard. I think yesterday scared the shit out of her, and she's got the baby and all the hormones. And Allison. She's on the other side of the pendulum. Your wife on the other hand, the way she crawled in that window, bruh. She once told me that I married the evil sister, and I'm telling you that I think you married the insane one. -J. Dawg

Colin snorted, finishing putting the sandwich together and wrapping it in a paper towel before putting it into the warming drawer. He pulled up his text thread to Olivia.

Come on baby we gotta eat so we can go. -C. Kent

Vincent responded.

Yes. We'll be there in maybe under an hour. There's a storm coming.-V

His ears pricked as he heard her bare feet hitting the wood floor as she padded down the hallway. He looked up from his phone as the juicer finished doing its thing with the oranges, filling the second glass.

His eyes tightened and his heart skipped a beat as she came around the corner, a cream suit jacket in between her teeth, her purse hanging from one hand, and her shoes dangling from the other. She tilted her head, draping the jacket across one of the stools on the island and plopping her purse down and bending to put her shoes on. Sky high heels, no doubt chosen specifically to test him.

Narrowing his eyes slightly, he reluctantly dragged his eyes up her body to land on hers.

"It's going to storm today," he said, fighting a rising desire that was settling inside of him, despite how viciously he'd just taken her. She was beautiful, dressed in a cream pantsuit with a soft pastel lavender purple silk top that her breasts did wonderful things to. The blouse was held up by delicate tiny straps on her shoulders.

"I know," Olivia breathed, bending down again and disappearing momentarily behind the island with the other shoe. She hopped as she put it on and stood up in a huff, blowing her perfectly blow-dried hair out of the way. She was wearing her pearls and diamonds again.

"Where's your diamond watch?" he asked inquisitively as he pulled their sandwiches out of the drawer and pushed hers towards her.Sh ortly after a crack of lightning, a boom of thunder made her jump.

He wished to God they could stay in today; he loved making love to her during a thunderstorm.

"It's upstairs," she replied, eyeing her sandwich and only picking up one half of it that he'd cut. Her nose crinkled as she picked the sandwich apart, smiling with joy as she saw all the mayonnaise he'd put on there for her. "Thank you baby," she sighed, putting her elbows on the island, leaning in so she could eat over the counter without getting anything on her blouse.

He tilted his head and licked his lips as the action caused her to stick her butt out far, giving him a generous view of her ass in the tight cream pants she was wearing.

"You're welcome. The watch?" he pressed, taking his own bite. They had breakfast together every day and he loved that.

"I've got too much money on today," she mumbled around the food in her mouth, swallowing it down with fresh squeezed orange juice. He raised his eyebrow in amusement.

She's so silly, it's adorable, but not acceptable, he thought to himself.

"Not enough for me. Go back upstairs when you're done eating and put it on, please," he demanded softly, taking another bite and mentally calculating how much he figured she was worth today by her clothes. His mental tally came up close to twelve thousand by her outfit, shoes, jewelry, and lingerie alone. The watch would push her to fifty grand, his sweet spot.

Though, she truly was priceless to him. However, he loved their little game.

"Ok fine," she grumbled, reaching around her purse and pulling out her back up pill case. She popped out several pills into her palm. Holding his sandwich aloof in the air, his eyes narrowed again as he fought the rising irritation, feeling it cancel out the desire that almost always ate at his soul when it came to Olivia.

"Why are there four pills instead of three?" he asked, strumming his fingers of his free hand irritably on the island, not bothering with his sandwich.

"Oh, it's depression medicine, birth control and ibuprofen," she said, washing it down with the juice. Colin's eyebrows hit the roof and he stood there stunned for a moment.

"What?" he asked, putting down his sandwich.

"Yeah, I got this from Stella, then I called my doctor to make an appointment. I've been crying a lot. Ever since China," she said quietly, sipping more of her juice. Her eyes shifted rather uncomfortably away from him. Guilt of hiding this from him plagued her.

"Okay...but that's really something you need to talk to me about, baby. I need to know these things," Colin said gently, taking her empty plate and cup from her and putting it in the dishwasher. He fought back the sudden wave of emotion threatening to overcome him. He couldn't stand to see her sad, it made him physically ill. Taking a second to himself, he contemplated their age gap, how hard it's been to let go of her independence.

The fact that she didn't tell him she added a medication to her daily pill routine bothered him. He took a deep breath, not wanting to rock the boat considering he'd just gotten her back.

"Is it because of all this stuff? We've been going through a lot of shit baby. I wish you would have told me you were feeling like this," he said, turning back to her and seeing her rub her hand down her arm. The rain pounded steadily against the skylight and the back of the house that the kitchen faced.

"Well, I'm just going to try it and see if it helps. Jonathan gave me his psychiatrist friend's name, Dr. Richardson, to contact if it gets to be too bad. But I'm starting with a therapist first, her name is Sarah Johnson...I'm sorry, I should have talked about it, but I didn't want to give you another reason to worry. You have a lot on your plate. Your life didn't use to be like this before I got here," she said quietly, her eyes falling to the island between them. Her lips pouted, betraying her emotion.

Colin pushed off the counter and rounded the island. *Fuck if we're dealing with unnecessary distance,* he thought to himself, pulling her into his arms.

"That's where you're wrong. It was worse. I had nothing to live for then," he said, putting his lips to her hair and smelling her strawberry vanilla shampoo. "I love you, Olivia."

"I love you too, baby," she sighed, hugging him tight.

"Now go put your watch on please," Colin said, giving her ass a pat, making her skip a step as she hobbled away. She tried to hide it but there was a visible limp in her gait. He smiled, turning to grab his keys.

***

Forty-five minutes later, they were in Vincent's security building in an obscure plot of land surrounded by trees and gates. They joined Vanessa and Jonathan in a plush, well decorated sitting room with leather seats and a huge aquarium that housed mini sharks which Jonathan was currently standing before staring at, fascinated.

Vanessa sat across from them with air pods on, listening intently to the band's rendition of her song she recorded for them a month ago. She'd taken up Elijah's offer and was demoing some covers for them while waiting for the baby to be born.

Olivia was reading a book and Colin's eyebrow went up as he snuck and read with her over her shoulder. He broke out in a grin, thinking that the main characters might give them a run for their money. Whatever she was reading was crazy. He looked at the side of her face, she was giving no indication she was reading smut. The woman could have a poker face sometimes, but not with him.

"That's very interesting baby, we should try that sometime," he whispered in her ear, and she turned off her phone with a gasp, the color coming up into her face finally. He chuckled, pressing her against his chest and kissing the side of her head.

Stella walked in, and Colin almost did a double take at the gorgeous statuesque African American beauty. He nodded in approval at her business suit.

They assessed each other for style every time they met up, and this had become his and Stella's own little game. He noted that she had traded her usual braided style for a flowing style, with hair halfway down her back and boasting a middle part. She looked like an African goddess in gold color that set off her skin tone perfectly.

You'd never know by looking at her that she was a brat and needed frequent punishments according to Vincent.

"Wow," Olivia breathed, standing up gracefully and walking into Stella, giving her a hug. "You look gorgeous, friend. This color is to die for!"

"Thanks girl. I'm loving that pantsuit. What are we clocking today? About forty-five grand it looks like?" Stella leaned in and whispered with a small giggle at her friend. Olivia had shared their daily vie for power, and it started with how much money she was ordered to wear on her person at all times.

Colin grinned, letting out a little chuckle. Thinking that the joke was on Olivia anyway, because her wedding ring alone was four times that much. But she didn't need to know that.

Stella thought it was cute.

"Are you all ready? Vincent is ready for the four of you in our big conference room," she said, holding the door open and letting them out into an expansive hallway. All the doors were wooden and there were no glass windows anywhere.

"So, Nessie, when are we dueee?" Stella crooned, stroking her hand down Vanessa's belly as they walked. Vanessa had the cutest waddle.

"Supposed to be seven weeks," Vanessa said with a little laugh. "But he feels like a freaking bowling ball so he can come out whenever. My god. The doctor said he's already eight pounds, can you believe it?" Vanessa said, placing a hand on her lower back and pressing.

"Girl that's what C-sections and vaginal tightening surgeries are for," Stella joked, making them all laugh as they rounded the corner. She opened another door and let them into a huge room with nineteen intimidating men and Vincent, making up the twentieth. He was sitting at the head of a thirty-foot table, a huge projector screen on the other side of the room across from him. The teams looked like they were split into two sides. Colin's and Olivia's on one side of the table, Jonathan's and Vanessa's on the other side.

Vincent stood up, welcoming them and waving them in.

Olivia's eyes perused every one of them. She stared hard, getting her bearings; and they stared back too. One of the men, closest to Vincent on the right side of the table, had an intimidating scar slashed across his face. He was extremely muscular, but not bulky. His hair was in a buzz cut and he wore all black. He stood there staring silently. No life in his eyes. She felt a shiver go up her spine. The man's aura was heavy and trained straight on hers. Her eyes widened.

Fucking God. Olivia whined in her head. *Please don't be ours,* she silently prayed.

She glanced at the other members; the guy next to him was intimidating but the bullshit didn't roll off of him like the first one. Everyone around the table looked lethal, in control, like they'd seen shit, did shit, and knew shit.

Shit, Olivia tightened her lips before taking Vincent's warm handshake, not quite able to look him in the eye. The testosterone in the room was killing her. She looked across the table at Vanessa, who was being helped into one of the empty chairs next to Vincent, on the same side as the intimidating scar face guy.

Olivia breathed a sigh of relief, settling into the chair that was on the opposite side.

Oh dear God, thank you. We can officially be friends again, she offered Vincent a tiny smile as she leaned back in her chair, waiting for them all to settle. Stella took the second seat at the head of the table, throwing Olivia a glance that made her look at her phone, seeing her friend had texted her.

I'm sorry-I just want you to know that I tried. -Stella.

Olivia's brows furrowed and she glanced up at Stella who was shooting her a little apologetic glance before turning her face to her husband who started speaking.

And then Olivia's stomach fell through the floor. She stood there, mute, trying to process what her friend's husband was saying. And when it finally clicked, she let out a hilarious laugh. Shaking her head.

Jonathan was looking rather alarmed at her, leaning in to whisper something to Vanessa who was shooting her a 'what the hell' glance.

Olivia sat in her chair giggling. Uncontrollably. Like about to pee-my-pants uncontrollably. So she looked at Colin and said it.

"If I fucking pee myself it's going to be all your fault. Because I can't believe what the fuck I just heard," she said leaning forward and putting her forehead very unlady-like against the table, shaking she was laughing so hard. She looked up at Vincent.

"I'm sorry Vincent, can you just say it again please. Because this is fucking crazy," she said to the African American man, who was sitting back, reaching into his pocket. He suddenly took out a small device and slid it across the table to the scarred man who he'd just introduced as Zero.

Her personal security detail. One of two.

Zero's hand reached out and snagged the object, spinning it around in front of him before he stopped it facing her. He picked it up and she heard a click. She raised her eyebrows before looking over at Stella, who had unconsciously scootched back in her seat. She looked back at Zero before sitting back in her seat and smiling.

Fuck this, Olivia thought.

"Click," she whispered across the table at him. She felt Colin stiffen before turning to look at her with an incredulous expression. She ignored him.

Zero picked up the device and clicked it again. She tilted her head.

"Click," she said louder as she crossed her arms and legs, throwing Zero a filthy stare. The other men on either side of the table watched this interaction carefully.

Zero clicked the device again. Still saying not a word.

"Cli-"

"Olivia," Colin said, his voice sounding so deep and hoarse. Like he was trying to keep from strangling her so he was strangling himself instead. "Fucking stop it,"

She turned and looked at him, her lips twisted. She looked back at Vincent.

"He's not coming on my team," she snarled.

"Why?" Vincent said, his baritone slightly louder than she was used to hearing from him.

"Because this is MY body and I fucking said I don't want him BODYGUARDING IT. That's why!" she leaned forward and hissed the words at her friend's husband.

Colin turned her in her chair abruptly, making her cry out in shock at the violent motion, her fingers curled under the lip of her seat and her eyes went wide. Colin leaned forward with an audible rumble that stopped her heart momentarily before he leaned even further forward, getting into her face. She paled, leaning back and scooching down in her chair. She shook her head minutely.

Not her body. *His.* Colin's. Olivia gasped as the words bounced around her head, making her dizzy.

"I'm sorry, I'm sorry, I'm sorry," she whispered, the words barely making it out. She understood him without him having to say anything. The clicker clicked two more times and her mouth dropped as she craned her neck to look around him at Zero. Still staring at her impassively.

Colin roughly grabbed her by her chin and firmly turned her face back to his. His eyes were cold as they stared into her. He remained silent and Olivia felt her heart rate ramp up so uncomfortably that it was almost choking her. She stared back, blinking the rising tears away.

"This is why," Vincent barked, slamming his hand down on the table so hard that Stella pushed back in her chair all the way to the wall behind them. "This is why we are having this meeting today all together instead of two separate meetings," he stood up, placing his hands behind his back in an intimidating stance.

"Olivia is a flight risk and she will put herself in danger when provoked. You *ALL* need to see the attitude and what she's capable of. If she is in your presence, you protect her just as if she was Vanessa. Do you understand me? She will engage with Carmichael. She threatened him just yesterday, bursting down his gate and breaking into his house. This is unacceptable, and anyone who is found lagging in regards to the safety of this family will be immediately terminated, and your security license revoked without question," Vincent boomed, his speech aimed at the Sinclair team, who was commissioned for Jonathan and Vanessa. Everyone at the table nodded, regardless of whose team they were on.

Oh my God, Olivia's eyes widened, still on Colin's. Whose eyes were unwavering on hers.

She turned her gaze back to Zero. *"Not him,"* she said out loud. Uncaring of the speech Vincent just made. She was going to be heard.

"Why?" Zero questioned her now, and Olivia felt her entire body stand at attention. It was as if a cord was attached to a string on her spine and someone was standing over her pulling her up. She cursed as she felt her nipples harden and she didn't know why. She wasn't even attracted to this man. She was suddenly grateful for her jacket, to hide it.

The man's voice sounded like Lucifer himself. It was scratchy, raw, unfiltered, and dangerous.

Her eyes widened. "That's why. You're too much like my husband and I don't like it," she hissed.

Zero nodded once standing up and brushing his hand down his shirt calmly, before rounding the table behind Vincent and coming up to her side. She moved quickly, scooting herself into Colin's lap and pulling her legs up, her heels digging into her husband's thighs. She watched as Zero sat on the table next to her and looked down at her with that cold stare of his.

"This is why I'm here. For you. To keep you in line. When you're not with Mr. McDermont, you answer to me," he said simply. His big hand reached out and she moaned as Colin reached forward to shake it.

"No. No. You're my security so you answer to *me,*" she whispered. The room was deathly quiet. Aside from a click.

"What?" Stella breathed from her seat across the room. "Why do I get a click?" she said tearfully.

"Because your friend is a pain in the ass," Vincent growled in reply, sitting back in his chair.

"You will answer to me, or you will get no freedom. I know you, Kat," he said quietly, his eyes on hers.

Olivia's jaw dropped. It clicked, quite literally, why she didn't like him.

He used to be security for one of her more prolific and powerful clients, and he would stand outside the door in the shadows and make sure she didn't go too far with the one particular client she had who liked more nefarious sessions than others.

"Oh my God, it's *you*," she breathed. Zero nodded with just the barest hint of a grin that betrayed a dimple in his cheek.

"So, I'm actually more qualified than everyone here in this room as to what you're capable of because I've actually seen you in action and let me tell you," his eyes slid to Colin's. "She's *wicked*. A fucking true born manipulator, Medusa herself. We nicknamed her Lilith."

Colin raised his eyebrow, amused by this. Lilith couldn't be dominated.

Olivia's mouth fell open as she bristled. *No the fuck this man didn't.*

"Lilith? What a fucking insult," she said, her face scrunched up as Zero continued, his eyes still trained on Colin, effectively ignoring her.

"She was the best, I'm talking *head honcho* status. Whatever she said to Carmichael yesterday, I'd take it as gospel. She's more than capable of it. How on earth did you manage to nail down this? I would pay good money to have seen that in action. Mad respect brother," his eyes slid to Olivia's and perused down Olivia's huddled form, still snuggled on top of Colin's.

Zero got up and resumed his seat and Olivia sat back down in hers quietly. Colin's rough style of domination this morning made sense. He already knew what was going to happen today.

She huddled tightly against herself, only looking up to nod to the rest of the folks on her team. The men had already vetted the teams, now they were going over their house layout, a security manual for the home and what guys would be on what shifts for the house. Mary was even brought into it somehow, but Olivia was already retreating in her head, looking to the side blankly, wondering how she could get away with killing Carmichael so they could be done with all this.

Then she knew. That's why they gave her who they gave her. She wasn't on her own anymore; she had multiple people's safety to look out for. She wasn't superwoman anymore, slaying dragons on her own and conquering demons. She bit her lip, chancing a look at her husband, aware of Zero's eyes on her every movement. Learning her.

Colin was in complete control. She reddened as she realized he even let her have her little outburst as a lesson to everyone there what they were dealing with. Her eyes narrowed.

Was she ever really in control with him? She couldn't tell.

Olivia felt physically sick when she was told she was basically going to always be followed from here on out. Until the Carmichael situation gets resolved, anyway. She couldn't go anywhere without a security detail. If she was driving, they had to be in the car, and one tailing her. They would be with her on campus, when she went on outings, the grocery store, she damn near wouldn't be able to go to the bathroom without someone knowing about it.

"Olivia!" Colin said sharply, shaking her out of her thoughts. She looked up from staring at the floor as if in a daze, noticing the place was silent. Her sister was looking at her with a melancholy expression. "What was that?" he asked, leaning into her with an eyebrow raised. She had said her thoughts out loud and didn't realize it. She blinked.

"I said, given the first chance, I'm going to find him and take his life away. Because he's taking mine, ours," she gritted, the tears finally falling through angry eyes and her breath hitched as she assessed her husband with emotion.

Pushing back in her seat, she stood up calmly, taking off her jacket, her earrings, her watch before pinning Zero boldly with a stare. The men all watched quietly.

"Olivia, you're foolish," Vanessa said across the table, her cat eyes narrowed at her sister.

Olivia leaned forward, placing her hands on the table, not even caring if her blouse gaped open for everyone to see.

"I'm a fucking survivor," she yelled, baring her teeth at her sister before turning her eyes to Zero. "You have no fucking clue what I'm capable of. He hasn't tamed me," she whispered, jerking her head to Colin who sat there quietly, crossing his ankle over his knee and remaining silent. Zero stood up.

"Let's go," she said. "You think you can handle this? Let's see what you got, since you know me so. Fucking. Well," she hissed this last part.

"Okay Lilith, after you," Zero said, his hands at attention behind his back.

"Let her go," Vincent said quietly to Colin. "and observe what you're paying for," he turned his eyes to Zero. "No hitting her in the face."

Colin sat back, nodding his head, accepting a drink from Jonathan, who had poured something for them to take the edge off.

Olivia turned and walked out of the room barefoot, hearing nothing behind her. She pushed through the other doors until she made her way out of the building into the storm outside. She turned on her heel, beginning to run, her red hair flying behind her as lightning cracked the sky around them.

She was quite literally going to give the security a run for their money.

***

Olivia laid back in the bathroom hours later, sitting back in a steaming hot tub with the window cracked, letting the sounds of the storm in. There were lit candles stationed in various spots in the spacious room and the recessed lights were dimmed. Grateful for the dark, moody atmosphere that matched her mood she turned back to her phone after taking a sip of wine. Her phone was on a holding receptacle that sat across the tub.

She was currently on a group facetime call with Vanessa, Stella, and Aaliyah and she moaned as she moved her aching muscles, closing her eyes on a wince.

"See that's what you get for being such a hard headed bitch," Stella said, angry with her.

Olivia winced, thinking she really showed out today. If she hadn't been in so much pain, she'd be rather proud of herself. She took both Zero and Byson on a straight up manhunt, though she could tell they were all toying with each other. She came to the conclusion that whatever they were getting paid for their services, it probably wasn't enough.

"Yo, you threw a brick at Zero?" Aaliyah gasped in shock. Stella had sent them the security footage of her episode today outside of the building and she was watching it on replay. "Girl, I didn't know you had moves like this oh my God,"

"Yeah, and he caught that shit with his bare hands then threw dirt at her face, blinding her," Stella said, a little eye roll breaking through.

"He fucked up my cream pantsuit," Olivia moaned, sinking further into the water.

"Serves you right," Vanessa said, annoyed.

"They were out there for over an hour fighting, running, being straight chaotic. One of our security cars has to be replaced," Stella said, huffing as she threw herself into a comfy looking bean bag that swallowed her whole. "But the best was when Zero kept calling her 'Lilith', he was chanting it while they were out in the storm being children. Apparently, that was your girl's nickname back in the day when she was head honcho of Esmerelda's Ring," Stella said, filling Aaliyah in on everything that came out in the boardroom today.

Aaliyah grunted and then was silent. She was still pissed and in disbelief that her oldest friend was involved to the extent that she was. "But you're a badass. So that's all that matters, eh Ollie?" Aaliyah finally spoke, breaking her silence.

All the women murmured their agreement, even Vanessa who didn't even want to talk to her right now.

"Well, enough about that please. Let's talk about Vanessa's vacation we're supposed to be going on in a week! We're decided on Bora Bora right?" Olivia said, pulling up her browser and looking up resorts.

"Yes," Vanessa said, a crash blared through the phone as she dropped something, followed by a rather unladylike grunt as bent down to pick it up. They saw her stoic looking security guard turn the corner and her irritated "I'm fine. Thank you," before he walked away.

"Jesus fucking Christ. I can't even have the pregnancy farts anymore," Vanessa huffed, sitting down at her island, and pushing her hair out of the way. They all busted out laughing.

"Okay, well there's a private Villa with a private beach near nice eateries, and it has a separate wing for the boys," Olivia stated, sharing her screen with them. She took a slow minute scrolling through all the pictures for them to see.

"For the boys?" Aaliyah said in an irritated tone. "This is supposed to be a not-a-baby-shower-girls-trip! Why are they coming?"

Stella shook her head, her beautiful mouth pouting, as Vincent suddenly appeared on the screen as he gave her a rather raunchy kiss followed by a hard slap that no one could tell where it landed.

"Owww, Goddammit V!" Stella complained, her face scrunching up.

Suddenly Colin came into the bathroom, and Jonathan appeared on the screen with Vanessa. Olivia hurriedly scooted down in the water hiding with a horrified look on her face.

"You guys what the fuck," Olivia hissed, her face now screwed up in annoyance. Her face was red on the screen. "Any one of us could be naked at any given time!" she said, pulling more bubbles to cover her chest.

"Well, then don't facetime while you're in the bathtub Ukhat!" Jonathan joked, giving her his toothiest smile yet. "Hey, I wanted to congratulate you on a job well done, huh? Vincent sent us all the security footage of you and Zero and man! Wow! Your ass should have been in the army, Lilith!"

Her jaw dropped and she cracked her head sharply to look at Colin, who'd squatted behind her and put his lips to her neck with an amused chuckle.

She turned back and scowled hard at the screen.

"Yes, we have to come, Beau," Colin replied, using Olivia's nickname for her best friend. "Everyone's under security watch right now. How bad would it be if while you're out of the state something detrimental happened. It would be hours before we could get to you," Colin said rather sternly, his fingers digging into Olivia's shoulders and massaging her sore muscles firmly.

Though Colin was pissed at her temper and outbursts today, the stories that Zero shared with him gave him a fresher perspective on this woman. She was a beast, and he'd tamed her somehow. A grin graced his face at the knowledge, and unbeknownst to her, his chest puffed out slightly with male triumph.

"Ladies, I'll take care of the arrangements, ok? You don't have to worry about anything. We'll sit back, out of your hair and smoke our cigars and just be men in Bora Bora," he smiled as Stella shot him a disbelieving look through the screen.

Aaliyah tsked. "I don't even believe that shit though forreal," she said with a slight laugh. "But uhm, bring me one of those cigars you like, and I'll smoke with yall and be friendly. Now, love yall but I gotta go eat some ass now. Bye," and with that she hung up.

They all either laughed uncontrollably or hid in embarrassment. Olivia did both.

"Bye you guys," she said with a little wave as she disconnected the call and sat back with a sigh. Colin stood up and disappeared, coming back with a warm towel.

"Up you get, Lilith," he joked, unplugging the tub and helping her up. Though he thought she'd put herself through it, he was sympathetic to her plight as she'd really been through a lot today. He wrapped the towel around her carefully, pulling her wet hair out from where it was snagged in the towel.

"*Oww,* and stop calling me that," she complained with a wince, her body smarting everywhere.

"Yikes, that's not a word that I'd have thought was in your vocabulary, beautiful," Colin said, a twinkle in his eyes. He'd been in a much better mood once he saw how well Zero handled Olivia. He didn't like him throwing dirt at her, but he wanted to see exactly how far she was wanting to push things, and what Zero's response would be to her.

Colin was worried that they'd wind up with a security guard that would be easily manipulated. However, because Zero knew Olivia's mannerisms, he had a heads up. He'd previously asked what the name Zero meant, knowing it wasn't his God given name. And Zero explained to Colin that he'd earned his name because he had zero failures. He scored every time.

Colin breathed a genuine sigh of relief for the first time in weeks. He picked her up carefully, ignoring her little whines as he carried her to the vanity and blow dried her hair. He took the brush and caught her eye, not wanting to trigger her. This was brand new between them, so he was going slow. Olivia gave him a little nod and he kissed her lightly in between brushes, telling her how amazing he thought she was.

She listened quietly as the brush whooshed through her hair stroke after stroke and he turned the blow dryer on. He gave her a cheeky grin and massaged the muscles at her nape as he dried her air, playfully blowing some warm air in her face to shock her. She giggled, the sound warming his heart.

Colin's eyes tightened as he regarded her beautiful face carefully, he did not like her on depression pills. They were going to have to seriously figure that out. Unfortunately, things were getting worse before they were getting better. They had all kinds of security, and yet it stole their freedom. Carmichael was still on a rampage, they were still in danger, and it didn't look like it was going to get better yet.

Not yet.

Colin carried her to bed. Where he took oil and massaged her body thoroughly, waiting until she drifted off to sleep before he stopped. Placing the covers over her and crawling into bed after her.

No, it was going to get worse before it got better. And he'd be here to hold her through it all.

Nineteen
Modus Operandi

THE WEEK FLEW BY quickly, and they all chartered the private plane to Bora Bora for Vanessa's vacation. Olivia was momentarily distracted, easing into having security, and finding herself thankful that constant surveillance wasn't as bad as she initially thought. It helped her to observe that Vanessa seemed much more at peace knowing they were protected, and seeing some of the stress leave Colin's features helped to soften her viewpoint as well.

They spent three days on vacation and between drinks with the girls and sex with Colin, she had a momentary lapse in her depression and let herself feel light for the first time in weeks. She went home feeling refreshed and made her and Colin the asian dish he'd come to love so much.

That night, while Olivia was getting ready for bed in their closet, she said a rare prayer of thanks for her new life, despite the struggles they were currently going through. Acknowledging that she could have been single, and left unprotected, attempting to fend herself off from Carmichael's advances. She wouldn't have stood a chance and could have easily been one of the millions of women who fell victim to a predator's tactics.

She was staring off into space, pondering where she would have been had Colin not entered into her life, when she heard a ping come from her phone, breaking her out of her daydream. Walking over to the island, she picked it up, opening it. Her eyes widened as she read the text from an unknown number.

There's only so long we can play this cat and mouse game. Will you only be satisfied when you are the last redhead left on Earth? Because if that's the way you want to play it, we can. We can play as long of a game as you want to, Olivia Alexandra. You know how to stop this. The more you resist me, the more people are going to die. Because of you. -ANIMUS POSSIDENDI

Carmichael! Olivia felt all the blood drain from her head.

She swayed and hit the floor hard with a pained gasp, dropping her phone with a muted thump onto the carpet. Seeing his text still staring up at her from the lit screen, Olivia's face contorted and she leaned her head into her hands and sobbed. *Not as bad as I thought? Wishful thinking.*

Worried that he hadn't seen her in a while, Colin searched for her, finding her in a ball on the closet floor, crying. His heart stopped in his chest when he saw her curled in on herself, shaking and crying inconsolably.

He walked swiftly towards her. "Olivia, what's happened, baby? Speak to me." He got down on his knees and reached for her face, brushing her hair out of the way and wiping her tears. His eyes widened in concern, seeing her tear-streaked face. She made a small sound and sniffed, curling in on herself and put trembling hands to his wrists, her slender fingers wrapped delicately around him.

"Olivia? Are you hurt? *Say something!*" Colin ordered, working hard to keep the alarm out of his voice. He hauled her to his chest and rocked her, hearing small gasping sounds escape her throat. His eyes swiftly glanced over her body before seeing the phone laying face up on the carpet next to them. Reaching over, he grabbed it quickly and opened it.

His eyes narrowed at the contents and a sharp snarl ripped from his own throat.

Motherfucker, he thought. Swallowing hard, he tightened his mental grip on his floundering sanity and breathed deeply, trying to right himself. Needing to be strong for Olivia.

His arm tightened hard around Olivia as he processed the words. Hauling them both up off the floor, he carried her into the bedroom and opened the door swiftly, seeing Zero stationed outside. He shoved Olivia's phone to him, his chocolate eyes furious as they landed onto Zero's cold impassive ones.

"Handle this. *AHORA!*" he barked, before slamming the door back shut. Turning with her in his arms, he carried her to their lounge and sat with her in his lap, rocking her until her tears subsided and she cried herself to sleep. Much like the first time he'd made love to her, he refused to placate her with senseless words of reassurance. He would never reassure her when he knew there was none to give. He made a vow in the beginning of their relationship that he would not give her any false hope if there was none. No, he knew this was a terrible predicament they were in. People were dying, children were being murdered.

And he'd be damned if Olivia or anyone in her family were going to be a victim.

***

Olivia refused to get out of bed the next morning. Mary and the security team messaged, letting him know that they were stationed in the home and outside on the property. Colin brought up breakfast, and tried to get Olivia to sit up and eat but she wasn't interested. She'd woken up crying in the middle of the night and he held her for a long time, until she'd exhausted herself once again and fell back asleep.

Worried, he sat on the edge of the bed and placed his hand on the side of Olivia's face, seeing her eyes, cheeks, and nose tinted red.

"Amor, you need to eat something," he said softly, stroking his thumb across her cheek.

"No," she sobbed, turning and pressing her face into her pillow.

Colin's features hardened painfully as she closed her eyes, and a tear escaped, falling to the pillow under her cheek. He turned, placing the oatmeal he'd made her to the side and crawled in next to her, sliding under the covers and wrapping himself around her.

He heard his phone ding, and he reached into his pocket, recognizing the tone for Jonathan.

Hey brother, are you meeting me and Alex for boxing later this evening? -J. Dawg

Colin pressed his lips together, seeing Olivia's quiet, slight form, hearing her sniffle. He wasn't leaving her like this.

Not tonight, tell Alexander I'm sorry. I'll have to meet him next time. Olivia is going through something. I don't want to leave her. -C. Kent

Anything we can do to help? -J. Dawg

Abandoning texting, he opened the microphone. Speaking softly into the phone, he sent a voice message to Jonathan, his hand rubbed Olivia's head gently, soothing her.

"Brother, I don't know what you are doing later, but can you cancel your plans? We have an errand to run. Someone needs to be paid a visit. I'm taking Olivia to her counseling appointment at three o'clock and we'll go right after I drop her off. Be ready, please." Colin turned on a soothing classical music station and put his phone down, turning back to Olivia.

"It's going to be ok, love. Everything is going to work out. I got you, always," he breathed, kissing the top of her head.

Olivia flipped over, pressing her face into his neck and curling her fingers into his t-shirt. Colin shifted, yanking his shirt off then settling back down, pressing his bare skin to hers, pulling her impossibly close. Pressing her head into his chest he rocked her against him, soothing her with broad strokes of his hand down her back and her hair.

"Colin," she whispered, her fingers gripping his neck hard. "He's getting too close!" her voice was muffled against his chest, thick with emotion and angst. She clutched at him, feeling fear and desperation fill her at the unfairness of why they were in this situation.

Judge Carmichael. She hated herself for getting into that lifestyle, and now her choices were coming back to haunt them all.

Colin held her like that for an hour, skin to skin, before making her get up. He carried her into the bathroom and straight into the bathtub, where he bathed her and washed her hair. He took his time to blow dry her hair, not even minding that she kept her eyes downcast. Leaning forward, giving her a kiss on each swollen eyelid, his hand splayed against the back of her head. His other hand curled around her waist.

"Whatever we have to face, my love, we're facing it together. *As one,*" he whispered, leaning his forehead against hers. Olivia nodded, sniffing and looping her arms around his neck in a desperate hug.

***

A few hours later, Colin and Jonathan pulled out from the therapist's office. Olivia had chosen a quaint, small therapy practice based in a nice residential area. The office was a small house, and Colin instructed both of Olivia's security guards to stay with her; one stationed outside, and the other in the lobby. Colin and Jonathan rode alone, with their security detail following in a separate vehicle. They were headed to see Carmichael, who was in his office today, according to inside intel. Jonathan had paid a pretty penny to guarantee they would be able to have an audience with the judge.

"Do you have any idea what you want to say to him? I would expect that we're not going to go to prison today and that you can control yourself?" Jonathan asked, looking over at his friend in concern. Colin's features were tight with worry for his wife. He briefly grimaced, hating that Jonathan even had to suggest that he couldn't control himself.

He turned efficiently into the parking space of the building he knew the judge's office was located in, and showed his ID to the security officer before they waved him in.

"Jon, I'm just going to speak to the man. Okay?" Colin cleared his throat as he pulled into a spot and put the car into park. He kept his eyes studiously off his best friend.

Jonathan grunted and opened his car door, sliding out smoothly. "Whatever you say, friend."

They made their way into the building, with their security tailing them, knowing that it was a stroke of luck they were able to get in to see the judge in a public setting at his office. Carmichael wouldn't be so careless as to outright refuse a call from two of the wealthiest men in the area without looking suspicious. Making their way down the hallway to Carmichael's office, they passed portrait after portrait of judges, flags, Latin sayings, and statues.

Jonathan reached an arm out and pulled Colin to a stop just before they got to the ornate wooden door.

"Hey," he said quietly, his brow furrowed as he regarded his friend closely. Colin arched an eyebrow in return and gave a long-suffering sigh. "Don't fucking do anything stupid. I know we have security, but we don't need to antagonize the man any further than he already is. Even though he hasn't gotten to our girls, there's still other people dying."

Colin gave him a short nod, always preferring to never verbalize promises he wasn't sure he could keep. Without knocking, he entered the expansive office, striding through confidently, his eyes narrowing in on Carmichael sitting behind his desk. Two armed guards were stationed against the wall behind him, and they each put a hand on their guns at the sight of Colin, Jonathan, and their two security guards tailing them.

Carmichael stood up from his desk, holding a hand up to call off the security behind him.

"No need, I've been expecting them," Judge Carmichael's deep voice called out to the two guards behind them. "Gentlemen, to what do I owe the honor?" Carmichael gave a sly grin as Colin confidently walked to the wide desk separating the two of them.

"Cut the niceties, Carmichael," Colin said sternly, narrowing his eyes at the man. "Killing children now, Judge? This is what your sick antics have come to?"

Carmichael's gray eyes turned cold, and a half grin appeared on his face before he cleared his throat and pushed some papers aside. "I have no clue what you're talking about, McDermont."

Colin and Carmichael stared each other down for a heartbeat before Colin leaned forward.

"Sure," he tilted his head, pinning Carmichael with a deathly cold stare. "You contact my wife again, and you'll regret it. I don't know what kind of crazy lies in that brain of yours, but trust me, you don't want to meet my brand of crazy. Because see, the only reason you are alive right now is so the authorities can have enough time to build a case against you and those victims you killed that need justice. But I will absolutely not stand by and watch my wife be tortured for too much longer. You'd do well to watch your fucking back." Colin arched an eyebrow at him.

Carmichael gave him a dismissive wave before leaning back in his seat. He steepled his hands together in front of him and regarded him for a couple seconds before he tilted his head, his gray eyes flashing almost manically. He licked his lips before speaking.

"Tell me, McDermont, is her pussy absolutely divine? What's she like to fuck? Do you think she's worth all the dead bodies? I bet she's nice and tight, a dream to screw," he smiled a bright, toothy grin at Colin. "The first time I fuck her I'm going to make her scream for you, may even take her in front of you, so you have the pleasure of personally watching me defile your wife." Carmichael taunted boldly, pulling a paper from a stack and beginning to sign it, his eyes no longer on Colin's.

Colin turned his head, looking over at Jonathan, who had walked a couple of steps closer to grab him if he needed to.

He smiled a purely evil smile before sliding his eyes back to Carmichael, who had now put the paper aside and trained his eyes back on him. Colin took a couple of steps towards him, ignoring his own security guards uncomfortably close. He leaned down over the desk and pinned him with a stare.

"The only reason, and I legit mean this with everything in my soul, that I'm not killing you right now, is because I have self-control and it wouldn't be fair to end us all in a bloodbath and leave Olivia and her family alone. So, you feel free to imagine what her pussy sounds like, feels like, tastes like all you want to; just understand that whatever you fantasize will never compare to the real thing. But know this Carmichael. *I'll kill the woman myself* first before I ever let you touch her," Colin ignored Jonathan's sharp intake of breath and continued as if he didn't just say the most fucked up thing imaginable. "Understand that, and maybe spend your time wondering how you're going to die. Because I plan on waiting just long enough for them to frame you for all these murders, and then I promise you, you won't make it into a prison. That's when I'll come get you. Enjoy," and with that, Colin turned on his heel and strode past his security and headed to the door.

He paused as Carmichael's voice rang out through the office.

"If I were you," Carmichael called, repeating the last words Colin said to him in his guesthouse weeks ago. Colin turned back to face the judge head on. Carmichael's eyes turned a stormy color, a sick look on his face as he assessed Colin, pure hatred in his face plain as day.

"I would fuck her good while you have the chance. Because once I have her, and I will, you'll never get the chance to see her again. I'll make her mine. And I'm going to damage her to the point you'll never want her again if I ever did choose to discard her. *You* enjoy."

Jonathan, who'd been silent for the entire interaction, looked at Colin, worry filling him anew for his friend's sanity. He observed Colin's eyes turn the coldest Jonathan had ever seen, and for the first time, Jonathan truly wondered if the man really was legitimately crazy, despite the psychological evaluations he'd made Colin go through stating he wasn't. He watched the mask leave Colin's face like a veil being lifted off a painting, showing what was underneath.

Colin's eyes turned downright lifeless. There was no civility, no humanity, nothing of a person left within his depths.

Jonathan shuddered, feeling bile rise up his esophagus and he fought against dry heaving. He'd only seen that look one time upon the face of a truly evil captive when he was a torture specialist, and he worked extensively over the years to get that look out of his nightmares. He'd never expected to see it again on his closest friend's face.

Colin slowly walked the few feet back to Carmichaels' desk. The two men flanking the judge put their finger on the trigger of the rifles they were holding. But Colin didn't care as he stepped towards the judge's desk and leaned down, putting his hands flat on the wood top. His fingers spread and his wedding band sparkled in the overhead lightning.

"I'm usually a man of many words," Colin said, his voice taking on a hollow, dangerous cadence. "Truly, I love to hear myself speak."

Colin saw an imperfection suddenly in the judge's desk and his eyes narrowed.

They all watched, riveted, as he suddenly took his right hand and twisted it, the nail on his pinky finger digging sharply under the tiny, exposed piece of wood, nicking it further. He grasped it in his fingers and started pulling slowly. The tiny narrow tan line looked glaringly sharp against the dark wood of the varnished desk.

"However, much like this small little detail here," he whispered, pulling steadily at the tiny strip. The men's eyes were narrowed intently, watching the line become broader as he continued to pull. The tan line slashed a sharp divot into Carmichael's desk, heading straight for him. "You too will make the smallest of mistakes. And when the time comes, I just want you to understand that I will absolutely relish killing you," Colin whispered, twisting his hand and plucking the several inches worth of exposed wood he was picking at, effectively snapping it off from the rest of the desk.

"And, as much as it pains me to say this," Colin said, his eyes now turning from the desk to meet Carmichael's, who was thunderous with rage. His gray eyes stared back at Colin from his seat in the brown leather studded chair of his office. "Killing you is going to give me more pleasure than being inside my wife. Which is Nirvana. So, I hope that whatever you plan on doing, If I were you, I'd really commit to it and make it worth it, brother. Matter of fact, I *praayyy* you do."

Jonathan felt sick.

"Because," Colin continued. "As my wife's body is my favorite destination on earth, and the thought of anything being better than that, well, it just doesn't sit right in my spirit. If I were you, I would make it a point to go to church on Sunday. You need to repent before you slip up, because when you do, and you see my face when the time comes, you won't have time to talk to God. And that's a promise. I'll be sure to say a prayer on your behalf as well. God and I have been tentatively acquainted as of late. If I were you, I'd make it right with Him, *while* you have the chance. And, just to show you how much I mean business," Colin moved, pulling something out of his pocket.

Jonathan groaned as he recognized the object hanging from his friend's hand, his eyes watered as they widened watching Colin toss it to the man. The object hit the judge's desk with a hard thud.

"This rosary is the only thing I have left of my mother's; you can borrow it. This is for you, to say your Hail Marys while you still have the chance. You need it more than I do. If I were you, I'd make each one count, from one sinner to another."

And with that, Colin turned and strode out of the office, walking past Jonathan without a second glance. Jonathan held a hand up to his personal security, stalling him, walking up to the desk and snatching the rosary back up. "I don't have anything to say, because it all goes without saying, really," he raised his eyebrows at Carmichael and shook his head slightly, turning his back on the man with a little whistle and striding out the room confidently behind his friend.

Colin waited until Jonathan got into the car before he spoke.

"You will never tell anyone what I said in there," he asserted quietly, keeping his gaze averted from his friend, every muscle tight with restraint.

"Of course not, brother. I would never. But you know I have to ask...did you mean that?" Jonathan said just as quietly, watching Colin's mask fall back into place as he worked to school his features into an impassive expression.

Colin started the car, not answering his friend's question, and drove off to pick Olivia up.

***

They returned home, and Colin remained quiet as he walked behind Olivia as she entered the kitchen through the mudroom. He curtly dismissed Mary and Beth for the day, ignoring Olivia's raised eyebrow as he walked past her and headed to his study.

He closed the door and leaned against it, shutting his eyes from the mental images that Carmicheal put into his head about his wife. Shaking, he went to his desk and got out his anxiety medication and took a pill, swishing it down with a bottle of water. He lowered himself into his chair and put his head into his hands, trying to breathe.

The urge to go and kill the man was quickly taking over.

Lowering his hands, Colin sat back in his chair and stared ahead of him at his wall of pictures, seeing the one he had of Olivia on his monitor at work, in the center of the wall of photos. His eyes pricked, thinking of the judge getting his hands on her.

His chest swelled painfully, and he put his hand to his heart, rubbing hard. *We've never even had a chance to have children, to have a life together.*

He made a rough, distressed sound, feeling his heartbeat ramp up as fear and anger warred for the dominant emotion inside of him. He let out a ragged inhale, clenching his jaw at the absolute feral desire to head back out the house and hunt the man down. Reaching under his desk, he opened his safe, pulling out the gun he stashed there. Opening the chamber, he checked the bullets in the gun before placing it on the desk in front of him. The metal gleamed in the light of his desk lamp, and he let himself go wild with thoughts of shooting the man who felt like he had any right to his wife.

"Colin?"

Yanked out of his musing, Colin turned his head slowly, seeing Olivia walk through his office door before pausing. She stood in the wide threshold, her eyes riveted to the gun on his desk. They widened, the color coming high into her face. Irritated, he snatched the gun back up, placing it into the safe and closing it quickly, not wanting to alarm her.

Too late.

"What are you doing?" Her voice was small with shock and her eyes bored into his, still standing in that spot.

"Nothing," he said gruffly, refusing to disclose just how close he was to leaving and potentially fucking up their lives. Olivia walked further into the room to stand on the other side of his desk, folding her arms.

"That wasn't nothing. That was a *gun*, Colin," she snapped, her brows furrowed as she regarded him from her spot standing up. "I didn't even know you had one of those. What else don't I know?" she bit out, her lips tightening, betraying her stress.

He paused, tilting his head at her as he regarded her angry, trembling form.

"What the hell do you mean 'what else don't you know?'" he said in a warning tone. It took everything in him to mask his own sudden surge of anger, an emotion that finally won the dominant spot in his body. He tensed, feeling his blood pressure skyrocket.

"I said what I said, you heard me! What *ELSE* don't I know, Colin?" Olivia said sharply, her face tight as she regarded him back just as intently.

Colin stood up slowly, placing his palms onto the desk as he leaned down, leveling her with a stare.

"I suggest you fix your tone-"

"You don't get to fucking tell me what-"

"*Olivia!*" Colin snapped, feeling his face darken with irritation. "*You will watch your tone with me woman,*" he tilted his head, and they stood for a few silent seconds facing each other down across the desk. Olivia leaned forward, placing her own hands down on the desk and staring at him. Her eyes were narrowed and her face was dusky pink, betraying her irritation. She sucked in an offended breath.

"Or what?" she taunted, her eyebrow arched haughtily. She slammed her palm on the desk between them, her face angry as she expressed her emotion to him. "*OR WHAT,* COLIN? *WHAT THE FUCK ARE YOU GOING TO DO-*" Olivia squeaked as he suddenly reached out and snatched her up by her throat, hauling her slowly onto the desktop. He relished her gasps and her scratching at his wrist as he pulled her to him, pressing her body to his as he flexed his hand around her throat threateningly.

He bent down to her ear, feeling his chest tighten even further, knowing he was so close to finally snapping. His voice was rough in her ear as his fingers flexed.

"You had better watch yourself. Fix your temper, *now*! I told you before, I have bent over backwards for you, I have coddled you, and I didn't even punish you the way I wanted to when you left me for four months to do who knows *what the fuck* in China. *So*, If I can manage to control myself, then *you will fucking mind your Goddamn place next to me*, and you will show me that respect as my wife," he said deathly quiet. His voice raspy, with the effort it was taking to lock his own vocal cords down from saying some seriously sick shit to her.

Olivia trembled, feeling her nipples tighten as her husband demonstrated that once again, he held control. He gave her nothing, while simultaneously giving her everything. She gasped for air as his fingers relaxed, letting her breathe, her knees slipped on the wood of his desk as she struggled to find purchase. His voice deepened, and Olivia whimpered as his beard scraped the sensitive skin of her jaw. His hand continued to press into her neck.

"I won't let him have you. Do you understand me, Olivia? He's not going to get the pleasure." He tightened his fingers once more, cutting off her air supply. Olivia trembled, her own fingers going to his belt buckle and tearing at his pants. She pulled his belt through the loops in his pants and he let go of her neck and grasped her shirt in his hands, tearing it off roughly and then snatching her up by the front of her bra, hauling her to him. "I will not let him have you," he repeated angrily. "We just found each other, goddamnit!"

Olivia keened, hearing her bra rip in half with the force of him tearing it off of her. She slipped with the movement, toppling forward, yelping as Colin snatched her up by her hair and hauled her up, making her land clumsily on her feet in front of him. He pulled back further, making her tilt her head up for him. Ignoring her ragged breathing, he bent into her face, staring into her wide eyes.

He leaned forward even more, giving her a chaste lingering kiss on her plump lips.

"I just found you," he repeated softly, pain lacing his voice as his hand left her throat and he wrapped both arms around her, pulling him flush to him. He pressed his lips hard to her temple, feeling his hands shaking against her, he groaned miserably. "Do you even know how much you mean to me? You're my world, Olivia. I am nothing if you aren't with me. I am nothing without you!" he gritted, feeling tremors wrack his own body. "It's taking everything in me not to go to that fucker and kill him."

"Colin," Olivia bit out, her voice desperate. She unbuttoned his pants and wiggled against him, struggling to lean back and lower them. He wouldn't give her the room to do so. "I love you, I need you! He won't win, he can't!" her voice shook, and she realized then that she wasn't confident in her words. No one knew the future.

There was definitely a chance Carmichael could win, if he found the right button to push.

Olivia sucked in a hot, desperate breath as she pushed against Colin. Her skin suddenly pricked, feeling too tight. A slightly painful buzzing ripped across her flesh and she put her hand to her forearm, scratching, digging her nails in.

Her eyes watered as he slammed his mouth over hers and pushed her back down onto his desk roughly. She squealed as he snatched off her pants and then lowered his own over his hips, freeing his cock. He crawled onto the desk, on top of her, and slammed himself home on a thrust so hard it sent her up the desk, knocking her into his monitor, sending it crashing to the floor as he began a merciless pounding into her.

Olivia arched her neck and screamed, taking her nails and scratching at her forearm again.

Seeing her dilemma, Colin leaned down and bit her arm right at the juncture of her elbow. Tightening his teeth hard, he felt his blood pressure rise at the tortured wail that arose from her.

"Yes, harder!" Olivia screamed, bucking hard against him as he worked over her. He moved to another spot on her arm and bit down there too, pulling at her flesh and sinking his teeth in. He growled, as he thrust inside her repeatedly, not letting up on the pace.

Olivia squeezed him tightly with her orgasm and she arched off the desk on a sharp cry before cutting it off in surprise at him roughly pushing her back down. He thrust harder, moving his mouth to a straining nipple before tightening his teeth around it and nibbling sharply. He groaned and jerked inside her as heat flooded his dick and he pulled away, trailing his mouth to the swell of her other breast where he bit down hard, hearing her squeal.

Olivia moaned, arching her neck as the pain of his actions settled deep inside. Her eyes rolled into the back of her head and she gasped as he tightened his teeth even further around her flesh. The hot stab of pain met the almost mind numbing pleasure he was beating between her legs and she felt her clit twinge right before she fell to pieces underneath him. She tilted her head back.

"Godddd!" she screamed, bending her knees back further as Colin continued to bounce off her pussy unrelentingly. She sobbed as he pulled himself out and then hauled her up by her hair.

"Suck me off. Now, Olivia. And make it sloppy," he commanded, giving her a look before his hand firmly pushed her mouth down onto his cock.

Olivia moaned in pure bliss as the first taste of their combined essence hit her tongue and she gagged as she swallowed him as deep as she could take him. She relished him shoving her on and off his cock and her mouth watered. Obediently, she purposely flooded her mouth, streams of drool and his precum hung down from her chin. She squealed as he suddenly slapped her hard across her hip and her clit twinged miserably.

She was used to him giving her foreplay, not neglecting that part of her body and the furiousness of the way he was taking her, the way they were taking each other, fueled her desire and she tried to raise off him to ask for more when she suddenly stiffened, feeling him slap her other hip sharply. His dick swelled a tiny bit more in her mouth, choking her, and she began to gag in earnest.

Tightening his lips, he pulled her off.

"Fucking can't handle it?" Colin whispered down at her. Hauling her up to her knees, he tightened his hand in her hair before he treated her to rough slaps across her breasts, making them burn. He watched her breasts bounce with the movement and his jaw ticked at how obviously turned on Olivia was from how he was treating her. He turned her roughly around and slammed back into her from behind, shoving her chest down onto his desk with a rough hand between her shoulder blades. "If you can't handle my cock in your mouth, then I'm going to punish you. Reach into the top drawer of my desk and get out my stapler."

Olivia felt all the blood drain from her head.

"W-w-wait...Colin *wait*!" she whispered, swallowing past the terrified lump suddenly lodged in her throat. She made a pained sound as he hauled her back up again by her hair and lowered his lips to her ear. His breath came out rough as he churned his hips hard against her, abandoning the hard thrusts from before.

"When I ask you to do something, all I expect to hear out of your mouth is "yes sir" or your safe word, that is all," he said, his voice deceptively calm. "Now get. The. Fucking. Stapler." He pushed her head away from him and grabbed her hips, beginning to thrust anew while she scrambled to reach into his top drawer to do as he requested.

Olivia's eyes were wide as she handed it to him, then he forced her back down on the desk again. She could feel her ass bouncing lewdly as he let go of her hips, and she flinched when she heard him toss the stapler carelessly to the floor. The stapler was open and all the little pieces fell out onto the hardwood. Her eyes widened as he placed a warm hand on her hip and stilled his movements.

There was a tense second while he made her wait, her eyes squeezed shut in anticipation as every nerve in her body strung tight, waiting for whatever he was planning to do to her. She fought hard to control the desperate pants and whines escaping her throat.

"God, I fucking love you helpless. You have no clue what I'm going to do to you and you're trusting me anyway, even though I can see you're scared." Colin's deep voice sounded tortured before he moved fast, taking her by surprise. She felt her body break out into a fresh coat of sweat with the delicious anticipation of what he was going to do.

She yelped as she felt two tiny pricks on her vulnerable skin of her back and then heat, as he dragged the staple down her back in a broad stroke. She fluttered around his cock at the sudden, intoxicating flash of heat that seared her. Moaning wildly, she gripped the edge of the desk hard as he began to treat her to those hard slapping thrusts that she loved so much. She lay there with her chest against the wood, in pure bliss as he dragged the stapler slowly and repeatedly over her back. Sometimes just up and down, sometimes side to side.

He kept the pressure light so as not to cause bleeding, but somehow it was just enough, yet not enough at the same time. Olivia felt a tear slip out of her eye at the relief the pain was giving her, and she shuddered hard, whimpering softly.

"More, please," she said, looking back at him, catching his eye.

Colin was shiny, covered in sweat, his body gleaming in the light of the office. His muscles were tight with tension and his facial features were pulled tight with desire. He nodded at her, before pressing the staple slightly deeper and dragging it down, his heart beat wildly hearing a sound that he'd never heard come from her before. She suddenly orgasmed hard as he repeated the movement. He hissed, feeling her vagina gripping him tightly and he followed her over with a harsh growl, leaning forward and pressing his lips to the tiny welts on her back.

"Thank you for trusting me, baby. Thank you," he whispered reverently. Laying his cheek on her back, he breathed deeply. Memorizing her feel, her scent.

They laid there like that for long moments, shuddering against each other, holding each other.

Praying that they could find a way out together.

Because they just had to.

TWENTY

Auntie Shenanigans

COLIN WOKE UP BEFORE Olivia and in a rare move, he texted Mary to bring them up a tray of coffee and tea so he wouldn't have to leave the room right away. Going through his morning grooming motions, he brushed his teeth and washed his face, replaying last night's sex session with the stapler.

He groaned, feeling himself swelling, needing release yet again.

Going back into the bedroom, he noted Olivia was still laying there, sleeping soundly, but she had moved slightly, letting him know she was close to waking up. He walked out of their bedroom and picked up the tray of drinks Mary placed on a little table outside and nodded at Bryson, who was almost done with his night shift. The muscular man was situated by the wall in a chair, with a computer system set up, monitoring their security feeds throughout the property and making sure the men outside weren't slacking on their job.

"Morning. How was last night? Any issues?" Colin asked, waiting patiently as the burly blond man clicked a couple of buttons.

"None on the property, but there were a couple unmarked cars going past the gate last night. We are installing more cameras around the property's fence line, and we have asked your surrounding neighbors for permission to monitor the outer edge of their property where their fence line meets yours. We'll be installing them sometime later today when the equipment comes in."

"Thank you. Let me know if you need anything from me," Colin said. Grabbing the tray and walking back into the room, he closed the door softly and set it down in the lounge. He picked up a cup of coffee and took a deep swallow, allowing his eyes to flick over Olivia again, seeing the cover had slipped off her body slightly and revealing the tiny welts on her back from the stapler.

Colin hissed, feeling his dick lengthen and thicken to its fullest extent and he hurriedly shoved his pants and briefs off, crawling back under the sheets. Uncaring she was still asleep, he rolled her firmly to her back and moved down her body to settle his head between her legs. Breathing deeply, he smelled her natural scent mixed with the body wash she'd used for her shower late last night and he lowered his head, sucking her clit into his mouth. He gave her a few slow sucks before he tightened his teeth.

Wake up beauty, Colin thought, pulling back to give her nice slow licks up her center before sealing his lips on her again and flicking with his tongue.

Olivia stirred, her thighs shifting against him restlessly as she struggled out of sleep. Her eyes popped open, and she sat up, gasping. "Colin, please tell me that's you!" she yanked at the covers, revealing Colin's brown hair, and then he lifted his head with an irritated look on his face.

"Why the fuck wouldn't it be me, wife?" he said, lowering his head to her thigh and taking a sharp bite out of her leg, making her cry out and fall back to the mattress on a small squeal.

"Because there's so many dicks walking around the place now I just wasn't sure," she said with a small smile, trying to hide behind her hand.

Colin snapped his head up again, throwing her a dangerous look as he abandoned her pussy to crawl up her body. "Why are you thinking about other men's dicks when mine is the only one that matters?"

Olivia's eyes widened. "Wait, I was just playing-" she screamed and jerked as he lowered his head once more to take a rough bite out of her neck. Olivia squirmed and bucked under the fierceness of it. This bite was slightly rougher than the one he'd treated her to the first time they'd had sex.

Olivia moaned, sagging against the mattress as she felt the swollen head of his cock brush the entrance of her sex. Her hands sank into his hair as she held on for dear life. "C-Colin," she gasped.

"Mine's the only one that matters, right?" he growled into her ear, waiting for her answer before he slammed into her so hard he pushed her up the mattress, knocking her pillows off the bed and onto the floor. In another rough movement, he swiped his hand outwards, pushing the other pillows away as he began to thrust hard. Olivia squealed at his actions, excited over how rough he was being first thing in the morning.

Oh my God, that means this is going to be a good day! She thought to herself as he leaned down and took her by her throat at the same time he wrapped a hand around their headboard and shoved his hips into hers so hard they raised off the bed. He held her there like that for a minute.

"You're going to stop thinking about the other men's dicks. I'll punish you if I even think you are," he spat out, tightening his hand around her minutely and watching her eyelashes flutter closed.

"Yes sir," she whispered through the hand around her throat. She trembled as he pulled back, letting her hips settle to the mattress.

"Are you ready to begin, baby?"

"Yes, sir." Olivia's heart soared, feeling with every thrust her abraded back scraped the mattress and she wrapped that feeling close to her. Protecting it and cherishing it. She ran her hands up and down Colin's arm with the hand around her throat. Vowing to protect and cherish him just as much as he did her.

***

Olivia shakily pulled on her pants, sitting on the edge of the couch in the lounge, trying to get her bearings after such a strenuous morning. She licked her lips as Colin walked up to her and handed her a cup of coffee.

"Sorry baby, it's cold now," he said, lowering to the table in front of her he reached forward and rubbed a hand down her hair. Olivia looked at him enviously, he was already dressed and ready for the day, and she was still trying to get her socks and shoes on.

"It's okay, I like cold coffee too," Olivia muttered around the mug. She giggled as he picked her foot up and slid a sock on, repeating it with the other foot before he put her shoes on for her.

"So, what are you doing today? Do you have any plans?"

"Well it's Sunday, I'm going to Vanessa's for a bit to see Allison and to give Jonathan and Vanessa some time to meet with their doula. You know they're only like a month away from having Ian? Can you believe it? Time's just flying!"

"Hmm-hmm, I know. We've been together just a bit over nine months," Colin stated suddenly.

Olivia paused and glanced at him, gleaming his hidden meaning. Staying silent, she nodded, not wanting to bring up that after nine months page three of their contract would take effect. She'd been studiously ignoring page three for months now. But with the subject being brought to the forefront of her mind, she felt those nerves come back, making her feel off center.

She placed a trembling hand on her tummy, hoping he didn't notice.

"So, do you want to come with me?" Olivia asked, standing up and placing her coffee back on the tray. She journeyed to the bathroom with him following close behind. She observed he'd been staying closer to her than normal and wondered if that's why she'd had a lapse in her crying spells.

"No sweetie, I spoke with Byson this morning, and he said that we had a couple unmarked cars go past the gate late last night, and they're installing more security and speaking with the neighbors so I'm going to stay behind this time. But next time, you can count on me being there. Maybe we can take Allison to the zoo or something fun?" he watched intently as she beat the brush rather hard on her head with every pass.

"Is that how you'd like me to brush your hair? Am I doing it right when I do it?" Colin asked her suddenly, cocking his head at her as she paused in her movements and blinked almost confusedly.

Olivia frowned, staring at the brush for a second before she set it down on the vanity. "Uh, no. Not really. I wasn't even aware I was doing it..." she flicked him an obviously embarrassed look before she reached forward for her perfume.

"You don't have to be embarrassed, love, it's okay," he reassured her. Reaching forward, he slicked a hand down her hair and pressed a kiss to her temple. He fisted his hand in her hair and gave her a small yank before smacking her ass hard.

Olivia jerked and gave him wide eyes. "Colin!" she admonished, laughing at him as he hightailed it out of the bathroom before she could smack him back.

"Have a good time baby, keep your phone on you and don't be upset at Zero when he drives, you know it's his job so just sit back and let him do it without complaining," he called out, grabbing his phone off the bed as she exited the bathroom and veered to the bedroom door.

"Fine!" she said sweetly, opening the door and then scrunching her face up as she walked out, seeing Zero sitting in the chair outside of their bedroom door. "Hi Zero, I've been told to be nice to you and let you do your job in peace, so can we go? Do you need a coffee or anything before we leave?"

She watched impassively as Zero turned cold eyes on her. He lifted up his coffee thermos and arched an eyebrow. "Good morning, Lilith. Nope, I'm good, thanks for asking. I'm ready when you are."

Olivia rolled her eyes and strolled to the elevator. "Bye Colin," she called out down the hallway. Colin had stayed behind in the bedroom to alert the team that Olivia was leaving the house and to have an extra escort.

"What the fuck?" Colin stuck his head out the door and gave her a stern look. "Did you just tell me goodbye? Take that shit back!" he said, giving her a once over.

Olivia shrugged her shoulder and laughed. "Okay," she laughed, winking at him.

"And give Ally a kiss for me," he yelled out to her, as she and Zero disappeared into the elevator.

***

Guy Group Chat

Yo, we have to freaking reinforce our fence. And bug the neighbors, now they think we're reclusive AND dangerous. What the hell?! -C. Kent

But other than that, are they guys holding up to your high standards? Stella got a heeelllll of a punishment due to your girl, so I hope to God they are. -V

Why're you punishing her anyways for something Olivia's doing? We're all good over here by the way, thanks for asking. -J. Dawg

Jesus, I sent you an email regarding how your team is doing so far. What crawled up your ass and died? -V

Whatever it was, I can guarantee you wasn't Halal, Jonathan would NEVER let anything forbidden up there. -C. Kent

Fuck you, asshole. -J. Dawg

Jesus...one would think YOU were the hormonal one having a baby, not Vanessa. -C. Kent

When did I get added in here? -Alexander

Pick a nickname, quickly! And welcome to the shit show, son! -V

Well, since you're trying to be useful and all, can one of you call me at like 9p if I send an SOS? Act like it's an emergency so I can get out of this date I'm going on. -Alexander The Great

Why're you trying to get OUT of a date? Isn't that normally something a woman does? Is there no chance for pussy or something? -V

Pardon me, but I am not feminine in any sense of the word. -Alexander the Great

Alex, you gotta stop doing this. We talked about this multiple times. How many times have you been out with this woman? -J. Dawg

Something's fishy here and I don't like it. You a fuck em and leave em type of man? -C. Kent

No, actually, he doesn't hang around long enough to even fuck 'em to see if they're worth leaving. -J. Dawg

Harsh bro. That was harsh. -V

Alex when's the last time you had any pussy? Is that why you're so strong =D you taking all the sexual tension built up in you out on the menfolk? -C. Kent

Jon, I've been out with her four times. That's enough for me. Superman, I'm knocking your teeth out of your face the next time I see you, dick. -Alexander The Great

Superman, if you need an extra security guard, please let me know. LMAO. -V

Yeah, Superman lol -J. Dawg

Superman where are you?-J. Dawg

Awww, don't be like that Superm-I mean COLIN. -Alexander the Great.

Colin?-V

Ok, you can keep your teeth, damn. Why so sensitive Colin? -Alexander The Great

Thanks a lot, cunt. -Colin

Aww, don't be like that. Go back to C. Kent. -V

***

"Jump Ally! Jump! You can do it sweetie!" Olivia held her jump rope and cheered Allison on at the nearby park where they were spending the day at the splash pad.

Seeing that she'd wanted to take Allison out in public, Jonathan ordered her to take extra security and so they had five men there swarming the perimeter. Olivia tried to not let that distract them from their play time and she laughed heartily as Allison got several successful jumps in without tripping.

"Look Aunt Ollie! I did it! Did you see me?" Allison's red hair swung in her pigtails as she began to jump again but quickly pouted when the rope hit the hem of her shirt and messed up her streak. "Oh no!" she complained, pouting her lips and throwing her rope down. "Stupid rope!"

Olivia smoothed her hand down her white tank top and took off her ball cap before crouching down and shoving it down onto Allison's head and chucking her chin. She took her finger and flicked her lips until Allison broke and began to giggle, showing off her two missing teeth.

"Now, that's better! Princesses don't give up do they?"

"No."

"What?" Olivia cupped her hand to her ear. "I can't hear you!" she said loudly, feigning deafness.

Allison heaved a deep breath and then leaned forward with all her might. "NOOO!" she yelled, her freckled face turned pink with her efforts.

Olivia winced as Zero honed in on her and shifted his sunglasses down to pierce her with his eyes. She childishly stuck her tongue out at him before turning back to Allison and standing up. Adjusting her own sunglasses, she stepped back, flicking her jump rope behind her and getting a tiny thrill at the thin rope slapping the back of her legs, making her think of Colin.

"Now, just a little more and then we'll get ice cream from that vendor over there! And then we can play in the splash pad."

Allison squealed with excitement and hurried to put her jump rope in place and they spent the next ten minutes trying to beat each other's scores of how many jumps in a row before they got tangled. Handing off their ropes to security, they walked and got an ice cream cone for Allison and an ice cream sandwich for Olivia and sat on a bench, watching all the kids and their families playing in the splash pad.

Olivia looked over, seeing Allison looking at the baby area.

"Whatcha thinking about, lil' bit?" She asked, bumping her shoulder into Allison, who looked up at her with a bright smile, ice cream smeared on her chin. Seeing their security moving around, she smiled, seeing how inconspicuous they managed to look.

"My little brother coming. I'm so happy. I can't wait to see him. I'm going to be the BEST big sister. I'm going to help mom feed him." Allison said simply.

Olivia bit back a grin, not feeling the need to tell Allison that she probably wouldn't be able to help in that way at least for a year. She bit off another bite of her ice cream sandwich and tilted it to Allison. "Want a bite?" she asked. Allison nodded her head and bit off a huge chunk, getting some onto her shirt.

Olivia reached forward and wiped it off with a napkin and smoothed her hand down her hair and leaned in to kiss the top of her head.

"I think you're going to be the best big sister in the whole world. You know, your mommy is *my* big sister, and I love her so much. Big sisters have such an important job, you know. And I think you're going to be amazing at it." Olivia encouraged, feeling the part of her soul that ached at giving her up begin to hurt slightly more.

Allison looked up at Olivia with wide eyes. "I'm ready Auntie Ollie!" she quipped with a serious expression on her face.

Olivia smiled down at her. "I know you are baby, I know you are! Let's go play in the water." Olivia grabbed her hand, and they took off running to splash the rest of the afternoon away, and when Allison laid her head wearily on Olivia's shoulder hours later, she picked her up and carried her to the black SUV and climbed in. She watched her sleep on her the entire way back to the house, allowing herself to feel what she could have had as Allison's mother, had events not turned out so wrong.

She took a moment to cry silently, keeping her face out of the eyeline of Zero, and let herself imagine she was about to carry her baby home to tuck into bed for a nap, instead of back to her sister and Jonathan, where she knew Allison really belonged.

Her heart ached, needing closure, but wasn't quite sure how to get it.

She feared she never would.

***

A week later brought more death, two redheaded toddler twins. As well as another text from Carmichael.

There's about thirty-five other redheads in the area. How many of them do you love and care about? Are you ready to give up and come to me? I will take you willingly. Matter of fact, I'd prefer it as I don't necessarily want to make you scream, but I will if this carries on for much longer. -Maleficia propositis distinguuntur

Zero sat both Colin and Olivia down in the study and reported the news to them both about the children's deaths.

Olivia stormed out in anger when Colin brought out his phone to call Jonathan to discuss the news with him. Zero was hot on her heels. She was taking it incredibly hard. It was clear that Carmichael wouldn't rest until he got what he wanted. At this point, she was ready to just go to him herself and stop the madness. The thought of Allison being hurt paralyzed her senses, making her unable to think straight. Walking into the kitchen and pausing at the pantry door, she whipped out her phone and pulled up her chat with Vanessa.

Nessie. Two more deaths, toddler twins. I just can't believe this! What do we do, it's like we're just sitting ducks. Is ANYONE going to go after this guy? -Olivia

Olivia's eyes flickered, seeing Zero standing a few feet away from her, arms behind his back. Just standing there regarding her quietly. Pissed off, she stared back at him, tired of having her privacy invaded. Her skin crawled and burned, demanding relief. Her phone dinged with Vanessa's quick reply.

Ollie, you have to let them do their thing. We are not vigilantes, this man is high up in Government, and even with the men's resources we have to tread very carefully. Please trust they know what they are doing and most of all STAY THE HELL OUT OF IT.-Nessie

Olivia threw her head back on a frustrated groan and then pursed her lips, seeing Zero still staring, assessing her. She narrowed her eyes.

"Zero, I swear to God if you don't leave me the fuck alone right this instant, I will find a way to drown your ass in your SLEEP!" Olivia hissed at him, she lingered in the doorway of the pantry in the kitchen. "There's no window or secret door in here, I have to come out the same way I come in so leave me the hell alone!" Olivia backed into the massive walk-in pantry and slammed the door in Zero's face, her eyes flashing.

She stood there, breathing hard as she finally let herself have her moment to cry.

Her face broke, her features contorting as she slapped both hands over her mouth to keep her ragged sobs in. She fell to her knees, trembling, her hands flat on the floor as she gritted her teeth hard. Ignoring the flash of pain that erupted in her skull at the vicious action.

What was it all for? Giving Allison up, killing myself to pay her doctor bills, Vanessa's marriage ending, and now she finally gets a liver? What was it all for if this man is going to take everything away from us? She lamented.

Crying hard, she gasped for air and slapped her hand to her forearm, squeezing the flesh tightly. She moaned, digging her nails in and scraping. Her heart beat out of control and she repeated the movement, not getting the relief she needed. Looking up, she spotted the shiny stainless steel knife handles gleaming in the light of the pantry and paused, feeling conflicted.

A nervous, excited tingle caressed her body, and she licked her lips, flicking her eyes nervously to the closed door, then to the knives again.

Colin wouldn't want me to do this.... Olivia thought to herself. She stayed unmoving, staring at the handle blades, knowing she would find relief if she could dig just deep enough.

Hauling herself off the floor with a grunt, she snatched one out of the knife block. Desperate, she laid her forearm on the counter and pressed the sharp tip of the blade into her forearm. She felt herself break out into a sheen of sweat and her hand shook, anticipating the burning sensation she knew would follow. Her hand trembled.

Just a tiny cut. He won't know if I make it small enough, she thought.

Olivia pressed down right as the pantry door swung open. Her head swung up just as the first speck of blood bubbled up out of her arm and Colin appeared, freezing as he saw her standing there silently with the knife to her arm. His eyes met hers and they stared at each other for a tense few seconds.

Olivia trembled, feeling the drop of blood drip slowly down her arm.

Eyes tight on hers, Colin walked in, closing the door softly behind him. "Is this what you need? This is why you've been scratching at yourself?" he asked quietly. The question hung uncomfortably in the air between them.

Olivia swallowed hard and felt a tear escape her eye, staying silent. Her lips quivered, and she gasped as the tip of the knife slid minutely deeper. Colin reached forward fast, taking the knife efficiently from her with one hand as he gripped her chin roughly with his other, hauling her face to the side to look at him dead on. He met her eyes and breathed deeply for half a second, smelling the fear on her, as well as her conflict.

This is unbelievably sexy, but I need us safe, amor, Colin thought to himself. He made a split-second decision. "Blood play and cutting are not in our contract except for page three. Do you trust me to do this for you, or do we need to add it in the other sections first? Tell me now," Colin bit out, his eyes hard as he looked at Olivia, seeing her eyes widen and her lips quiver as she struggled with her emotions.

"I trust you," Olivia whispered. "Colin, I t-trust you, please give this to me! Please..." she sobbed, her tears hot on her cheeks, her lips pressed together tightly as she tried to stem the extent of her emotions. Colin's eyes roamed, taking in her face. His nostrils flared slightly at her desperation.

"Then only me. You come to me and ask me for what you need. You are not allowed to do this to yourself. Do you understand me, amor?" Colin asked, seeing her lips tightened. She shook her head yes, then gasped as he rather roughly tightened his hand on her wrist. Moving fast, he made a shallow cut horizontally on her arm, so fast she barely felt it until after it was done.

Riveted, she stared at her arm, the thin shallow line pebbling up with dots of blood. She sagged in relief.

"Another one, please," she begged, refusing to look him in the eye.

Olivia winced slightly and let out a breath as he moved fast, giving her a cut parallel to the first one. She leaned forward on a groan and rested her head on his shoulder. "Thank you," she whispered, feeling the tears receding as sadness gave way to desire. Her hands came up to grip his forearms hard and Colin tensed as she kissed her way to his neck. He pulled away slightly, his eyes hard on hers.

"Why didn't you come to me and talk to me about this?" he breathed, his eyes searching hers.

Olivia stared rather blankly as shame filled her and she stayed silent for a few seconds too long for his comfort. Colin's eyes narrowed.

He snapped his fingers abruptly and Olivia stood there, semi-shocked as her green eyes met Colin's plainly, not blinking. Tilting his head, he regarded her for a silent moment. Pushing off the counter, he walked into her body. Bending his head to her ear, he spoke softly, dangerously low.

"You really think because we're married it changes anything between us, baby?"

Olivia's breath audibly hitched, and she shook her head no, her eyes now watering as her body began to burn as it finally recognized the danger that was her husband.

"Okay," he said calmly, his face turning to meet her eyes. "So when I snap my fingers, what is it I expect you to do?"

"Kneel," she answered, swallowing hard.

"Kneel *what*, Olivia?"

"Sir," she trembled, feeling a very different energy than she ever felt from him before.

Colin stepped back, opening the pantry door and then leaning a shoulder against the frame.

Olivia could see a sliver of Zero's shoulder and the back of his head standing right outside the pantry door.

Colin stared hard at her, snapping his fingers once more. Arms folded, he crossed an ankle over his leg as Olivia sank to the floor at the exact moment Zero turned to face Colin and he froze seeing her in a submissive pose. Colin still held the knife in his hand, nonchalantly, as if he stood casually holding knives every day. The tip of the blade was still red with her blood.

Zero's cold eyes snapped from the blade in Colin's hands to the blood pebbled up on her arms, and for a heart-stopping second their eyes met and they shared something that Olivia couldn't explain. Staring at Zero, Olivia mentally freaked out, thinking for some reason that Colin might try to share her with Zero, knowing it was crazy. But was it really when they were both seemingly unhinged, a match made in heaven? Then Colin spoke.

"Olivia may need protection from Carmichael, the world, hell, even *herself* at times, but Zero," Colin turned his head to regard the dangerous, scary looking lethal killer. Olivia shook as the men locked eyes. "Understand me clearly, when I say that I am the one person on this Earth you will not be able to protect *Lilith* from."

So shocked she couldn't even feel relief that he wasn't about to force her to be with Zero, Olivia felt herself free fall into hell at his words and watched almost as if she was outside of her own body as they two men stared at each other, their own look being communicated between the two of them. And in that moment, she decided she'd never share with him her secret thought, ashamed she was apparently that currently insane enough in her head to think Colin was capable of something like that without even discussing it with her first.

Her hands trembled as she clutched them tightly together.

Zero nodded once, then turned on his heel, without another glance back at them, and exited the home quietly to join the other guards outside. Olivia glanced away quickly as Colin turned his eyes back to her, seeing she was struggling trying to get her breath and unable to find her bearings. Cold, his eyes were merciless. That beast he'd kept successfully chained up all these months finally let free, summoned by Lilith herself.

He walked the few feet back to her and stood there silently, the blade eye level with her for a second, before he squatted down. Olivia's heart pounded and her breath hitched when he took the blade of the knife and tilted her head up to meet his eyes.

"From here on out, you call me 'sir'."

Olivia's eyes raised to meet his, stunned.

"It's time for page three, baby."

TWENTY-ONE
Page III

COLIN HELPED OLIVIA PREPARE, having them both shower, and then dressed her lightly in a thin short dress and nothing else. He pulled her hair up and clipped the mass onto the top of her head and carried her into the room off their closet that he'd had built for this purpose but hadn't yet shown her. He bent slightly, setting her on her feet with an arm around her arm to help her balance.

She had the green tie she'd gifted him around her eyes, blocking her sight so she was unable to see anything. Her flesh pebbled up as Colin helped her kneel on a cushion.

"You don't know where we are because I haven't yet shown you this room. But before I take the tie off, we need to have a talk. First of all, are you comfortable, baby?"

"Yes."

"Scared?"

"...No. Nervous, but not scared." Olivia licked her lips, adjusting her weight on her knees. She was thankful for the thin dress he'd had her put on before carrying her to the room.

"Good." Olivia heard a thunk as Colin put a chair in front of where she knelt and sat momentarily. He lit a cigar and puffed for a second before speaking. "Tell me what you remember of page three of our contract."

Olivia hesitated, not expecting the question. "Uhm...we can only do this two times a year. There's stuff in there like suspension, board binding, water, fire use, electricity use." She stopped and swallowed hard, feeling her skin become hot. She shivered, feeling her nipples distend.

His words from when they were signing the contract came to the forefront of her mind.

"Now, imagine tiny bolts of electricity on these sensitive nipples while I have my lips wrapped around your clit, making you orgasm over and over again. Making you take it like the good girl I know you can be."

Olivia bit her lip, feeling dizzy.

"Yes. Toys too, whips, rope, other things...but I'm curious as to which one of these things scares or intimidates you the most?" Colin tilted his head, regarding her sitting quietly on the cushion.

"I think...I think the fire makes me scared."

"What about it scares you?"

"I'm okay with being hit. I just don't want to be burned," she said a little louder.

"What if I told you I could make it feel good?"

Olivia gave a half laugh. "Come on, Sir. I know you're good at sex, but even you can't control the elements?"

Colin leaned forward and took the tie off, staring at her.

"Can't I?" he whispered, and Olivia felt the sweet hot weight of desire weighing her down at his blatantly confident tone. His eyes flickered from her eyes to her lips as her jaw dropped open and her eyes widened, taking in their surroundings.

"What is this place?" she breathed, her face and chest flushing as her eyes darted here and there, trying to take everything in at once.

"I was busy having this built, while we were looking for you," Colin said simply, standing up and moving the chair to the other side of the room. He walked back to her and spread his legs. Folding his arms behind his back. "It took a lot of my time and did much to keep me sane. Sometimes the only thing keeping me going was knowing that I was going to get you back, and then beat the fuck out of you for running."

He stood silent, watching her breathing deepen the more she was able to take in and process.

Olivia shivered, seeing the entire room the size of their bedroom colored in a deep charcoal gray color. Even the ceiling was the same color as the walls, making the room feel more intimate. The floor was huge tiles of gray slate and the walls were lit with recessed lighting in the perimeter of the room, currently on a dimmed setting creating a romantic atmosphere. The lights highlighted a wall of wooden cabinets, and a floor to ceiling wall of mirrors behind Colin's back.

Suddenly, her eyes landed on a spot above his head, and he smiled as she stilled, seeing a huge, formidable looking iron rack, her eyes lowered, seeing ropes that hung down, the pulley system that controlled them, and what was underneath. Just a simple, small elegant looking firepit that was covered.

"S-Sir, where's the bed? Why is there no bed?" she breathed. Her eyes went impossibly wide.

"We have a bed sweetie, it's in our bedroom. This room is not for comfort. It's for pain." he stood there calmly while her eyes did another slow perusal. Olivia nodded almost absentmindedly. "The room leads out into our bathroom... if we need it."

Her eyes traveled back up his body before meeting his. She stayed silent.

"I need you to trust me, Olivia. Do you trust me?" he said, his voice coming out hoarse. "I can give you what we both so desperately need. I know your body hurts, let me make it better." He brought a hand up to her cheek, caressing her gently.

Olivia stared into his eyes, seeing the love there. Feeling nurtured. "Please don't hurt me, not like that," she whispered, her lips tightened.

"I'll make it hurt just enough. Just enough baby...to give you relief." His fingers tightened on her cheek.

Olivia stayed quiet, but her chest heaved nervously. She licked her trembling lips, trying to speak, to say something.

Colin squatted in front of her, placing his lips harshly to hers, and Olivia could feel the tension within him, the same tension that mirrored her own. The knowledge that this situation they were partaking in excited him made her feel powerful, almost giddy. He pulled away from her mouth too soon and placed a hand along her jaw.

"I'm going to hang you from that rack," his eyes settled unwaveringly on hers, lending her comfort. "And I'm going to warm you up for a bit. Then, I'm going to use the thruster machine on you while I am whipping your back, while I have the electrical clamps attached to your nipples."

Olivia suddenly made a keening sound at his words, her arms wrapped around her torso and she bowed her head, bending slightly as the weight of his words entered her brain and began a torturing echo.

Oh fuck yes, I need it. I want it, she whimpered to herself, rocking back and forth gently.

"Do you know how to use one of those?" Olivia asked. Her voice was small, shaky.

Her body tightened, imagining the lick of the whip as it touched her skin and she moaned miserably, feeling her essence slick down her thighs. The thought excited her almost unbearably and she gritted her teeth as her sex began to throb. "Please tell me you know how to use a whip," her voice came out strangled and she bit back a sob, her mind's eye going back to the porn video of the woman being whipped while she sat on a dildo. The banging between her legs ramped up.

"Honey, I just need you to trust me," he said quietly. "Just trust me,"

Trust me to give this to the both of us amor, he thought to himself. His chest swelled uncomfortably tight as he waited.

"Yes," she sobbed.

"Red is the safe word. Say that, and everything stops. Do you remember why you use red? It's not your normal safe word. You cannot use that one."

Olivia nodded, remembering very well. "Yes, sir. Red, only for if I feel like injury is imminent, like a broken or dislocated bone. That's it. No safe word permissible,"

"Why? Olivia, I need to hear it," Colin stayed quiet.

"Because this is the ultimate act of trust. I have to trust myself entirely with you," she said just as quietly.

"Correct, let us begin," Colin waited as Olivia stood up and walked to his outstretched hand. He paused for a second, staring down at her. Her eyes flickered from his, to the suspension ropes and then back again. "Is there anything you need from me, amor, before we begin?"

Olivia rolled her lips and nodded. "Yes, sir. Can you please kiss me. Just for a little while?" she spoke the words softly. Colin smiled wickedly, taking her wrists and hauling her to the chair that he abandoned earlier. Turning, he sat down lazily, stretching his legs out.

Olivia squealed as he yanked her to him and crashed her into his chest before he hauled her into his lap, making her legs straddle his thick thighs. Placing a broad hand onto the back of her head, he pushed her lips onto hers and slanted his head, licking into her mouth lewdly with a groan.

"God, I love your mouth baby, you're so delectable," he gritted in between wet kisses.

Olivia ground herself against him, her dress riding up her thighs. "Sir..."

"What is it baby?"

"It turned me on when you used the knife on me," she whispered against his lips, sucking his bottom lip into her mouth and giving it a sharp nibble. She gasped as he jerked her even harder against him.

"Oh yeah? Qué otros deseos secretos se esconden en estas profundidades?" he growled, lost in desire he pulled his lips away and sank his teeth into the juncture of her shoulder and neck, making her jerk on top of him.

Olivia moaned, her eyes fluttering shut as she fought her body's instincts to protect her neck. She wiggled on top of him, feeling his lips and teeth pull strongly at her.

"What sir? I don't understand..." she said breathlessly as her hands came up to sink into his hair.

"I said what other secret desires are hidden within these depths? What else are you hiding from me, huh Lilith?" he whispered, his hand trailed down her stomach to the plump flesh between her legs. He found her clit and grasped it, rolling it between his fingers. "Hmmm. God you're always so wet for me." Thrusting two fingers into her, he scissored them slightly, pulling back to regard her face tightly.

"Nothing...I'm not hiding anything sir," she said before biting her lip, feeling him manipulate her g-spot.

"Hmm..." he conceded. Cocking his head, he looked down between them and saw her nipples standing out against her thin dress.

"Sir, please suck them," she moaned, pushing up higher on her knees. She thrust her breasts out, offering them to him.

Any other time he'd gladly take the bait, but not right now. Colin glanced at her sharply, his thumb fluttered against her clit, making her skin feel hot, too tight for her body to handle. He smiled at her gently, seeing her eyes dilate.

"No. I'm getting ready to take care of you, amor. How I want to. What I've been waiting for all these months," his thumb rubbed harder, and he reveled in the feel of her clenching his fingers tighter. She came suddenly, gushing wetly over his fingers.

He put them to his mouth quickly, sucking her juices off. He grasped her under her buttocks and stood swiftly, carrying her to a small mat by the center of the room, next to a small pile of ropes.

"Onto your side and bend your legs back," he ordered, grasping a rope and waiting for her to comply. He worked swiftly, ignoring her gasps of shock as he tied a rope around her lower thigh and her calf, bending her heel to her thigh and tying another rope around her ankle and her upper thigh. He did the other leg, and then began to loop a complicated tie around her torso, roping it around her shoulders and breasts.

Olivia lay patiently quiet as he worked, concentrating on his work. Her eyes landed on a wall that was nothing but mirrors and watched enraptured as he continued to efficiently tie her into several more complicated knots. Standing, he hauled her up and sat her on her knees on a padded raised table. Reaching over to grab a rope, he attached the fastener at the end to the back of the rope, one on each side of her legs, and then hit a button on a remote, causing her to suddenly lift a couple inches off the table.

Olivia's mouth dropped at the feeling of her body weight settling into the ropes.

"How is it, are you ok? Anything hurt, or pulling?" Colin asked, standing before her with his arms folded, he assessed every rope and where they were attached to the suspension ropes hanging from the iron railing above them.

"No sir..." she said, biting her lip as he suddenly reached forward and pushed her hard, sending her flying through the air. She squealed, feeling her heart slam into her chest, stealing her breath. He caught her easily, making her motionless again.

"Just to get the blood pumping," he said with a wicked grin. And with that he stepped back and walked to a side of the room where there was a cabinet, and out of it he grabbed a fire extinguisher.

Olivia's eyes widened at the sight as she panted, still feeling shocked after swinging around. "Wait!" she whispered, clearing her throat of her nerves. "Coli-" she cut her words off at his sudden sharp, narrow eyed stare. "Sir," she said quietly. "Please don't set me on fire."

"What if I want to set you on fire, amor?" he tilted his head at her. "Are you within your rights to tell me no?" he asked calmly, placing the extinguisher down with a clunk he stood back up and regarded her once again.

Olivia turned her eyes to the wall of mirrors again and paused, seeing herself for the first time. *Oh my god*...she said quietly in her head. She swallowed thickly. "No sir, I'm not."

She was hanging from ropes in the middle of the room, her legs completely restrained and spread open, her pussy just there, for whatever he wanted; vulnerable, not able to call any shots. She began to pant as he walked around the room and grabbed more things, putting them on the table he'd sat her on before he hauled her into the air.

"You know, I wasn't going to go this easy on you, but I think I'll let you be able to clench your fingers and toes for this, so I won't be binding them...this time," Colin said nonchalantly as he fiddled with a machine. He put the machine down then turned and walked to her, bending down and hauling the device that was under her up a few feet, about five feet beneath her. He took the lid off the device and pushed a button, starting a flame under her.

Olivia gasped as the heat met her sensitive skin and wiggled hard, trying to move but only managing to make herself swing slightly. "Colin!" she screeched, feeling the warmth lick at her pussy.

Oh fuck, fuck, fuck, fuck, fuck! she screamed inside of her head, feeling her body temperature begin to rise. She moaned miserably, not able to get away from the heat tormenting her. She jerked, feeling a sudden slap on her pussy.

"What's my name?" Colin said calmly, his eyes staring up at her as she began to pant. He lowered his hand palm down just under her vagina, holding it there for several long seconds, making sure the heat wasn't too hot. Despite what she thought, he didn't want to burn her.

"It's sir...I'm sorry sirrrr..." Olivia panted, knowing without looking that her face and chest were turning red.

"Are you ok Olivia, is it too hot? Tell me the truth," he murmured, removing his hand from the source of the heat, and giving it back to her full force.

Olivia shook her head slowly, not wanting to lie to him. Not while she was currently in the state she was in.

"Good girl. Now that we're getting that pussy warmed up, let's give your nipples a little love, hmm? How does that sound, amor?" he waited till she raised her head and trained her green eyes on his before he gave her a devilish smile and turned back to his table. He pushed it closer, taking a clamp that was connected by a wire to the small machine and he slowly reached for her nipple, clamping it down. Olivia hissed and then moaned, the pain feeling so good. He waited a second, watching her reaction carefully before attaching the other clamp.

"Now, these are going to send little electrical currents through your nipples. I'm going to start off light, because in a minute, I'm going to place the thruster machine inside you and then I'm going to start working on your back. Are you listening to me, Amor?"

Olivia, who'd begun shaking at the knowledge of what she knew was about to be one hell of a sexual experience at the hands of her husband who didn't just have a sadistic side, but a crazy, wildly imaginative one as well.

"Yes, I hear you," she whispered. "You did NOT tell me you were like this. Who thinks like this, sir?" she chanced, not meaning to be offensive, but she couldn't think straight with the fires of hell right at her pussy.

Colin's eyes met hers, a flash of surprise crossing his features before he began to laugh. A truly dark chuckle that he couldn't stop.

"Sweetheart, you signed the contract. You knew what was in there," he said through his laughter. He reached over and turned the current on to the second to lowest setting, and his smile became brighter as she suddenly threw her head back on a harsh wail.

Olivia jerked in the ropes as the current ran through her nipples and exploded on her clit, which was currently burning up from the inside out. She heaved a harsh breath, feeling her skin shrink too small for her body.

"FFUUUCCCKKKK!" Olivia screamed, not able to stop wiggling as she hung there miserably. Inhaling hard, she screamed again, feeling Colins wet lips wrap around her clit and suckle her strongly into his mouth. Shocked at the unexpected contact, she came almost immediately. Her face flushed bright red when she heard her essence splash against the ground. She stared rather unseeingly at the mirrors behind him, her chest heaving as she struggled to right all the sensations rolling through her at once.

Pulling away, he looked down at the floor under them. Amused, his eyes raised back to hers, seeing her body had broken out into a sheen of sweat. He turned, leaving her to it and walked to another cabinet, grabbing a small package and what looked to be a small briefcase. Returning to the table by her again, he opened it, setting it up and pulling out the various attachments.

Taking a small plastic structure attached to some straps he turned to her and wrapped the straps around her hips, snapping it in place, then settling a fleshy soft silicone piece against her clit. He took a remote and clicked a button and it began to buzz on her clit. Olivia felt her temperature rise even higher and a sheen of sweat broke out on her body, making her feel slightly dizzy. He turned back to the briefcase dismissively.

Olivia looked miserably at him working, wanting to cry, feeling like she was strung so tight. She licked her lips on a soft whimper.

"Siiirrrrr," she pleaded. "I don't think...I don't know..." she tried, not able to express herself.

Colin remained quiet. Listening, but not feeling the need to respond. He took out a medium-large dildo and attached it to the thruster machine.

Olivia's eyes widened once more and her mouth fell open, seeing him work over the machine, preparing it for her. Colin looked at her, a small smile on his face when he caught her facial expression.

"I'm just going to venture to guess you didn't know what a thruster machine was when you signed page three, huh?" he chuckled again. The sadistic side of him was truly getting a kick out of rendering her speechless, knowing the state of her emotions had to be quite interesting and discombobulating. "That's unfortunate. I'm going to teach you all about contracts, pretty thing. We won't be making this mistake again,"

Shaking her head no, Olivia began trembling as he turned the fire onto a lower setting, giving her a very small temporary relief. He pushed the table closer, aiming the dildo at her twitching pussy.

"I'm turning it down because I don't want the machine to get hot and potentially burn you," he explained simply.

"Coliiinnnnn-sir, sir, sir, sir..." closing her eyes, she shut him from her sight, suddenly feeling almost too vulnerable. She tensed, feeling the thick silicone head of the toy nudge her entrance. Her mouth dropped open as he moved it closer, shoving it gently forward inch by inch until it was almost completely inside of her. She couldn't meet his eyes. Something about him using a sex machine on her shattered all her defenses and that last wall between them that she'd kept erected subconsciously.

Oh my Gooooood-

Jerking in the ropes, Olivia threw her head back, screaming in earnest as Colin turned the toy on and it began to thrust inside of her at the same time he turned up the current on her nipples. He watched her face carefully, before turning it slightly higher. Olivia made a small sound as her eyes began to water and her vagina throbbed as a heavy pressure settled into her sex, wanting to be fulfilled.

Oh fuuuck, it's painful but it feels so good.

Colin appeared next to her face, yanking her to the side by her hair to look at him. His own features were pulled tight with desire as he struggled to not undo all the work it took to get her to this point so he could take her body the way he wanted. With a firm hand, he adjusted his painful erection and a muscle ticked in his jaw as he groaned, seemingly barely able to restrain himself. Olivia opened her eyes in shock and there was a tense moment where they just stared silently at each other. Him, letting her know that she was his to do with as he pleased. Her, helpless, giving up control she knew he so desperately needed and craved.

Olivia gasped, feeling her face snap to the side as he suddenly smacked her, turning her face away from him. She inhaled through her nose as she orgasmed again, gritting her teeth hard. She blew out a breath as her toes and fingers clenched hard against the hot heady feeling weighing her down.

"You say my name again, then you're truly in trouble. Do you understand?" he whispered, bringing her head back to face him.

"Yes sirrrrrr," Olivia sighed weakly.

"Now, are you okay? Answer me truthfully, amor."

"Yes sir," Olivia squeezed her eyes shut, feeling her heartbeat ramp up uncomfortably.

Colin nodded, leaning over to smack a hard kiss onto her lips before turning away from her once more. He clicked a button on the remote and the clit vibrator ramped up slightly making her wail in pleasured agony. Ignoring her, he walked to another cabinet and pulled a long, deadly looking single tailed whip out.

Oh God, I've never even used one of those, she whispered to herself, licking her lips.

Olivia threw her head back, shuddering at the sight. Already feeling the tip hitting her, even though he was still standing a few feet away uncoiling it. She flinched again, hearing the deadly snap of the whip as he gave it a test and then his voice as he spoke loudly to her from across the room.

"Olivia, you must breathe. Breathe, amor."

She relaxed, not even realizing she'd been holding her breath in anticipation. Obediently she let out a whimpering breath, eyeing the machine thrusting steadily inside of her. Throwing her head back, she bit her lip, moaning in earnest as she struggled, attempting to refrain from orgasming again. She twitched, fearing she wasn't going to make it through this experience. Her nipples burned, the electrical current like a live wire from her breasts to her clit, which was enduring a burning of its own under the vibrator's ministrations. She shuddered, feeling a bead of sweat work its way down her temple and between her breasts.

"Enjoy them amor, they may slow down a bit, depending on how hard I hit you. We're about to find out just how you react to what I love most," Colin said to her, his voice confident as he got himself into position several feet behind her.

Olivia raised her head to look at them in the mirror and her eyes widened, seeing the change in her husband. The shift had happened so incrementally that she'd missed it. She assessed his reflection greedily.

Colin's features were standing out in sharp relief, his muscles tight with tension, and the veins in his arms roped almost sensually up under his tattoos. He rolled his neck as he slowly took his stance several feet behind her. He was calm, collected, and seemed at peace.

He'd taken his shirt off, exposing his tattoos and bare skin to her gaze. His thick muscles rippled, his skin shiny as he put one foot in front of the other and ground his foot slightly against the floor. She watched, entranced, as he took the tail of the whip in his hand and pulled it slowly through the space in between his thumb and forefinger, caressing it almost lovingly with his hand before he tossed it behind him. His eyes met hers briefly in the mirror and he treated her to a slow, wicked smile before his arm snapped forward on a quiet grunt.

And as if in slow motion, Olivia watched the tail of the whip come closer and closer to her, and an almost feral look crossed over Colin's face before the tip connected with her back.

Too stunned to make a sound, Olivia flinched and readjusted her grip on the ropes as her heart expanded painfully in her chest. She closed her eyes, rejoicing as she felt something in her soul slowly shift into place.

She took a slow steadying breath as the whip connected lightly once more and she relaxed. She hung there silent, feeling her pussy clamp on the dildo hard as he snapped the whip against her repeatedly, giving her warmup taps against her skin. She yelped and inhaled sharply as the next one made contact hard on the delicate skin of her left shoulder blade, hey eyes flying open, meeting his in surprise. He gave her another sexy grin as the next one hit just as hard.

She kept her eyes on him, crying out as the next lash licked the top of her shin.

"What was that, amor?" Colin said in his elegant voice, as he brought the whip forward again, this time landing on her right buttock. Olivia's head fell to the side and she twitched, biting her lip hard and squealing as his hits came faster and slightly harder. Her back smarted and she took joy in the feeling.

"I said it feels so good sir, m-magical," she moaned, she wiggled, feeling herself orgasm on the dildo. Her eyes narrowed, as her pussy suddenly felt overstimulated. The soles of her feet burned, and her fingernails dug into her palms as she tensed up hard. She almost choked on the next sharp inhale of breath as she screamed almost manically as she orgasmed once more, right as Colin hit her the hardest he'd hit her so far, right on the fleshy skin of her left buttock.

Oh my God is this what I've been missing my whole life? She shivered with happiness as the next lash landed almost whisper soft against her shoulder blade, reminding her of Colin's loving touches as he soothed her through her sad moments.

She was struck aback at the realization that she hadn't felt the need to tell him how hard or soft to hit, it was like he just knew.

He knew what she needed.

"There we go, amor! That's what I'm talking about. Now it's time to really play," Colin said, tossing the whip down. Walking swiftly to the table, he turned the speed on the dildo up one more notch, turned the vibrator down a bit, and turned the flame completely off. Olivia blinked at the duality of the switching of sensations and licked her lips as he then took one of the clamps off one her nipples and left the other one attached, making her feel suddenly off kilter.

"No, *oh no please*," she whispered, her eyes widening in surprise. Her heart began to beat painfully as shockwaves rolled through her body, and she felt her sex spasm painfully around the dildo which suddenly felt thicker inside her, battering against her tender, swollen tissues. She almost choked on a shocked breath as her body temperature rose almost unbearably.

"No!" she screamed, panicking as her body fell out of control, the loss of some of the sensation, and the increase of the thrusting making her body confused. She swallowed hard, feeling tears come to her eyes. Colin walked swiftly past her and grabbed the whip once more.

"I'm about to make it all better, Olivia," he assured her right as he swung the whip forward and Olivia barely had time to hear the sharp crack before she began screaming as he really let loose. Every crack rendered the air around them, confusing her even further. Some hit her back, others hit on her legs, on her arm, her shoulder, her buttocks. He varied between light taps, and harsh ones. Her body burned, despite the lack of flame under her, and she could hear her juices hit the floor as she squirted in earnest. She struggled against the ropes, fighting the next orgasm, the strength of it making her dizzy.

She blinked hazily, seeing his arm raise the whip before he flicked it and she screamed hard, feeling drool hitting her chin as she suddenly orgasmed the hardest she ever had in her life.

She barely heard him drop the whip as he walked up behind her and swiped his hands gently down her back and legs, soothing her.

"So fucking beautiful amor," he praised as her screams broke off into sobs as she began to cry. He smoothed his hand to her front and manipulated her free nipple with the fingers of one hand, and moved the vibrator aside he grasped her clit with the other, rolling them both. "Almost done, beautiful," Olivia thrashed her head, her back was burning, her nipples were so tight they were painful, and her clit was so engorged every tug and flick made her gush wetly.

"Sir plleeaassseeeee," she moaned miserably, tensing up as he dug his fingernail into her nipple and twisted it gently. Colin chuckled.

"I don't even know what you're begging for, because once I turn everything off, it's my turn. You know that right?" he whispered against her ear, hiding his smile.

Joy. It was a beautiful feeling, and he took pleasure in her shocked eyes meeting his before she turned away, screwing her face up in another orgasm, this one sounding like a torturous one.

He bent to her, licking into her mouth, licking up her chin that was covered in her spit and swallowing her screams as he played with her some more, loving the hot feel of her skin from being pleasured too long. He pulled away reluctantly and turned off the machines, freeing her from them gently. Not able to help himself, he leaned forward and softly sucked her overstimulated nipples, eating up her small whimpers as she hung there helplessly. He smiled as her cum splashed against the ground once more when he pulled the dildo out.

Helping her out of the suspension and the ropes, he stretched her out on the mat and massaged her lovingly. Wrapping her up in a robe hanging by the door, he carried her through the closet and into their bedroom where he laid her down and talked to her while he fucked her nice and soft, chasing his own release.

"Do you have any idea how settled you make me feel? How long I've waited for you baby?" he whispered to her, his hips moving slowly against hers as he ran a hand through her hair, cupping her head to keep her still while he moved his lips just as slow against her.

Olivia moaned, arching under him and running her hands down his back. She smiled against his mouth. "Well, I know it wasn't near as long as I waited for you. You are thirty nine years old after all."

They shared a chuckle and he gave her a surprisingly rough circle of his hips.

"Aahh," she sighed, feeling sore and on such a high.

"Yeah?" he chuckled against her lips. "You like when I do that?"

Olivia nodded. Licking along his bottom lip, she nibbled on it before pulling back and looking into his dark eyes. "As long as you keep it nice and slow for me." She tightened hard around him, making him grunt. He gave her a smile.

"Yes Ma'am." he chuckled again and feathered his finger across her cheek as he repeated the movement.

"Ohhh..." she gave him a teasing look, arching her eyebrow. "I think I like the sound of that."

Colin raised his eyebrows as he kept his movements nice and slow. "Hmmm...I wouldn't get used to it." He leaned further into her face and kissed the side of her mouth. "Did you like me whipping you baby? What was your favorite thing we did in there? Tell me...you know I want to hear." Colin ceased moving as she suddenly flooded his dick. He lowered his head to her neck and breathed deeply as he held himself high and hard inside of her. "God, that was such a great nonverbal answer... you feel so *hot*."

Olivia whimpered through a slow wicked orgasm, replaying the way the whip felt hitting her back, and the way he looked when he welded it. "Oh Colin, you looked so sexy behind me, whipping me." She rippled around him again, getting off on replaying what happened just an hour before. She looped her arms around his neck and held him close. "You're the most handsome man I've ever seen. And you're all mine."

Colin pulled back, and gave her a wicked smile. Noting that their Page III session brought out a different side of Olivia than he was used to getting. "Oh baby, nothing beats how you looked up there, your red hair, pink flushed cheeks, the way your skin reddened for me so deliciously. Ohhhh." He groaned, the sound almost her undoing and Colin hissed as he felt her slick over him once more. "There's way more to come. I hope you're ready."

Olivia's eyes flashed in a challenge at him. "I was *born* ready." She licked her lips, throwing her head back as he suddenly leaned down and took a sensitive distended nipple into his wet, warm mouth and suckled at her. He took a second to switch between her breasts, giving her love there before he settled even deeper into her and placed his lips to her ear.

"Once upon a time, there was a lonely man who, despite all his wealth and connections, seemed to live a life with only half of a heart in his chest. And every day he searched for the other half. He would walk around and look for it within other people, seeing theirs didn't quite fit. They were too whole, not cracked like his."

Olivia whimpered, slapping a hand to her mouth as her eyes welled up with tears. Colin continued, still moving nice and slow against her, feeling tremors begin to rack her body.

"Or they were a different color, a different size. He looked every-where he could, coffee shops, parties, book stores. And still, no one could help him. Their hearts all belonged to someone else. The man became desperate, looking for the other half of his heart in things instead of people, so he began to search elsewhere, and yet still nothing fulfilled him. Eventually, his light became dimmer and dimmer as the years went on until he gave up, fearing that no one would ever see and match his light."

Olivia quietly cried, his admission and the way he was working her body so sweetly after making her so discombobulated in their sex room unraveling her.

"One day, he went for a ride and saw a beautiful red flame in the window of a diner, and when he got closer, realized a woman was inside. And when she stood up, he saw her chest glowed just like his, the same color. When he got closer, he saw her heart's cracks matched his. And the man felt bone shattering relief knowing that he finally found her. He found the other half of his soul. And baby, you light me up *so* bright."

He moved his lips to hers and kissed her deeply through her tears, now telling her without words what she meant to him. Olivia wrapped her arms and legs around him, holding him close while they shared something much deeper than sex. Deeper than love.

By the time he disengaged from her, he was of the opinion that their first venture into the Page III activities was successful, and turned his mind to wanting her to help plan the next one, wondering if she would like to do this more than twice a year.

Her answer was a resounding yes, but she didn't want to help plan it every time. He chuckled at her request for him to always surprise her with something new, as she adored how creative he was in the bedroom. They'd decided to make Page III a monthly venture and would revise the contract accordingly.

And Olivia's revision? For him to make up a new fairytale for them every time, and tell it to her while they got busy.

TWENTY-TWO

Parental Reckonings

"HEY JONATHAN, YO' WHAT'S up, you good?" Colin was sitting in his study going over some paperwork for his company when Jonathan's ringtone lit up the silent area.

"Yes," Jonathan replied in a solemn tone. Colin felt the hair on the back of his neck stand up, and he put his papers down at the almost wary tone that was present in his friend's voice. "But I have something to tell you, my friend."

"What is it? Are the girls okay?" Colin felt his heart begin to race as he sat forward, about to jump up out of his seat to find Olivia.

"Yes... but, Colin... it's your father, Henry."

There were a tense few moments of silence while Colin's heart decided to slow down and skip a beat instead. He swallowed hard as all the blood drained from his face, leaving him slightly lightheaded. Out of all the things in the world he would have expected his friend to present him with, this was not in the realm of possibilities.

"What do you mean, my father? What are you talking about, Jonathan?" Colin worked hard to try to keep his voice level, but the strain was present.

"I don't mean to have kept this from you brother, but...I've been keeping tabs on your father for you. I know you said you didn't want to have anything to do with him and I respected that. But I thought it might be smart to have a general idea of his whereabouts just in case anything happened..."

Of course you fucking did, Jonathan. Colin thought to himself, leaning forward and placing his head wearily in his hand. He took a deep breath, weary of the extent his friend meddled, but knew that he was right more often than not. He chose not to let it bother him. *"And?"*

"And he's in a hospital in New York, dying of late-stage pancreatic cancer. I just thought you should know so you could..." Jonathan went silent, not sure how to approach his best friend's feelings. "I am truly sorry if I've overstepped my boundaries regarding this, but I know how this bothers you deep down inside. Brother, you have a chance for closure if you should want it. *But if you do,* you need to hurry. It doesn't seem Henry's got very long."

Colin cleared his throat and sat back in his chair with a deep huff, feeling his eyes prick with unshed tears. "Thank you, Jonathan. Please send me the information so I can inform our security team. I'll let you know what I end up doing." And with that, he hung up the phone. Placing it softly on the desktop, he let his eyes meander to his picture wall, where he'd put the canvases that had previously been hung in his guesthouse. The image of his dad stared back at him. Healthy. What would he look like sick?

Giving the canvas a few more seconds of perusal, he picked his phone back up when he saw Jonathan had texted him the information for his father and he got up swiftly, heading out the door to speak to his team and grab Olivia.

***

Three hours later, Colin walked into the hospital room with Olivia hanging back in the hallway, feeling his stomach drop further with every step as the end of his father's bed came into view. He paused, hearing the muted click of his shoes on the tile mixing with the muted beeping of the monitors in the dimmed lighting of the room.

He felt Olivia's presence, even though he didn't physically have her next to him. He was nervous and wanted to approach his father alone, terrified of the depth of emotions he feared would consume him.

Swallowing thickly, he closed his eyes, feeling his throat clog up as the old feelings of inadequacy swamped him suddenly, and he could hear his father yelling the last words he ever heard him speak at him like it was yesterday.

"You're worthless! You killed her! *YOU!* You're not my son anymore! Get out of my sight."

Colin's hand fisted as he took a steadying breath and resumed walking deeper into the room, seeing his father's hands, his arms, and then his head come into view. He stopped just as his father's gray eyes flickered heavily, aware that he was no longer alone in the room.

"Hey Dad," Colin said, his deep voice sounding unsure, but no longer bitter. Pity began to swell inside him as he locked eyes with the man he'd last seen twenty-three years ago. Surprise filled him with how dilapidated he looked. Weak. No longer the boisterous, strapping, broad man he'd remembered from his adolescence.

"Son?" Henry McDermont's gaunt face filled with surprise as he took Colin in. His face showed disbelief and then sorrow suddenly pulled his features tight. "Oh Colin, please tell me that's you, that I'm not hallucinating again." He began to sob, closing his eyes and putting shaking fingers to the bridge of his nose, letting out a ragged exhale before suddenly fumbling for the nurse's button.

"Help me! I'm seeing things again." Henry suddenly groaned, trying to hit the button on the cord to summon the nurse.

Colin crossed the few feet of space between them, grabbing the cord and pulling it away. He placed his hand over his father's shaky, frail one.

Why didn't I reach out sooner? Colin lamented to himself sadly, feeling his father's clammy skin underneath his fingertips.

"Colin?! It's really you?" Henry gasped, his eyes tightening as he laid there, trying to maneuver himself to get a better look, but he was just too weak. Colin leaned further into his eyesight and let his father lock eyes with him momentarily before he stepped back. He turned his face away and cleared his throat, which suddenly clogged up, seeing the depth of regret in his father's eyes.

It was painful to see.

"Yes Dad, I'm here. I would ask how you're doing but...it doesn't look like that really needs to be answered," Colin said softly. Looking to the side and seeing a recliner, he reached for it, dragging it over to the bed. Sitting, he tugged the lapels of his suit jacket before placing an ankle over a knee and making himself comfortable.

Henry shook his head minutely, taking a deep breath and looking like the very action was tiring him out.

"I'm not doing good, son. I've missed you so much. So much, I am so sorry. I have so many regrets." Henry laid his head back against the pillow, taking another gasping breath, collecting himself. "I've been following you for a while, but you became really successful, and I didn't want you to think I was just showing up because of your status." He turned his eyes to Colin again, a tear fell out and down his cheek making Colin's chest tighten with pain. "Son, I am so e-extraordinarily *p-proud* of you. And your mother would be too. I am so sorry that I wasn't able to humble myself enough to be there when you needed me the most." Henry's next breath sounded painful.

Colin sat there silently with his gaze tight on the floor. He put his fist against his lips as he struggled to process his father, giving him the closure he'd spent years praying for. Leaning forward, he bowed his head and clasped his hands between his knees. Lost in his thoughts and memories, he startled, feeling a soft hand land on the back of his neck.

Olivia.

Settling immediately, he reached out to his father and placed his hand around his, making the older man turn his head to the side warily, opening his eyes which rounded as he saw Olivia.

"I've died?" he whispered, his eyes going wide.

Olivia smiled and shook her head. "No sir, you're still with us. I'm Colin's wife, Olivia. It's nice to meet you," she said, leaning forward herself and placing her hand over Colin's and squeezing Henry's fingers.

Henry's mouth fell open.

"Do Elena and I have grandkids?" the man gasped, his face looking incredulous. Colin glanced up, piercing him with his stare.

"Not yet, dad," Colin said, his voice coming out stronger with the realization his father never moved on, stuck in the pain of the past. He'd seemingly died right along with her all those years ago. Jonathan's information had revealed that he'd never remarried, had no more kids, and worked as a janitor in a middle school until he'd come down with cancer.

Henry visited Elena's grave and had dinner in the cemetery three times a week, every week, until he couldn't make the trip anymore.

Colin's heart suddenly ached for him. He knew what it would be like to fall into a well of misery that seemed never ending. It didn't take but four months to feel like he was an empty shell of the man he once was when Olivia had been gone. Though it still hurt, a fresh understanding entered his heart regarding his father. He had to endure twenty-three years without the love of his life.

"Son...do you forgive me?" he gasped tiredly, his face looking sunken in as he reached out his other hand for him. "I love you so much. You're my boy, my only boy. I was so foolish...so foolish. Of course...it wasn't your fault. It wasn't. I was wrong... I wasn't strong enough for you, not a man," Henry moaned, his head lolling against the pillow as he squeezed his eyes shut and then a lone tear fell out of his eye, spilling onto his cheek. His breaths labored, his chest falling and rising raggedly, and his broad hand shook in Colin's.

Colin bowed his head again, placing his head into his hand as he was suddenly overcome himself, his body trembled, and he swallowed back a sob.

"I forgive you, of course I forgive you dad. I love you too. You'll always be my father, siempre. La Muerte no cambiara eso, papi. La distancia tampoco. Te amo," Colin gritted out.

Death wont change that. Distance didn't either. I love you.

"I love you too son...my boy-" Henry's weak voice suddenly trailed off.

Colin rocked in the chair, struggling with trying to hold back in his tears. When he looked up, his dad was gone, and his hand went slack in his. The monitor beeped, showing no heart activity.

Colin's tears broke free at the knowledge he hadn't been too late.

Olivia bent down, kissing the top of his head and running her hand soothingly down his back as he heaved big breaths, feeling the pain washing over him in overwhelming waves.

"Honey," Olivia said softly, squatting down and placing herself in front of him. She placed her forehead against his. "I'm here baby," she squeezed his hands and pressed closer, putting her head onto his shoulder and sighing when Colin suddenly banded both arms around her and let out a tortured sound. He hauled her to him tightly and shuddered. Olivia felt his tears hot on her shoulder.

"They're together now, him and your mom. They're happy, there's peace here. I can feel it, love," she whispered, rocking him, pressing her lips to his neck and breathing him in.

"I would never live that long without you," Colin said suddenly, pulling back. "I refuse, Olivia. If you go, I go," he said simply, knowing it was true.

"I'm not going anywhere. I'm right here, my love," Olivia whispered as the nurse came in, alerted that Henry was gone. They ignored her, lost in comforting each other.

"We're going to get through this. Carmichael can't win, he won't," Colin said, placing his hand on the side of her face. Olivia nodded, the sadness in her heart pulsing, feeling like a thorn was shoved in there that she couldn't remove.

She wondered if she ever would.

Colin stood up, holding his hand out for her and helping her up gently. She watched as he turned his eyes back to his father and then reached forward, running his hand down the back of his dad's head, feeling his hair before pulling away.

They made the two hour drive back in silence, after Colin had settled his father's instructions away. His funeral would be in a few days, and he would be buried next to his mother. Colin planned on having a tombstone of the two of them sitting on a bench, facing every sunrise and sunset together.

They arrived home and Olivia ran a bath, undressing Colin quietly and treating him to soft kisses all over his body. She murmured to him gently and held him while they sat in the hot water, and she pressed her ear against his chest, feeling his heartbeat steadily against her ear, thanking God for His strength and praying that He would keep them all safe.

***

A few days later, Olivia stood at the cherry wood casket with Colin, holding hands with him while he said his final goodbyes to his father before the ushers closed the casket and replaced the flowers on top. Through the lace on her black veil, she regarded his solemn face tightly and looked over at her sister, Jonathan, and Allison who were sitting on the front pew, dressed all in black when suddenly Vanessa let out a gasp and jerked, looking down.

Olivia's jaw dropped, and Colin turned, looking over seeing something was going on. His hand tightened on hers as Jonathan suddenly stood up and glanced at him briefly before turning his attention back to Vanessa.

"My water just broke. Ohhh my God, I am so sorry Colin," she whispered, struggling to stand up and then yelping slightly as Jonathan picked her up swiftly in his arms. Colin turned and spoke to the funeral director quietly before turning and grabbing Allison with his other hand. He pulled Olivia and Allison after him as he began to walk briskly to the entrance of the cathedral they were in.

"Let's go!" he said sharply, jerking his head at their security. "Where there's death, there's life," he said almost reverently as he led the way out the door, waiting for Zero to go first. He yanked open the door to their armored SUV and ushered them in. They drove off, headed to the Sinclair household, to watch baby Ian be born.

"Is my brother coming?" Allison said, looking over from her spot in her booster seat, she had a big smile on her face, showing she was missing two teeth.

Olivia looked over at her and grabbed her hand smiling.

"Yes baby, little Ian will be here anytime today! Are you as excited as I am?" she leaned in and whispered conspiratorially to her as Allison giggled and nodded her head. "You know, you'll always be my little girl right, no one will ever take your place, especially some stinky little boy," Olivia wrinkled her nose at the little girl, and they all shared a laugh until Allison spoke again.

"I know momma."

The car went quiet, and Allison turned her head to look out the window at the trees whizzing by. Olivia turned shocked eyes to Colin who furrowed his brow and gave her a 'what the hell look'.

"Allison, baby... did you just call me momma..." Olivia whispered, her face going pale.

Allison looked over at her. "Yes, a pretty angel came to me when I was in the pool and said my mommy was coming to get me, and she would keep me warm while we waited for you." She turned her head back to the window. "But, I still want to live with mommy, and daddy, and baby Ian. I love my little brother," she said simply.

Olivia leaned back in her seat with wide eyes and reached out a shaky hand to Allison, wrapping her fingers with hers, staying silent. Colin reached back in concern and placed a hand on her leg, seeing her stare rather blankly off in the distance with a shocked expression on her face. A tear fell from her eye and to her breast, soaking the fabric there. Making himself stay quiet, he gave her knee a squeeze and as soon as they got to the house he jumped out, ripped Olivia's car door open and hauled her out and to him, hugging her to him hard.

He bent to her lips, kissing her softly. He rubbed his hands through her hair, trying to soothe her.

"Amor, are you okay?" he asked quietly, seeing her face still pale. She sniffled and nodded her head, bringing up a shaky hand to wipe a tear away. Her green eyes looked tortured as they met his chocolate colored ones.

"I am, but this isn't about me right now. Please let's just be here for Vanessa and Jonathan right now."

Colin nodded, giving her another soft kiss, seeing Jonathan carry Vanessa out of the SUV and another vehicle pull up with their doula. They helped Allison out of the car, and they all went inside the big mansion to watch life enter the world.

***

"Push Nessie! Fucking *PUSH!*" Olivia gasped into Vanessa's ear as she felt her squeeze her hand so hard that a knuckle cracked. She'd done exactly what she said she wouldn't do and got in the birthing tub with her. And there was goo everywhere.

She wiggled her toes, feeling them brush Jonathan's knee who was in there with them. The only ones who weren't were Colin and Allison. Colin said he had to draw the line somewhere, and Allison turned her nose up at the nasty water as she sat there quietly with her hand in Colin's.

Vanessa let out a pained groan and a whimper. "Oh my God, I'm going to *die!*" she lamented loudly before letting out another scream. Her face turned bright red as she suddenly cut off her screams and pushed hard. Olivia winced, her eyes sliding over to Colin's in sympathy. Vanessa collapsed, leaning back against Olivia weakly. Tears were trailing down her face.

"No you're not mommy! That man that was at the church today said you were going to be fine."

"Huh?" Olivia and Vanessa said the word at the same time, throwing Allison a confused glance.

"What man? Someone talked to you? When? How?" Vanessa gaped at Jonathan, who suddenly looked angry. "We had security everywhere! Who the hell could have talked-"

Olivia's eyebrows raised as Vanessa let out a sharp scream and contorted her body in the tub and Olivia gagged as some goo got stuck to her arm. She blinked her watering eyes away and sniffed, swallowing the nausea that was threatening to spew forth.

"No, the man that was in the pretty shiny box, he's right there. See?" Allison turned and pointed a few feet away from Colin. "He doesn't look like that though, like how he was in the box. He looks kinda like Uncle Colin, except there was a pretty lady with him. She said she loves you, Uncle Colin. She's *reaallllyyy* pretty." Allison had a goofy smile on her face as she clutched her beyond destroyed pink bunny to her chest. Her eyes looked far away as she stared off into the corner of the room they were in.

Colin stiffened and turned to look behind him, the hair on the back of his neck standing up as he glanced over to where she was looking. As if he expected to suddenly be able to see spirits.

Everyone went quiet as they turned too, to look where she was pointing. There was nothing.

"Allah..." Jonathan breathed, looking between Vanessa and Colin.

Vanessa suddenly gritted her teeth and bore down hard, straining silently.

"Ohhhh there's the head. Just give us a few hard pushes dear." The doula announced, plunging her hand in the water and feeling in between Vanessa's legs who was now gasping. She looked up at them. "You'd be surprised how often this happens; kids have the ability to see a lot of stuff. They tend to lose that as they get older, though. Some don't. Ah, okay daddy, ready to catch your son?" She stood back, wiping her hands on a towel as Jonathan positioned himself between Vanessa's legs.

Olivia shuddered, knowing a bunch of other gunk was about to fly out along with the baby, and she locked eyes with Colin and gave him a weak smile. It was seriously something special they were sharing and despite how disgusted she felt, she knew she'd never forget this day. He gave her a smile back, reaching out a dry hand to touch her cheek as he held her gaze and she knew what he was thinking in that moment.

When was it going to be their turn?

Olivia wasn't sure, but she was positive it wasn't going to be in a tub where she could feel all the yucky stuff floating and sticking to her skin. She gasped, breaking her eye contact with Colin and smiled brightly, seeing the baby come out and into Jonathan's arms. Vanessa sagged against her once more and she gave her a smacking kiss against her cheek.

"Thank you, sis." Vanessa panted tiredly, smiling as Jonathan raised baby Ian out of the tub and laid him on her chest before the doula got to work on the baby, cleaning and suctioning. "I know you think it's disgusting but I couldn't have done this without you. I love you."

"I love you too, Nessie, sisters forever."

"Sisters forever." Vanessa giggled as they both looked down at baby Ian, who was now crying.

Olivia ran a finger down his cheek and arm, remembering the day she had Allison. It was the happiest day of her life. She felt a tear fall down her face and she sniffled, closing her eyes briefly against the memory. She opened them again and found Allison, who was staring at her brother with such a look of adoration that she felt that place inside her heart shift. The place that held so much hurt, and made her cry almost daily. The pain suddenly lessened, its vicious grip easing away from her as Allison's eyes filled with so much joy at the sight of her brother. She clutched her bunny to her chest hard and kept glancing at the water as if she wanted to get in.

"Ok, little one. Let's do this," Colin said in his deep confident voice. He suddenly reached forward and helped Allison out of her shoes and toed his own off before picking her up in his arms and stepping carefully into the bath.

Olivia's mouth dropped, seeing him settle with Allison into the tub, and she swallowed back tears as Allison leaned forward and put her lips to the back of baby Ian's head. Colin turned his eyes and caught her gaze, love pouring into her from his, and he reached a hand out and laid it heavily on the back of her head, squeezing tightly.

Overcome, Olivia placed her face against Vanessa's shoulder and openly sobbed, beginning to heal.

And yes, healing is painful, too.

TWENTY-THREE

The Clock Is Ticking

TWO WEEKS LATER, COLIN was in Jonathan's rec room with Jonathan and Alexander, sharing a drink and a laugh with the two men when a text from an unknown number came through on his phone. His blood ran cold as he opened his phone to read the message.

McDermont, How much is she worth to you? Is she worth your sanity? You may be able to keep it if you know she is alive, rather than dead. Do you want to keep wondering every night when it'll be her turn? I know there's more redheads in the family, another newest little one has been born. Congratulations. What can I offer you, to ease your suffering? Because trust me, you're going to suffer. -Quid Pro Quo

Slamming his phone on the side table and standing up, Colin threw his glass across the room. Jonathan looked at him with a thunderous expression as the sounds of glass shattering echoed around them loudly.

"Let me see," Jonathan said angrily, snagging up Colin's phone to read the message. Jonathan glanced up with a murderous expression on his face. Alexander looked over, his blue eyes assessing the two men coolly.

Colin and Olivia had been staying at Jonathan's house so they could be close to the new family. And because they'd been rigid with their schedule, not making any unnecessary trips and having staff handle home deliveries and groceries just in case of any assassination attempts, Alexander met them there for some guy time. Colin tensed as Alexander stood up quickly to face him.

Colin felt his blood run cold as his demeanor became fiercely agitated. His eyes met Alexander's and narrowed. "I have no problem killing you if you don't let me the fuck out of this room." Colin's chest heaved as he squared off with the psychiatrist.

Alexander slid his abnormally cold eyes to Jonathan before speaking. "Jonathan, go get your security, I can hold him off for a few minutes." He pushed the sleeves of his shirt up. "Colin, remember what we talked about? You need to calm do-"

Jonathan hurried out the room to alert the security, staff, and their family. Alexander narrowed his eyes at Colin, opening his stance as he faced him head on.

"DO NOT TELL ME WHAT THE FUCK TO DO!" Colin roared at him, his face flushing dark as he squared up with the man. He got into Alexander's face, his lip curling and his features tight as he went toe to toe with the man who'd helped him get through Olivia's disappearance.

He knew the psychiatrist was right, but he was done. He was going to get Carmichael.

"Colin, I'm not telling you what to do, but you need to get a hold of yourself!" Alexander hissed at him, reaching forward to place a cautious hand on his shoulder. "They need you to keep it together."

"No, keeping it together is keeping these people dying" Colin's chest heaved as he stared at the cold man. "If he was close before, then he's right on our front step now. Tell me how the fuck he knows about baby Ian? None of us had announced his birth! How does he know!?"

Alexander's face paled as he saw Colin's true fear. They either had a spy in the home, or he had been following them, picking off the other redheads around town for fun. A true psychopath.

"We need to get the fuck out of here. They know where we are! He has to know!"

Just then, Olivia burst into the room.

"We need to go," she said shortly, turning away from him and addressing Zero who was hot on her heels. "Z, tell our security team to get ready to evacuate the Sinclair household and we are going to head to Gypsy's compound. We need to take an additional two SUVs, and we all need to leave at the same time and head in different directions. We've been followed, that's the only explanation." She turned her head to Alexander, assessing him sharply. "Did you fucking tell anyone? We haven't been anywhere. No one knows Ian was born early!"

Alexander shook his head. "No, Olivia, I wouldn't have done that. I know what's been going on, I wouldn't betray you all like that."

Olivia stared at the man for another second and nodded her head.

Colin screwed his brows together. "Olivia-"

"I'm going upstairs to pack," she turned to Byson. "Let the Sinclair team know that we will be heading out. I've already contacted Gypsy for use of her panic house and pulled my favor with her and her client I offered a service to."

"Olivia, slow the fuck down for a second. I don't know these people! You don't get to just-"

Olivia rounded on him with a wild look on her face. "Do not talk to me any kind of way in front of these people."

Colin narrowed his eyes and regarded her tightly.

"You do not understand this man, Colin. We need to move. Someone call Vincent. Now."

Colin was torn, having a moment of pride and fear that warred within him. He felt out of control, but at the same time, seeing Olivia so in control, so obviously in her element, let him know just what Zero meant when he said he didn't understand how he was able to tame her. In that moment he felt calm, knowing that this woman would be the perfect mother. Seeing how effortlessly she took over when chaos ensued, solidified for him that this was the woman he was meant to be with.

He could tame her because she understood and submitted to the chaos that was within him. That's why they worked.

He nodded his head. "I agree, let's get the fuck out of here," he turned to Alexander. "You coming with us?" Alexander threw him a wry look with an arched eyebrow. "Nah, I think I'll be okay. Thanks though." Alexander reached forward, clasping his forearm in a harsh grip. They shared a look before Alexander turned to give Olivia a brief hug before letting himself out the door.

Olivia turned on her heel, pulling out her phone. She dialed a number, snapping a finger at Zero. "Get to fucking moving!" she said harshly, flicking her hair behind her shoulder as she put the phone on speaker.

"Carmichael," she spat out. All the air left the room as she addressed the man through the phone.

Colin felt his blood pressure skyrocket.

"Kat! It's so good to hear-" the man stopped talking as Olivia hissed into the phone. A look unlike any other Colin had ever seen graced her face. She began to tap onto her phone during the call as she interrupted him easily.

"I have warned you. I have even graced you with my presence, and you have the fucking nerve to reach out to my husband. *How fucking dare you*. I told you to leave my family alone!"

"All you have to do is come to me. You know where I am."

Colin hurriedly walked to Olivia, snatching the phone out of her hand to see the number she dialed, he waved over another security who came forward.

"Write this number down," he snapped quietly, tilting the phone so the security could see. Colin felt an icy blanket over his heart as she continued to address the man.

"So this is how you want to play it? You just won't let go, even though I am telling you no?" Olivia's hands began to shake as she attempted to take a breath to ground herself. She began to walk towards the door swiftly, seeing the staff of the household rushing around, getting the families together.

"Well, you haven't even given us a chance-"

"THERE IS NO US!" Olivia suddenly screamed into the phone, shocking them all.

Jonathan came around the corner and raced up the steps after Olivia and Colin. Olivia burst into their room and began to throw her clothes into a bag, mixing Colin's clothes in.

"Baby," Colin whispered, shaking her shoulder, trying to get her attention.

"You are fucking around with the wrong one, Carmichael! I will fucking-"

Jonathan snatched the phone from her and hung up on the man. "We're almost ready to leave. Olivia, tell me. Can we trust this Gypsy woman?"

Olivia snapped her head up and narrowed her eyes at Colin and Jonathan. "I can trust this woman with my life," her face was beat red, and her lips were tight against her face as she regarded them with her chest heaving. There was a crash from the bedroom door as the door banged into the wall.

Colin and Jonathan's gazes were momentarily torn from Olivia as Zero burst into the room, commanding their attention.

"Sir, Gypsy just forwarded the safe house's information," Zero came up behind Colin, standing there stoically. "Apparently, a few members of royalty use the residence. It checks out, very obscure. We're able to hunker down together in the same household. It is a massive compound."

Colin felt his features harden as the chaos of everything seeped in. *"Olivia!"*

She whirled on him, her red hair flicking as she snapped her neck to address him. Colin's eyes flickered across her face as they both stood there, off center, their world tearing apart right before their eyes.

"NO! Colin, I'm tired of sitting back waiting and waiting for justice or for someone to handle this man. Punish me later if you must, but you told me you wanted me to give you respect as your wife, well you will give me respect as my husband," Olivia stood there next to the bed, her heaving chest betraying her emotion.

He gave her a nice, slow smile. "Oh no, babe, you're mistaken. I'm not mad at you. I am so incredibly in awe of you. But," he tilted his head as he assessed her. "You're probably going to get a punishment, regardless. Let's go."

They finished packing up and several SUVs and routes later; they wound up at Gypsy's compound.

Gypsy was standing at the front of the heavily gated and armed drive, with several bodyguards flanking her and the lights of the massive mansion glowing against her back in the background. She stood there stoically as a dozen SUVs pulled into the circular drive.

Olivia jumped out, walking swiftly to the woman. She threw her arms around her, hugging her tightly.

"Thank you," Olivia whispered, pressing her temple against Gypsy's before she stepped back, rubbing her hands down her arms, sensing Colin come up behind her.

"It's no problem Olivia, you know I said I'm only a phone call away," Gypsy said softly, turning towards Colin and holding out her hand.

"It's nice to finally meet you in person, Mr. McDermont," she said, eyeing him coolly.

Jonathan appeared next to them holding Allison's hand who was soon joined by Vanessa holding baby Ian.

"Hello Sinclair's, I've heard so much about you," Gypsy stepped forward and squatted down to get eye level with Allison and her demeanor changed, going from cold to softening at the sight of the young freckled, redheaded child. "Especially *you*, little one. Your auntie loves you so much," Gypsy reached forward and bopped her on the nose gently, giving her a pretty, rosy smile. Allison smiled back and giggled.

"You're preetttyyy," Allison whispered to Gypsy as she reached over and sank her hand into Shadow's fur. The little dog sat obediently next to her, his tail wagging.

"Thank you, you're pretty as well," Gypsy whispered back, giving her another smile before she straightened up and took a couple of steps back to get a better look at the group. She folded her arms behind her back and her posture commanded respect. Her entire demeanor was that of a military officer of the highest order.

Jesus fuck, Colin thought, his eyebrows raising in surprise.

"You may use my place as long as you need, I have multiple security checkpoints. No one is allowed in or out, staff will not be allowed to venture outside of the grounds. If this is a concern, then let them know now so they can leave while I am here," she looked out the corner of her eye at Mary, Beth, and Jonathan's staff who had come up behind them, "I will have my own security taking over on the outer grounds, and your security will take over inside the home. Whoever does not like my rules, feel free to leave now. If you choose to go, you have one hour to get your plans in order and to depart." She turned towards Zero. "We have run surveillance on Carmichael's job and his home. We are assessing points of weakness. Until this is figured out, no one leaves."

"Uh, what about Allison? She needs school... normalcy," Vanessa said quietly, stepping forward.

Gypsy narrowed her eyes. "Beth, take Allison inside and show her her room while I speak with her parents, please," Olivia and Colin turned stunned eyes to Beth, who walked up to Allison and took her hand gently.

Beth looked at Gypsy and they shared a glance before Gypsy looked away coolly. "You are dismissed."

Beth walked into the home with Allison and Shadow without another word.

"Uhh...lo siento, do you and Beth know each other?" Colin asked, with a shocked look on his face.

Gypsy turned an arched eyebrow to Olivia, ignoring Colin. "You can't possibly have thought that I was going to let my top girl just fuck off with some *man*, disappear off the face of the earth, and I wouldn't keep tabs on her to make sure she's safe now, do you? This is not how Esmerelda's Ring operates. *You* know this, and *should* have known better." She turned a haughty eyebrow to Colin. "I had Beth, my sister, planted in your house weeks before to sus you out before you moved Olivia in. When I found out you were following and pursuing Olivia, I had you followed and vetted as well," Olivia's eyes almost bugged out of her head as she turned to look at Colin, who had settled his features into a calm, almost respectful expression.

Olivia's eyes widened. *That's why she dyes her hair brunette!* she thought, putting her arms around her torso and squeezing.

"Goddamn," Jonathan breathed. "You had a spy in your house this whole time."

Colin frowned and Gypsy continued, as if the big man hadn't spoken.

"AND, I want to thank you for taking such good care of Olivia. You make one almost believe that love might be an actual, obtainable thing," she gave the couple a tip of her mouth, not quite a smile. She turned her attention back to Vanessa and Jonathan.

"She will be allowed to go to school, and then come straight back here. However, this is against my better judgment, but I get that kids need stability. Also, this ban on freedom is only temporary. We need time to take Carmichael down. It should only take about a week seeing he's got men behind him, but my men are better." Gypsy reached forward and grasped all their hands before turning on her heel and leaving.

"Gypsy!" Colin called out, walking forward a few steps and addressing the petite, blonde woman, "Thank you, how can I repay you?" his eyes searched hers shrewdly.

"No offense, Colin, but you can't afford me. Olivia, however, has paid this debt several times over. Don't worry your pretty little heart. We're even." Gypsy dismissively turned her eyes to Olivia once more.

"Red, you know how to get a hold of me if you need me," she said, sidling up to one of their SUV's and sliding in the back smoothly as an officer shut the door behind her. They drove off without another word, leaving them all standing in shock in the driveway.

They went into the house and were shown around by other staff and Beth to their rooms. Allison and Ian slept in the room with Vanessa and Jonathan, they were taking no chances with their safety.

***

By the third day, they were all going stir crazy. Colin and Jonathan were holed up in an office of the mansion and were trying to run their businesses remotely. Neither one of them was happy about it.

Gypsy dropped by briefly to give them an update, letting them know her people were watching Carmichael's house and so far there's been no activity out of the ordinary. He went to work with his guards, then came back home. There was nothing that they could sus out.

Until the fourth day.

Olivia was reading a book in the library, trying to take her mind off things when the first text came through her phone. However, her phone was on silent on the table and she didn't get it.

Kat, I just want you to know, I have tried to reach out to you. I have given you chance after chance to be amicable and to make the right decision. We can be so good together, and I hate that it has to come to this. A bloodbath shouldn't be necessary for you to do what you should have done in the first place. I hope that we can come to some sort of understanding that will be mutual for the both of us. Maybe this way, we can both get what we want. But when you push my buttons, I will definitely push yours back. This game ends today. -Qui facit per alium facit per se

***

Olivia was turning the page in the afternoon, thoroughly lost in her book, when Vanessa barrelled around the corner.

"Olivia!" she screamed. She was clutching baby Ian to her and the nanny was on her heels, flapping around her trying to take him, but Vanessa was shaking too hard to give him up.

Olivia jumped up and with wide eyes she reached for baby Ian. "Oh my God *is he okay*?" Olivia said. Her fingers trembled as she moved his blanket aside.

"No-" Vanessa choked, "NO! It's Allison, she was kidnapped from the school!" Vanessa yelled, finally giving up Ian who was being tugged out of her hands by the nanny.

Time stood still as the news processed and Olivia paled. She shook her head, "No, she has too much security, this doesn't make sense-"

"A bomb! She was in the bathroom and *they bombed the fucking-*" Vanessa bent over choking on her tears.

Olivia's heart ramped into overdrive and she dove for her phone, checking it just as Zero barreled around the corner. Suddenly their phones went off with the unmistakable blare of the amber alert sound. The high pitched noise triggering panic in her chest. Olivia paled further, her fingers trembling as she struggled with her phone.

"No, this can't be right-" she paled, stumbling back a step as the text from that morning hit her phone. Her eyes widened, just as Colin and Jonathan tore into the room.

Colin stepped up to her and snatched her phone out of her hand, reading it quickly.

"FUCKING HEEEELLLLLLL!" Colin roared, grabbing at his neck he spun on his heel and faced Zero. "What do we know? Do we know anything yet?"

Zero narrowed his eyes. "From my intel right now all we've got is a "parent" of an enrolled child was in the bathroom during break with Allison at the time of the explosion, there are no child fatalities but there are several injuries, and three teachers are dead, including the "parent". Whoever was on the other side of the bomb got her through the debris and chaos and she was able to get out before the security could get to her. Sir, we are sorry," Zero faced Jonathan and gave him a discrete nod.

"For the love of GOD." Jonathan breathed, his face was stricken with fear for his baby girl. "Do we know where she could have been taken?"

"No sir, she had a tracker in her backpack, but since she was in the bathroom she didn't have the backpack with her." Zero's eyes slid to Olivia who looked to be vibrating she was so angry. She snatched her phone back from Colin with a rough sound and beat her hand into the phone. She held it up to her ear.

"Where the fuck are you?" she spoke into the phone, panting hard.

"Are you alone? Am I on speaker?"

"Yes, No," Olivia replied. She held up her hand and jerked away as Colin went to grab the phone, flashing him a warning glance.

"So I've got your attention now?"

"Yes." *Keep cool. He's got Allison. Keep calm.*

"I want just you, that's all. They can have her back, but you need to come to me. Alone."

"That's not possible. I can't get out of here Carmichael. There's too many people guarding me and you know it. Give me the coordinates, and I will exchange myself for her."

"I have men stationed everywhere. I will pick them all off if you bring a swarm of security."

"Only me and my security guy," she whispered. Seeing Colin's eyes flashing, she spoke quickly. "And Colin, and my sister, she will need to go back with my sister. That's all."

"Hmmm....I like the thought of seeing your husband again. I promised him something delicious when he paid me a visit. Maybe I can make good on it. Okay, meet me here, and don't fuck around. If you bring extra people, I will kill her. I'm sending you a photo from another number to show you just how serious I am. That's why so many little ones had to perish, so you can see just what I'm capable of if you don't cooperate. If you all are armed, you will die. Don't take all night now. I'm giving you exactly two hours and five minutes to get here," Carmicheal hung up.

Just then, multiple phones rang and they pulled them out, opening up the message.

"O-o-ohhh-ohhh my G-God," Vanessa said, falling to her knees and staring hard at her phone in shock.

Olivia kept her eyes on Colin. "I am not looking, and neither are you. Whatever he sent, I believe him. Nessie, put the fucking phone away. *Put it away, goddamn it*, looking at it isn't going to help and we need to move," she opened up the coordinates and set the GPS. "We're exactly two hours away. Get the fastest fucking car you can find and lets roll out. Two vehicles."

"He fucking did that so we wouldn't have time to set up a perimeter or scope out the place, god fucking damn it." Jonathan said bitterly, taking a deep breath and trading a hot glance with Colin.

"The five minute grace was to get security out of the way." Olivia dialed another number.

"Gypsy." They all listened as she rattled off what Carmicheal said, after some back and forth, Zero put his hand to his ear listening to his earpiece.

"Gypsy's men will open the gates and not pursue. But they will be on standby."

Colin shook his head and looked to the heavens. He said a quick prayer.

"Let's go," he growled, they flew out of the house into the vehicles and their tires squealed as they took off, racing against the clock.

***

Olivia and Colin went in one car, and Vanessa, Jonathan, and Zero followed the location that Carmichael sent. However, about twenty minutes from their destination Carmichael called.

Olivia answered over the speaker phone.

"What," she growled, steering the car efficiently through traffic, they'd been so lucky as to avoid cops so far.

"I am sending you another coordinate. Good girl, I see you're finally following instructions. However, I wonder why you didn't drive in one car?"

"Because, you dumbass-"

"Now be nice," Carmichael drawled, "Allison, does your auntie always use bad language?"

Olivia's eyes widened and her heart skipped a beat hearing Allison whimper in the background.

Colin clenched his fists and reached a hand over, grasping her thigh hard. Olivia's chest heaved as she tried to calm down. "Don't fucking touch her, Carmichael!"

"Nooo, I wouldn't dream of it. She's so sweet. We're taking such good care of her. I heard she got a new liver?" Carmichael's voice was sickeningly sweet.

Olivia's lips trembled as a tear spilled over onto her cheek. "Why are you giving me a new coordinate?"

"Because I needed to make sure you weren't going to sic anyone onto my location. It's being sent to your phone. Bye now," Carmichael hung up the phone and Colin snatched it up, hurriedly sending it to Zero and Jonathan.

"Baby-" Colin spoke, but Olivia was looking lost, far away, almost as if she was retreating into herself, going on autopilot. "Amor, *listen to me*, I love you. No matter what happens tonight, I fucking love you, baby. We're getting out of this, okay? Come on, let's focus, take a deep breath. We need to be *clear headed*." He squeezed her thigh, moving his hand up to the nape of her neck and squeezing hard.

"Colin, what if he kills her anyway? What do we do?" Olivia's eyes flickered all over the road as she took a sharp turn, narrowly missing a truck.

Colin grabbed the grab bar hard and turned to face her. Looking at the dash, he saw they only had five more minutes to go.

"When we get there, let me go first with Zero, we will scope out the area and verify any weaknesses," he spoke rapidly, trying to get as much out as he can. "Do not let him touch you Olivia, he might not let her go and could keep her to control you."

Olivia's blood raced in her veins as she took another sharp turn. Looking into the rearview mirror, she saw Zero was almost on her bumper.

"I have to get her out of there. That's why I brought two cars. One for us, one for her. I'm getting her out of there, Colin," she shot him a look full of pain and Colin winced. "Colin, we might not make it out of there, but *she has to*." Her voice cracked. "Do you understand what I'm trying to say?" she sniffed, her fingers tightened on the steering wheel hard as she struggled to not let fear overwhelm her.

Colin stared hard at her before nodding once. "I'm not leaving you baby, you have to know that. I will never leave you. It's you and me baby," Olivia nodded, and a fresh tear fell down her check. Colin leaned over the middle and kissed the side of her mouth, breathing her in.

"B-but if I have a chance to get you out of there, Colin, I need you to take it-"

"No, you've lost your fucking mind asking me that."

"COLIN," Olivia bit out, her lips were tight as she spoke to him. "Colin he wont kill me, but I'll never survive if something happens to you. I can take care of myself out there baby. I won't like it but I will get away eventually. *But if you die*, I won't survive that. If tonight doesn't go well I need you to please, *please* listen to me."

Colin watched as her tears dried up. They turned into a forestry area, the diminishing sun disappeared behind them and they were in sudden darkness.

"If you fucking love me, you'll listen to me. Get the fuck out of here if things go bad. Don't be a fucking hero." Her eyes flew to the dash just as they were swallowed by trees. "Two minutes to go."

She held her hand out and gave him a hard, lingering look as the car bumped over potholes in the darkness.

Colin scowled, his spider senses tingling, letting him know that they were being lured into a trap. Part of him wanted to call Jonathan and tell them to turn around, worried about him and Vanessa, but he knew he had a better chance of getting the man to eat pork before that would happen.

The hair on the back of his neck stood up as they slowly approached a clearing, seeing several cars with headlights casting everyone into a silhouette. His heart stopped, seeing five henchmen with rifles, and Allison in front of Carmichael. He was standing there patiently, his hand wrapped around Allison's hair so hard she was on her tiptoes.

Holding onto her bunny for dear life.

Olivia felt her heart crack in such a way she wasn't sure it would ever be repaired, seeing the little girl with blood and tear stained cheeks, snot running down her face. Her lips were trembling and her little eyes flickered back and forth, looking for someone to save her.

Her eyes narrowed and she let out a snarl, seeing a red dot trained on the little girl's chest.

Colin glanced at her for a heartbeat and narrowed his eyes as she started talking.

"You will let me get out of the car first. If you get out first he will kill you with no hesitation. I need to get in front and start talking. Do not lean into me or kiss me, do not provoke this man. You let me get my baby out of here first and then I am okay with however tonight turns out. Are you hearing me baby?"

Colin narrowed his eyes and licked his lips, knowing all bets were off. Seeing Allison the way she was turned some switch on in Olivia that he wasn't sure he'd be able to turn back off if they made it out alive.

Which he planned to.

"When we get the fuck out of here, I'm going to *skin you alive* for the way you've been ordering me around for the last two hours. Like I said, it's you and me baby." he repeated his words from earlier.

Olivia closed her eyes and tilted her head back, and for a second, time stood still as she breathed deeply, listening to her heartbeat and welcoming the hot loud rush of blood in her ears. Opening her eyes back up on a slow exhale, she turned her head to Colin.

"Comfortable chaos," she breathed, turning her eyes back to her daughter. "I know you know what I'm talking about. You feel it every time we're together. I'm getting my daughter out of here and then I'm going for the sweet spot. As soon as you feel it, you're free to do whatever the fuck you need to." She turned her eyes to him and they shared a mutual understanding that didn't need to be verbalized.

With a nod, she opened the door and then walked around the car, holding her hand up to stall Zero, Vanessa, and Jonathan, who had opened the door. She turned her face to the side and pinned them with a stare.

Stay, let me go first, she implored with her eyes, making sure they got the memo before she began to walk forward, her gait confident.

Colin narrowed his eyes, feeling his entire soul wanting to reach out for his wife.

But all he could do right now was watch as her alter ego, Lilith, walked into the lion's den.

TWENTY-FOUR

Lilith Reborn

OLIVIA LOWERED HER ARM and began to walk confidently towards the group, seemingly uncaring that four weapons were trained on her.

Ignoring Carmichael's gray gaze on her, she locked eyes with Allison, narrowing her eyes at the little girl's state, and her fear. She softened her gaze and took another step towards them, seeing three men turn their rifles to her family behind her.

However, one stayed on her and another on Allison. She refused to raise her hands, not showing any weakness at all. They didn't deserve to see it.

Allison's trembling became worse as she whimpered, slipping on her tiptoes as Carmichael hauled her up slightly higher by her hair. Her little fingers were clawed around the bunny.

"Mommy I'm scared, but Uncle Colin's daddy is here with me," she said in a little trembling voice.

Olivia fought back a wave of nausea, not knowing if that was a comforting thing or a bad omen. They couldn't quite figure out this new found gift of hers yet.

"Hi, baby. I'm so sorry that one of the bad guys got you, but I'm here now. And we're going to slay this dragon together, okay?" she said with a wink. She saw Allison's trembling start to slow as she held her bunny to her mouth, seemingly unable to speak any longer.

Olivia took a few more steps toward Carmichael and narrowed her eyes even more. The headlights from the cars illuminated over all of them brightly and her hair flickered around her face in the wind.

Colin felt his chest tighten and moved to go to her. He audibly growled as Jonathan reached a hand out and stilled him with a vicious look. The other henchman momentarily trained his rifle onto Colin's chest and a muscle ticked in his jaw as his muscles locked up, fighting every instinct, wanting to go to Olivia, who was speaking.

"Let my baby go, Carmichael," she hissed. The air was thick with tension as her entire demeanor changed in front of everyone. Her features became sharp and tight as she regarded the stoic, regally held man in front of her. Her green eyes looked vicious and confident. No sign of the submissive inside of her was presently visible to other people.

Carmichael's eyes flashed at her as he tightened his hand on Allison's hair. The henchman's gun stayed trained on Allison, unwavering.

"Allison, close your ears now baby. Don't take your fingers out for anything, love," she crooned softly. She waited until the little girl put shaky hands up to her ears and plugged her ears hard.

Colin chanced a quick look at the four henchmen that were bracketing him, Jonathan, and Vanessa. Two on the left of Colin and Jonathan, and two on the right, near Vanessa. Vanessa clung to Jonathan's arm hard, barely holding back whimpers. Her eyes kept flitting from Olivia to Allison. That red dot from the fifth henchman stayed trained steady on Allison's forehead now.

There was complete silence as everyone held their breath in anticipation. The car headlights glowed brightly, highlighting the gnats in the woodsy humid air which buzzed within the lights that were also illuminating Olivia, Allison, and Carmicheal.

Carmichael took a tiny step backwards, his grip on Allison's hair yanking her with him.

"Carmichael," she said sharply, the man narrowing his eyes on her. "I hope you realize, if you hurt her, no one is making it out of here alive. I will kill you first. This entire operation is going to end in a blood bath. So I want you to think very, very hard about what your next moves will be. And what you truly want."

Carmichael curled his lip as she stepped further towards him. Colin's chest tightened; his blood boiled.

"You don't get to make demands! This goes how *I want it*," Carmichael spit out and Allison cried as he gripped her hair tighter. The little girl had snot running down her nose and was visibly shivering. Little whimpers escaped her lips as she stared at Olivia in fear.

Olivia narrowed her eyes before flicking them to Carmichael once more. Her nostrils flared as her lip curled.

"You should have thought about who gets to make commands when you kidnapped *my daughter* then. Shouldn't you have, Carmichael?" Olivia said, her voice sickly sweet.

Carmichael's eyes widened before narrowing, his face flushed red as his eyes glanced from Olivia to Vanessa and then back again. "Your daughter? I thought this was your *niece*?" the man said, disbelief in his eyes. His gaze flitted now from the little girl to Vanessa.

"Then that's what your dumbass gets for thinking. Do you know what happens when you fuck with a mother's child? Do you want to find out, Carmichael? I'm horribly offended right now, and I mean I am greatly displeased. The only reason why I know you is *because* of her. I had to enter Esmeralda's ring to take care of her. You've majorly fucked up," she whispered, taking a step forward. Her head cocked as she spoke, and Colin noticed she sounded completely different.

"Wel-Well. I didn't know. I'm sorry Kat," Carmichael said. His face was red in the light, sweat dotted his forehead.

"Olivia," Colin growled at her, his whole body tensing as he took a step towards her. She put her hand out to still him. He gritted his teeth hard as the henchman shoved the gun into his chest.

"Watch yourself, before you get a bullet in your chest," the henchman said threateningly.

Colin took a deep breath and willed himself to calm down. He turned his head back to Olivia as she continued to speak, addressing Carmicheal.

"I will go with you willingly, but only if you will let them all go, unharmed, and alive. Including Colin," she said softly, her voice turned deadly. She sounded different, confident, in charge.

Carmichael's eyebrow raised. "And what are you going to give me in exchange?" he said haughtily, stepping back minutely with Allison, his grip on her hair unrelenting. That red dot stayed steady on Allison's forehead.

Colin's own forehead broke out in a sweat and his hands clenched.

"*Oh no*, Carmichael. If I go with you, it's going to be all about what you give me, isn't it?" Olivia said, her voice sweet as a siren as she steadily walked another step towards Carmichael and Allison, and a step further from Colin.

Colin's lungs burned as Carmichael nodded.

"Yes Kat," he said, his voice changing, becoming deeper, sexual.

Colin snarled.

"Good boy," she crooned at Carmichael, running her hand sensually down her hair and her chest. She took another cautious step forward, her steps light and easy. Her hand paused at her belly. "Matter of fact, I think you can give me something now," she purred. Looking through her lashes at the older man.

"Tell me," he said, stepping forward towards her with Allison. Eager.

"I'm going to come with you, and you're going to make sure my baby gets out of here before we leave. And if you let everyone go, I'll do that thing you like, that you always begged me for. Ohhhh, how I miss you *begging,*" she trailed off with a sensual whisper.

"The *thi-thing* I-I-I-wanted?" Carmichael stuttered, his hands loosening on Allison's hair.

"Yes, you know what I'm referring to. And to sweeten the deal, I'll even give you a taste of what you want before we even leave here, if you let them watch me do it to you. All I want is to be able to say goodbye to my husband after he watches me give you what you've been wanting from me this whole time," she said softly, her voice turning sexual, her breathing audibly hitched.

Carmichael shook his head.

"Yesss," she hissed, her hands coming up to play with her hair. She preened for him, coming closer until the dot trained on her back instead of Allison's head. Colin visibly shook.

"Let her go, baby," she whispered, swaying her hips as she stepped even closer, she reached out her hand to caress it down Carmichael's shoulder and arm until her hand wrapped around his, plucking it off Allisons head and pulling the little girl to her with her other arm. In one swift move, she turned them, placing her back against Carmichael and pushing Allison towards Vanessa.

Allison ran, her little legs pumping hard as she ran sobbing, barreling into Vanessa.

"Zero get her to the car now, and drive," Olivia called to her security agent. Raising her hand gently, placing it on Carmichael's cheek. He'd buried his nose into her hair and closed his eyes breathing deeply.

Zero barreled forward, all of Carmichael's men's guns trained on him as he took the screaming little girl and ran to one of the cars not even bothering to put Allison in her own seat. He held her close to his chest and sped off, dust kicking up behind them.

Colin's chest relaxed minutely, glad that if anyone got out of this alive tonight, that it was that little girl.

"Carmichael. If I even get a whiff that you hurt her, I'll fuck you up so bad you will wish you would have killed me," Olivia said quietly, starting to rock slightly.

Carmichael's arm came around her torso to hold her tighter to him.

Two red lights trained on her now, Colin glanced around, looking for the other three.

Looking down, he saw one on his chest, and another two on Jonathan and Vanessa. The henchman closest to his side had turned his gun as well as his gaze to him.

Fuck, we're in serious trouble.

"I just wanted you, baby. I wouldn't have hurt her. I knew you'd come," Carmichael said, his hand pressing into her stomach pressing her harder into him.

Colin's heartbeat went into overdrive as he tensed, every muscle standing in sharp relief.

"Don't," Jonathan said quietly. "Colin, let her do her thing," he breathed the words across the foot of space between them.

Colin watched as Olivia nodded, turning her head to look up at the older man. "Are you ready for them all to watch Carmichael?"

"Call me Daniel."

Colin felt nauseated.

"Ok, Daniel. Are you ready?" she said, hearing the car with Allison fading away into the night.

"Yes, God. Yes."

"Good boy," she whispered, her eyes on Carmichael's. She turned fast as shit and before anyone saw it, they heard a sharp crack echo around the clearing. The man's head whipped violently to the side as she slapped her hand as hard as she could across his face.

"That's for my daughter," she snarled.

Vanessa let out a shocked gasp. Colin's eyes widened.

The henchman who had his gun trained on Colin glanced up in surprise and over at Olivia and Carmichael, but still kept his gun trained on his chest.

Carmichael turned back to her, caressing his jaw lovingly. He was looking at her with a sick adoration. The wind blew slightly, ruffling her red hair like a flickering flame around her body.

"This is how this is going to go. I'm going to punish you for daring to hurt my baby. You scared her, Daniel. And as a mother, tell me how I'm supposed to accept that lying down?" Olivia said, her hands lifting to his belt and unbuckling it, the sound loud around the space. Everyone was so quiet, no one dared move. Carmichael's men shifted uncomfortably as she whipped the belt out of his pants so fast it made a cracking sound.

"I-I don't know. I don't expect you to," Carmichael sniveled, and as Olivia looked up at him, her eyes narrowed.

"*On your knees!*" she barked so loud that Vanessa flinched in shock next to him and Jonathan. Jonathan inched slightly closer to Colin, their shoulders almost touching.

They all watched in disbelief as the man obediently sank to the ground in front of her.

Olivia moved, walking around him slowly. She went behind him and kicked his legs further apart, making his stance wider and Carmichael made a sick sound that turned Colin's stomach. She finished her circle, coming to his left side and squatting down next to him.

Carmichael went to turn his head to find her.

"No no," Olivia said sharply, with a small laugh. She tilted her head. "You know how this goes; you don't get to look at me when I hurt you," she said, her teeth baring as her tongue came out to lick her lips. She snapped her head forward, sinking her teeth into his earlobe and growling.

Carmichael cried out, trying to reach for his ear but Olivia slapped a hand forward, stilling him. Colin scrunched his nose, feeling his blood pressure rise impossibly high.

"What are you fucking crying for, you piece of shit? This is what you wanted, isn't it?" she sneered at him, wiping blood off her mouth.

Colin regarded Olivia quietly, seeing that she'd lost it. She didn't even look like herself.

If we get out of this, she's going to have tetanus shots, a blood transfusion, blood tests, and anything else medical that I can think of to make her go through, Colin thought.

The sight of that man's blood on her mouth, in her mouth, made him think about just going ahead and ending this whole thing in a bloodbath. In this moment he hated that he'd spent so many years with horrible anxiety and suicidal ideations. It made him too comfortable accepting the end, however it needed to end.

There were a tense few seconds as she crouched there next to him, regarding him from the side. She inched closer. The dots all relocated to the ground now, as the henchmen were now invested in watching the drama between their boss and Olivia play out.

"Are you going to rape me, Daniel?" Olivia said in an excited tone, her eyes wild. She licked her lips, as if she liked the thought.

The man nodded, trying to look out the side of his eye to watch her. Olivia smiled, standing up and then walking in front of him. She stood silent for a second before she looped the belt and then slapped Carmicheal aside the face with it. The crack echoing much like when she used her hand. One of the henchman's guns went off as he squeezed the trigger in shock. The bullet dug into the ground.

One less bullet to worry about going into one of them.

Jonathan's hand came up to cover his mouth, grimacing slightly. Colin heard Vanessa fall behind them to the dewy grass with a gasp, but he couldn't move, couldn't look away from his wife.

Carmichael roared out in anger.

"I said you can't look at me. Did you think I was playing with you or something?" Olivia hissed, squatting down again. She took his jaw in her hands, her fingers clawed, digging into his skin. She pulled him slowly to her, shuffling, backing up two steps, making him crawl on his knees towards her. She sighed.

"Bad boooyyyy," she said, like she was disappointed. "I was hoping you could show my family how well I'd trained you," she huffed, closing her eyes. She slapped the belt rather absentmindedly against her hand and then opened her eyes back up before tsking. "I mean, aren't I worth all this you went through to get me?" she said, placing a hand against her breath and sniffing. A tear rolled down her face and she shoved her face slightly into his and lowered her voice, as if she only wanted Carmichael to hear her. "Why are you embarrassing me, huh?"

Colin's jaw dropped. Vanessa was moaning and dry heaving in the background.

Carmichael's eyes widened as he gasped. A horrified expression passed over his features. Colin could see a vicious welt raised across his cheek and temple.

He felt joy, pure and unadulterated.

"Yes! Yes you are, I love you, Kat. I would never embarrass you," Carmichael implored, shuffling forward slightly, his eyes wary, almost hurt.

Olivia nodded, wiping her tear away. She leaned forward and pressed her forehead into his. "Then why can't you behave like I taught you? I mean, we spent four years together. Was it all for nothing?" she whimpered, rocking a little, like she was in distress.

Carmichael's henchmen were now watching in earnest, rapt, with their guns still lowered.

Colin looked over at Jonathan, who had something akin to pride in his eyes watching the whole thing. For some reason, Jonathan's look calmed him and he took a brief reprieve in the feeling.

"Wow, she's good," Jonathan said under his breath. Giving his head a little shake. Colin looked back at Olivia. She was stroking the man's chest. Murmuring.

She stood up from her crouch looking down at Carmichael.

"You have to know, that every time you rape me, the beating you ask for afterwards is going to make you question your entire existence. The more you rape me, the worse it will get. Until there will be nothing of either one of us left. I bite, Daniel. That will never change. I don't give pleasure, I give pain. You already know this," Olivia said softly. "Pull your shirt up. Let's finish this so we can go." She stepped back, crossing her arms as the man hurriedly complied.

She made a disgusted noise. "Fucking embarrassment. Hold your screams in. You sicken me and I don't want to hear you. I only want to hear this belt, do you understand?" she hissed at him; the man nodded.

Closing his eyes, it was clear he was mentally getting ready for her. Olivia took the opportunity to turn to look behind her, locking eyes with Colin momentarily. The look she exchanged with him was one of pure love before her eyes hardened, almost turning black.

Olivia walked around Carmichael, before standing behind him and giving her arms a little shake. She snapped the belt a few times, warming up, making the tension grow. She spread her feet about two feet apart and with a little huff, she pulled her arm back and let loose, the belt slapping harshly against his back. Carmichael tensed, his face going tight as he clenched his jaw so hard Colin heard his teeth grind. She pulled back her arm again, striking him repeatedly. The slaps echoing sickeningly throughout the small clearing they were in. Colin shook his head in a slight motion, disbelieving what he was seeing.

Slap after slap echoed out, and nary a sound escaped from Carmichael's lips as he knelt there, enduring what was the worst beating Olivia had ever given anyone in four years of her servicing Esmerelda's ring.

The henchman's jaws dropped watching her whip their boss. Colin had to admit, it was incredibly confusing even to him how the tables turned.

Colin watched stony faced as Olivia let out a little grunt with every whip of the belt. Carmichael let out a little whimper on a particularly vicious downstroke and she stopped mid swing. Standing there and breathing hard.

"What did I say?" she asked incredulously, almost with a laugh.

Carmichael's eyes widened, and he started sniveling.

"*Wait, no*. I didn't Kat! I didn't!" he said, his deep voice a few octaves higher. Colin grimaced as he saw his pants were tented. The man was getting off on this. He almost swallowed his tongue.

Motherfucker.

She walked around to face him, standing slightly to the same side the two henchmen were next to him, watching enraptured. Olivia looked at Carmichael with a stunned expression on her face.

"Yes you did. *Yes you did!*" Olivia said with a laugh. "Soooo, now you're an embarrassment *and* a liar? Daniel, what happened to you while I was gone sweetheart? What the hell? I'm so confused. You got us all out here in the fucking woods, in the fucking *DARK!*" she gasped, sounding annoyed. "Trying to make me prove to everyone how good and worthy I am, and you can't even fucking do what I asked you to do?" she bent to stare in his eyes for a second before she looked away scoffing, placing her hand on her head pensively.

In turmoil, she stared off at the trees in the distance before suddenly nodding to herself and dropping the belt. It hit with a thud and clank as it hit a spot of dirt where grass refused to grow. Her arm lowered and she turned her wild eyes to Carmichael once more.

"You know what, have him kill me!" she snarled into his face. "Apparently, I'm not worth it after all," she said, turning and pointing to one of the henchmen.

Carmichael just kneeled there, his eyes flickering from Olivia's to his men then back again. He shook his head minutely, disagreeing.

When no one moved, she walked up to the nearest man next to Colin, who was standing there shocked, giving her the opportunity to grab his gun and place the end of the barrel to her forehead.

Oh fuck no. No! Colin felt his heart stop. He let out a pained groan. Jonathan's hand wrapped around his forearm and clenched down.

"Nooo!" Carmichael screamed, shuffling forward. "Derrick, don't you fucking dare," he roared. "She's MINE!"

"I'm not good enough," Olivia cried, closing her eyes, pressing the barrel of the gun harder into her head. "Pull the trigger Derrick!" she screamed at the henchman. Everyone jumped at her wild, unexpected shriek.

Oh my God, I could kill her myself. Matter of fact, I am. As soon as I get out of this, I'm burying her in the backyard so she can't go crazy ever again. Colin felt his heart suddenly racing at a breakneck speed, watching Olivia hold the man's gun to her head as if she was fearless.

"NO!" Carmichael yelled, clamoring awkwardly to his feet.

"I SAID PULL THE FUCKING TRIGGER!" she screeched, spit flying out of her mouth as she stared at the blue-eyed henchman in his eyes down the barrel of his gun. *"Pull it,"* she whispered, both of her hands now wrapped around the barrel of the gun and taking a step forward, making her and the henchman move back about four feet behind Colin, Vanessa, and Jonathan.

"Pull it, pull it, pull it, pull it," she began chanting, a little growl emitting from her throat. The henchman's blue eyes widened, looking truly afraid, and his finger twitched on the trigger in the light of the car's headlights. Their silhouettes stood in sharp relief of the lights, the only color visible was Olivia's fiery red hair.

And in that brief moment, he saw what everyone else saw. Lilith. Chaotic, demonic, man eater Lilith. He shivered.

Fuck she was beautiful... otherworldly.

"Don't you fucking *DARE*," Carmichael screamed, pulling a gun out of nowhere and shooting Derrick in the head, missing Olivia by a fraction.

Colin watched in slow motion as blood sprayed everywhere, and the man hit the ground, his gun falling to the side unnoticed in the chaos erupting around them.

The three other henchmen slightly shuffled away with confused looks on their faces as they stared at their fellow comrade on the ground, a part of his face gone and blood pooling onto the ground under him.

Colin felt Jonathan wrap his arms around him and squeeze so hard that he felt a rib crack. He heard roaring echoing around the clearing, realizing it was coming from him. Jonathan yanked him back a few feet.

"Calm the fuck down. Look at what she's doing stupid!" Jonathan growled in his ear. "Look at the power she has over this man. Chill the fuck out. Or you're going to get us killed," Jonathan hissed.

Colin panted, shaking in Jonathan's hold, eyes straining to stay on Olivia.

Covered in blood, Olivia twisted around as if a man didn't just get shot in front of her and looked at Carmichael, who was panting for air himself, looking half out of his mind.

"You naughty boy. Would you like me to help you stop making noise? I can do that thing you like now," she said quietly, walking to him. Not even minding the gun in his hand. Carmichael sniveled; his eyes wide as he stared up at her in awe.

"Yes. Yes, please," he whispered roughly. "I'd like that very much."

"Okay Daniel, I have a question for you," Olivia asked softly, reaching forward to caress his cheek, she let him maintain eye contact with her for several seconds before she bent at the waist and put her lips dangerously close to his.

"Anything Kat, ask me!" Daniel sniveled, trying to lean down closer to close the gap between their mouths. Olivia turned slightly, and placed her eyes on Colin's.

"Would you shoot him if I asked you to?" she whispered, turning to look back at Carmichael.

He nodded, and his arm raised. Carmichael tilted his head as his eyes found Colin's.

Colin kept very still.

"No, no... I just wanted to see if you would do it. I don't want you to kill any of them," she said, whipping out her arm. She slapped it over his forearm, making his gun lower back down, and with the action, another bang rendered the air as another bullet wasted into the ground next to them. Olivia smiled almost tenderly at the man. "Put the gun in the back of your pants baby, and get back on your knees," she said, her voice coming out soft, almost the same voice she used to talk to Allison or baby Ian.

Carmichael hurried to comply.

"Oh, can Colin put some music on real quick? I want to play his favorite song while I do this to you. I think it'd be such a sweet ending don't you think? Then, every time he hears it, he'll think of you. And me together. That way he'll never forget me," she said, bending down to press her lips softly to the side of his mouth. Colin felt bile rise in his throat. "He needs his phone," she called out to the other henchman.

"Give it to him," Carmichael bit out, almost angrily.

The henchman dug into his pocket before pulling out his phone and tossing it to him. Colin stared incredulously at her, his eyes narrowing. He was seething on the inside.

"Oh and don't even think about calling the police, Colin. This is going to be too good to interrupt," she said in a sultry voice as she looked down at Carmichael, licking her lips.

Colin growled as Jonathan gave him a little shove.

He reluctantly walked to the car, one of the henchman's guns trained on him as he opened his car door and took his phone, putting it into the docking station and turning the volume on high. The music blasted through the trees. He hit the button that signaled help through the car's software, also activating the signal that indicated the need for help but with an SOS for help to be silent. He prayed quietly that his decision didn't just sign all their death certificates.

Breathing a small sigh of relief that no one came over the speaker, he saw the dash light up, letting him know that the message was sent. He didn't know at this point if help would make it in time.

Colin walked back to where he was and groaned as he saw Olivia beginning to dance, her eyes on Carmicheal. She gave her hips a little wiggle before moving her body in such a sexual way that as much as he hated to admit it, he got hard. Even in this very fucked up situation where they might die, he still wanted her. His jaw dropped as she suddenly got on her hands and knees and crawled seductively towards Carmicheal, the belt dragging next to her in her hands.

She sat back on her knees and dragged her hand slowly up the man's stomach, up to his throat before squeezing lightly, almost like she was giving him a massage. Her breaths came out ragged, like she was enjoying it. Her nails dug in and she suddenly squeezed hard, making him whimper and tense up.

"Don't worry Daniel, I'm going to make it so, so much better. You just let me know when you're ready," she moaned. The sexual sound scared them all as it was so unexpected. Carmichael groaned as she kept going, making breathless, moaning noises.

Colin's eyes narrowed as he saw the man suddenly twitch, a wet spot spreading on the front of his pants.

"Oh my God, this is *sick*. This is so fucked up," Vanessa whispered from her spot on the ground. She was leaning against Jonathan's leg, wrapped around him, trembling.

"Patience," Jonathan whispered back. So low Colin wondered if he even heard him right over the music.

Olivia looked down at Carmichael's pants and tsked.

"Oh noo. What have you done? Daniel, I didn't say you could come," Olivia whispered. "You took the good part away from me," she slapped him across the face once more with one hand, then followed up with a slap with the other hand, the element of surprise catching him off guard. "Oh well, you ready? I'm only going to do this once," she said, a little hurt look on her face.

"No, no! More than once, Kat. Please?" the man whined.

Whined. A grown man sniveling and whining like a bitch, Colin fought hard against dry heaving like Vanessa was. It was truly disgusting to watch.

She shook her head. "I said once," she hissed.

"But please. Please," he whined, sounding like a child.

Olivia paused, everything was silent for several seconds as she tilted her head slowly, tapping her fingers against her arm. "Ok," she said. "since you begged so nicely. JONATHAN!" she suddenly barked.

Jonathan raised his eyebrows, turning his eyes onto hers.

"I need Colin to turn around and look the other way. Make sure he doesn't see this part. There are just some things a girl's gotta keep to herself you know?" she said this last part rather quietly, and Colin's stomach turned.

Olivia began unbuttoning her pants. The henchman watched, riveted with their guns lowered once more. Colin's vision went red. Jonathan turned him quickly, putting his back to the scene and getting into his face. Jonathan wrapped a hand around his throat warningly.

"She's doing this to be a distraction. We are going to die if we don't find a way out of this," he whispered very low so as to not be overheard.

Colin started shaking as he heard Olivia pull her pants off, the shuffling noise barely able to be heard over the music. He saw Vanessa stand and take four steps backwards, her eyes wide, hand over her mouth.

"Lay down on your back and open your mouth, you filthy, disgusting, sick son of a bitch," Colin heard Olivia hiss from behind him.

"She's buying us some time. Look at me. Look at me, brother," Jonathan whispered.

Vanessa suddenly turned pale, then gray. Both of the henchmen made a startled sound, backing up in surprise themselves, they were spread out in a crescent moon shape, flanking Olivia and Carmichael.

Colin's ears strained. He could hear a trickling noise, then rough gurgling as if the man were choking on liquid.

Vanessa's eyes rolled into the back of her head and she fainted, hitting the ground with a sick thud. But Jonathan kept his eyes on him. The man continued to gurgle and Colin swore he was going to die of a heart attack just like his mom. This night had taken several years off his life. But Jonathan was still talking, and Colin needed to pay attention.

"Swallow it," Olivia hissed suddenly. "Stop being disgusting, *you're spilling it,* fuck."

Colin blinked, not sure he could vomit past Jonathan's grip on his neck, but they were all about to find out if this shit didn't stop soon.

"I'm going to let you go in a minute, and I'm going to get the gun from the dead man next to us," Jonathan said, peeking over Colin's shoulder before turning his eyes back to Colin. "Then I'm going to give it to you. But we need to wait for her signal. She has one, I just haven't seen it yet," Carmichael let out a deep groan before chuckling. The sound moving through him like someone was shoving razor blades in Colin's ears.

Colin nodded minutely, not bothering to tell Jonathan that he wasn't waiting for a signal. After what he just heard, he figured he'd be happy for them all to die tonight.

Jonathan looked back behind his shoulder and Colin heard the unmistakable sound of her pulling her pants back on. He turned his head to look at the henchman, they were not even looking or caring about them at this point. Jonathan nodded at him and let him go, and he turned, his eyes flicking all over Olivia and the surrounding area. He stiffened, seeing the ground was wet beneath where Daniel was now raising himself up from. He looked dazed.

Holy fuck. No. She didn't. No way, there has to be some other explanation. Colin thought.

Olivia sniffed as she backed away a few steps, waiting for him to get back into position for her. She didn't raise her eyes to Colins.

Moving behind Carmichael, she placed her feet on either side of the man's legs in a wide stance. Slowly, almost erotically, she wrapped the belt around his neck, slipping the end through the buckle and pulling. She held the belt with one hand and fisted her hand in his silver hair, pulling his neck all the way back to look at her.

"Are you ready, dear?" she asked with a little giggle. "It's going to hurt."

Colin suddenly realized that Jonathan had disappeared, unnoticed. He'd slipped away quietly while everyone was distracted. Colin didn't move, not wanting to call attention to their area lest the three other henchmen notice he left. He waited for a second before he felt Jonathan's presence come back, slightly behind him and pressing the dead man's rifle into his hand. He grasped it, his fingers feeling alongside it as he held it behind his back. Learning without sight the gun's mechanism, he prayed the other henchmen didn't realize anything suspicious was going on while their attention was diverted.

Colin moved fast, crouching down and swiveling, aiming at the henchman next to him and shooting him between his eyes. The man groaned, hitting the floor. Dead.

With a loud cry, Olivia slammed her foot into Carmichaels back, pushing him forward and tugging on the belt with a growl, choking the man hard. She'd bent down, with a harsh grunt, shocking everyone. Standing back up with the gun Carmichael had in the back of his pants, she pressed it to the back of his head.

Vanessa was sitting up, startled by the sudden commotion.

Colin swiveled fast, taking out the third henchman in a millisecond before he could pull the trigger. Hearing the thud of his body, he turned swiftly to train his weapon on the fourth man who he saw Jonathan was currently active with, with no weapon. He turned back to Olivia who was currently grappling on the ground with Carmichael, the gun she'd had was nowhere to be found.

The hair on the back of his neck stood up as he saw Jonathan fake a grab and then leap for the henchman.

Jonathan lunged at the henchman as his gun went off and he fell to his knees with a grunt, hand across his chest. The henchman turned with his gun, the red dot racing across the ground towards Olivia.

Colin's heart swelled with pain, the panic almost choking him. He took aim at the henchman aiming for Olivia and shot him down fast. Then it was just them and Carmichael, who was straddling Olivia and had his hands around her throat. She was yanking on the belt hard, trying to find purchase.

As enraged as he was, Colin calmly stood up and walked to the man, who was so intent on hurting Olivia that he didn't notice him at first. Colin came up to his side and put the barrel of the gun to his head, stilling the former judge's actions. He heard Olivia wheeze for air.

"Look at me," Colin said sharply, smiling evilly as the man turned. The second Carmichael's eyes met his and widened, he pulled the trigger and heard a slight click, quickly realizing there were no more bullets. Carmichael laughed.

Unfazed, Colin turned the rifle quickly and knocked him hard across the face with it, hearing a crunch and a sickening scream come from the man. He fell to the side and Colin bent forward, grabbing the man's hair with a harsh grunt and dragging him several feet away from Olivia, who was scrambling trying to get up.

She ran towards Jonathan and her sister.

Colin dropped the weapon and pulled his fist back before snapping forward and sinking his fist into the man's stunned face with a sharp crack, feeling bones crunch. He repeated the motion again and again, uncaring of the man's screaming. He didn't stop until he quieted, and he let him go, watching the man slump to the ground. He was moaning, twitching.

Colin stood up to go to one of the other henchmen to grab their gun but then there was a deadly silence.

He heard the music suddenly stop; the song turning off. No other sound except for Vanessa's crying and Olivia's wheezing. He turned once more, scanning the area quickly for help, hearing sirens way off in the distance. Too far.

"Colin!" Olivia suddenly screamed as Jonathan moaned, tipping to the side. Vanessa caught him, holding him upright.

Colin ran over to Jonathan in a hurry, seeing that Vanessa had taken her shirt off and was pressing it against the wound at his chest.

Jonathan looked at Vanessa, smiling, placing a bloody hand on her cheek. "I love you," Jonathan said to Vanessa weakly.

"Olivia, get the phone," Colin said sharply, seeing his friend's face pinch, his eyes shutting.

Olivia tore off in the direction of the car and a second later, he could hear her yelling. Colin turned his head slightly, hearing Carmichael groaning in the distance.

Colin pulled Vanessa out of the way before hauling his fist back and punching Jonathan square in the face. Jonathan's eyes fluttered open, looking angry. He inhaled on a deep ragged breath, shuddering.

"Motherfucker, you are not allowed to die. Not today, pussy," Colin snarled, putting himself under Jonathan's good side and hauling him up. He got the big man to the SUV on adrenaline and the grace of God.

"Get in," he yelled at Vanessa, who launched herself into the hatchback, unable to crawl into the backseat with the way Jonathan was laying across it. Olivia crawled into the passenger seat, shaking as she tried to tell the police where to find them. Colin slammed his hand into a few buttons on the car's computer system and a weird sounding noise filled the car, disconnecting the current call with the police.

"Your location has been sent to all local police stations, and the nearest cop has been alerted to your area. Do you need medical assistance?" A disembodied woman came over the phone.

Olivia gaped at him as Colin said, "Yes,"

He roared the engine before backing up several feet, turning the car harshly.

Olivia's eyes widened as he trained the headlights on Carmichael's barely moving form. He had lifted his head off the ground, his face looked unrecognizable. The engine roared again as Colin stomped on the gas and they shot forward, the tires kicking up dirt and squealing beneath them. They shot forward and Olivia braced herself. Colin hit the man straight on and the car bounced as it went over him, going airborne slightly.

Colin put the car into reverse before turning, placing his arm on the back of Olivia's headrest and looking behind him as he stomped the pedal again, sending them flying backwards over the man again. Olivia held a shaking hand to her mouth and leaned backwards, shuddering.

He glanced at her, meeting her eye before putting the car back into drive and sitting there for a second, panting. He revved the engine a few times before stomping down and the car bounced hard as he ran Carmichael over for the third time.

He looked in the rearview mirror, catching Vanessa's eye and her mouthed 'thank you' to him. He nodded tightly.

He spun the car quickly, tearing off into the night, the engine roaring, the dirt road kicking up behind them. As he looked at Olivia sharply, his features hardened.

"Baby, did you do what I think you did to that man back there?" he said quietly, not even able to say the Judge's name. Filled with rage, he revved the engine harder, pushing it as hard as he could.

Colin just needed to know.

He knew they lost precious seconds while he filled his need to run over the sick fucker repeatedly. One time for Olivia, one time for Jonathan, and one time for Allison.

Olivia looked at him with a haunted look on her face.

"Yes," she said on a tortured moan, her voice sounding very far away.

"So, we need to have a conversation about whether or not we need to fix that memory for you. If you catch my drift."

Olivia's face turned the reddest he'd ever seen it. He would have told her he was joking, if he was. He'd do anything to reroute her memories and take away her trauma.

Vanessa suddenly laughed in the backseat.

"You know bro, EMDR is so much more effective than that you sick freak," Jonathan said weakly from the backseat, his voice also sounding very far away but for a different reason.

"Oh my Gooooddd, you are one sick fucking man Colin," Vanessa said.

Colin grinned suddenly feeling very elated. He knew they were going to all be ok. He just knew it deep down.

"Jonathan's passed out," Olivia said suddenly, turning to reach into the backseat.

He pressed the pedal harder, thanking God for sports cars.

They heard multiple sirens after a few minutes. Once they turned onto a blacktop road, they faced an onslaught of lights. There were several cop cars, an ambulance, a firetruck, and several black SUVs.

Colin screeched the car to a stop and got out, yanking the back door open and pulling Jonathan's limp body out of the car quickly. He placed him gently on the ground, careful not to crack his head onto the asphalt.

"He's been shot in the chest, unresponsive," he yelled to the cops that came running. Vincent and their team followed close behind. "Vanessa, you need to go with Jonathan to the hospital. I'll show the authorities the crime scene." He turned to Olivia, who looked shocked. She turned towards Jonathan as the paramedics started swarming.

"I couldn't do it. I'm so sorry, I had the gun in my hand and couldn't do it. Jonathan wouldn't be hurt if I had just shot him. Oh Jonathan, I'm so sorry. I've never killed anyone before! I'm so sorry," she cried, fat tears falling down her face. She stumbled over to him and sank to her knees next to the injured man who was fighting to stay conscious.

Colin pulled her out of the way, hauling her up to his chest again.

"Baby," he whispered, placing his forehead against hers. "You did so good. You did so good, mami. My beautiful fucking smart wife. You saved our lives." He pressed his lips against hers, kissing her again and again, his hands cradling her face, feeling her tremble and whimper.

She gripped his shirt hard, trembling. He continued to speak, keeping his eyes on hers.

"Honey, I need you to keep it together now. You have to go to Allison. She needs you," he whispered, kissing her forehead. "I'll be right back, ok?" he said as he nodded at Vincent, who pulled Olivia to him, quickly ushering her away to the authorities and his team. Colin watched as they carefully maneuvered her to safety before he turned and nodded at the police officer who was trying to get his attention.

As Colin got in an unmarked SUV, he was unaware that the lit-up lights and sirens hasn't bothered him in the slightest as he gave them directions to where they all almost lost their lives that night.

TWENTY-FIVE

There Are No Endings

COLIN AND OLIVIA WALKED hand in hand through the cemetery, with Zero as their only security lurking in the background, staying behind in the unmarked SUV, parked behind Colin's dusky blue vehicle. Olivia looked up at him with a slight smile and squeezed his arm as they made their way to the bench that Colin had erected in his parent's honor.

They approached his parents' gravesite and Colin took the blanket he had tucked under his arm and spread it out before the bench and the statues of his parents' likeness.

"Careful," he said as he helped Olivia down onto the blanket, thankful for once she wasn't wearing the heels that liked to test his patience.

"Thanks love," she said, putting down the picnic basket she'd been carrying and opening it as Colin settled next to her. She carefully took out the heated bowl of paella she'd packed and the wine bottle and wine glasses, giving him a spoon. She kept the bundle she'd wrapped and hid amongst the basket carefully tucked away, replacing the lid and pushing it to the side.

She held up her wine glass. "Let's toast!" She stated, clinking their glasses together and blushing as Colin looked at her with an expression akin to reverence. They sipped their wine and she watched as he took a spoon and dug it into the seafood and rice.

"So, what's next for us, love? What grand adventure awaits you and me do you think?" Colin asked, looking across the bowl they were sharing. His eyebrow arched and he gave her a teasing grin as she took the shell of a seafood muscle and sucked on it.

"Well, school starts back up in another month. And other than that...I guess we just have to see where life takes us." She looked over at the faces of his parents, seeing they were wrapped around each other and staring at the sunset in the distance, getting ready to go down.

That's a beautiful sentiment. She thought, feeling her heart tug.

"Hmm-hmm....the house should be done within the next couple of years. That was a big project baby." Colin teased, leaning forward and lowering his voice, he motioned for her to come closer. Olivia leaned in on a giggle, realizing he didn't want his parents to hear.

Silly man, she thought, hiding a grin.

"The final cost ended up being about twenty-one million dollars, and you know what it did to me when I got the invoice, don't you?"

Olivia let out a hilarious giggle and put another bite of rice into her mouth, chewing slowly. Her eyes sparkled as she regarded him through her lashes. "Oh noo...tell me. I can only imagine, knowing you."

"Good think you've got a great imagination then, huh?"

Smirking at his words, she took out her phone and texted Zero.

Now. Just like we talked about. -Olivia

"Oh, it's time for another page three adventure sweetheart. As soon as we get home." Colin leaned in further and took her earlobe between his teeth on another growl.

"Ohhh sir. I don't know if tonight's going to work. I think we've got plans." Olivia said with a small pout on her face.

Colin pulled back with an arched eyebrow. "What? What plans?" He frowned, trying to remember if he missed something.

Olivia reached forward into the basket and pulled out the bundle she'd stowed away and handed it to him, trying to hurry.

Colin frowned again, putting down his spoon and taking it from her. His eyes flickered to hers as he began to tear the tissue paper open slowly.

Hurry up slow poke! Olivia silently urged him to go faster. Her eyes scanned the horizon for Zero.

"Oh baby." Colin's eyes widened as he breathed the endearment out slowly as the leather bound collar with a simple heart charm fell into his hand. His eyes fell to her neck and there was a brief pause as she realized he misinterpreted the gift. Her own breath froze in her lungs as they locked eyes for a second, and she almost forgot why she even gave it to him until a big black and white mass slammed itself into Colin's front, knocking him backwards.

Olivia raised to her knees, clapping and cheering as the Dalmatian puppy pounced all over Colin, who was sputtering and squirming on the ground, trying to get his bearings.

"Olivia! Woman, help me!"

Olivia laughed and whistled. Getting the dog's attention, she scooped some of the rice into a small bowl and giggled as the puppy came over, wagging her tail excitedly. Her entire body was shaking. Colin sat up, thrusting a hand through his hair as he looked rather bewildered at the dog then at Olivia before a huge smile graced his face.

"You got us a dog?" Colin said incredulously, rising up to his knees and shuffling next to her. He reached forward and petted her. "She's beautiful. What should we name her?"

"Well, I was thinking we could name her Ginger...she didn't come with a name. She's an orphan, just like us," Olivia said, looking up at him. "I love you, husband," she whispered, touching his cheek, "my other half."

Colin's eyes watered as he stared down at her. Feeling a lump swell in his throat.

"God, I love you. Are you as complete as I am, amor?" He choked out, leaning forward to press his lips to hers. Olivia wrapped her arms around him and squeezed, letting him know without words that she was. Finally.

And for a moment, their souls lit up brightly, finally connected.

Knowing this was only the beginning of their love story.

TWENTY-SIX
Epilogue

WHAT? OLIVIA THOUGHT, HER eyebrows furrowing.

"This isn't the song I'm walking to?" she whispered to Jonathan, not able to turn and look at her wedding party proceeding her.

She scowled in slight confusion as the sounds of "I can't help falling in love with you" accompanied by a lone guitar drifted throughout, Allison leading the way with her basket of flowers, and Stella and Vanessa quickly taking their turns after. They looked gorgeous in their deep green dresses. She could hear the murmur of the guests through the curtain and it made her butterflies worse. She brought a shaky hand up and smoothed it over the delicate lace of her veil, a choice that she'd wavered on. But since her boat neck dress was satin and simple, just flowing over her body and down her arms, she'd splurged on a beautiful, expensive long veil to complete the look, and it made her red hair stand out beautifully.

"Relax, Ollie. This is how it was designed to go. There's no mess up," Jonathan replied, tucking her hand into his arm and leaning down to press his head against hers. That'd become their thing as they got closer. The brotherly gesture was doing much to soothe her.

"Ok, but if that's the song they're walking to, then what's my song?" she whispered back, curious.

Olivia and Jonathan were off to the side, not facing the entrance as Colin had instructed them that he didn't want her to get a peek of anything before the curtains raised. Olivia closed her eyes and breathed deeply, taking Jonathan's arm in a harder grip. As nervous as she felt, this was the biggest day in her life and she didn't know what she was about to walk into. Only that Jonathan and Vanessa had assured her she wouldn't be disappointed.

Colin had taken over every detail of the wedding ceremony and wouldn't let her peek at anything. He'd converted the office room at the guest house and changed the code on the lock so she couldn't snoop, using that space for wedding planning.

"Breathe, Ukhat," Jonathan said softly, leaning forward to press his temple against hers. Jonathan was Colin's best man, but had offered to walk Olivia down the aisle so she wouldn't be alone. He would hand her off and join behind Colin once they got to the top of the isle. And after Colin told him his plans for the ceremony, he was validated in his decision, knowing Olivia would need the support.

The guitar slowly transitioned into the song that they were meant to walk down the aisle to and he'd turned her to face the beautiful satin white curtains that blocked her from the view of the venue and entry way. Olivia's eyes smarted as the lights completely dimmed behind her and the curtain began to rise, showing her sparkling gold light that started off muted but then became brighter and brighter as the curtain raised, casting her and Jonathan in a warm glow.

The aisle in front of her was lit with twinkling fairy lights of all sizes, hanging down in sporadic spots all around in front of her from the ceiling of a humongous glass dome. The stars above them twinkled in the night sky. The rest of the venue was dark, and she couldn't see anything beyond the lights, the floor on either side of them was lit by chunky candles of all sizes and beautiful white and pink Earth Angel roses spread all over. She gasped, and the tears she'd been holding back fell down her cheek as the lone singer began to sing "Yellow" by Cold Play. Her sweet, breathy voice transitioned the song romantically.

The singer began as she and Jonathan took their first steps forward onto the white carpet. On the first set of the bundles of lights were small polaroid photographs clipped to the strands, and she bit her lip as she took in the first photo. It was of her through the window of the diner the night they first met in the storm. She gasped again as her eyes landed on another picture of her, smiling at her phone as she texted while she sat in a seat nearby him while they waited for his ride to drop off his car.

A small sob escaped her throat as they got to the next cluster of lights and their pictures. Her, looking lost outside of the food bank, her leaning against her car as she stared off into the woods next to the diner pensively, her looking up to the heavens as she tried not to pray for a miracle, her green eyes conveying so much emotion.

The next cluster of lights held various pictures of her that he'd taken at the diner during all the times he'd come in trying to convince her to go out with him. Some of the pictures showed her smiling at her customers as she poured a cup of coffee, another was of her at the cash register trying to get the correct change, another one was of her sweetly touching a baby's face.

Her tears came freely, her hand was shaking, covering her mouth under her veil. The next cluster of lights was of her the day she'd come to his office and was staring at the trees through his windows, struck by their beauty. The next one was of her bent over their agreement, a scowl on her face. The next one was of her sleeping peacefully in his car as he took her to his home for the first time.

The next cluster of pictures were of her curled in on herself in the bathtub the first night, her sleeping peacefully in bed, even her in her hideous hospital gown and cap as she waited to be wheeled away for her surgery. She giggled a little at that. She and Jonathan shared a small smile as they continued.

More pictures of her, Colin, Allison,Vanessa and Jonathan. Kissing in front of their decorated house for Halloween, them all sharing a drink the day of Thanksgiving over the turkey, them all in front of a vast fireplace and Christmas tree. The two of them dancing at the New Year's party where he'd picked her up and they were spinning, pure joy on their faces. And a candid picture she'd never seen of the two of them kissing at their secret wedding at the house. She looked over, seeing Jonathan was handing her a handkerchief so she could dab her eyes. She smiled thankfully.

As she continued, she saw herself bent over a focaccia bread with small tweezers, trying to place a design perfectly, the tip of her tongue stuck out as she concentrated. Her watching a movie in the lounge of their bedroom. Her dressed up in her red dress, inspecting her heels. Her first day at university, standing in the front of the fridge, trying to figure out a snack to take with her. Then she was in front of Colin, she was panting, gasping for breaths, emotional and crying. She peeked up at him through the veil and saw that his face was just as emotional, and he was holding back tears of his own.

The singer trailed off the song as the lights dimmed slowly on the guests. Until this point, she hadn't even known the layout and looked in shock as she realized they were on a platform in the middle of a circular dome, their guests spread out in a three sixty degrees around them. She shivered, feeling very laid open. He stepped into her and placed his palm on her cheek over her veil and leaned in, pressing his forehead into hers.

"That was so beautiful, Colin," she whispered, her breath hitching. "Thank you so much, baby." More tears slid down her cheeks. She dabbed at them again, not wanting to get her veil wet, thankful that

Vanessa had commissioned a celebrity make-up artist to come and do her makeup for the big day. The woman had focused on a minimal natural look while still making her look otherworldly beautiful, and not a speck of makeup was out of place or smeared. She felt like a princess.

As they said their vows and kissed, sealing their union, fireworks exploded in the air above them and they tilted their heads up, looking at the spectacle through the glass dome.

Colin reached forward and caressed her cheek, bringing her eyes back down to his. "Happy ever after, baby." He whispered, lowering his lips to hers once more.

"Happy ever after," she mumbled back as they smiled and rocked against each other.

Lost in their own fairy tale.

Also by

In You

Mounted (2026)

INTERCONNECTED WORLDS

The Romancing Me Series

Coming 2026

Alexander and Sarah's story

The Billionaire's Assurance Series

The Pain We Nurture (Book 1)

The Pain We Allow (Book 2)

Unmasking Me Series:

Lola Unmasked part. 1

Lola Unmasked part. 2

Lola Unmasked part 3

The King Dynasty Series:

The Heir

The Spare

The Reign (2026)

Christmas Novella

Surrender at The Snowflake Inn

Acknowledgements
Beautiful Readers

Where can I even bein to express my thanks and gratitude to those of you who have taken me under your wing and have shown me what friendship is, understanding, compassion, and just the itty gritty acceptance that we all want and strive for?

To my parents, you'll always be first, because you were the first. The first to help me to bloom and to make me believe that I could do just about anything I could set my mind to.

To my family, especially my family, who can never let me catch a break, haha, thank you for your continued patience, and believing in me and my dream. To my beagle, sometimes you staring up at me intently with those big brown eyes causes me to have breakthroughs in my writing dry spells. You have to be giving your accolades too, my sweet fur baby.

Ashli, Des, Jodi, Cheryl, Lisa you five are amazing and I can never thank you enough for the endless hours of conversations about books, story ideas, book cover agonizing, and everything literature seeped fun.

To my beta and alpha readers, you keep a girl sane and excited to keep writing. I hope you enjoy the process as much as I do.

To my girlfriends Gina, Blair, Erica, you are so cherished, and I hope you know that. Thank you for always believing me, and not letting me give up.

Lastly, to my beautiful, sweet readers, do you know how awesome you are? How special, cherished, amazing, and just down right loved you are? Well, now you do. I couldn't and wouldn't be able to do this without you. And I hope to continue to be able to deliver books just as amazing as I believe each and every one of you are.

And as always, remember to take care of yourself always.

Love,

SKP